STAINED MIRROR

A SERIAL KILLER MEMOIR

GIANNI FRANCO

ISBN-13: 9781736621707 (paperback)
ISBN-13: 9781736621714 (e-book)

Cover Photo by Jeremy Bishop on Unsplash
Library of Congress Control Number: 2021902435
First Edition, Printed in the United States of America.

The diary of a madman is buried within the mirror into which they muse.

Gianni Franco

Content and Trigger Warnings

Before reading, please be aware of the following:

Alcohol and drug abuse
Smoking
Graphic Consensual Sex Scenes
Graphic Death Scenes
Violence
Self-harm
Suicide
Mental Illness

April 13

Halos ascend towards the ceiling between each drag from the smoldering cigarette sagging between my lips. Ashes fall like snowflakes onto the kitchen table, missing their ceramic fate. Above, where I'm seated, a haze of smoke blurs the dangling fluorescent.

I've been instructed to create a journal by my psychiatrist, Doctor Matilda Brazen—*the/rapist* of the mind. She prides herself as the best doctor money can buy. My salary doesn't qualify and the civil servant discount makes no tangible dent in her hourly rate. I work the justice system the best way possible, stealing from criminals. A Robin Hood scheme to pay for a doctor who's convinced she can treat and cure me.

I'm an officer at the Rochester, New York Police Department, Precinct 13. We call it RPD for short. It's been a turbulent fifteen years, and within the last three, I became

Sergeant. I passed the psyche exam when I first started, but due to a few missed days this past year and alcohol on my breath, the Captain suggested I seek help.

Many years have passed since I've written. I'll attempt to write as often as possible. She insists with my great memory and investigative skills, I should be able to pinpoint and solve my problems. I do *not* believe this to be true. She also says the more I write, the more I'll be able to better understand myself. I do *not* believe this to be true either. For me, psychological issues reflect a lapse in judgement, a plethora of uncontrollable thoughts with consequences. Mine—well… those thoughts—those actions—they're all calculated. Only time will tell if she can convince me my mind is broken.

She says to write when negative situations arise, as they did tonight, but my mind refuses to instruct my hand again. The pen, strangled by a three-fingered death grip, bleeds blue from its needle tip through blank pages. My fingers spasm, snapping the pen into an upright position. I must write, must continue. Made an agreement and must stick to it. I can't continue. The box of memories has one more addition. I must rest.

I

Most of my mornings never went well. Hell, most of my days and nights were just as bad, but the mornings, the toughest. I needed to shake off the two-ton weights on my eyelids, and pull the bales of hay wrapped in barbed wire from my throat. Sporadic coughs between cigarette drags produced blotches in my hand as dark as ink. Dad always used to say, "The less you know about your health, the healthier you'll be." That sure as hell made sense to me.

My first stop of the day at a bodega named Diego's. Not my usual, but closer than Pat's Drive-In and en route to the police station. I needed Visine to clear away the burning eyes, nicotine sticks to stay awake, and hot coffee to melt the razors scraping my throat and stomach. Once through the entrance, I bowed my head to avoid eye contact and rushed towards the back of the store.

A dozen glazed doughnuts glistened under a warming lamp next to the coffee makers. I couldn't resist their temptation. Glazed, my favorite. No fillings or creams, just molten sugarcane dripping from their edges like wax. The sugar rush certain to jolt me through the morning, especially when combined with nicotine and caffeine.

Three carafes sat atop separate warming plates. They hadn't been washed in months, only refilled, creating a thick film on the glass like plastic. Each had a string label attached to the handle: bold, medium, and weak. I picked bold, of course. The coffee flowed into the Styrofoam cup black like tar and almost as thick. No cream or sugar for me. I like keeping it pure like my alcohol so as not to weaken the effect. I mumbled my cigarette order at the register, refusing to look up. Once he slid them across the counter, I snagged them, threw him a ten, and stormed out.

Precinct 13 only a couple miles ahead. April mornings in Rochester, New York had an early sunrise, but on most days overbearing grey clouds swallowed the sun and spat gloom. As I came upon the entrance and huffed a final drag, last night's liquor indulgence paid me a visit, spinning my mind like a Tilt-a-Whirl. My foot slipped from the brake and pounced the gas. The right-front wheel jumped the curb and it didn't land until I slammed the brakes, locking up the rear wheels and stopping the front bumper inches from the building.

"Damn it. Damn you. Damn me. Damn everything."

The Styrofoam cup had slipped from my hand and spilled onto my leg. The burn stung at first, but quickly subsided, replaced with a soothing, tingling ripple flowing around my thighs through to my feet. What used to hurt now aroused me. Hopefully, the opposite didn't ring true.

The car radio glowed 6:55 a.m. I exited the vehicle and shuffled towards the Precinct entrance. My shift didn't start until 8:00. The Visine had worn off. My eyes burned like a fever, so I trickled a few magic drops to cool them. I kept my head down hoping to fend off any cops hanging outside. If they acquired a quick glance, their snooping minds would send me to the interrogation room, or perhaps the Captain's office. It wouldn't be the first time, but I wasn't in the mood this morning. I peeked towards the door making sure not to run into the exterior wall and noticed Joe walking ahead of me.

He'd been on the force several months and clueless about working at the Precinct. He arrived early every damn day trying to get bonus points from the Captain. We, more so I, called him Joe Rook, rook short for rookie. Russo, his real last name. A good ole *I—talian* boy, first or second generation, who grew up in Gates, the Little Italy district of Rochester.

I'm not sure why he left Gates to work in downtown Rochester. That town had it all: amazing food, friendly people who flailed their hands every time they met you, and beautiful men and women who could've posed in *Vogue*. I loved them, but they didn't love me. Their excuses endless, but the ones that stuck: too burly, too quiet, or not to the level of their definition of a man. One girl even told me in a high-pitched twang, "You're not *I—talian* enough, so you can't be with me." Well, I wasn't *I—talian*. Joe received the same treatment from me because he wasn't cop enough. After spending fifteen years on the force, I knew being early made no difference. I wanted him to learn the hard way and suffer like I did, but I never turned away help from an oblivious newbie. Welcome to downtown, Mr. Joe Rook.

"Hey, Joe Rook," I said with a rasp. My eyes steadfast on my boots, making certain not to miss a step. "Can you hold the door for me?"

"Yes, of course." He smiled and lunged for the door handle like a lizard's tongue. "You're like a doughnut delivery boy today, Sergeant." His pitch exaggerated like a typical twenty-something who's in love with life and his job. "What are you going to do about that coffee stain?"

"Nothing. Whatever, Rook. Anyway... I guess, thanks. Next time, open the door faster."

As I walked through the entrance, my focus turned to balancing the half-filled coffee cup and doughnuts, hands fumbling like they were still under the influence. I didn't want to drop them and bring attention to me, so instead of slowing down, I sped up the pace to my desk. The alcohol must've flowed from my arms to my legs because once I reached the edge of the desk they shimmied like jelly. I dropped into the faux-leather chair. It must've looked as tired as I: crusted, cracked, and peeling.

My body might not have been working, but my stomach growled for a sugar rush. I ripped open the doughnut box like an eight-year-old on Christmas Day. The glazed ring went down in one bite, followed by a long swig of coffee. A few minutes passed and the doughnut didn't settle as it burned its way up my throat. I barreled the bathroom door, reaching the porcelain throne just in time. Scotch, doughnuts, coffee, and thick speckles of something made for a colorful splash, reminiscent of a Pollock painting. It could've been blood from my lungs, but more than one diagnosis per day is too much. It'll make any layman go crazy. I'll stick to my dad's advice.

I struggled to the sink and spun the faucet. The cold water provided a temporary sanctuary to my burning face. I rinsed my mouth and took a sip. Mid-rinse and the toilet bowl beckoned again. Damn water made me sick, or maybe it was the putrid blend of toxicity emanating from the bowl. In either case, a lost cause. I replenished the bowl with the same contents as before. I hunched my way towards the sink, slamming my body into stall doors and walls. The second splash of water a charm, settling my stomach. I dug into the paper-towel dispenser like a squirrel and found no nuts. A punch to the faded, aluminum container weakened to a tap. I turned to re-enter the stall and whirled half a roll of toilet paper to dry myself.

Luckily, the coffee spill from the car had already dried, so I didn't bother with it.

I lit a cigarette and entered the locker room for some peace and quiet. Tucked in the rear of the locker room, under a makeshift, cardboard canopy, existed the longest and most comfortable bench at Precinct 13. Granted, its finish had lost its luster, suffering the wrath of a thousand cop asses, but it worked. I swiped the bench clean with one hand, while the other attempted to stabilize my tired back onto the wood, but it slipped and my body flopped. I stretched my legs and propped my boots, took a deep drag from the cigarette, dropped it to the ground, and fell asleep.

The dream must've started not too long after. "You're a pig. I hate you. Go to hell. I hope you die," she said. Each piercing word lingering like a mountain echo.

"This can't be… You're dead. Leave me alone. Why are you here?" My voice mimicking her fervent pitch.

She didn't respond but her face appeared, then her body. It was Maria. And just as fast as she entered, she disappeared.

"Get away from me, Maria. Die."

Images of her body in the bathtub and my blood-soaked hands circled around me like a high-speed camera roll. I stretched to grab the pictures, to stop their torment, but with each spin, they inched further and further away.

"Hey, Sergeant. Sarge. Are you okay? Frank, wake up."

"You're dead. Die. What... what's going on?" My eyelids crept open and noticed a blurred silhouette of Joe standing above me. "Yeah... I'm okay." I continued grasping fistfuls of air. "I dozed off. Sorry for the noise."

"Sergeant. Sir. You said *die* in your dream over and over. Are you sure you're okay?"

"Yes, Rook. I'm fine." Typical interrogation from a rookie. I have the right to sleep and say *die*. It's not like I said Joe Rook die. I played him with an easy excuse. "I think I was dreaming about a movie. *The Shining* or something. I really can't remember. Thanks for waking me."

"Hey, no problem, Sergeant. As long as you're okay. That's all that matters. Our shift is starting in a few. I'll see you at your desk."

Being awake for the top brass held priority. With a white-knuckled grip, I pulled myself along the ragged pew. Staggering to stand, I stooped, and fumbled through my pockets looking for a quick nicotine rush. A snap of the Zippo and a deep breath burned the tip red. I gazed the lungful of smoke twirling the arms of the ceiling fan and within seconds the synapses with my mind exploded like a shotgun. That rush never quite made it to my strides, boots lugging across the floor towards the desk.

Across the office, I noticed Joe scrabbling the coffee maker and dropping unopened sugar packets into his mug. I grinned with a bit of relief. In hindsight, it was good that Joe found me. A great cop, like Daniels or the Captain, would've asked more questions and demanded more answers about my dream. They live and breathe the five W's: what, who, where, when, and why. Joe can't even pour himself a coffee, especially when multitasking includes talking to coworkers. He poured a full mug of coffee onto the floor, missing the oversized countertop as well.

The main entrance caught my eye. "Speak of the devil himself," I mumbled.

In polished designer shoes, Detective Daniels strutted like he owned the Precinct. His stern shoulders fit square into a pressed, white shirt under a dark blazer, accented by a red tie. Clean-shaven, his pronounced jaw barked orders and condemnations behind wide smiles. Everyone loved him, everyone hated him, and everyone feared him.

He approached my desk. "Good morning, Detective Daniels."

His glare sized me up in seconds. "Doesn't look like a good one for you. Did you have another rough night?"

I changed the topic as I had done many times in the past. Deep down in his heart, I think he was jealous. I didn't have to peacock around the Precinct, nor did I have any interest to start.

"You always dress so damn good. I'm impressed. I don't think I can wear a suit like you." I offered a quasi-smile.

"Well... maybe you can." Daniels fanned his chin. "But you should probably start by taking off that stupid ring. I think you wear it too much and it certainly won't flatter any suit." His pleasant smile never reduced the sting of his vocal jabs.

"Come on. Don't pick on the ring. It's my good luck charm." I fought back for approval. "My dad gave it to me after high school. It's Saint Gabriel. He's the saint of mercy."

"I don't think so, Stark. Pretty sure your Dad lied. If you look closely, you'll see it's Belial, which befits you well."

"Anyway." Smoke billowed from my mouth and nose as I heaved a sigh. "Do you want a doughnut? I brought them for the Precinct." He didn't need to know they were just for me and not anyone else.

"You know I don't eat that garbage, Sergeant. That shit's bad for you and so is smoking. You should work on fixing those vices."

"Yeah, but they say everything's bad for you." I slid my hand over the ashtray in an attempt to hide the mountain of logs formed from all the extinguished butts.

"I don't know who *they* are, Sergeant." He waved me off, changing to a more important conversation. "Did you hear what happened last night? I received the call this morning at five."

"No one's told me anything."

"Well, Sergeant. There's been a homicide in the Park Ave neighborhood. Maybe you can help me out with this one since you're familiar with the area."

My thoughts raced to keep up with my pulse while my lungs scrounged for a breath. He knows. This can't be possible. I double and triple checked the body. I searched my memory like a file cabinet. There should be no trace. I'm a cop, damn it. I know how to clean evidence. I know what to do.

"Sergeant. Snap out of it. Do you want to help me or not?"

"Yes…" I gargled phlegm. "I'm awake. Of course, I'll help." I lit another cigarette, downed the coffee like my last, and headed to the crime scene with Daniels.

II

We drove to the crime scene in separate cars. His, the updated, unmarked police cruiser, and mine, the older model by ten years with peeling paint and mismatched lights. Daniels took the lead following the speed limit. He didn't break laws.

We never rode together because he complained about the second-hand smoke, and the ashes flying inside the car like confetti. He'd always say it made him nauseous, and most of the time, he interjected that statement with a few choice vulgarities. I never disagreed with him. The smoke made me sick as well, but I ignored it. Considering everything else I put into my body, the cigarettes were probably healthy. Nicotine helped reduce my throbbing headaches and bilious hangovers, especially in a car. Good thing the lights and sirens were off for our short trip or I'd probably be puking a trail down the rear fender.

We approached my apartment. The Park Avenue area and a murder last night, too coincidental. My eyes blinked with confirmation in the rearview. Damn it. The steering wheel exchanged for a speed bag, matching the pace of my heart. I should break free from the convoy and speed off. A head start allowing ample time to escape. Dealing with the consequences is an option as well, since I deserve the punishment. We came within a hundred feet of my apartment on South Goodman Street, but didn't stop. As the apartment faded into the mirror, a calmness enveloped me. Good to go on this one. My stomach eased and heartrate dropped. We drove one more block north, then a right onto Park Avenue and pulled onto the driveway.

My eyes met the rearview once more, this time blinking to confirm victory. I exited the car with a large plume of smoke trailing behind, flicking the lit butt over the car's hood and onto the wet walkway of Apartment 363, where it fizzled.

Up the steps, I paused at the enclosed porch, prepping myself for whatever resided beyond the door. As I entered the home, I noticed the door showed no signs of a break-in. Daniels barked orders at the Forensic team, commanding the crime scene like a Marine Corps drill sergeant. I surveilled the apartment for any signs of a struggle, but it was too dark. The only light came from a single, table lamp with a missing shade and a flickering bulb sitting on the floor in the far corner of the room.

Rubbing alcohol, mothballs, mold, and latex soaked the air. A continuous barrage of camera flashes bounced off the walls like strobe lights, amplifying my pounding headache and squeezing my stomach. The scotch and doughnuts reemerged from my stomach with brute force, gluing themselves to the inside of my chest.

"Are you okay, Sergeant?"

"Other than those bright lights and that foul smell, I'm fine. Why, are you actually concerned?"

"You better take some aspirin or put on your shades. I ask, because I saw you banging your steering wheel in my rearview. Are you sure you're okay?"

I'm not even in his presence and he still suspects I did something wrong.

"You don't miss a thing, do you Daniels?" I paused as a hundred excuses came to mind. "Well... I... I was mad at a radio host on WCMF. He kept complaining about the cops. You might know him. They call him Dopie. He's a dumbass."

"No, I *don't* miss a thing, and yes, I know the guy." Daniels scanned each corner of the room. "I met him at a charity event. A stumbling, bumbling drunk, knocking over tables. He's just as bad in person as on the radio. I think he's a druggie too, so the moniker makes sense."

Another close call. Damn it, Daniels. I need to be smarter and stay one step ahead. Daniels continued to look over the crime scene, mumbling and scribbling onto a flimsy notepad. The girl's head hung over the armrest of the couch centered in the living room. Her arm draped over the cushion parallel to the floor, but not touching it. The other had a bloodied syringe dangling from a vein. Her fingernails chipped, frayed, and blotted. A camisole, with both straps sagging, covered the body. Although young, her greyish skin showed prominent signs of wear and tear from a hard life.

"This looks like a case of a young girl at the wrong place at the wrong time."

"That was quick, Detective," I said stunned. "How did you figure that out?"

"She isn't stabbed or beaten. There's some trauma to the right cheek. Do you see the red and blue marks around her neck?" He pointed at her face from multiple angles. "These marks suggest strangulation, which means an intimate murder. Probably her partner. I think male. That's my first guess. What do you think?"

"I agree. They must've known each other to die like that. I took a course a few years back and they said about fifty percent of the time it's domestic. I do have one question. How do you know it's a *he* who killed her?"

"Simple. I found a male's flannel shirt tucked under the couch. He inadvertently kicked it after he realized what he did and forgot it. He's a sloppy killer."

"Good catch."

The flashbulbs kept clicking, burning spots into my eyes, followed by a piercing throb inside my brain after each one.

"What the hell? Aren't you done with those cameras yet? Be more efficient. It's my turn with the body. Stop taking pictures."

The forensic team murmured a few slurs and walked away. I knew they weren't happy with me, but my point is valid. They click a thousand pictures and only five are presented at trial. They waste time and money, and give me headaches.

I searched her jeans for anything to give us a clue. We needed a name to put to the Jane Doe. I came upon a small baggy of cocaine, another syringe, and heroin from her left. I palmed the baggy of cocaine, sliding it up my sleeve, and into my jacket like a magician. I left the heroin for forensics. It's not my choice drug. I'm sure they'd match it to what's in her arm. Inside her right pocket, I located an identification card.

"Got it, Detective." I waved the ID card like a winning lottery ticket.

"Okay. This isn't a celebration. So, what's her name?" Daniels's brow tightened.

"Alright, man. Name is Maggie May. Address: 151 East Main Street, Waterloo, New York 13165. No date of birth listed. That's quite a distance from good ole Rochester."

"Sure is, Sergeant. Drugs bring people a long way."

"I guess they do. Found heroin in her pocket. I'll leave it for the coroner."

"Good idea. They'll take care of the specifics. Let's move on with this case. I need you to check the local shelters for leads. You got it?"

"Yes. I'm on the move."

I left the crime scene and rushed home. In a frenzy, I checked the apartment for any residue as if I were Daniels. Everything looked clean: the sinks, the kitchen, and the bathroom. Damn you, Daniels. I poured a double scotch neat into a rocks glass to cool the nerves. As I shut the cupboard, I noticed a speck on the door handle. A microscopic review suggested it was dried blood. Only one way to be certain. I wet my finger and swiped the spot, tabbing the tip of my tongue. Sure is blood. Salty with a hint of iron.

I need to be more careful. No more haphazard clean ups. Everything must be done to perfection, just like a professional, just like Daniels, just like Dad. I lit a cigarette and plopped onto the couch. Before heading to the shelters, I opted to take a well-deserved nap to shake the hangover from the prior night. Finding leads for Maggie May required energy.

III

I'd slept longer than expected. Late evening had arrived. Luckily, the homeless havens are on South Avenue, a few minutes' drive from my apartment. Rochesterians referred to this strip as Shelter Avenue. They'd petitioned the city a few years ago to separate the homeless population from the general. The measure was brought to the City Council after multiple business owners ran an advertising campaign making any politician's mouth water. The commercial, "Their kind don't belong with our kind. Keep them out!" flashed across every television station. The citizens cheered and the City Council slammed the gavel, approving the statute while they shook their heads with disappointment.

Months later, after the Council revisited the ordinance, they realized omitting an important piece of legislation, the wear-and-tear clause. Most of the street lamps buzzed and flickered an array of colors while others yearned to light. I swerved the car, attempting to avoid the various sized potholes littering the road like exploded landmines. Most of the time I missed, but when I didn't, the wheels and seats shuddered like a jackhammer.

Focusing on the road is important, but an eye on the homeless stragglers is key. They offer the best street intelligence. Any evidence is valuable at this point in the case. In the past, Jacob Smith assisted me with all the information. Jacob was as plain as his last name and had a simple story: divorce took all his money, alcohol took his soul, and the heroin made him forget the prior two.

New Horizons, the first shelter on the list, and coincidentally, the place Jacob frequented. As I turned the handle, its casing collapsed into the hollow of the metal door. Pulling it open, its top hinges snapped, the edge slicing the sidewalk. I slithered through the angled gap like an oiled snake commissioned by the circus.

Inside, the skunky, sweet-leaf aroma filled my lungs, and within a few steps, piss and stale cigarette smoke replaced it. Two homeless men holding half-filled fifths broke from their huddle in the tiny lobby, bumping two plastic, lawn chairs. They refused to raise their heads, and instead garbled a few words before taking healthy swigs.

I inched towards one of the men. Although an adult, his oversized winter jacket diminished him to a child. "You look like a guy I know. Are you Jacob Smith?" I nudged his shoulder with my finger.

"No and I don't know him."

"Alright. Can you help me find another person?"

"No, man. We don't know anyone." He turned and swilled from the bottle.

"Will this help make you friendlier?" I dug into my pocket and pulled out a twenty.

"Yeah, man." He attempted to snatch the money, but I yanked it away. "Not that fast, friend. I need to show you a picture. Raise your head. Your eyes looking at mine. Got it?"

"Yup." His cricked neck tilted upward.

I pulled out Maggie May's identification. His cadaverous eyes attempted a glimpse. Each blink begging to return to a life that once existed.

"Never seen her," he said, scratching a scab on his pallid cheek. "Can I have my money now?"

"Yeah. Thanks for the useless info. Get some help." I handed him the twenty and walked towards the sign-in desk.

Bulbs swayed from the ceiling hallway, attached to frayed wires that buzzed and sparked. I stopped at an oblong desk pieced together like papier-mâché. The building didn't meet code, but no one cared enough to check. The flip side of that coin: hundreds of homeless people sleeping under cardboard boxes, or worse, dead due to cold weather. The city decided to keep them open, rather than making the national news for destitute death.

At the front desk sat a white, heavyset man with a bushy, greying beard. His leather vest had as many patches as he had tattoos. Once he stood, the heaviness disappeared. His intimidating stature reduced me to a teenager. For once in my police career, the gun I carried wouldn't win a fight with this guy. His biceps inflated like two balloons as he crossed his arms. His left featured a black sword with *Death to All* wrapped around the shaft. The end of the sword tapered into a skull, which blanketed his elbow. His right covered with an analog clock labeled with gothic numerals and shaped like a skull. Below it, a large swastika. On either side of the clock, lengthwise, *RED DEATH*. The tattoos represented a motorcycle gang of the same name, who funded their organization through the sale of narcotics, extortion, and violence. The gang used this shelter as a distribution point. I didn't care about their activity and only wanted leads.

I craned my head to meet his eyes. "Hey, I'm looking for someone." He ignored my presence, glancing beyond me at the unhinged metal door. "Hey. I'm looking for someone. Are you going to help me or what?"

"I pick *or what.* You broke the damn door, copper. Who's going to pay to fix it?" He flexed his biceps; the bulges firm like steel rods.

"I didn't break it. I'm looking for leads on a case I'm working. You're my first stop."

"You shouldn't have come here. Turn around and walk through the exit you busted." He extended his arm, pointing his tentacled finger towards the teetering door.

"I didn't come here to break up your business." I glimpsed the shelter license hanging on the wall with his picture and name. "Look, Mr. Richard Wagner. I'm looking for information on a girl who was murdered."

He turned his head towards the plaque on the wall and returned with a grin. "If you say *please* I might consider helping you."

"Fine." I sighed. "*Please,* can you help me find a lead for this girl?"

"That's better. Let me see a picture of this chick." He leaned over the counter and extended an open hand.

"All I have is this ID. Her name is Maggie May. Take a good look. Think hard. *Please.*"

He swiped the card from my fingers and raised it towards his eyes. He huffed and grunted a couple times, squinting for a better view. I noticed the movement late. His other hand had reached into an inside pocket within his leather vest.

"Stop!" Fearing he was about to show a gun, I pulled mine. "Put your hands where I can see them. Richard!" He continued into his pocket, as my finger released the safety and slid over the trigger.

"Relax, copper. Just getting my lighter so I can see the picture."

I returned the gun into its holster. He spun the flint and continued to peruse the ID. A few moments later, a rumbling echoed from the backroom, and not more than a few seconds after that, a crash. A young girl, wearing only panties, broke through the cloaked entranceway separating the front desk from the sleeping quarters. She stumbled, falling onto Richard.

"Are you okay?" I asked.

She murmured some gibberish as her body fell backwards and her head snapped the opposite way. Richard's hands latched onto her arms like two oversized vise grips, squaring her limp body against the wall. As her arms dropped, I noticed a needle dangling from the cusp of her arm.

"What the hell?"

"We don't need any help. Mind your business, copper. Hey, Vince. Come get this bitch out of here. Now!" A shirtless man larger than Richard, with hair the length of his back, appeared from the room, each step like a cinder block. Various placed tattoos and scars blanketed his face and body. He didn't say a word and threw the girl over his shoulders, walking away like Frankenstein. "Good job, Vince. Do what you need to do to her. Make it feel good. Don't kill her either with that monster you got." Richard turned his attention to me with a devilish glare. "Alright. I haven't seen her and you haven't seen anything here. Go try the next luxury hotel on this strip. Good luck."

"I'm sure you've seen Maggie. Probably handled her like that girl."

"Let me make this clear. We know everything about you and every other copper in this city. There's a file on each of you in the backroom." He glanced at my nametag. "Frank—Stark. We know you love your cocaine and booze. And we know you like your women *and* men. The one thing we haven't figured out is why those people you're with sometimes disappear." He turned towards the backroom. "Hey, Vince! We should put a tail on this copper. I know he's up to no good." Richard turned towards me with a piercing stare. "That girl from the ID didn't come here. Even if she did, she wasn't pretty enough to stay. We keep all the pretty ones here because they like their drugs, and like to be shared just like a joint. Red Death can do whatever we want in this city. Be gone. If you feel someone following you, it's me." He crossed his arms and flexed once again, making certain his intimidation tactics were well received.

I stumbled backwards, shocked by his accurate revelations. I composed myself and lit a cigarette, submitting to his request. "Fine. Clean this shithole shelter. I'll ignore what happened this time. Give me a call if you hear anything on Maggie May." I slid my business card onto the counter.

He snagged the card, crumpled it, and flung it over his shoulder. "Not a chance, copper."

I stormed the exit, shoving the two homeless guys standing at the entrance, then kicked the broken door, snapping a screw from the hinge, and burrowing it deeper into the pavement.

IV

A cold, stinging drizzle moistened the uneven blacktop with a reflective, rainbow glaze. The next stop about a half block west. The top of the sign faded and peeling: New Beginnings for Life. A bare incandescent bulb provided sporadic light to the entrance. It dangled from two bare wires affixed to the ceiling by electrical tape. A sturdier handle opened this door. Three hanging bells, attached by a rope to the push bar, created a crude alarm against the rotting jamb.

The front desk, a few feet from the entrance, formed a large square barrier to the backroom. A New Age religious sect ran this shelter. Their motto, Inspire healing from within, hung from the ceiling by two frayed strings within a paisley frame. Healing couldn't be that easy or I'd sign up to clear the toxic soup within me.

"Good evening, Officer." She greeted me with a wide smile. "How are you?"

"I'm fine. I'm looking for someone. Hope you can help."

"I'll do my best. My name is Desiree Despotta. So who are we looking to find?" A sexy, southern tone awoke the fine hairs on my neck.

"Her name is Maggie May." I handed her the identification card.

Desiree beamed beauty. A gem within the filthy Shelter Avenue haystack. Her olive complexion smooth like silk, surrounded by a dark, curly mane. A puffy winter jacket hid her body, probably just as perfect as her smile. Coconut oil exuded from her pores, reminiscent of a Hawaiian Tropic summer at the Lake Ontario beaches. She'd be the one lying on the beach with macho guys jostling to get a blanket space next to her. Not me, though. A woman as beautiful as she isn't interested in a guy like me. Those women and men from Little Italy taught me all the excuses.

A dim, dancing fluorescent provided the only light for our space. She twisted and turned the ID within inches of thick-framed glasses. "Sorry, I'm taking so long. She looks familiar. I'm trying to remember if, or when I saw her." She removed her specs, easing them onto the counter.

"No problem, ma'am. Take your time. It's important. You can borrow my flashlight." I slid it from the utility belt and accidentally shone the light into her eyes.

The sight of her mesmerizing hazel irises proved the fiasco successful.

"Whoa. I need a minute just to see again."

"I'm sorry." I handed her the flashlight with its brightness reversed.

"She does look familiar. She might've been here one or two nights." Desiree slid her hand through her hair and nibbled her lower lip. "I think around January, give or take."

"Are you sure, ma'am?"

"I'm pretty sure. And you don't have to call me ma'am." Her cheeks rose as her eyes surveyed me. "Officer Stark."

"Yes, that's my name." I slid my finger under the name tag, propping it like a medal. "By the way... you have a beautiful name—Desiree. I like it."

"Thank you, Officer." Blushing, she smirked. "I like it too."

"Your accent isn't from Rochester. Where are you from?"

"I'm from Georgia. Kennesaw to be exact. Near Atlanta."

"Nice. I've never been, but I heard Georgia is beautiful, and obviously, so are the ladies. So far I have one out of two. By the way, my name is Frank." Our eyes locked and we exchanged smiles, time suspended.

"Well, awfully cute of you."

"Thank you, ma'am. I mean Desiree. Your accent... but—" I cleared my throat. "—let's get back to the case. Did you notice anything suspicious? Was she with anyone?"

She pursed her plump, red lips and creased her brow. "I'm not a hundred percent sure. She may have met someone. Well, maybe she didn't actually *meet* someone. I really don't know. I think she talked to everyone at the shelter."

"Anything strange about her? Did she look nervous or lost?"

"Everyone here is lost to some degree. Why so many questions? Is she in serious trouble?"

I hesitated to respond. "Yes... She was murdered. We're trying to find the killer."

"Oh my, Officer. Is—"

"You don't have to be alarmed. We think this is an isolated incident."

"Good to know, but why are you here?"

"She was from Waterloo. Probably a transient, so the shelters are first on our list. We need to find the killer and give Maggie peace. Of course, that's when I—I mean *we* find the killer."

"That's so sad. Sometimes happens around here." She shifted her eyes towards the ceiling, then traced a blank stare into the darkness. "Momma used to say, 'can't bite the elbow that feeds you. Ain't no point in trying to move forward when you can't move an inch.' Those old southern women are smart from experience. Do you know what I mean?"

"Yes. I deal with this kind of shit, I mean thing, every day. It's horrible, but it's just the way things are. I'm numb to it." I slumped my shoulders. "I've seen and done a lot of things I'm not proud of. Well, Desiree, I don't want to take up too much more of your time." I handed her my business card. "Anything that comes to mind will help. I'm heading to the other shelter."

"Oh, don't leave so soon. I'll get you a coffee. Maybe we can sit and chitchat for a bit. I promise not to keep you here all night. Let's just have one. Gets lonely around here. Do you know what I mean? You want cream and sugar?"

"I don't know. I really have to take care of this case. I don't want to lose any leads. People forget things. We have a forty-eight hour rule."

"Frank, I don't care about any stupid rules." She stepped back, tilted her head, and braced her hips. "A few minutes with me isn't going change anything that happened to that girl."

She's correct. A gorgeous woman from the South is asking me to stay, but I'm arguing about when I should leave. Maggie's dead just like Maria. No one can bring them back. What's done is done.

Come on, Frank. Wake up. Make this work, Frank.

"Sure, let's have a coffee. We'll extend the rules because I can't say no to your smile. No cream, milk, or sugar. Black please. I start mixing and the caffeine stops working. It's like my liquor. Neat, no mixers."

"Great. I'll be back in a second. Faster than a cat on a lizard. The pot's in the backroom."

"No problem. I'll be here." I nodded and winked.

I ogled her strut until she disappeared into the diminishing light. Opposite the backroom, the homeless dorms. The entryway covered by a flimsy curtain, which rippled every few seconds from the gargling thunders. I'm not sure how they slept through the rumbling, let alone on single cots probably not cleaned in decades. I couldn't blame Maggie for leaving the shelter, considering the noise and whatever else occurred, but she made a choice and now she's dead. Her murderer may have been here as well. Barging through the curtain an option, but ruining the chance with Desiree outweighed it. Indecision twitched my gut, accustomed to living without restraint.

The nicotine fix called not too long after. Hard to resist after whiffing a hint of smoke. I slid the tobacco stick between my lips and flipped the Zippo. Exhaling, I noticed the sign tacked to the wall: *NO SMOKING*.

"Hey, hon." Desiree's silhouette scuffled towards me. "I got the coffee. Black and hot. Just how you like it."

"You bet I like it that way. I have a question." Like a magician, I palmed the cigarette in front of my back. "Can I smoke in this place? I couldn't find an ashtray anywhere on the counter."

"Yes, you can smoke here." She curled her lips. "I'm not sure why you're asking, since there's smoke rising from your rear."

"Busted. My bad."

"By the way, I smoke all the time. Everyone does. I hide the ashtray because everyone likes to steal it."

"I'm stressed. I should've waited."

"I understand. I do the same when shit gets that way. Better to smoke than do drugs. At least that's what they tell me at those weekly meetings at the center. My momma always said, 'it can always be worse.'"

"You're right, Desiree. It *can* always be worse. Thank you for all the information you've given me tonight."

"No problem. I always try to help. Which reminds me..." She patted her jacket, fumbling through each pocket.

"Do you need a smoke?"

"Yes... What kind you do you have?"

"Regulars."

"Thanks for the offer but not my cup of tea. I prefer menthols."

"Those are good. It's like smoking a cough drop. What brought you to Rochester?"

"My story is long and short. Which version do you want?"

"You pick." I leaned onto the counter and propped up a leg.

"Okay, short. I moved up here for my brother, Darnell. He's sick with an addiction. All the stress from Darnell caused my mom to have a stroke, so then it became my responsibility to take care of them." She leaned back, flush against the wall, and closed her eyes. "The weight from the pain fell on me like a boulder. My brother kept getting high and my mother sicker."

"The name, Darnell, sounds familiar."

"You've probably arrested him before." She jived, but a stern face showed a hint of truth.

"I suppose that's possible. I think it's somewhere else, though. Just can't place it. Anyway, go on. Sorry. Sounds like you're in a tough situation."

"Do you still have your parents, Frank?"

I can't tell her about my past. There's no way she'll understand the hell I've lived. Mom... Dad... Their fates ended differently but the same. The table... the flickering fluorescent lights... the leather apron... the animals... the humans... the basement... the blood... the journal... Maria... the darkness at the end of the tunnel...

"Frank... Are you still with me? Frank... Snap out of it."

"What's going on? Where am I?" I refocused my vision and shuddered.

"Frank. It's okay. I just asked you a question about your parents and you disappeared on me."

"Right. I remember. Yes, they're still around, much older now. They're in good health, considering their ages.

I think they're both in their 80s. I know their end is near. I'll deal with it someday. But enough about me. What do you think you're going to do with your mom?"

"I don't know yet. I'm scared losing my only parent. The whole dying thing. Do you know what I mean?"

I do, but I couldn't tell her. I'd already lied about my parents. They died years ago and my hands played a role, although not directly. Death is a fruitless thought. When it's over, it's really over. No happy skies, no perfect weather, and no wings to fly with unicorns. After you've seen a few people die or caused their deaths, you learn how to sever that part of the brain. I try to find its remnants, but they've disappeared, left me only with an idea of what used to be. Life is similar: trying to get a rise out of anything and everything to keep pushing through to the next day. Once that runs out, well, the only option is to take your own life, but that's easier said than done. Takes a lot of courage to cross that line and each time I reach it, I back away. I wanted to be blunt with her, but I couldn't. It'd scare her off. I decided to give her simple "heal from within" advice.

"I think you should go with your heart, Desiree. It'll work out either way. I believe you're strong enough to weather the storm."

She retrieved a single cigarette, flipping it between her fingers like a drumstick, and stared at the ceiling. Across from her, I waited for the perfect opportunity to swoop in like Romeo and light it. She took a deep drag and exhaled a blooming cloud.

"I'm slightly relieved. I'm going to consider your advice."

"Great. I'm here to help if I can. Are your family members going to be okay with your decisions?"

"I don't have any family, so it doesn't matter." She diverted her attention to the wall of the ashtray, rolling the cigarette tip into a smoldering point. She followed with a nonchalant shrug.

No family, Frankie. This one's a keeper.

"It will all work out for you. I promise."

"You're right. I'll figure it out in the next week or so. By the way, something just came to mind. I think Darnell may have talked to Maggie a couple of times. When she was here, of course."

"Did Darnell ever mention anything about her?"

"No, he didn't. He's always high and only sleeps here when it gets too cold, or the drug house is full. We can talk to him during the day, if he's available and sober. My guess is they probably talked about scoring dope. Nothing more, nothing less."

"That sounds like a plan. You have my card so call me anytime. They'll put you through no matter where I am."

We exchanged amusing smiles and she winked.

"Sounds good, Officer."

"Great. I'm going to head to the next shelter. Thank you for the coffee and the company."

"You're welcome. Have a good and peaceful night. I hope we talk soon."

"Me too. I'm looking forward to it."

I subtly waved from hip height. Once outside, I leaned against the brick wall and gazed into the starless sky. The drizzle had changed to ice, stinging my hands and face like a million pin pricks. I lit a cigarette and puffed a cloud into the open air. It floated towards a flickering street lamp, then lifted higher and merged with its larger brethren. Inside the drifting mass, Desiree's face appeared, her smile as wide as ten city blocks with hypnotic eyes just as vast. She batted her eyelids and blew me a kiss. I returned it without hesitation. She wants to be with me. I just know it. I wouldn't mind being with her. She'd be a positive change in my life and I'll forget my past. We can move forward together. You've treated me well, opposite of most. I raised my hand to stroke her supple cheek against the backdrop of the heavens —"Damn it!" I waggled my arm on instinct, awakening from the trance. The cigarette butt had burned its impression between my fingers. The remains falling onto the wet pavement, fizzling next to my boot.

V

Bits of icy drizzle crunched under my boots, providing the only commotion on the desolate street. The next and last shelter, less than half a block west, located on the corner of South Avenue and Alexander Street. It encompassed the intersection and resembled an apartment complex. Multiple flood lights illuminated its brick façade, which could be seen from anywhere on the avenue. As I neared, a wooden sign, as large as the wall and thick as a concrete block, radiated with freshly painted letters: The Catholic Open Arms Mission. Its monstrous frame supported by a hundred, handcrafted bolts and brackets. The overflowing coffers from Sunday mass certainly paid for the installation. "A Home for the Homeless, All are Welcome" blanketed a pitch-black window to the right the entrance, which resembled a church door made of maple or oak.

Prior to now, I'd never been to this shelter, interacting with them by phone for several hate crimes at a discothèque I frequented: the Milky Oyster, formerly known as Club Marcella. Some volunteers at the Catholic Mission, less than a half mile from the Oyster, helped the LGBTQ community, even though their religion suggested otherwise.

Some Rochesterians, from all walks of life, hurled derogatory slurs at the LGBTQ community. Within the vicinity of the club, the vitriol escalated. I responded to many calls where a gay or transgender person was beaten to the point of death. The hate crimes typically occurring during closing time. Drunk, straight guys, or guys in the closet looking to prove their manhood stalked the bar. Once people exited the establishment, the violent prowlers jumped them in a dark alley not far from the entrance. Unfortunately, the main thoroughfare to the parking lot and street lacked security due to funding. Every so often, we captured one or two, but most of the time they escaped. The patrols in the area weak, since the Captain regarded LGBTQ humans as lower class. His focus, the white neighborhoods. Hopefully, the Rochester Catholics would assist the Maggie May case as they do the LGBTQ community.

"What the hell? Open shelter my ass."

I tugged the slender pull-handle several times, but it didn't open. I opted for a different approach, kicking the door with steel-toe boots, hoping to get a response from the missing attendant. No luck. A few steps into my retreat, I spun and returned to the door with an alternative, swinging my baton like a hammer. Each strike louder than the last, reverberating the avenue like a bending handsaw.

I paused to rest, then a faint call arrived. "I'm coming. Wait a minute. One second, please." I retreated the club and the metal lock disengaged like the slide of a gun. The shelter keeper appeared, out of breath and disheveled. "Hello." He scanned me head to toe, stopping at my badge. "Hello––Officer. Sorry about the wait." He raised his sleeve and cleaned a white residue from his lips. "I was tidying the shelter and had to lock the door."

"Not a problem. *Father?*" He caught me off guard dressed in an unbuttoned cassock, a black shirt, and a clerical collar, which hung over his chest. "I'm hoping you can assist me. I have a couple questions to ask about someone who may have stayed at this shelter."

"Yes. Sure… I'll help you the best I can."

"Don't be nervous. I'm not here to stir any pots. Only want information."

"No problem, Officer." His stammer transitioned into a high-pitched lisp. "I'm here to help."

"May I have your name?"

"Brandon, sir. Father Brandon Biloxi."

"How long have you been working here, Father?"

"About six months."

I hadn't envisioned a priest like Brandon. The cassock draped over his lanky build like a bed sheet covering a ghost. Pink lipstick blotted the clerical collar. Yellowed teeth speckled with black sprinkles juxtaposed his sapphire eyes. Smudged eyeliner trailed over his thin-bridged nose. The caked foundation, matching the peroxided hair, formed creases across his hairless face and boney cheeks.

"Six months. Great. You might be able to help. Her name is Maggie May. Can you take a look?" I handed him the identification.

"I don't recognize the name. Maybe I've seen her. On the other hand, never mind. A lot of people come through here. Too… hard to tell. Wasn't her."

His stutter had returned. After fifteen years of interrogating all walks of life, I knew he had information. "Well, look harder and focus. It's important. Anything you can provide will help with our investigation. Can we move inside? It's too cold near the door."

"Sure. Right this way."

Taking the bait allowed an opportunity to find clues. He turned, leading the way down the narrow corridor permeating incense. Handmade, bronze sconces lined the hallway. Between them, crucifixes and blue-eyed, blonde Jesus posters hung like the Stations of the Cross. An odd selection of pictures for a Jewish man from Bethlehem in Palestine.

"If you… don't mind me asking, what happened to her?"

"Well, she's dead. Murdered. I know you have information." I pounded the wall, rattling a few of the crucifixes. Intimidation a useful tool for those who are scared.

"I understand, Officer. Give me a second. I'll have another look."

He fumbled the ID, spinning it like a wand towards his eyes. While he decided his angles of view, I ventured towards the check-in counter. I lit a cigarette and searched for an ashtray, which led me to a clue, not for Maggie May but for Father Brandon. A bottle of vodka, two glasses, and a Playgirl magazine.

"Hey. What are you doing? Get away from there... That's none of your concern." His footsteps thumped towards me.

I lifted the Playgirl magazine and several Polaroids of partially clothed children fell from between the pages. As I collected the photos, I glanced towards the sleeping area, blinking several times to clear my vision. A teenager peered from behind a door frame. The room opposite the sleeping area. He must've been fourteen. Once our eyes met, he quickly disappeared. I now knew why the door was locked. Fury filled my being.

"Damn, scumbag priest. You're a sad excuse for a human. Worse than the shit floating on the Genesee River." I flailed my hands grazing the asbestos ceiling. "Two glasses, a bottle of vodka, and a Playgirl. What the hell is wrong with you, man?"

"I… didn't do anything. I'm allowed to drink and look at magazines. It's none of your business."

I rushed him, stopping within centimeters of his flushing cheeks. "It is my business when you have two glasses of vodka and a kid staring at me from the backroom." Spit splashed across his clerical shirt and onto his face as my tirade continued. "Is that the real fucking reason why the door was locked? You were busy in the back room with a child. Taking advantage of him to satisfy your sexual needs."

"I did nothing of the sort." His stutter changed into persistent denial. "He's eighteen and legal."

I sucked a deep drag of the cigarette and unleashed a winded breath, swarming every crevice of his face. I latched onto his clerical shirt, swatting the collar from his neck, and smashed his body against the wall. A crucifix crashed to the floor and splintered. His death had crossed my mind, but I needed information.

"Father fucking molester. You're a disgrace. You have no shame. You're worse than a murderer. At least they kill their prey. You make yours suffer the burden of consequence."

"I didn't do anything, Officer."

"You're a liar. How about I go to the backroom and talk to that teen. Do you want me to do that? Do you?"

"No. Nothing happened. Please don't. We were just talking."

"You were not *just* talking and you know it. Your makeup is smeared and I bet it's on him too. Kid. Come out here, kid." My demand echoed the hallway.

"No... Stop!" He called down the hallway. "Don't listen to him, baby. Stay in the back, sweetie. I'll take care of everything up here. Just stay in the back." The child didn't approach, nor did he peer from the door. Father Brandon dropped to his knees. His face siphoned of what little color it had before I entered. "Please forgive me for I have sinned. Please... What do you want from me? Our father who art in hea—"

"Shut the fuck up. What I want to do is kill you. Give me all the information you have on Maggie May. Do that and I won't haul you to jail where you'll get raped every goddamn day. On second thought, you'll probably like that option."

"How do you know she was here? There are other shelters."

"I've been to them. She was next door, so I know she ended up here. There's nowhere else to go in this damn city."

"Fine. I'll talk, but you have to leave me alone. Do we have a deal?"

Silence filled the space between us as I weighed the options. Taking him to jail or killing him would be the right thing to do, but I needed to handle Maggie May's killer first. Father molester wasn't going anywhere, and he wasn't going to touch anymore kids, at least not in the near future.

"Understand, you're not special. You're a piece of shit. The only reason I'm doing this is for Maggie. Yes, we have a deal."

"Okay..."

I threw my cigarette towards him, and, while midair, stomped it against his knee. The cartilage popped. He gasped and moaned.

"Now, tell me what I need to know."

"Fine," he said, regaining some of his breath. "Maggie was here a few times in the last couple months, strung out on dope. Sometimes she talked, sometimes she nodded off. We talked a bit when she wasn't intoxicated. She didn't have much to say, loose conversation."

"What did she say? I need to know everything." I lunged and he flinched.

"Okay." He surrendered, then retreated into a Catholic clasp. "She talked about how she had no family, except a brother. Waterloo was too boring for her. She hitchhiked to Rochester where she found better drugs and a different life."

"What else?"

"She introduced me to her guy friend a couple weeks ago. Cute. He could've passed for gay, especially when you put drinks in him. He'd get really touchy-feely with the guys."

"What was his name?" I hit the wall again and shook several crucifixes.

"I think… Mario."

"Did he have a last name?"

"No. Last names aren't good for business."

"I get it. What did he look like?"

"Six feet tall, maybe a little less, reddish brown hair and a scruff to match. Tired green eyes with a large scar on his face."

"Is there anything else?"

He paused. "Yes. He mentioned a bar a few times. I think it's called Magpie Irish Pub. He likes his liquor when he has the cash."

"Got it. That bit of information should help. If he returns, call me as soon as possible. Guy is dangerous." I flipped my card onto the counter.

"I will. I promise."

"I have some advice. Stop with the little boys. I'll be watching you, and so will all the other cops. I'm right around the corner and we'll come for you."

"I understand. Forgive me," he said, gazing at the floor, hands clasped in front of his back.

I remained silent. My stay at the shelter had run its course. I shoved the door and lit a cigarette. Dragging my boots against the pavement, I wobbled to the police cruiser a few blocks from Shelter Avenue. The shelters requested we park out of plain sight because they spooked the homeless people. The Captain refuted their request because he hated everyone except his white buddies, but I obliged. I didn't want to come back to this area for a frozen body.

I plopped onto the seat like a slab of meat. Searching three shelters with a hangover drained my remaining energy that I had gained from the earlier nap. I lowered the window and slammed the shifter into drive, hoping the cold wind roused me during the ride home. Red lights blurred and street signs melded into street lamps as the pedal touched the floorboard.

Up over the hill of the expressway, I glimpsed the neon spire glowing: KODAK. George Eastman, the multimillionaire and founder of Eastman Kodak, had the right idea. When he decided he'd had enough, he shot himself in the heart. Takes plenty of courage to make that happen, which I lack.

Several minutes later the front tire jumped the curb in front of my apartment. I hammered the shifter into park, shaking the car to a halt. I left three wheels on the street and one up top. I didn't care. I needed a drink, or two. After three, tall scotches, I stumbled into bed in full uniform, hoping for better days ahead.

VI

Tossing and turning, the bed sheets entwined with the blanket fell to the floor at some point during sleep. Not a dream nor nightmare, nor bizarre events occurred during the early morning hours. At least not to the best of my memory. Reposing with my eyes closed, I pondered the mental anguish from the last several weeks. The conclusion: things never go as planned and sometimes it's best not to plan and just go with the flow.

I rose from bed, lit a cigarette, and focused on my first priority: stripping the uniform I'd worn day and night for the last few months. Its polyester blend infested with scotch, musk, and an unknown, molded-cheese strain. My options slim. The spare uniforms hanging in the closet and piled upon the floor suffered the same afflictions. Hopefully, those around me sniffed more musk than anything else.

I burned off the final drag of the cig and hobbled into the bathroom. A shower certain to clear the mind. Steam filled the room, condensing upon the grime plastered onto the ceiling. Eyes wide, I stepped into the bathtub. Rippling chills rolled my scalding skin, as black mold flaked from the tiled walls into the drain. The initial shock subsided into pleasure, while I slathered Ivory soap across my body. I smacked the faucet handle. The cold water spritzed my body like the baptismal fountain I swam in as a child.

I fell to my knees, hands clasped, and wailed. "Why has this happened? Why can't it be fixed? Let me feel the cure." I awoke a short time later spewing water from my lungs. Gasping for breath, I brushed the droplets from my eyes, and tottered along the tub, stretching and searching for the rim to rest my head. After several minutes, I mustered just enough strength to rise to my feet and exit.

I craned towards the vanity and swiped the remnants of fog, leaving streaks in the process. My reflection difficult to comprehend between the smears, the stained mirror unbearable. The whites of my eyes resembled a map, the roads chiseled in crimson. My lower eyelids sagged into my cheeks, surrendering to gravity. I nudged the skin to awaken it, but the attempt failed, bruised and battered like a thirteen-round boxer. I stopped prodding for fear of an explosion. An array of wrinkles pathed my face and stubble like carvings on a tree trunk hidden by dense moss.

I hobbled from the bathroom to the bedroom, sifting through uniforms with a scratch-and-sniff technique. The best one, or least odorous, was the one I'd slept in last night. I doused myself and the uniform with cologne, then slipped it on.

In the kitchen, I brewed a carafe of dark roast. A much needed caffeine spike to figure out the next options for the Maggie May case. The information I gathered from Father Brandon posed an issue, only because of the potential outcomes. If I gave Detective Daniels the lead, then they'll arrest the killer. Best case scenario: he gets life in prison. Worst case scenario: he spends a couple years at the Monroe County jail for manslaughter. Neither option provided Maggie May justice. That can only be served when an eye is exchanged for an eye.

I sat at the kitchen table with a full cup of coffee and lit a cigarette. I followed its trail of smoke towards the ceiling as it spun and curved like a hypnotic cobra. The pop and crackle of the smoldering tobacco awoke me from the trance. I sucked another drag as my other hand glided over my chin.

Springing from the chair with an idea in mind, I lunged towards the cupboards, rummaging through each one for game bags and tarps. Maria's unfortunate set of events had used my primary stash. I located one tarp and two game bags, stowing them in the closet. Certainly not enough for a human. A stop at Chase Pitkin, the local hardware store, would resolve the problem. I poured a glass of scotch in celebration, chasing it with a sip of coffee, and I was out the door.

Job well done, Frank. Time to head to work.

Pat's Drive-In, located on Main Street, deserved a visit. A much better locale than Diego's bodega. Pat always welcomed cops with open arms. He took care of the Blue Brotherhood and we reciprocated. That mutual relationship worked well for Pat. He had the only place in the city without any criminal incidents.

Pat, a short, brawny, Italian fellow, arrived from Italy about twenty years ago and never shook the accent, but spoke English well. His real name Pasquale Lucchese. He treated all his customers, especially cops, with the Italian code, paralleling New York City and the Chicago mafia during the 1930s. If anyone violated it, then certain unspeakable consequences followed. We didn't know the exact ramifications, nor did we know if he was *connected*. We'd heard rumors about cutting, shooting, and breaking bones but never asked to confirm.

The interior of Pat's Drive-In was built during the 1960s. Wire racks filled with chips and cookies lined the store aisles. Across from the racks, mammoth coolers built into the walls housed the beer. Bright orange tiles lined the floor, matching the color of the counter where Pat stood, guarding the cigarettes, coffee, and liquor.

"How are you Pat?" I asked, standing across the counter.

"I'm good today. No problems this week. Hope it stays that way."

"Me too, Pat." I nodded and let out a grumbling sigh. "This city is rough. It reminds me of a mini New York City. These damn criminals are horrible. Trust me when I say, I wish they were all dead."

"Sign me up for that crew." He crossed his large, disproportionate arms atop a jutting stomach, which formed a shelf below his chest. Those biceps may have hammered megatons of steel during a former life in Italy. "I'll join you in a minute. We'll take 'em all down together." He scrunched his wide nose like a boxer and threw a jab into the air.

"I'll let you know, buddy."

"What can I get for you, Frank?"

"I need a couple packs of smokes and a large coffee. Add some chips, donettes, and a fifth of scotch."

"You got it, Officer. Coming right up." He moved pretty damn quick for a squatty fellow, and had everything on the counter in less than a minute.

"Keep the change." I handed him forty, which included a tip.

"Thanks. Have a good day." He offered up a two-finger salute. "Stay safe and see you soon."

Most cops tipped Pat. He knew people in all the right and wrong places and always helped us get leads for big cases. If someone needed something they couldn't find, then Pat made a call, and voila, he delivered the goods. We never questioned his connections, nor did we care. Helping the Blue Brotherhood meant more than anything, so we all turned a blind eye or two towards him.

* * * * * * * * * * * * *

I sat at my desk puffing smoke and looking at the wall clock. The long, black pointer lollygagged forward, pulling the weight of its shorter brother, until it snapped to 8:00 a.m. And like clockwork, Detective Daniels entered through the door, swaggering and swaying through the precinct. Jet-black hair parted firm to the right, his suit pressed like plywood. The ensemble accented by a sturdy half-Windsor knot.

"Good morning, Detective."

"Is it, Sergeant Stark? Is it *really* a good morning?"

"I think so, Detective."

"You don't look any better than prior days. Actually, you look worse. Better keep shades on them eyes. So, I ask you again, is it *really* a good morning?"

"Shut up, Detective. Can't you just be nice? I said good morning. Just say the same in return."

"Alright. Good morning," he said with a deadpan tone. "Any new leads on the Maggie May case?"

Get it right, Frank. Get—it—right, Frankie.

"I've got nothing." I squared my shoulders, back taut, with a convincing stare. "The shelters had zero. I spent hours interrogating them and they didn't remember her. It's a shame. I hope this case doesn't go cold."

"Well, if it does, then there's nothing we can do about it," he said with a somber tone. "You have to remember it's not our fault. We try every day to get these things resolved."

Daniels spun towards his office, slumping his shoulders, and mumbling to himself. I reorganized a few papers on my desk, avoiding what was underneath, and turned towards the wall. This time the minutes of the clock fought a losing battle with the seconds. Cigarettes filtered through my fingers and mouth like a chain gang, while the dark coffee chased away the smoke lodged in my throat. I finally cleared the files from my desk and Maggie May's murder photos appeared. Her images spun in my mind like a Rolodex. I hammered the desk with my fist. The coffee mug, pictures, and ashtray jumped in unison.

A muffled voice called out, each syllable blurring into the next. The pounding in my eardrums escalated into booms against my skull while my chest caved, ribs snapped, their jagged edges piercing my lungs.

"Are you okay? Sarge!"

A shoulder tap shook the haze, but the voice as muddled as the face. "Yeah... what do you want?"

"Are you okay, Sarge? I've been calling out to you and you haven't responded."

The shoulder tap turned into a shallow massage, while a puff of hot air curled my neck. "Stop touching me." Joe Rook's face came into focus as he moved from behind me. "I'm fine. I was... just thinking. You know, deep thought."

"That must've been important, Sarge. Did you even hear me?"

"I'm fine. Move on, Rook. All good here. Nothing to see." Silence overcame the Precinct as every officer grimaced.

"Will do. Just making sure you're fine. You look stressed. Maybe you need more rest."

"Don't worry about me." I pounded the desk with both hands. "Do you understand?"

"Yes, Sarge. I get it. Okay. Sorry, man."

"Good. Move on, you damn Rook."

I exited not long thereafter, fed up with Maggie May's pictures and the Precinct's atmosphere. Damn Joe Rook always in my face. With sirens blaring from the car, I ran every red light to my apartment. The bottle of scotch calling for a drink and my bed for a nap. I parked and dashed to the door, fumbling the keys into the lock, then hurrying through the entrance and into the kitchen. Panting at the counter, I grabbed the bottle of scotch and spun the cap. Several dirty tumblers scattered throughout kitchen still had liquor from weeks ago. I grabbed two and poured triple shots of scotch into each, then downed them like water. I stumbled the hallway, crashing onto the bed in full uniform.

At some point, Maggie and Maria appeared, partying at the kitchen table. As Maria hunched to snort a line, Maggie struck her head with my baton, then fell onto the hardwood floor unconscious. I tried speaking, but my tongue had been removed. I tried charging, but my arms and legs had been nailed. She knelt beside Maria and slid her hand along her thigh, grabbing a handful of Maria's dress and lifting. She drove the baton between Maria's legs, each thrust more potent than the last. Maria didn't wake as Maggie retracted the dripping staff. She slithered Maria's body and straddled her chest, raising the baton and ramming Maria's mouth like a jackhammer. Maria's jaw crunched and crackled into pieces, while her neck snapped like a branch.

Maggie smiled with terror-filled eyes. "What do we do now, Sarge?"

I moaned, jouncing to escape, the nails stretching and tearing my skin. Maggie raised the baton, then whirled it like a wand. Seconds later, my tongue reformed, extended my chest, and retracted into my mouth.

"I don't know."

Maggie didn't take that too well. "If you don't answer correctly, you'll suffer just like Maria. Tell me, what do we do now, *Sarge*?"

"Cut her up, Maggie?" I squirmed, but the nails tugged harder. "If that's the right answer, let me go."

At that instance, Maria woke bloodied and broken. "Yeah, *Sarge*. What do we do now? Are you sure you want to cut me up?" She smirked, then part of her jaw dropped to the floor. "You're free for now, but I'll see you soon enough." She teased with a demonic laugh.

"What the hell—?" I sprung from bed soaked in sweat and ran from the bedroom.

"Maria… Maria!"

I stumbled across the corridor and a door handle greeted my temple. A frantic search commenced—closets, rooms, under the bed—but no trace of her existed. I dashed into the kitchen. Frantic pours and sips of scotch dribbled along my arm and onto the floor.

You'll be fine, Frank. I will not be fine. Just a dream. Not a dream.

I ran my fingers through my hair, stretching clumps from the scalp. Perhaps the/*rapist* of the mind wants to decipher these mental spasms at a later date. On the other hand, that's doubtful. She'll demean me with her overbearing and insincere know-it-all attitude. Tell me I'm flawed and the best solution is medication. "You need to stop drinking and drugging," she says. "It's not healthy for you, Frank. I have better drugs for you. I promise they'll cure you." She doesn't know a damn thing except what's in those books on her shelf. She doesn't know real life, *my life*. There's no time to figure all of this out now. The setting sun signals the bar. At least there I'm respected and we all share a common bond.

VII

Killing two birds with one stone is the goal for tonight: catch a buzz and follow up on Father Brandon's lead. I removed the malodorous uniform and threw it atop the unwashed pile of other fatigues in the closet. Always best going to a bar in civilian attire. Big Brother surveilling people getting wasted creates a tense atmosphere. I slipped into a dress shirt, a pair of weathered jeans, and a leather jacket. After drenching my body and clothing with cologne, I brushed my hair and headed to the kitchen. I pulled a prefilled flask of scotch from the cupboard and swigged. Elation greeted me at the door. Freedom from the Precinct this evening and perhaps several mental health days to extend the ride.

Thin, cold air and a light dusting of snow chilled the bones during the short trot to the bar. A few sips from the flask and a cigarette provided just enough body warmth to get me to the entrance of Magpie Irish Pub. I sat at my usual faded stool at the corner of the bar.

"Hey, Frank. How goes it?" Mike, the bartender, offered a weakhanded wave.

Everybody knew everyone's name at Magpie, as the regulars called it, and the bar had a reputation of priding itself on drunken debauchery. At times, the patrons stood shoulder to shoulder, at others, only three people kept Mike's skills sharp. The three consisted of myself, Chuck, and Jack. Tonight's crowd fell somewhere between. The drinks flowed like the roaring Genesee River.

"Going well, Mike. I think I want to get drunk." We exchanged a handshake.

"Good for you. Nothing new then? What can I get for you?"

"I'll take a couple shots of scotch and a beer chaser."

"Sounds good. Coming right up."

"Thanks, man. I really need the drinks tonight."

"You can always use the drinks, Frank." His gaudy laugh spread like contagion.

Mike Bates, a high school librarian, bartended as a side gig. The tips paid for hundreds of trips to music festivals as well as all the drugs filling his traveling backpack. He had an impressive store of knowledge and knew the names of all the patrons entering Magpie.

"I suppose you're right. Can I ask you a question, Mike?"

"Sure. What's up?" He perked up, which was a rare sight.

"Have you seen a guy with reddish hair and a beard to match? About six feet tall, maybe a little less, with a scar on his right cheek?"

"I might've seen him, but a lot of people come through here. Got a name?"

"He's a lead on a case. Might go by Mario."

"I'll keep an eye out and let you know. I promise." He played the counter like a bongo, took two steps away, stopped and turned towards me. "I have a question for you, Frank."

"What's that?"

"Whatever happened with that beautiful girl the other night?"

"Which one?" I belted out a laugh and sipped the scotch.

"I don't remember her name. I think it started with an M. She was wearing that tight outfit. Italian looking girl."

"Oh… her. I think her name was Mary or Maria. I can't keep track of names. She was in Rochester just for the night, then moved to New York City or something."

"That's too bad. I think you both had a shot for something long term. You looked good together."

"Thanks, but we'll never see her again. On to the next one. You know I can't settle down." I raised the glass and rolled my eyes.

"Okay then." Mike tapped the bar, then glided to a group of college kids and poured shots.

If he knew what happened to her, he wouldn't be serving you drinks.

A couple hours passed. The scene as busy as a funeral home. Two beautiful women exchanged some small talk with me, amounting to nothing. I think they wanted me to buy drinks, but I had someone else on my mind. Mario. I stepped out front for some fresh nicotine and encountered Katie huddled under the front awning, mumbling to herself. A cute local barista with a toned body and long legs snug inside black leggings. The heavy cocaine use and liquor diet kept her weight around a hundred pounds. That type of diet keeps you thin, but I don't think it works for everyone, because my waist keeps expanding. We exchanged a few words, then her speech faded into a beer bottle.

I headed into Magpie and straight to the bar. "Hey, Mike. Can I get another round of scotches and a beer chaser?"

"Of course."

"How's your night? Good tips?"

"Going well. By the way, I think that guy you're trying to find entered through the back door about ten minutes ago. Seems to fit your description. He's drinking alone." Mike slid the drinks towards me, pointing his eyes with a nod towards the back corner of the bar. "Over there."

"Alright. Thanks. I'll go talk to him."

"Sounds good, Frank. Just one thing."

"What's that?" My buzz kicked in as I downed the shot.

"Please, no trouble tonight." He grinned and slapped the bar.

I stretched one hand across the bar and we exchanged a handshake, while my other hand offered a Boy Scout salute. "You have my word. No trouble. Let me buy him a beer. I'll make it a peace offering."

Mike handed me the beer with a subtle nod and smirked. I hobbled to the back of the bar with two drinks in hand, a beer for him and a neat scotch for me. "Hey.... How's it going? Are you up for another beer?"

"Yeah... man. I'll take the beer, if you're offering. I'm running low." His eyes as glossy as the lips of a porn star.

"No problem." I slid into the booth. "I saw you sitting alone, so I figured I'd get you a drink. What's your name?"

"I'm laying low tonight. I figured the back room would be quiet. My name is..." He paused and slurred. "Mario—Mario Solari. What's your name, sweetie?"

"The name's Louie."

There's a go-to alias for all cops on the force. I chose *Louie* after a drug bust. We arrested a three-hundred-pound man on the toilet snorting lines while playing with himself. That cartoon stuck in my mind. Every so often I'd use his name for an inside laugh.

"What brings you to Magpie tonight?" I sipped the scotch.

"Drinks… to cure the soul. I'm in the dumps tonight. I've been reminiscing about a girl. A woman I used to know. Her name was Maggie May. She was a good friend of mine."

I hit the jackpot with Maggie's killer sitting next to me, drunk as a chipmunk in a barrel of whiskey. I desired more information. I needed to know why.

"What happened to her?"

"I don't know. She left out of the blue. I don't think she's coming back… People come and go quite a bit in my life."

"I feel your pain, man. Shit happens. I guess that's why we drink."

"You're right." He attempted to smile but stopped short. "We drink to kill the pain and cure the soul. My sister used to come here too. I thought she'd be here tonight, but I guess I was wrong. She comes—and goes—as well."

"What's your sister's name?"

Mario's eyes brightened. A broad smile made an appearance, exposing brownish teeth and greying gums. "Her name is… Maria. She's a pretty little thing. I love her more than life, even though she has a temper sometimes. She took care of me growing up."

"Do you have a picture of her?"

"I think I do." He dug into his jacket, retrieving and unfolding a picture. "Here she is."

"She's beautiful," I said awestruck, staring at the creased color photo of them holding hands shoreside.

"Was this taken at Lake Ontario?"

"Yup. When we first moved here. Seems like forever." He sighed and turned away.

Maria's never coming back, Mister Mario. She sunk like a rock.

"Maria. She's just as pretty as her name." I patted his back. "Well, let's have drinks for them. I'll call out an order." I swung towards the bar. "Mike! Send over a bunch of shots and beers. We're going to be here a while."

"Will do, Frank. Give me a couple minutes." He gave a thumbs up.

Damn it, Mike. So much for using an alias. Play it cool.

"So… where you from Mario?"

"Waterloo. A small town out east. My sister and I were inseparable. No parents and a small town wasn't fun." He closed his eyes and bowed his head. "We moved from home to home." He took a long sip of beer, then a shot, which shivered him. "We saved a few dollars and escaped to Rochester."

Good deal. He's too drunk to recognize names.

"That's too bad."

A sliver of my heart ached for him. I'm not emotionless, but such is life, and it never serves you a perfect platter. My dad threw me against the wall a few times while he beat Mom. He almost choked me to death on other occasions, but I turned out just fine without any sympathy.

Mario paused for a few moments. "Don't be sorry." His lips firmed. "It can always be worse. Anyway, I need to sober up. Hope I'm not slurring too much."

"You're fine, and welcome to Rochester. I'm not sure it's the big city, but it's better than Waterloo."

"You're right, but to me it's like New York City. There's a lot less trouble in Rochester than New York City. Don't you think, *Louie*?"

Maggie May and Maria disagree.

"Yes, and no. An old man once told me, 'Trouble is all around. It'll always find you whether you want it to or not.'" I grunted behind a devilish grin and gazed into his eyes.

The drinks arrived, thankfully interrupting our deep conversation. We each raised a shot glass, slurped the scotch, followed by long swigs of beer. "Cheers!" we said in unison, as we raised the second set of shots.

VIII

Mike poured drinks like an Olympian and viewed any refusal sacrilegious. Inevitably, we stayed until closing. Before that time arrived, we staggered out to the back alley to smoke a cigarette. I pulled one from my pack, lit it, and handed it to him. He raised it slow, his drunken hand snaking through the air to his lips. After the first drag, he stumbled towards me and crashed into my arms. I caught him, propping his body against the concrete wall. I steadied his shoulders and stepped away. He mumbled some gibberish, looked at me cross-eyed, and puffed the cigarette. This was my opportunity to dig into his mind for information on Maggie May.

"Are you doing okay?"

"Sure... Are... you?"

"Yeah. We need a few more drinks." I raised my glass, taking a sip. "Can I ask you a couple questions about Maggie?"

"Sure. …shoot."

He raised the cig, then lost his balance, flailing his hands like an orchestra conductor, then, in one grand motion, he stood like a military man saluting a general.

"What happened with you and Maggie at the apartment that night?"

"Nothing. What do you mean?" He flexed his brow.

"I know something transpired. You can tell me. Just trust me." My inviting grin probably made no difference to his drunken eyes.

"Okay. Fine! Maggie had an accident. That's all I know."

"What kind of accident?"

"We were all getting high and drinking, then she just went… quiet. I don't know anything else."

"Yes you do. By quiet, you mean dead, right?"

"Yes. Sure. Now, can we get more drinks? I need one to relax." He waved me towards the entrance, but stopped as I called. "Hold on, Mario! Not yet. I need to know the specifics. You can trust me, friend."

"Okay. One of my buddies was there and we were all shooting up."

"And then? Did you or your buddy kill her?" I inched closer to him and massaged his shoulder. "It's okay.

You can tell me. We've all done bad things. I won't tell anyone."

"Okay. Do you promise?"

"Yes, of course." I lit another cigarette and handed it to him.

"We were doing all sorts of things. Drugs, some kissing, some sex. My buddy was there and my sister—Maria. She left to meet someone at the bar. A few minutes later he left to go—"

"And, go on. Why did your sister go to the bar?"

"—to go somewhere. I don't know. Why do you care what she does?"

"It's important. Tell me."

"She meets guys at bars. I don't know why or what she does. It's none of my business." He scuffed the pavement with his battered shoe peeling at the sole. "Come on. Let's get another drink."

"We will. I promise. You can have some of mine after you tell me what happened to Maggie May."

"Okay... She took my dope and wouldn't give it back. I begged her. I didn't have any left and needed a fix. She'd already shot up and wanted more." Drooping his head, he rubbed the scar on his cheek.

"Couldn't you just buy more dope?" I belted out.

"No, man. I had no money. I saw her shooting the dope she stole from me, so I took a bump of meth. The next thing I know, I'm on top of her. My hands are tight around her neck. She's trying to scream, but I don't hear any sounds. The last thing I remember is our eyes meeting, hers laden with terror like she was a demon or something, then she stopped moving. I jumped to my feet and looked at her body. She still had the needle in her arm. I didn't know what to do, so I ran. That's all I know. That's all I remember."

"Are you sure?"

"Yeah, man. I swear. Can I have that drink?" He stretched his limp arm towards me. A loose bracelet glistened from his wrist.

"Let's make a deal." I smirked, inviting an additional option for his desperation.

"Okay. What is it?"

"Let me borrow that bracelet of yours."

"I'm not sure I can do that. It's from my sister."

"It'll be fine. She won't mind. I just want to see it for a second. I'll give you the drink for the bracelet."

He paused for a few moments and swung his hand around, eyeing each flexing link. "Alright. Fine. I need the drink. We'll trade for a second. Just a second." He raised his wrist to eye level, fidgeting for almost a minute before disengaging the clasp.

"Of course." I handed him my drink, which he swallowed in one gulp. I slipped the souvenir into my pocket and deflected to our original conversation. "Thanks for telling me everything. I owe you a couple more rounds. Stay here and I'll be right back."

"Okay. Can I have another cigarette?"

I handed him the smoke and rushed inside to buy more drinks.

Don't doubt, Frank. Take care of him, Frankie. For Maggie May.

"Thanks, Mike." With an armful of drinks I waddled to the alley. Mario hadn't fallen, although close, he had somehow found a stable contortion for his body against the wall. "I'm back, buddy." I handed him a full glass of scotch and set another aside.

"Thank you. I really need that drink after our talk. That was a weight I couldn't hold any longer. Hope I don't get in trouble." He let out a deep sigh followed by a cackle. He finished his first full scotch in two gulps and picked up his second from a crude shelf between the door and alley. "Can I ask *you* a question now?"

"Sure."

"I've been thinking the whole time you were getting us drinks." He eyed the pavement, then me, then back to the pavement. With his drink in hand he moved towards me, hugged me, and kissed my cheek. "Thank you."

"You're welcome." I obliged the odd interaction.

His next move startled me. He placed his hand around my neck and pulled me towards him. Our lips met. The kiss lasted only a few seconds. Awed, I pushed him away. Father Brandon wasn't kidding when he said a couple drinks made him gay.

"For fuck's sake. What the hell just happened?" My face filled with fever.

"It's okay, baby," he said, his rotting teeth fully displayed. "Be free. I'm free now. We can do whatever we want."

He approached once again. His fingers swept my hair, then he kissed my forehead. I attempted a shove, but all my strength escaped me. His mischievous grin suggested more. He licked my cheek, then pecked my lips. He gracefully retreated, studying me with his drunken eyes.

"It'll be okay," he whispered.

This encounter didn't faze me. Well, actually it did, but not for the evident reason. I've been in these types of situations. I've met guys at The Milky Oyster and dated several as well. Usually, it's a slower process, a cat and mouse game. This one occurred after talking about someone he killed. Granted, I'm not a saint and more of a demon, but flirting or foreplay is required. Plus, he wasn't my type, especially with those teeth. Hope he's ready for the after party.

We stood in silence as the cloud of smoke filled the space between us. Flicking our cigarettes to the ground, we watched them spark, bounce, and fizzle. I led the way inside.

As I crossed the threshold to the interior of the bar, he brushed my back and shoulder. "Let's have a toast. We made progress tonight."

"Alright. Whatever… Let's have a toast."

The rocks glasses clanged midair and alcohol spilled. What had happened earlier remained in the alley where it occurred. Several trips to the bathroom allowed our cocaine indulgence to take the reins of our make-believe nighttime carriage. We sat in the rear, enjoying the ride, hoping it wouldn't turn into a pumpkin.

"Let's party, Mario!" I lifted another shot to my lips.

"Okay… *Frank*, let's do it at your place. I don't like it here anymore."

"How do you know my name? I don't think I ever gave it to you," I said stupefied.

"Well, first you gave me that fake name, Louie. If your body resembled a pear, it would've worked, plus I heard Mike use your real name. Relax. Frank is sexier. I don't know what you were thinking." He chuckled, then growled like a cat in heat. "Let's have more drinks, then go party at your place."

"Let's go, Mario. It's going to be a great night for you."

I can taste him, Frank. It's almost time, Frankie.

IX

We lurched snow-dusted sidewalks like two Frankensteinian drunks, the subzero windchill providing enough sobriety to sustain mobility. Waning coordination followed me up the icy steps to the apartment. I grasped the handrails, steadying the climb, but my boots slid in opposite directions. At the door, I dug into every pocket for the keys.

"Hey... Come on! I'm cold..." The numbing effects of alcohol disappearing by the second as Mario shivered and rubbed his hands.

"Alright, man. Give me a second." Which turned into minutes. "I got them." Stretching to place the key into the slit proved more of a challenge than I thought. With every attempt, my hand undulated like a yoyo. "I can do it, man. One more minute." The key found its mate and the door flung open, sending a gust of hot air across our faces.

We exchanged a look of relief. I waved him along and we proceeded towards the kitchen.

"Take a seat." I pointed towards the chairs. He accepted the offer, plumping against the backrest, and sighed. I snagged a large baggie of cocaine from a cupboard and dangled it like a string for a cat. "Do you want some?"

"Yes! Bring it on." We grinned like two devils playing in a kiln. "Give it all to me."

I sprinkled the crystals into an uneven mound. He swiped a rusted razor leaning against a bottle of scotch, flipped it between his fingers, then chopped like a Ginsu master. He separated the final cuts into pinky-length lines as wide as a rose stem and snorted the first set of strips. I followed, and with newfound energy, snatched the bottle of scotch and poured shots.

Mario slammed the glass, shaking the table. Amped with courage, he inched along the table's edge and rubbed my thigh. "Did you like what we did at the bar?"

I paused. "Yes. I suppose."

"Good to know. We should continue more of it now." His gentle rub morphed into a stranglehold, digging into the bone.

Hesitant, I squeezed his hand, yanking it from my thigh. "Sounds like a plan, but only after a couple more drinks and a few more lines. Then, I'm all yours."

"Yes, you're all mine. That's a hot plan, you naughty boy. Another shot?"

We stood, spied each other, and raised the shots, blenching as we gulped.

"Frank, I think the alcohol has caught up to me." His violent sway attempted to find a center between the floor and the table. "I'm drunk and you're cute." I withheld a response, occupied with acquiring balance from the chair ahead. "Come on, baby. I have something for you." He curled his finger with a seductive stammer, lurching towards the couch.

I traced his path through my drunken haze like a Weeble. He gained control of me before I sat, pressing his lips against mine. The cocaine kick had subsided, erasing any chance to fight his advances. His tongue enveloped mine in angles never perceived. Sweat soaked our stubble, rubbing like wet sandpaper. He unhinged the button from my jeans, inching them down, brushing the ballooning bulge.

His hands wandered for something to hold, then he alternated, crashing to his knees and latching onto my waistband, lowering it like a garter belt. His elbows slithered atop my thighs, head hovering below my waist. I closed my eyes, swimming in a warm euphoric ocean, his touch evoking Maria. He rose, worming along my body, ending with a sensual kiss upon my lips. He retreated, sliding his fingers across my chest.

"Will you fuck me?"

"Yes." My vision blurred and heart raced, uncured by deep breaths. "Do you want to get kinky?"

"What do you have in mind?" His brow rose with an intriguing smirk.

"How about oils and toys."

"Perfect. I'm going to love whatever you do to me." His molded smile appeared, shocking my vision into clarity.

"Oh—you will—Mario. You will."

I gained my composure and doddered to the bathroom unclothed, searching the vanity for various oils. Standing with a bottle of baby oil and a jar of Vaseline, my reflection appeared, albeit by accident. I traced the mirror, following the deep lines like rolling valleys. Recessed ember eyes begged to live again, but I soon realized that hope disappeared long ago.

Frank, the stained mirror holds no answers. You need to move on.

I did, sauntering to the closet, retrieving a tarp to lay for Mario. "What's that, Frank?" His face stunned, yet captivated. "Are you going to get *rough* with me?"

Oh—yes, Mario. This will get rough. Soon, you'll know.

"Maybe, I will." I nodded with a wink. "I don't want to damage the hardwoods or the couch."

"Good idea, Frank. You're smart, and impressive."

"You have *no* idea. I hope you're ready."

We kissed and fondled each other, more heated than our prior exchanges. He broke free and pawed my chest. "Frank… I want you. I want to feel you."

Mario stretched the length of the couch, his back arched and extended. I poured oil onto his shoulders and watched it stream down the small of his back, around his thighs, and onto the tarp. Grabbing his hips, I stabilized myself. He released a howl, instructing me deeper.

"Give it to me, Frank. More!"

I slung my hand around his neck, grasping locks of hair, and pulled him towards me like the reins on a horse. His screams pitched. I thrusted like an immortal giant. I, Zeus, and he, my peasant. His guttural moans escalated, resonating within my skull.

Slipping during the throws, we repositioned our bodies. In an attempt to get better traction for another round, my foot bumped an object protruding from the couch. A second glance confirmed a police baton. With my senses intoxicated, I swung it to waist level, stepped back, and hesitated for a brief moment, focusing on the vicious pain I'd unleash upon him. The fool oblivious to his impending doom. I oiled the rod.

"Come on, baby. Why did you stop?" His gasps slowed to rhythmic breaths as he stretched over the armrest.

I didn't respond, inserting the staff to prime and tease him. His moans of pleasure continued without notice. I howled and drove deep. His fate sealed. The rounded edge jammed and recoiled as if hitting latex. I heaved a breath, and with every fiber within my body, I thrusted. His insides popped like bubble wrap through the maze of organs, stopping with most of my forearm engrossed. As I retracted, blood trickled his thighs and pooled the tarp.

"Stop! Please, stop." His desperate appeals faded into a faint whimper. "Stop... Stop..."

With the staff still in hand, I grabbed a fistful of his hair, snapping his neck towards me. His lifeless eyes paralleled his flaccid body. Flipping him onto his back, I pried his mouth, jamming the blood-soaked staff into his throat, snapping bones as it pierced the back of his head.

"How do you like that motherfucker? This was for Maggie May. Even the dead can get revenge."

No response followed. Blood streamed upon the tarp, submerging the soles of my feet. I flicked his bits from my body and backed away. I released the baton and watched it crash onto the floor, bouncing several times before resting in a puddle of blood.

A breather beckoned. I clutched a soaked pack of cigarettes from the coffee table and removed a stick. The wet paper between my fingers impossible to light, and the lighter had suffered the same fate. Tapping dislodged the clots from the flint and several spins produced a flame. I extinguished the cigarette in his eye, situated his body onto the tarp and towed it into the bathroom, setting it parallel to the bathtub. That last bit of exertion burned every muscle.

Starving for rest, both hands struggled to negotiate a faucet turn. A steady stream to my face awoke the skin, sending chills along my scalp and back. Scrubbing feverishly failed to win the match against the dried blood glued to my body. I swiped the toothbrush from the sink and, with determined precision, scoured. The saturated bristles, now red, curled and the drain clogged. I scooped his bits onto the tarp, then studied the channeling whirlpool to the sewer.

The laborious exfoliation reignited the torch within my muscles, body beckoning for medication. I searched the vanity for a remedy, but none existed. Refilling the shelves a future priority. The next best options, cocaine and alcohol, awaited in the kitchen. Good to numb, but not to cure. Then again, I'll never be cured.

I miscalculated a step atop the bathmat, scraping my shins against the sharp, ceramic rim of the tub. Waddling wet to the closet, I grabbed the leather bag, no larger than a small suitcase, from the bottom shelf. It held the tools of the trade, handed down generation to generation, to make body parts portable. I'd reassembled its contents after Maria. Cleaning her brother's mess imperative, but pain relief held precedence. I poured four shots of scotch, and between each, snorted a line of cocaine. As the buzz titillated my brain, the aching throughout subsided, allowing the process of disposal to continue.

I hobbled to the bathroom and set the tool bag next to Mario's feet, unhinging the pewter lock and pulling its flaps open. The smorgasbord glistened, scalpel to sledgehammer. No corpse a match for their strengths. The next step crucial. I caressed the sharp ends and dull items until an inner feeling, a shiver combined with a stare faded into blackness, directing me towards the proper tool for the corpse. I referred to it as *psyching*, although Dad never named it. Learning the technique required a multitude of practice. The selections for this cleanup: a sledgehammer, a hand saw, a set of pliers, and a mini axe.

Mario's body lay motionless. I jabbed his ribs with my foot, making certain there'd be no surprises. The only movement, a drivel of blood from his mouth after every nudge. His peacefulness extraordinary, considering his night. I thought about Maggie May, who justified my actions. Everyone deserves a chance, unless of course, you do something wrong, then again, humans are the most erred species. I knelt beside Mario and squeezed his lifeless cheeks. The trickling blood spurted, then ceased.

"To hell with you, Mario. You deserved everything you received."

I cradled his body and threw it into the bathtub. The sledgehammer, with its mammoth handle, tight in my grip. I raised it overhead, paused for a deep breath, and exhaled with a blow onto his skull. Swing after mighty swing, his skull cracked and crumbled, brains splattering along the tub. Each clump like snails slithering the dewy plant stalks during cool Rochester mornings. The strikes continued across his chest, arms, and legs, creating deep craters, spritzing blood onto my face and body.

A work cessation long overdue. I ambled to the kitchen and poured two shots and smoked a cig. I prepped an extra round for the bathroom. A line of cocaine bolstered the energy required to rid his pathetic body before rigor mortis set. If that occurred, the cutting process could challenge any blade and tire the user. Leaning against the bathroom sink, I sipped the drink and ogled my reflection. My vision faded into darkness, *Remember Dismember* glowing.

I plugged the bathtub drain with a small towel and returned to work. The pounding sledgehammer transformed him into a meaty playdough. With no time to waste, I grabbed the pliers and removed the intricate cartilage from the skull to his feet. The pieces curled and crackled as they hit the porcelain. The throws from the handsaw sliced through the smaller bones like tenderloin, while the axe severed the spinal cord and larger bones like twigs. The head snapped from the spine with two simple chops, falling into the corner of the tub. His modeled eyes steadfast upon me and what remained of his torso.

Piece by piece, Mario filled the empty spaces in the bathtub: lungs, intestines, and meters of serrated skin. Only his hands and feet remained, which melted in mine after the sledgehammer had its way. I separated each flaking digit, utilizing the pliers to peel the fingerprints like a sticker. I placed them in the toilet, pissed, and flushed.

A review of the scene suggested body packaging couldn't occur. The lack of materials posed a problem, which I received as a blessing. The time spent on Mario's body had drained me. My hands like two scorching logs as

I washed them under cold water. A restart to this process best served during a different day.

I splashed my face and cleaned his remnants from my body before returning to the kitchen for a final nightcap. Piercing sunlight filtering through the mustard-stained blinds conjured a headache. A definite signal from the gods for bed.

Dawdling towards the bedroom, the pungent aroma of the rotting carcass caused me to choke. Dizzied, I almost collapsed to the floor. Mario's meat not safe for human or animal consumption due to the existence of toxins. It reminded me of certain days spent in my childhood basement. I soaked a towel with bleach and detergent, snugging it against the base of the bathroom door.

April 18

My only option is to write today. The prior night's events didn't go as well as I planned, or perhaps they did. I don't know anymore. Does my mind control my actions or do my actions control my mind? I can no longer tell, and to be honest, I no longer care.

X

I couldn't tell if I'd slept for days or just one night: steadfast lassitude. I suppose it didn't matter. I rolled onto my side and remnants of scotch bubbled into my throat. Putrescent flesh pierced my lungs. I swung my legs over the edge of the bed and cupped a hand over my mouth. The towel, soaked in disinfectant at the base of the bathroom door, was now as dry as Mario's bones. I lit a cigarette and strutted about the room puffing and waving it like a stick of incense.

With reluctance, I opened the door. A rush of dizzying pungent air swarmed my face. I lunged over the blood-soaked tarp, swiping a washcloth hanging on a hook next to the sink, and steeped it, creating a temporary oxygen mask. After several minutes, the venomous aroma subsided.

I draped the towel over the sink and splashed my face with cold water. Several drops of Visine missed their mark, dribbling upon my chin. I squinted at the mirror. This, the last thing I wanted in the morning, but just like a horrifying car crash, one stares. The reflection told a story of a tired man, who even with three months of sleep, would never regain the youthfulness of his prior self. The furrowing crescents below my eyes had transformed into black swells. Thick creases as wide as scars covered my forehead and cheeks. Scrutinizing each imperfection, I expected ESP to resolve them, but it didn't. With each finger, I poked and stretched the skin, hoping with careful realignment my facial deformities would snap back into place, but they didn't.

"Wake the hell up, Frank. What's wrong with you, man?"

The mirror didn't respond. Mario's reflection appeared. His body stacked in neat order along the length of the tub. His head propped in the corner, glossed eyes overlooking his sloshy remains. We exchanged a subtle smile, his lined with perfect white teeth, followed by a nod.

"It's time to go, Mario."

"No—Frank. I want to have more fun. Last night... perfection."

"It's time to go, Mario."

"But... Frank. I like you. I think we had something."

"It's time to go, Mario. We're not lovers. It's over," I said, shaking my head.

"Fine. When?"

"Soon."

Relieved, I closed my eyes to plan the next steps. The mission as evident as snow in Upstate New York: remove this mess and avoid all else at whatever cost. Work would have to wait, perhaps a few days or weeks, give or take.

With a rejuvenated sense of direction, I marched into the kitchen for a pot of dark roast. As I awaited the brew, an open bottle of scotch, abut to an empty tumbler, enticed me. I filled it halfway, and with one swift motion gulped. Before I poured a second, the coffee maker burbled to completion. I filled the glass with coffee and guzzled. The burn, which seared my throat, subsided into a soothing sensation as I huffed a cigarette. By the third cup, my heart pumped a thousand volts, ready to face the day.

I marched to the bathroom and surveyed the tub. The decomposition intensifying by the minute. Although, I'd become accustomed, introducing the neighbors to Mario's scent without a proper greeting would be as rude as it is criminal.

Dressed in street clothing, I dashed the apartment with such pace, my boot clipped the door jamb and I tripped down the stairs. The tires thumped from the curb and I punched the gas, rotating a plume of smoke at the rear. Destination: Chase Pitkin, a locally-owned hardware depot adjacent to Wegmans Food Markets. Its location on the outskirts of the city in the town of Chili.

* * * * * * * * * * * * *

I positioned the car onto a corner space farthest from the entrance. A quick glance into the rearview suggested aviators. Once through the automatic doors, diesel and dirt welcomed the shoppers. I yanked a cart from the train rail. The tiled floors, when first opened, as white as snow, but after the second week, they conceded to the muddied boots and never returned.

Not more than a few steps, and a girl with bold, purple-rimmed glasses approached me. She wore the typical multi-pocketed apron, which hung like a bed sheet on her tiny, teen frame.

"Can I help you find something, sir?" Her voice sounded like an out of tune trumpet.

I suppose I could've asked her to point me in the direction of the tarps, totes, and bleach, but I decided to keep it short. "No. I'm all set." My voice crackled through phlegm. "Thanks."

No fell on deaf ears as she proceeded with a medical diagnosis. "Sir? You sound sick. Do you need cough drops?"

I scanned her without a response, then clutched the cart handle and bolted. Most found locating items in this store as easy as a drunken mouse finding a sliver of cheese in a cornfield maze. For me, it was a walk in the park. Aisle by aisle, I filled the cart: totes, meat bags, concrete blocks, bleach, epoxy, and duct tape. With each push, the items clanged, the wheels squealing and twisting every which way but straight ahead. At the checkout line, the cart thundered into the counter.

A pimpled, scrawny teen manning the register greeted me. "Hello, Mister." His apron two sizes too big as well. Mark W. stickered onto the name tag in bold, mismatched and misplaced letters. "You have a lot of stuff in that cart, Mister."

Rolling my neck produced several pops. "Obviously. I'm taking care of something. What's the *W* stand for anyway?"

"Worchestermire. What kind of something, Mister?"

"Never mind what I'm doing. You need to fix that last name."

"Anyway…" He sighed, not appreciating my joke or laughter. "My name is just fine. I'm just trying to have a conversation. "

"Are you for real, kid?"

"Mister, the name's Mark W." His pubescent pitch peaked. "Not *kid*. Thank you."

I huffed, fanning his hair from across the counter. "Look, kid—Mark W—or whatever. I have hunting meat to store before it spoils."

"A little weird so late in the season. Hunting is an interesting sport. You go into the woods and shoot at animals that are weaponless." He creased his brow, slitting his eyelids.

"Yes, Mark W. I'm well aware. Can we move along? I don't have all day."

I leaned over the counter. His virgin nostrils twitched, probably from my breath. He stumbled into the corner of the booth.

"We'll continue soon, but I have a question. This is all interesting, *Mister*. Maybe someday, I'll hunt as you do. What do you do with the concrete blocks and bleach?"

"Look, kid—Mark W—I'm not here to train you, and you don't want to do what I do. Cash me out. I don't have fucking time for an interrogation."

One hand white-knuckled the counter, while my other raised a clenched fist, stretching towards his head. Cowering, his face drained of all color.

"Okay, *Mister*. Relax. I was kidding, just conversation to move the day along. It's boring being a cashier." His clever grin hinted he knew more about me than I did. "Use the stuff for whatever. I don't care. Just, one more thing. Don't get mad."

"What's that kid?"

"You need to clean the white stuff from your nose and upper lip."

"Damn it." I rushed to wipe it with my jacket. The residue glistened atop the dark cuff. "Mark W., will you please cash me out and I'll be on my way?"

"Yes. All you had to do was ask, *Mister.*" He scanned the items and tallied the total. We exchanged funds and I wished him a good day.

I launched from the cash register towards the exit. Drunk, and at a furious pace, I crashed the cart into the automatic, sliding doors.

In the background, Mark W. shrieked. "*Mister.* Do you need help to your car?"

The doors hit the cart a couple times as I tried to force it through like a battering ram. Each push mis-timing the intervals. Blank stares and deafening silence from the spectators frazzled me further. Refocused on my escape, the last thrust forced the sliders open, the cart snagging the edges of the glass. Good thing it didn't crack. I darted to the car yelling screw all of you, then loaded the items like an assembly line worker while cursing everyone at Chase Pitkin. With light traffic, I sped home unfettered.

Stay focused, Frank. You have only one agenda.

* * * * * * * * * * * * *

In front of the apartment, I ground the shifter to park, stopping the car on a dime, and smoking the rear wheels. I unloaded all the items with several sprints to and from the door. I poured a double scotch and headed to Mario, situating the tarps and totes in the bathroom and along the hallway.

A piece of a lung here combined with a chunk of leg there. His bones, muscle, and the rest of his useless body stacked tight into the portable, plastic chests. Before snapping the totes closed, I squeezed a bead of quick-drying, marine epoxy around their edges. Once set, I affixed long strips of duct tape to reinforce the epoxy seal. The job complete within a few hours. It's amazing to realize how a body fits into a few totes. We stand tall and weigh hundreds of pounds, but with a few snips and cuts, we're as compact as little boxes.

With Mario out of the way, the time arrived to clean the bathtub and remove any trace of his existence. Hot water mixed with bleach streamed the basin. The rising steam created a toxic mixture burning my eyes and throat with each whiff. I curtailed some of the effects by holding my breath for several seconds at a time. I soaked two towels in bleach to clear errant blood spots: one for the kitchen and one for the living room. The unwelcomed intoxication caused me to keel onto the couch after swiping a few spots around its base.

Not too long after closing my eyes a dream ensued. This dream much different than the others. A dark room lit by one candle whose tall flame swayed but without wind. To my left, Maria, to my right Maggie May, and straight ahead Mario. All ashen and translucent. Eyes fixed upon mine without uttering a word. I questioned them. Their lips moved but without sound. Moments passed, the time uncertain. "What's *happening*? Answer me. Answer me!"

No response. Their eyes spewed blood, forming puddles at the base of their feet, then, without notice, the blood flow stopped. Bare skulls with hollowed eyes as black as night replaced their faces.

I jumped from the couch, sweat soaking my forehead, dribbling over my lips and onto my chest. I cupped one hand to clear my face, while the other combed the hair matted to my brow. Smoothing my hands along my trousers left gooey handprints.

"What do you want?" Silence followed. "I have nothing for you. Leave me alone. You're all scared to talk. Fine! It's time to be gone," I said caterwauling.

Dressed in my police uniform, I peered the front door to confirm no passersby. Time to move. I hurried the totes into the car, filling the trunk and a portion of the backseat. I returned inside, gulped two, generous shots of scotch, and locked the deadbolts. This disposal should be as easy as pie, just as it was for his sister, Maria, and all the rest. I sped away with only one detour: Pat's Drive-In.

* * * * * * * * * * * * *

Pat sat behind the orange countertop on a padded stool in his usual shoulder-dropped stance, against the backdrop of liquor bottles and cigarettes.

"Hey, Pat. How's it going?"

"Okay," he mumbled in his Italian accent. "I've been slow tonight. How about you?"

I nodded to confirm. "Same. Can I get a large coffee, couple packs of smokes, and a fifth of scotch?"

"Yeah. No problem, Frank. Do you want cream and sugar?"

"No. Black. You know I always drink it straight."

"I know. I was just checking to make sure." He crossed his arms and blinked. Pat's an interesting man. Sometimes he'd wink, sometimes blink, and sometimes both. Must be an *I–talian* thing. "I didn't know if you wanted a change. Change is good."

"I guess so, Pat, but I'm never changing." I shrugged. "Life's dealt me these cards. Is what it is."

"Are you going to be alright? You seem sad."

"Yeah…" I crimped my lips, struggling to convert a smile. "I'll be okay. Busy night ahead. Thanks for everything." I left the store before he could respond.

Inside the car, I swigged the coffee and lit a cigarette to warm my insides. I gazed beyond the windshield at the building's wall and a greyish haze of nothingness formed.

"Hey… are you okay, buddy? Hey—"

A muffled humming mixed with cracking bones and rampant screams filled my mind.

"Are you—"

One last snap delivered me out of the daze. I slanted my head in slow motion towards the driver's window. From out of nowhere, Pat glared and tapped the glass. "Pat… Yeah…," I said garbled. His mouth moved like a frenzied fish, but his words muzzled by that damn humming. That damn humming burning my ear drum.

"Turn off the car. Turn off the car."

His stubby fingers pointed towards the pavement. I followed the pantomiming through the gap in the steering wheel. My foot welded to the floorboard, where carpet once existed, now rusted steel. I lifted the weight of my foot and the humming ceased. Pat's voice clear.

"Are you—okay? You've been in your car a long time staring at nothing."

"Yes... Pat. I'm good. Dozed off. Job... You know?"

Pat didn't respond. An about-face led him into the store shaking his head. I hurried to the river. Good thing he didn't look in the backseat and see the totes, or at least, I hoped he didn't see them.

Don't worry, Frank. Stay focused. He didn't see anything.

* * * * * * * * * * * *

I circled the confines of Genesee Park, crossing soccer fields and street paths, checking for potential onlookers sexing or shooting dope. The cold weather on my side tonight and the park empty. I lined up the cruiser to the river's edge, opened the trunk, and both rear doors. Tote by tote, block by block, the ropes slipped and wound, forming centered crosses. The filth-infested current swallowed them into the riverbed muck within seconds. A well-known Rochester rumor stated cars and cows rested at the bottom of this section of the Genesee River. A haven for dumping because it's the deepest part of the river intersecting the Erie Canal. Humans need to be added to the distinctive list. If only those joggers, bicyclists, and families knew dead bodies lay beside their joyful daily excursions to the park and canal paths.

I raised my boot onto a jagged boulder near the rear tire, a few inches from the bank. Leaning against the fender, I lit a cigarette and puffed a plume of smoke. It floated over the river and in an instant sucked down by the force of a large rippling wave, buoyed by a cluster of smaller waves. I followed its path down the river, the white crest illuminated by the car's taillights. Mario's face appeared in the mist, as did Maria's, and to my surprise, Desiree's. The churning swell rose higher and higher, growing tenfold in size as tall as a tree, then, with the brute force of a whale, it crashed into the river splashing as wide as a football field.

Discombobulated by the series of prior events, I rushed home. The blistering cold from the open windows provided no waking affect to decipher why Desiree was in the mist. The engine revved. My foot hit the throttle like a bag of concrete, barreling down the 490 West Highway. Tears welled around my tired eyes, blurring lamps and signs. With every attempt to swipe them away, I'd lose the steering wheel, sending the car into a violent swerve. At high speed, I exited the off-ramp at South Goodman Street, fishtailing the back end into oncoming traffic, almost clipping the front of a random vehicle. The driver pounced the horn, flashing the headlights like a strobe.

As I approached 310 South Goodman Street, I let off the gas, coasting the car into the curb. Rigid fingers slipped from the handle several times. I pulled myself up from the lip of the door, then fell backwards, slamming it shut. Hunched over, carrying the weight of hundreds of bodies on my shoulders, I teetered through the entrance, knocking chairs in my quest to reach the kitchen counter for a single sip of scotch. The bottle trembled in my hand as the liquor trickled into the shot glass and onto the counter. I couldn't lift it. I leaned forward, wrapped my lips around the glass, and tilted. As the warmth exploded my stomach, I realized I'd left the fifth I purchased from Pat in the car. The night would've been easier, if I had drank earlier.

Step by unsteady step, using the walls as guides, I entered the bedroom, still in uniform, and fell onto my side. I garnered the strength to roll onto my back. The stained, stucco ceiling drew my glare. With each breath my chest sunk, through my back, into the mattress, then the floor, then to the river bottom. Paralyzed, my screams confined to my mind. And without notice, I awoke gasping. I hoped the future held better days. A cure from Doctor Brazen or a scribble into my journal to cleanse the kaleidoscope of memories, dreams, and nightmares. Time to rest.

April 20

I'm sorry for what has happened. The world in which I live is as clear as night. Soon I'll visit with Doctor Brazen because my mind doesn't feel comfortable within its surroundings, but for now, I must move forward. When we talk, we'll find a cure, or we'll talk about nothing. Help me Doctor. Help me Mom and Dad. Someone, please help. On the other hand, help may be a hindrance. I've taken some time away from work to rest, although, I want to sleep for years.

XI

I'd covered the sole bedroom window with cardboard and duct tape months ago. An inkling of sunlight, even on cloudy days, brought unfettering angst, whereas darkness comforted my mind. Restless sleep abound for uncounted hours. Subtle taps transitioning into thumps, juddering the deadbolts like a hysterical martini shaker, lured me from the drowse. Between each strike a familiar voice shouted.

"Sergeant Stark. Are you okay? Alive? It's Joe Rook."

Luck despised me. I'd rather have been dead than have this guy at my door. The fool didn't even use his proper last name. The Precinct opted not to send a cavalry of sirens or a SWAT battalion for a safety check. Instead, they sent the loitering, office donkey, who kissed everyone's ass, and I hated. The value of my life less important than a missing dog.

A bout of puckering and a tongue roll cleared the bale of cotton stuffing my mouth. "I'm fine."

I'm not fine.

"I can't hear you, sir. What'd you say? Speak up."

I propped myself against the headboard, mustering enough energy to bark a response. "What the hell, Rook. I'm fine. Go away." Drips of fluid, thick like syrup, trickled my shredded throat.

"Great, Sarge. Glad to hear your voice or what's left of it. You're doing well, then?"

"Leave me alone, Rook. Go away." More drips dribbled. It might've been blood, but I couldn't tell nor did I care.

"Are you coming back to work soon? We've been trying to call you. Seems your phone isn't working."

"Go away!" Choking, I gargled viscous blotches like oil onto my hand. "I feel better now."

"Did you say something, sir? I'm here to help. We want you back at the Precinct."

The veins atop my sweating forehead throbbed as I heaved each word from my bowels across the length of the apartment. "Leave—me—alone." Pressure filled my skull, then exploded like bombs filled with needles.

"I'm not leaving, Sarge. Anything I can do for you?"

"Fine. Bring me vodka, scotch, and a carton of smokes. Leave it on the doorstep."

"Sarge. Are you sure that's all you need?"

"Yes." I slid from the headboard onto the bed.

"Okay, Sarge. I'll do that straight away."

"Whatever, Rook. Get the hell out."

A few moments after situating my back into a comfortable position, a numbness crawled like a centipede the length of my arms, across my chest, and enveloped my lips. A violent throbbing filled the space behind my eyes, rising to my brow.

Frank, take it easy. Breathe.

I raised my pulsating head and scanned the bedroom. The bed sheets soiled and socks stained. My legs twitching and tremoring. Telepathy failing to lift them from the deep crevices of the bed.

"Come on. Move. Goddamn it."

With limp arms, I extended to the mattress ledge. My legs flopped to the floor. Standing failed. My body dropped like a rock, headfirst, against the hardwoods. Blurred vision added to the list.

I lunged, latching onto the door handle with two fingers, crawling the doorframe like a slug. Grasping the top of the door, pigeon-toed with buckling knees, I swung my weight on its hinges to the hallway. Hunched, a few deep breaths, and a thigh massage revived them enough to waggle to the bathroom. One hand on the wall, and the other lowering the begrimed underwear. Ammonia and sulfur flowed like a waterfall, forming amber pools around the toilet bowl. Bile shot into my mouth and a convulsing gulp scorched my chest.

I spun the faucet, sipping a handful of water. The vanity invited me for a review. Flaking lips, bloodshot eyes, and snarled hair crimped an overgrown, peppered beard. I shivered and twitched, bowing to follow the circling drain.

Damn it. Frank, you're not fine at all. You need a drink.

Another nip cleared the leg pain. I trickled several eye drops and thought about the kitchen, realizing without any liquor it was best to head back to bed. I fell to my knees at the door, breath expelled. Urine, feces, and body odor had been shaken in a jar and strewn across the mattress and walls. I hadn't noticed prior, too involved with trying to walk. I regained my composure and noticed the bed sheets stained like a chalk line at a murder scene. Somnolent, I crawled onto the bed, assuming the same position as the outline. The viscid, unkempt sheets adhered to my overheated skin like masking tape. Not more than ten minutes into sleep, and the door shook.

"Sergeant. Come open the door. I have everything you requested."

"Leave it on the porch, Rook. Go away."

Unrelenting in his quest to destroy any ounce of sanity left in me, he continued. "Come to the door. Just for a minute. Someone might steal this stuff if I leave it."

The Rook made a valid point. The potential loss of those items placed me in a fatal predicament.

"Fine. I'll come to the door for only one minute."

"Great, Sarge. Can't wait to see you." His voice as chipper as a boy singing in the school choir.

Each leg like a stilt on ice as I traversed the hallway. Slinking hands stuck to the walls like suction cups for support. The chairs and couch substitutive canes. Panting, I fumbled the deadbolts ajar. A whirlwind of cold air evacuated the stale stench. The sun, hidden behind the clouds, hovered at a quarter turn in the sky, suggesting morning. I leaned against the door jamb.

"Hey, Rook."

Joe's eyes popped as his gaping mouth sucked a lungful of the apartment air. He lost his footing, gripping the trim above my hand. His face, drained of color, morphed into multiple shapes while dry heaving and fanning his nose.

"Holy shit, Sarge. Man, you don't look good. That smell. What's happened to you?"

"Nothing, Rook. I need a drink," I said with a guttural voice.

"I really don't think you do, Sarge. You look pretty bad." He stopped heaving and regained some color, but his eyes held bewilderment. "You need to take care of yourself. Maybe go see a doctor." I appreciated his legitimate concern.

"No way, Rook. Just need what you brought. I'll be good as new."

I dove into the grab bag and came away with a pack of smokes. I tapped the box against the door frame, ripped the seal, and pulled out a cigarette. "See, Joe Rook. That hits the spot." A large plume encircled his head. "Almost like heaven." The nicotine like miniature shot of adrenaline. Joe didn't say anything, too occupied with coughing and waving the smoke.

He spun, gulped a breath of clean air, and returned to the door. "You know… I used to smoke, Sarge." He wiped his watering eyes.

"Really, Rook? I can tell. You're a comic on your spare time too. Show me how you hold one."

He fumbled the cigarette with both hands, placing the paper end in his mouth, then realizing to flip it to the butt. I had zero respect for Joe but appreciated his longing to be cool. He handed me the cigarette shaking his head.

"When are you going to learn, Rook?"

"Whatever, Sarge. Hey, don't get offended. But have you looked in the mirror?"

"I try not to." I bowed my head, staring at my bare foot scuffing the rusted lip at the base of the door. "You know, Joe… there's a saying. If you don't see something, then it never happened. I haven't seen anything."

"If you say so, Sarge."

"I'll be fine. Go back to work and I'll see you soon."

"Aren't you worried about losing your job?"

"Nope. They can't fire me. There are some things a rookie just doesn't know yet. Unions and medical leave make you untouchable. Take notes."

"Okay."

"Worry about yourself. I'll be fine." I winked, then crept my eyelids closed.

"I do, but I still think you need help."

"Enough." I drummed the frame. "I think it's time for you to go. I need to be alone."

"Okay, Sarge. There's food and aspirin, plus a bottle of vodka and scotch."

"Good deal. Tell Daniels I'm fine. I'm sure he's not missing me."

"He asked about you a few times. I'm guessing he needs your help with some of the cases since you have the streets locked down. He mentioned Maggie May and some guy Mario."

"Well, those cases are closed," I said with surety and satisfaction.

"Closed? Daniels is looking for leads to solve the case."

"I didn't mean it like that. I meant I have good leads. I'm sure Daniels will find the killer. He's a smart guy."

Don't make mistakes, Frank.

"Alright… See you later, I guess. Stay strong and get well soon."

"Okay. Don't send my regards to anyone. Got it?"

"Yes, Sir."

"Hey, Rook. I do have one more question for you."

"Anything, Sarge. Go ahead."

"Where did you buy the stuff?"

"Pat's, of course. I know where all the cops go."

"Good job, Rook. Now leave."

I slammed the door as he was about to rattle another sentence. He called me an asshole for acting rude. I thought about reopening the door but was too tired to argue. I snapped the deadbolts shut and shuffled to the kitchen. The first drink I poured, a scotch. The second, a scotch and vodka. The ScoVo is always splashed with lime, but Rook forgot to buy them. Mike always twists his face when I order it, but it's popular in the right circles, even if the circle consists of one today. The ScoVo packs double the kick, putting anyone to bed quick. With the alcohol taking effect, I raised my glass and toasted for better days ahead. I swayed to bed, slithering atop the gummy bed sheets.

May 05

I like and loathe writing in a journal. I need to stay focused
and write more often. Hopefully, you'll heal me. I must see
the Doctor soon. I believe I'm doing better, slowly
improving. The dark imprints below my eyes have turned
a timid grey, but the road traveled has been difficult. I've
had to hurt a few people, including myself, to arrive at this
point of success. I teeter on the fulcrum of good and bad,
right and wrong. Luckily for me, I've been able to confide
in my friend, alcohol, who makes me happy and keeps me
from depression. Until next time.

XII

I awoke refreshed. No dreams or nightmares, and no hangover. Hopping out of bed, I bolted to the kitchen to make coffee and smoke a cigarette. A burst of frigid air greeted me from an ajar window near the sink, which must've remained as such throughout the night. I had no recollection of ever wandering near the damn thing.

The temperature hovered above freezing, spring on the heels of winter. Snowflakes dusted the warming ground, swallowing them whole and regurgitating a moist film. Atop the blades of grass a round of thirsty robins gathered to peck the droplets. A certain omen for good fortune.

I hung outside the opening, rubbing my hands and gazing at the sky, while white crystals sprinkled my cheeks and melted. Learning to live like this should be easy. The last puffs of the cigarette trailed towards the clouds like ropes to the heavens. If only I could grab one to ascend, then all my problems would be forgotten, perhaps even resolved.

Optimism pulsed throughout my body, the future bright. No police uniform today, opting for an affable, yet impressive, approach for Doctor Brazen. At the bathroom vanity, I prepped, skipping the eye drops, scrubbing every crevice of my face with soap, and even washing my hair. I buttoned a well-ironed, blue shirt, slipped on the best polyester slacks I owned, buffed my shoes, and parted my hair to resemble Daniels. The mirror didn't lie this morning. Today's goal: walk into her office to tell her I'm healthy and no longer need treatment. I rehearsed my statement in the mirror.

"I'm cured, Doctor Brazen. I—am—cured."

I exited the apartment, flipped up my collar, and stopped, surprised by the freeze blanketing the car. Instead of scraping the ice, I decided to sit with the window rolled down and a lukewarm heater blowing. Twenty minutes and two cigarettes later, the car defrosted. I headed towards the 1600 block of Monroe Avenue, passing Mark's Texas Hots, a diner I'd frequented in the past that served cheeseburger plates. The complex housed multiple doctor offices and she had the biggest sign. The letters stood tall, highlighted in navy blue against a beige background, DOCTOR BRAZEN A PLACE TO HEAL. She offered one perk: call her any day of the week at any hour, but I never did. The thought had crossed my mind many times.

From inside my apartment the phone would ring a handful of times before she answered.

"Hello, Doctor Brazen," I'd say, followed by a villainous laugh. "I have Maria and Mario here with a few other corpses. They're all having drinks, enjoying themselves. Can you help me decide how to handle their bodies in the bathtub?"

She'd sit on the phone silent, pondering the proper mind-boggling jargon to convince me I'm mental. "You need to relax, Frank. Try some meds. I hope you're not high again."

I'd stare at whomever in the bathtub, sipping scotch, and smoking a cigarette. I want to respond, but every time I think of something to say, I retreat the receiver. I want to proclaim something intelligent, so she'll have no verbal comeback. I flick the hot cigarette ashes into the pool of blood. Some flake onto their bones and bloodied heads as well. They sizzle on contact. I figure out a smart response.

"I'm all set, Doctor. I'm cured. My friends don't need your help anymore and neither do I. They're happy sleeping and swimming."

She doesn't respond, but her breathing escalates, heavier with each passing minute, of which there are several. I've refilled the empty glass of scotch and lit another cigarette. Finally, she'd say, "Your only cure is to stop living."

The exact response I didn't want from the wretched Doctor Brazen. I take a large gulp and extinguish the cigarette into a severed head's eye. I lower the receiver to the floor without hanging up. I want her attentive to my work. She'd stay on the line, hyperventilating and exploding into horrific screams. She'd understand then, why those calls are never made to her.

"Doctor, can you—"

The apartment had disappeared: no phone, no bodies. Bewildered, I realized the car had jumped the median on Monroe Avenue. While kneading my eyes I swerved onto the road and yanked the steering wheel, almost missing the entrance. The parking lot void of any visitors. I chose a random spot and headed to the office. With the sun poking through the clouds, I stood outside with my back to the door for a few minutes warming my face, reminiscing summer, who'd been murdered by the icy spears of winter and soon to be born again.

Without notice, Doctor Brazen's door slammed behind me, whirling air around my face. A silhouette raised its hand and brushed my hair. I opened my eyes but couldn't focus. The sun's rays had permeated my eyelids with blinding starbursts. I flailed my hands hoping to acquire contact.

"Why do you smoke and drink? You're a loser. You're disgusting. Screw you, Frank. I hope you *die*. You *hurt* me." The voice female. A translucent figure I couldn't quite place walked ahead of me, then darted.

"What the—? Who are you?" Silence, not even a rustling leaf or chirping bird. "Why do I need to die?"

My vision crept into focus. I sprinted the length of the parking lot, then checking between bushes and other entrances. No one.

The voice arrived once again. "Frankie. Frankie. You need to *die*. That Doctor can't help you."

"Who's there? Show yourself to me. Stop hiding."

I rushed to the center of the parking lot to gather a perimeter view. Again, nothing. I scurried to the Doctor's entrance. Out of breath, I leaned against the adjoining wall to the door. I slid my hands over my face, rattled my head, and turned towards the office.

"That was strange. For fuck's sake, why is this happening?"

Doctor Brazen's door handle squeaked while I turned it with care. The bright blue office door creaking with a slight pull. The plush carpet absorbed each creeping footstep into her office. I scanned the waiting room, hoping to find a patient who could place a face to the harassing voice. The chairs empty, just like the parking lot. Distressed, I sat, awaiting *the/rapist* of the mind to emerge from her treatment room.

XIII

Doctor Brazen exited her office, chased by wafting vanilla. Probably an expensive coffee from a fancy Park Avenue café. Paid by my contributions to her savings account because of the ridiculous hourly rate.

"Who was your previous patient?"

"*Hello*, Mr Stark. We usually start with a greeting but never mind. What patient?" A welcoming smile contrasted her perplexed eyes.

"The screaming one. She yelled at me at your entrance. Told me to die."

"Mr Stark. I didn't have a patient."

"What do you mean you didn't have—a—I saw her outside."

"Mr Stark. My schedule has been clear for over an hour. I hoped for your early arrival as I do every time we have an appointment, but you're always late," she said, swinging her arm like a windmill. "Come into the office."

The inviting vanilla replaced with moth balls, baby powder, and a hint of peppermint. The same type of mint I've used to gargle and usually swallow. Blanketing three walls, degrees and certifications framed in Cherrywood hung alongside self-help poems. Beneath them, a faded, black and white wallpaper. Surrounding the door, handwritten cards and notes from satisfied patients. Overlooking the office, an antique Howard Miller pendulum clock.

"Are you sure no one?"

"Take a seat, Mr Stark."

"No. I'm not ready. Are you sure?"

"Yes, Mr Stark." She sighed, annoyed by my questioning. "No one else visited. I only have one door for people to come and go. Are you okay, Mr Stark?"

"Yes. Call me Frank. I know what I saw." I pressed my palms against my eyelids and shuddered.

"Frank. Are you sure you're not having another episode?"

She eased onto a luxurious, leather chair with armrests as tall as a throne. The Queen of Hearts Brazen sitting behind a mammoth, oak desk, staring at me as if I'm crazy and clueless to the world around me. Of course, I know what I saw. I couldn't pinpoint the exact person, but they were there, somewhere in front or behind me. Yes, I admit it's happened before, and I know for certain each time it happened someone or something chased me, touched me. This is why coming to the/rapist of the mind is ill advised.

"No. It wasn't an episode."

"Well… if no one was in my office and no one walked out the door, then it's an episode." Crossing her arms, she nodded with certainty. "It's okay to have an episode. The ability to realize you're having an episode is progress. We don't want to ignore them. We want to fix them."

"I understand, Doctor, but I don't think I had one." I glared at her. If I focused long enough, she'd believe me. The tactic always worked on criminals.

"Frank... Come now. Work with me. Having an episode doesn't make you a bad person. *We* will fix *you* together."

"I know." Humming, I turned to one of her poems on the wall. The silver body of the frame tarnished, its edges opposite, glistening from a ray of light seeping through the sheer, vertical blinds.

"Steps to the Future
If your footsteps fade behind you
Do not fear
Continue your strides
And your future will become clear"

The poem, more of a Hallmark card, not Dante, Neruda, or Lord Byron. But it served a purpose to get its point to the reader. Just like everything else in life, it's always easier said than done. The more the footsteps fade, the happier I am. Keep everything in the past. The future will never be clear, or maybe it is clear and I just don't want to see it. I need to tell Doctor Brazen I'm cured so I don't have to see her anymore. Being cured, I won't have to worry about the future and I can forget the past. Maria and Mario just hiccups in my quest to be healed. The others, prior to them, were of no significance. I'd been doing well for so long I can't count the others in the grand scheme of things. I arrived at Dante's *Purgatorio*, soon to be promoted to *Paradiso*. Someone was following me and wanted to kill me, wanted me to die. Doctor, you must believe me. Doc—

"Frank! Come back to me." She clapped. "Let me ask you once more. Did you have an episode?"

Our eyes met, mine admitting defeat. "Yes, Doctor. It was an episode. I just…"

"It's okay. Like I said, we'll try to fix this. Take a seat. Take off your jacket. Relax and stay a bit."

"I will." I hung the jacket over the backrest of the only other chair in the office, strategically placed across from her desk. In the movies and on television, the doctors have plush couches or recliners but not in this office. The chair suffered years of neglect, its purple, vinyl cushion flattened into a pancake and splintering at each corner. The Oriental rug below my boots, which covered most of the office floor, had lost its ornate luster at the expense of too many impatient, grinding heels.

"Great. Are you feeling better now that you're seated?"

"Yes. I seem to—"

"Frank. Remember what I said about using certain words. *Seems* means not real. You can tell and trust me. Let's try again. Are you feeling better?"

"Sometimes good, sometimes bad," I said, bowing my head.

She never accepted any of my responses and always pointed out my failures. Her trademark vitriol consisted of overusing my name combined with "okay," and following it with the phony response "you're doing great."

"It's okay. It's progress. I have to ask how you're feeling because you don't look so great."

"What do you mean, Doctor?" I raised my head and scowled. "I showered and dressed well."

"Certainly positive, but you look tired and drawn out. Sometimes, when people are used to seeing the same thing in the mirror, they don't see anything different." She readjusted her arms, folding them atop the oak finish, front and centered.

"I swear I feel fine and the mirror didn't lie. You told me to listen to it."

"I did. I'll reword it for you." She rolled her neck and eyes in unison, searching for a focal point in the room other than me. "You have to understand sometimes when people look in the mirror they want to see something positive, so they convince themselves it's true, even though it's not."

I shook my head and dug my elbows into my thighs. My heels carved another notch into the worn crevices of the Oriental rug. "That's not good, Doctor. I now understand what you're telling me. How about this? How does *your* mirror respond?"

Father time requested payment for services rendered for her beauty. Red lipstick, on her thin lips, covered the chapped ridges, some of it smeared onto her teeth. Purple eyeshadow failed to make full contact with her weathering eyelids. Mascara clumped onto parts of her eyelashes while others remained sans the black goo. Wrinkled, ashen skin failed to absorb the mismatched foundation and blush, especially the area rimming an overhanging nose where the pores resembled a thimble.

"No need to stare, Frank. Let's move on. Don't look at my statement negatively. It's an observation. If you feel good inside, then that's all that matters. Stay positive."

"How can I?" I said, gritting my teeth. "You just stated I look horrible."

She parted her lips with an exasperated breath. "Okay. It's just an observation. Not a big deal. Let's talk about you. How is Frank feeling?"

"It's *so* typical. You never answer any of my questions. You only want me to answer *your* questions."

"Frank. Come on now. Let's not make this a big deal. My statements are about building progress within your mind and soul. One more time. How is Frank feeling?"

"Answer *my* question. How can I not be negative, if you told me I look horrible?"

"Well… Have you even looked at your eyes? They're bloodshot." She folded her hands and propped up her chin. "Please, let's move forward. We don't need to act this way."

"My eyes are fine, Doctor."

"How is Frank feeling?"

Damn it Doctor. I loathe you most of the time, all of the time. You can't give me the common courtesy of answering my questions. I want to jump across the desk and grab your encrusted face and shake it like a Christmas present. What's inside is certain to excite me. Your aerosol-infested hair might pose a problem, gluing my fingers. I'd peel those cemented strands like bloodied gauze. As I squeeze your throat, the weeping mascara will fill the crevices on your lips as you gasp for air. I can't do it. I need her. I have to focus.

"Frank. Snap out of it. Please answer the question."

"Yes… Sometimes really up, sometimes really down. My downs outnumber my ups. I'm doing fine. Great, in fact."

"Okay, but how are you dealing with these swings?" Her hands slid up her cheeks, pressing her eyelids and pinching the bridge of her nose.

"I don't. I just go with the flow and hope they work themselves out."

"Frank. You can't do that with emotions. You have to face each emotion and adjust to the situation. Do you remember when we first started?" Her eyes reappeared wide and piercing. "I told you, we're trying to keep you in the middle mood. We don't want them to swing. Then, you'll be fine."

"I get it," I said with a subtle nod. "The moods are tough to control sometimes. It's not as easy as you say it is."

"Okay, but we need to fix them consistently. If we don't work on them, then the bad ones will overtake the good ones. Do you remember what I told you if that happens?"

"Yes. It'll be *bad* for me."

"I don't need sarcasm, but you're correct. The negative moods are stronger than the positive. You may get stuck in the negative moods for quite a long time, which will cause you harm. Those moods will cause excessive physical and emotional damage. I've seen people never return to normalcy. That *will* be dangerous for you." She plucked a pink pencil from a grey holder resembling melted wax.

"Did you get that pencil holder at a used candle shop? It's pretty bad."

"Frank. Stop trying to change the topic. If you must know, one of my younger patients created it. She listens more than you. If you decide to listen, you too could make something just as beautiful. Let's return to the moods. You had a question before you interrupted our flow."

"How *long* do people stay in those negative moods?"

"A long time. A couple days, weeks, months, maybe a whole lifetime."

"Interesting."

"Frank, you decided not to take medication. Medication will stabilize your moods forever, allowing us to work on your other problems."

"Absolutely not." I slid my fingers through my hair, grabbing and releasing clumps until I reached my neck, then squeezed some more.

"I understand, but without the meds you'll need to focus harder to try and fix yourself." She scraped her pink pencil across the notepad, pausing, then scribbling again.

"What's the worst case scenario you've seen?"

I sat firm in the chair awaiting the positive response I needed to hear, hoping she wouldn't disappoint me with more negativity.

"Okay, I'll be blunt. I've seen everything from getting addicted to drugs to becoming violent and committing crimes like murder, even suicide. The outcomes are never good. Medication is preventative. How bad have your ups and downs been? Be honest."

"I see, Doctor." I regarded Dr Brazen's blue eyes, calculating my response. "Well... now that I think about it, the ups and downs haven't been that bad," I said with an assertive grin. "I try to keep them in the middle as often as possible. I'm a cop so I won't commit any crimes. I'll do my best to keep everything in check. I promise."

"Okay. Great. That's an awesome attitude. Exactly what I want to hear. And the door is always open for meds."

"No more medication talk. The side effects are worse than the positive outcomes. Plus, I like liquids better than pills."

"Since you mentioned it. Have you been controlling your drinking?"

"Yes." I locked my arms across my chest and glanced at the stippled ceiling.

"Are you sure? I smell alcohol right now." She pursed her lips as her index finger tilted her chin.

"Maybe it's you. It's not me," I said, mimicking her movements.

"Okay, Frank. Whatever you say. Stop with the sarcasm. Drinking isn't good for people suffering from your ailments. It usually intensifies the effects."

"I'm not sick," I said with finality. Her desk pictures shook in unison with her pencils as the coffee mug jumped and spilled.

"Frank, please don't kick my desk." She released a disgruntled sigh, snapping a handful of tissues from a paisley, Kleenex holder, laying them squarely to soak up the coffee. "You're not sick with the flu. Things *do not* work properly in your mind, which is opposite of normal people." She leaned across the desk, adjusting the pictures and pencils into their original positions with utmost care. With the sopping tissues raised in her hand she said, "Look at me. You must come to grips with your diagnosis. If you *do not*, then it'll devastate your general health and mental well-being. Everyone around you will suffer as well."

"Whatever." I flailed my arms.

"Frank. Let's move on again. What have you been doing with your life?"

"I've been keeping busy with things."

"Do those things make you happy?"

"From what you've told me, everything's bad."

"Stop it. We've discussed your emotional comfort since you started visiting. What I've said today is no different than what we've talked about in the past. Tell me Frank, what specific things have you been up to?"

"I've been working many hours. When I'm not working, I hang out with friends to keep busy and my moods steady. I've met a girl. Actually, I've met a couple girls, but one didn't work out."

"Okay. That's a great answer. What are their names?"

"One of the girls, Maria. We didn't work out. She ended up moving away. The other girl is Desiree. She's cute. I'll have to wait and see."

"That's great, positive news." She clapped like a seal. "I'm sorry Maria didn't work out. I hope it does with Desiree. Do you think you like her or maybe even *love* her?"

"Too early to tell. We'll have to wait and see. Love is difficult for me."

"Why is it problematic?"

"Love to me is like sex. If we don't have sex, then there's no love. Relationship over."

"I really don't know how to respond to that comment, but I'll try. Sex doesn't last forever, so you need to learn to love. Was there anything in your past that may have caused you to feel this way about love?"

"No! Nothing. What are you insinuating, Doctor? Are you trying to go down the road of sexual abuse?"

"Not necessarily. I never mentioned abuse, let alone sexual. You did. Was there any type of abuse in your past? Do you need me to go down that road with you, since you brought it up?

"No. It's simple. Sex, to me, is equal to love, and vice versa. No sex equals no love. I'll never change."

"You should really try to work on that, Frank." Her pink pencil, dried of any coffee remnants, etched new lines onto the notepad. "Here is some important advice for you—*do not* forget to look at your past to fix your future. Let's move on for now. I sense tension. What else? Have you been writing in your diary?"

"Do you really have to ask that question?" I slithered my hands over my slacks, wiping my sweaty palms. "And it's called a journal. I try to write as much as I can. Sometimes I don't have time, and sometimes I just don't feel like it." I adjusted the flared cuffs hanging over my boots.

"Frank, you have to write all the time, even when you don't want to. Writing is the only way to expand your mind and workout your issues. Writing is a way to free yourself from your thoughts, both positive and negative. Please try to keep it up."

"I'll try."

"Okay, great. You're attempting to make progress, which is positive. Take small steps, and before you know it, you'll be on your way to a healthy mind and body. If you keep writing in your diary every day, who knows, you might put all the entries together and write a book like Mr Stephen King. A memoir of sorts. Did you bring your diary for me to read?" She leaned over the desk. Her batting eyelids hoping for the correct response.

"I didn't. I want to keep it personal. Do you know what I mean? And it's a journal."

"To each their own, Frank. I do, but I can always hope," she said, the disappointment evident in her voice. "It's okay. Bring the… journal next time. Just keep writing. Trying is half the battle. How's work?"

"Work is work. I'm a cop. Always stressful. Murder, rapes, assaults, and everything between. Damn tough job. I know one thing: being a cop doesn't always help my moods and mind. I took a couple mental health days to relax."

"I understand, Frank. Have you ever thought about leaving the force?"

"We all want to quit our jobs at some point." I paused with a deep breath. "Sometimes I wish I could be more like my dad."

"What did he do?"

Your question should be, what didn't he do? The list of atrocities are endless but at least he seemed happy. Seemed or was? What's the difference? Don't bother me, Doctor, with the word inconsistencies. Let me continue. The animals in the basement, the humans, Mom, the blood, the meat bags, the freezer, and the dissecting tables. The pep in his step faded as he aged, scuttling up and down the stairs carrying his catch of the day. The glimmering desire etched onto his eyes until his final breath. That's what he did. That's who I want to be like, yet I'm here in front of you awaiting your decisions on how to treat and fix me. The all-knowing the/rapist of the mind. If only Dad would've met you during one of his excursions, then I'd be free from your hold today.

"Come back to me, Frank! Mr Stark. What did he do?"

"What? Oh yes… this and that. He was a butcher, I think."

"That's an interesting occupation. It's never too late to follow in his footsteps. Your well-being is more important than the job. Let's take me, for example. I like my job and don't want to leave. I'm fairly stable, emotionally and physically. Don't get me wrong, we all have our ups and downs, but mine aren't as severe as yours."

Her smugness seethed her pores. She wanted me to inhale the aroma of her superiority, to teach me the difference between me and their kind.

"Always easier said than done. Good for you and your happiness, but I don't care. I'll figure out my job situation as time passes. I need the money. I like the power. I'm in a brotherhood. We never get in trouble. We do what we want, when we want. We're like a legal militia, a legal mafia. It's hard to give up."

"I don't need to know specifics, but I understand what you're saying. Power and ethics should play a role when you think about your job. I can only hope your power doesn't compromise those who do *not* have that power."

"I suppose."

I remember during our first appointment she told me she didn't wear a watch because she cared about her patients. Her furtive peer at the wall clock behind me proved she didn't care.

"Our time is up now, Frank. I hope to see you soon and we can work on your problems."

"Okay."

"Great, Frank. We're making progress. Good luck with Desiree. Make sure you call me if you have any pressing situations."

"Will do."

I exited as quickly as my feet allowed without any attempt at looking back. Her damn office appointments reminded me of an interrogation room: bright lights with repetitive questions, which always led to a jaded judgement. The inquiries led nowhere and each appointment left more doubt in my mind than the prior. I needed to keep seeing her so the department would stay off my case and my job stayed secure. The immense stress from the appointment signaled a time for a quick drink. I patted my pockets. No flask to be found. The next best option, a smoke to calm the nerves.

* * * * * * * * * * * * *

I drove the on-ramps and off-ramps for hours, east and west on the 490 expressway, until I tired. The oversized, burnt umber sun setting stole my attention, and as I attempted to park the damn car it jumped the curb again. I jutted into the apartment, stripping my clothes with each step until I reached the kitchen. A quick shot, then with the bottle tucked under my arm I headed to bed. Staring at the ceiling, my vision blurred and my mind spun like a hurricane with Doctor Brazen's words slipping in and out of consciousness. "You need to look back to fix your future. You need to write." Both options not the best ideas, but I'll do what she wants. I stretched towards the nightstand and clasped the journal, or diary I suppose, sliding the pencil from the separated binding and flipping the book to the first blank page I came across.

May 06

Doctor Brazen, *the/rapist* of the mind, continued pressing me to write. Her chapped lips flapping like a duck bill: "you need to look at your past to fix your future and heal." My history isn't the brightest spot from memory. It's best to avoid it in my case. Doesn't she understand how difficult it is to write all the time? Sentences, paragraphs, words, subjects, and verbs. I'm drunk and tired, and all the names from my past are blurred except for Maggie May, Mario, and Maria. Damn you, Maria. Damn you! Ask Maria, Doctor Brazen. Bet you can't find her. I can't write anymore. The weather is bothering me. I tried Doctor Brazen.

XIV

The howling wind brought a pelting rain; the flimsy windows and paper-thin roof suffering a pebble bombardment. The dim light in the bedroom flickered after each thunderous roar and beaming bolt. The final blast, as bright as day, severed the room into darkness.

I returned the pencil inside the binding and placed the journal onto the night table. I struggled with the weight of my eyelids, but my zigzagging eyes forced me to remain awake. Maria, it's you who did this to me. All was fine before we met. I'd been free from harming others for months, perhaps even years. You could've walked, left me alone. Your brother, Mario, killed Maggie May the same weekend we met. I handled him with the vengeance of a thousand men.

The grotesque image of Mario in the bathtub appeared within my mind. Provoked, I arose, trudging the hallway, guided along the walls by the sway of my shoulders. Sporadic lightning provided adequate glow to find the kitchen table and a bottle of scotch. As I poured my second, a flash lit the wall ahead of me. Maria appeared.

Frank—when you look back, you'll see it was your fault.

Friday, the 13th of April. I had attempted writing in my journal that evening, but my mind wouldn't allow it, so l left the apartment after a few paragraphs. I'd been to random pubs throughout the Park Avenue neighborhood, and as last call approached, I ventured to Magpie Irish Pub. Last call at Magpie guaranteed heavy pours and no line at the door. I flipped my thick leather collar, lowered my head, and like a freight train barreled down the street. The cold rain peppering my face made the jaunt unbearable. Several cocaine bumps and flask swigs allowed me to continue forward, numbing the effects from the weather and giving me an excuse to overindulge. I rifled my pockets for a pack of smokes and found my badge. I should've left it home this particular night.

Two steps inside Magpie and Mike waved, standing tall against the backdrop of liquor bottles. He'd been waiting for me, or so I hoped. I approached the counter and we exchanged a handshake.

"Hey, Mike. I'll take a shot of scotch, a beer to chase, and a double scotch neat to chase the chaser."

"No problem. Good to see you again. What's it been, a day?"

"Oh... at least two days." I chortled and slapped the countertop. To my dismay my hand landed in a puddle of liquor. "Damn it."

"I'll get your drinks in a second." He nodded, grabbed a dry cloth from behind the bar and threw it at me.

As I dried my hand, he snagged a rag from the other end of the bar and wiped the area ahead of my stool. With each swoosh of the tattered cloth, a trail of alcohol, bleach, and anise shaken and stirred under a heat lamp, lifted towards my face. He must've soaked his hands in a bowl of detergent for days to remove the stench. He lined up a set of glasses, filling them with a hovering pour, and with a slight of hand delivered an open beer bottle.

"Let's have one together."

"Thanks." I flipped the empty shot glass onto the bar, exchanging it for the beer. He replied with a thumbs up, then headed towards the center of the bar to serve the next drunkard.

I sat on the stool smoking cigarettes and drinking scotch. A woman at the far end of the bar caught my eye like a stripper in a church procession. Strutting and wobbling on red stilettos, she trekked towards me, balancing herself every few steps with the counter's ledge. I couldn't help gawking, but I don't think she noticed. The closer, the prettier, too lean for some but perfect for me. Tall, with curly, strawberry blonde hair flowing to the middle of her back. Pink tip strands matched her nails. A spandex dress exposed her upper thighs. Within two steps of me, I raised my hand and waved.

"How's it going tonight?" She ignored my greeting and continued past. "Damn it," I whispered.

"I'm just kidding." She stopped and spun towards me. "I noticed you staring at me. That's cute." Her smile more of a drunken smirk, but still sexy to me.

"Thanks. I hoped you'd notice. I watched you strut like a model on a mission." That was a lie. More like a drunken sailor on a listing ship. She inched closer. The top of her dress losing the battle with her ballooning bust. "I was worried you were going to leave." I slid an empty stool next to mine and tapped it. "Please, have a seat." With a whimsical grin, I eyed her plump rear as she sat.

"You're so sweet." She placed her hand on my shoulder, more for balance than an advance. "Do you want to buy me a drink, hot stuff?"

"Of course. Let's have a shot."

Both beyond drunk, but once you've arrived at this point an extra dousing never hurts. I motioned to Mike. He mouthed one second, busy pouring a handful of beers from the tap.

"What kind of shot do you want?"

"Good question. How about lemon drops?" She parted her lips, licking the top one like a lizard.

"Great choice."

Lemon drops, at least from my experience, are always everyone's favorite. I liked them, but then again,

I'm not too picky. Sucking the lemon removed any of the vodka aftertaste. As Mike arrived, I called out the order. We swooped the shots and downed them with drunken grace, spilling some atop the counter, some along our arms, and the rest into our mouths.

"Yummy. I love those sour drinks. Thank you, sir."

I nodded to Mike. In a blink of an eye, he placed two more atop the bar. "Glad you liked them. Look… we have more. Just like magic."

"Those were on me, Frank," Mike said.

She plucked a pack of cigarettes from between her braless breasts and lit one. Her chiseled chin rose as she puffed towards the ceiling. She raised the shot glass, dribbling the last drop onto the tip of her acrobatic tongue.

"Do you want more?"

"Yes, I'm parched." She grasped the other empty shot glass and lapped its edge.

"Mike. A tall vodka on the rocks with lemon." Mike didn't respond, instead serving it with a swizzle stick and straw.

"Thank you." She pushed away the straw with her lips and gulped from the glass. "By the way, what's your name, sweetie?"

"Frank—Frank Stark. And yours pretty lady?"

"Oh… I like Frank. Sounds so manly. I'm Maria."

"Are you Italian?"

"Well, yes I am. Good guessing, Mr Frank."

"Do you have a last name, Miss Maria?"

"Oh...," she said, fanning her face, "we don't worry about last names."

I found it odd she didn't want to give me her surname. At that point in time, I brushed it off, more interested in hooking up. Additional questioning could've shut down that possibility. Her beauty superseded any name games we could play. In hindsight, I shouldn't have divulged mine. I suppose it didn't matter since she was drunk, and what happened later in the night would put the whole argument to rest.

"Okay. No problem. No last names. You can forget mine too," I said with a growling laugh.

"No problem. I only know Frank. Frank the shot taker." She giggled and took another sip, looking about the bar. She espied each patron as if searching for someone specific.

"What brings you to Magpie tonight?"

"Oh... you know. Many reasons. Something here. Something there."

"What somethings are you looking to find?"

"Since you mentioned it. Do you like to party?"

"Yeah. Everyone likes to party."

"I mean, do you like to *party*?" She slid her finger over the edge of the glass, brought it to her gums, then fixated on my eyes.

"*Party*. Yes, I party. It's the only way I stay awake."

"Do you mind if I have some of yours?" Her fingernails grazed the top of my hand.

"Well… I don't know."

"Come on, baby. I'll make it worth your while." Her gaping smile filtered a thousand options through my mind. She deserved plenty of credit for being upfront in her quest to get high, although, I shouldn't have said yes. If I would've just ended the night, then all of this wouldn't have happened.

"Alright, but I can't give it to you here." I raised my chin and glared towards the rear of Magpie.

"You're amazing. Where in the back?" Her giddiness rivaled a teen at prom.

"Here's my plan. We alternate going to the bathroom. I'll leave some lines for you on the sink. I'll go first, then you go."

"Okay. Sounds like a plan. Make sure you leave me plenty."

I entered the bathroom and cleaned a corner section of the sink. I laid out two lines for myself and two ample lines for her. After I returned, she went. It didn't take her more than thirty seconds and she was back at the bar asking for more. I should've said no, but I couldn't to the gorgeous Italian girl. Proving the Little Italy women wrong, who'd rejected me so many times, meant more. I kept feeding her needs, hoping she'd give me what I wanted. Between conversations, the treks continued until closing time.

"Mike. Another round." As she approached, I spun the stool to face her. "Glad you made it back. Are you feeling good?"

"Yes, baby. I'm as a high as a blue moon." Her widening eyes proved that to be true.

"Good to hear. Have you lived in Rochester your whole life?"

"No. Originally from Waterloo. Do you know where that is?"

"East of here about forty minutes, right?"

"You got it. Do I look like I don't belong?"

"You belong just fine. I hadn't ever seen you at Magpie, so I figured I'd ask."

"You're right again. It's my first time. My brother, Mario, suggested it. I had an appointment to meet someone, but he never showed." She frowned for a second, regaining the smile as she sipped the glass.

"Odd, anyone would stand you up?"

"Why is that *odd*?" She sneered, eyeballing the ceiling, then wound her hand and leaned in to slap me.

I raised my elbows. "Whoa... I'm not trying to upset you. I meant I'd never leave a beautiful woman like yourself alone at the bar."

"That's what all the guys say, until they don't show up."

"I wouldn't do that to you. I promise."

"Alright. Good." She retracted her swing, placing her hand atop mine. Our gazes entranced. Mike startled us from the spell.

"Last call! Last call for alcohol! Everyone. Last call for alcohol. You don't have to go home, but you can't stay here. Finish up your drinks, boys and girls. Thank you. Have a good night."

"Mike. Couple more rounds and we'll be on our way." I turned towards Maria and placed my hand onto her shoulder. "Do you need to call someone for a ride?"

"No, baby. It's fine. I have no one to miss me. Maybe you can be my *ride*?" Besides, I have to pay you back for the blow somehow, right?"

"That's a good plan." My smile masked the arena cheers roaring within my mind.

"I had a feeling you'd agree with me. Let's finish our drinks, have a few more lines, then go to your place. I can't wait for *you* to get into *me*."

I couldn't return from this point, full steam ahead. We wanted each other. I miscalculated how it could go so wrong. Prior to tonight, my negative thoughts were at bay, and these days, those are the only thoughts I can't remove. After our last bathroom break, we headed towards the exit. At the door, she kissed me. As patrons brushed past, I returned the affection with the best of my drunken abilities, which she didn't mind.

I scanned the road for a cab and not one in sight. I led the way with her arm around mine, overstepping random, ice patches from the drizzle. We plodded to my apartment at 310 South Goodman Street, wriggling the concrete steps like two simians. Her contorting body tugging my arm as I searched my pockets for the keys. My first attempt failed. She climbed atop my shoulders. The keys crashed the concrete. I peeled her from me and leaned her against the wall adjacent to the door.

"You need to stay off of me, if you want to get inside," I said louder than I'd expected.

With keys in hand, the second attempt proved a success. We stumbled through the front door. I went to the kitchen and poured us drinks. Spinning with the grace of a drunken ballerina, she kicked her heels across the living room, then collapsed onto the couch.

"This is comfortable. It feels good against my body. I hope you feel this good against my body too."

"I think we'll both feel good, Maria. I can't wait."

As I tottered towards her with drinks in hand she called, "Hey. Stop!" She arched her long legs, spreading them far enough to expose the inside of her upper thigh. "Do you like what you see?"

She wore no panties. I wanted to give her a hundred responses, but none rolled from my tongue. I nodded with an enormous smile, stretching my cheeks like a rubber band and handed her the drink.

"Thank you, Frank."

We inched closer upon the couch. She invited my hand upon her icy, bare thigh. I followed with a passionate kiss. The tip of my tongue caressed her neck. With each heaving breath, I swallowed her scent. Fields of lavender, orchids, and vanilla intertwined with a sensual perfume fed the rise between my thighs. I glided one hand up her skirt while the other fondled her breasts. Her fingernails drifted over my chest, onto my stomach, and around my thighs. She pawed at my hips, then missing the bulge between my legs, and by an erroneous chance, her hand landed in my pocket. The next set of events took a horrific turn. I should've left the bar earlier. I shouldn't have engaged with the beautiful Italian woman from Waterloo. I could've done so many different things. Such is life. Remedying the situation impossible.

She yanked her hand and raised the metal oval to her eyes.

"What's this?" She knew what it was, and to this day, I don't know why she asked. It's as if she wanted a confession to its ownership.

I tried swiping it from her, but, oddly, her drunken reflexes quicker than a cat. "It's my badge. Give it back. I'm a cop. What's the big deal?"

Within seconds, her prior lust catapulted to hatred. She scooted into the corner of the couch and unleashed an unprovoked tirade. "Get away from me."

"Get away from you? What do you mean, Maria? I didn't do anything."

She jumped from the sofa and continued her diatribe as she stood before me. My shirt unbuttoned, my belt unbuckled.

"I hate you. Cops are cancer."

"We're not. Give me the badge. Look… let's just call it a night."

I was stern but not overzealous, latching onto her hand. She ignored my statement and attempted to slither free.

"Yes—you—are. That's the same thing the cops said after they gang-raped me in Waterloo. You're all the same. Get away from me. Let me go."

"Come on, Maria. I'm not like that. I've never hurt anyone." Regardless of the statement's validity, I tried amending the situation.

"*Pigs* and *Nazis*. That's exactly what we call your kind in my hometown. I hope you die. You all belong in hell." I approached, grabbing her shoulders. "Leave me alone. Stop touching me." She pushed and pounded my chest.

"Come on, Maria. It'll be fine. Stop talking… just— stop—talking. If you don't, you'll regret it. I'm warning you."

"You were going to rape me. I hope you die for everything you've done to all the innocent people. Your mother should've killed you at birth."

To be fair, rape hadn't crossed my mind. I'd been doing well. I'm not sure how she knew about the innocent people. I suppose some were and some weren't, but that's neither here nor there. We etched new lines in the sand as every minute passed, ensuring no points of return.

I heaved a deep breath, my heart beating into my stomach. I lifted my hand, wound it around my body, and with all my weight, I unleashed a backhand so powerful it could've snapped a tree trunk. Her jaw, like jelly, caved on impact as her teeth splintered like wood.

Blood spewed from her mouth and her garbled rant continued. "Garbage, pig. You're hurting me."

Two teeth dribbled her chin, bouncing like marbles from the hardwood floor. With one swift glide of my hand, I scooped them into my pocket.

"You're going to kill me. Stop. Please stop." Her pleading didn't faze my rage.

"I'm the pig who's going to blow your house to hell. You just couldn't listen, could you? Now, it's all regret."

I pummeled her face, swinging like a manic pendulum, spraying blood across my forehead and chest. Body punches compressed her breath into shrills. I cradled her body, and threw her into the bathtub, snapping her neck against the porcelain rim. I wrapped my fingers around her tiny neck like tentacles and squeezed. Bones popped and snapped against my palm. Then, nothing. I stepped from the tub and regained my composure. As my panting subsided, I watched the white porcelain swarm red around her motionless body.

I spun the sink faucet. While the water flowed, the vanity called. An unnerving reflection, I hadn't viewed in quite some time, greeted me. The five o'clock shadow had turned twelve. The whites of my eyes like the pool overflowing Maria, the tops of my cheeks sagging to my chin, and each wrinkle an irremovable excrescence. At first, I thought the man in the mirror was an illusion of the mind caused by the booze and drugs, but as the frigid water splashed my face, I realized it wasn't a dream, but a nightmare, and this nightmare, my reality.

Welcome back, Frankie. You'll be fine, Frank.

Only two options existed to resolve the issue: cut her up or dispose her whole. The former a more logical route to remove evidence. It's what I'd done many times in the past. Just like riding a bike. I piled blades from various drawers and cupboards atop the kitchen table and initiated *psyching*, plucking a hatchet, a butcher knife, and a ten inch, serrated blade. From the closet I retrieved two new tarps, several game bags, and totes. I spread one tarp in the kitchen and one in the bathroom.

A series of deep stab wounds targeted the veins and arteries. Part two included the tools: hatchet to chop, butcher knife to slice the meat, and the serrated blade to saw the bone. I stuffed her into the game bags and sorted those into totes. Women usually fit into two or three, while men typically filled three or more. The largest one filled eight.

STAINED MIRROR

I returned from the river that night and all was normal, except for the turmoil within my mind. I tried to finish my journal entry, but couldn't because I was too tired from Maria. I filled a tall tumbler with scotch and drank half in one gulp. No different than what I'm doing tonight, gazing at the wall and reflecting, just as Doctor Brazen suggested. The lightning stopped and the power flickered to life. Maria's image had disappeared and the buzz had run its course. I tramped to the bedroom and rolled atop the bed. As I closed my eyes, I promised myself not to move and only to sleep, hoping for better days.

XV

I awoke to blackness. Searching for a splinter of light futile. My eyelids had fused to my cheeks. Tears seeped their corners, flooding the eardrums. I attempted a lunge, my appendages arrested to the mattress by invisible handcuffs, a million ants burrowing tunnels beneath the skin. A scream impossible without breath, nostrils pinched with unseen hands, lips laced, skull expanding like a zeppelin. Maria's butchered face appeared, then evanesced.

Gasp. Must breathe. Alarms blared like an ambulance trapped inside a scream box. Pops and bursts reverberated like a fireworks display. Pleading with throaty shrieks to flex any muscle, I willed the ring finger adorned with Gabriel to flinch. The twitch electrified every fiber within my corpse, freeing the paralysis.

Sight still impossible. A viscid crust had cemented my eyelashes. With precise care, I peeled each fine hair like a scab, plucking several in the process. The bedroom blurred through brining eyes. I thrashed my arm like an eagle's wing towards the cacophony booming from the nightstand, each strike bouncing the clock and the cigarette pack beside it. A fortunate swat sent it crashing to the floor, silencing the clamor.

The strenuous arousing deserved rewards: cigarettes, coffee, and a stiff drink, or two. The blend robust, as if it had just been ground, although it wasn't. I couldn't afford the fancy beans. I crammed the filter for strength, hoping to eradicate this morning's stresses. I filled half a mug with scotch, drinking most of it by the time the spouts of steam signaled readiness.

The blend of scotch and coffee coated my throat like syrup, bringing much needed relief. The day had taken a turn for the better, or so I thought, then when I went for another sip, the liquid had changed from black to red and as salty as an ocean. A drop dripped like a glob of paint onto the table. As I set my index finger atop it, the liquid spread like tributaries along my arm and neck, then another set sprouted from my other hand, circling the table and filling the kitchen like a pool. From the cup, it multiplied and within minutes my head was submerged in a pond of blood, drowning me, and with a blink of an eye it disappeared; the mug refilled with scotch and coffee. The panic didn't subside, with each heartbeat came the thrust of a bayonet.

I lowered my damp forehead to the edge of the table, digging the wrinkled skin onto the splintered trim, but the action provided no reprieve, except to bleed, which I dabbed onto my tongue.

They're not episodes, Frank. They're only thoughts. You'll be fine as time passes.

I put out the cigarette and sighed. Dwelling on the topic served no purpose. It was just a fantastical thought that swelled the imagination and ended. A shower certain to shake this mythical lull and prep me for work. Water spritzed through the showerhead, cleansing the grime. As I waited for pressure to build, I dipped a toothbrush into a cup filled with mouthwash and scotch. After brushing away the morning funk, I gargled and swallowed. Each eye rejuvenated with ample amounts of Visine. As I lowered my head, I noticed the vanity mirror was muddled with steam. A stroke of luck because I didn't want to see my face this morning, although within the haze, if I gazed at just the proper angle, a skull appeared with glowing embers. I clenched my fist, wound my arm, and drove it toward the mirror. I stopped within centimeters of the stained reflector. Breaking it served no purpose. Reality would not be changed. I crept into the bathtub, subjugating myself to the hot and cold water treatment: castigation and redemption.

I swaddled my body in a towel and headed to the bedroom with mug in hand. I plucked the smelly uniform from the floor and suited up, returning to the kitchen for a refill. This time more scotch, less coffee. Sitting at the table, I wished for the events to reoccur, but nothing happened.

"What the hell? What are you afraid of? Show yourself to me." I punched the tabletop, spreading ashes over my head. "I don't have time for your games."

Outside, frost had blanketed the car windows even though it was approaching May. Leave it to Rochester to forget spring. The early morning sun dimmed behind a wall of grey. The blades of grass standing like needles frozen in time from the prior season. I slotted the key into the ignition. After several clicks, whines, and squeals the engine roared to life.

Frank—the blood—it was an episode.

"Shut up! They're only random thoughts."

The Precinct empty as usual at this early hour, which meant I could rest. I pulled the entrance a crack and surveilled the office. Joe Rook, the last person I wanted to see. With the coast clear, I sprang into a quick step, heading to the locker room for a bit of comfort at the usual corner spot with the long bench. A couple swigs of scotch and I swooned.

"Good morning, Sergeant," a mumbling, male voice called. I couldn't tell who it was, nor did I care.

"What do you want?" I growled, while my eyelids flittered.

"Just saying good morning. You don't have to get mad." His tone like a scolded child talking to his parent. "It's me... Joe."

I kept my eyes closed. He deserved a response for bringing me the liquor and smokes, but we weren't going to make this an all-day event. "Sorry, Rook. Don't you see I'm sleeping?" I wasn't sorry, but for some reason everyone likes to hear that stupid word.

"Are you sure you're okay, Sarge? You don't look or sound too good."

Rook's face came into focus and I tore into him. "You're like a talking doll. Yes, I'm fine. Are you okay? Maybe you should try looking in the mirror once in a while."

"I do, Sarge. I look fine. I'm healthy. I don't even drink. You look like you had a rough night. You know… like staying up too late with the bottle." He tilted an open thumb towards his mouth.

"Go to hell, Rook. I'm always fine. Are you my girlfriend now? Shut the hell up. You're a fool." My chest heaved and shuddered with a cracking chuckle.

"Alright, man. Just take care. Let me know if you need anything."

"For the last time… I'm—fine. Nothing's going to happen to me. There's an old saying, Rook. Do you want to know what it is?"

He crimped his forehead and shrugged. "Sure, Sarge?"

"Only the good die young. I'm neither good nor young." A cigarette dangled between my sly grin that told a thousand tales. If only he could read the book within my mind, or watch the movie with a tub of buttered popcorn. The statement rang true the more I repeated it to myself, which brought me a sense of ease. Perhaps, the worries that Doctor Brazen instilled upon me are a bit overblown.

"Okay, Sarge. Whatever you say. Have a good one. Time for me to get to work."

"I will. Make sure you *don't* have a good morning. I'll be out in a few minutes after a little more shuteye."

As I closed my eyes, Joe Rook's conversation with the front desk officer, Geoff Sullivan, filtered through the heating vent in the locker room. Sullivan, a plain-faced rookie with thin lips and full cheeks, answered all the phone calls to the Precinct, whether from civilians checking on detainees, other police divisions, or a spouse tracking down their police partner.

"What the hell is wrong with that guy? Why is he such an asshole? Tell me, Geoff," he howled.

"I don't know and don't care." Geoff plead amnesia to Joe and mostly everything else occurring within the Precinct.

"What do you mean, Geoff? How can you not care? That guy has some serious mental issues. Someone needs to address them. Fix them now." I imagined Joe's morphing facial configurations during this rant.

"It is what it is, Joe. Don't let it bother you. We all have problems and we all deal with them differently."

"Well, Frank is on a whole other level. He projects all his problems onto others. He's a walking aura of negativity. He wants to drag you down to his abyss. You're right, we all have problems. But we know how to keep to ourselves and fix them. If this guy doesn't get help, he needs to leave the RPD."

"Joe, just relax. Don't worry about him so much. Frank's cool with you. At least he talks to you. He doesn't even know who I am. No one does. I answer phones for chrissake. Let people be. You know, if he hears you talking about him, he's going to flip out."

"I don't give a crap if he hears me, or if no one knows you. Cops like Frank give the Brotherhood a bad name. You're either with us or against us. There's no room for them in our ranks. I've tried to help him. The only thing he cares about is alcohol and cigarettes."

"Don't forget drugs, Rook," I whispered, still resting on the bench in the locker room. I wasn't quite ready to venture into the Precinct and confront the Rook.

"I get it, Joe, but I don't care," Geoff said.

"Can you imagine Frank's childhood?"

"No, Joe. I don't care."

"Didn't he have normal parents? I bet they were the worst, probably beat him senseless every damn day. No other reason why he ended up the way he did."

"Rook. You have no idea," I said, debating if I should exit the locker room. He brought up a valid point.

My parents weren't the best role models, then again, a good role model is only a concept relative to its surroundings. I spent most of my time alone in a small room with four, white walls and a brown door. When I wasn't in that room, I was with Dad in the basement. Outside the home, the pickings even slimmer. I ended up hating school and people in general. I skipped college and joined the police force. I knew if I joined, they'd accept and respect me without any question. For once in my life, I could finally belong to something.

"Whatever the situation, it doesn't matter. You probably shouldn't bring his parents into this," Geoff said.

"The truth hurts most of the time. And he needs to hear it."

"I get it, Joe. You have to understand that sometimes you can't fix people that don't want fixing. Leave it at that. Move on with your day. Forget Frank. Just worry about you."

"Alright. I'm done complaining. I'll talk to Frank later, I guess. The phone's ringing. Better answer it."

"Don't tell me what to do, Joe. Screw you, asshole. You're still a rookie," Geoff said, snickering like a child.

"Yeah. Screw you, Rook," I bellowed, stomping from the locker room. The cops milling about the office stopped in their tracks and silence overtook the Precinct.

Joe Rook retreated a few steps, his back against a supporting beam at the center of the office. "What are you doing here, Frank? I thought you were sleeping."

"I'm awake, buddy," I sneered. "Don't ever talk about me or my parents. You've crossed the line, Rook. My life is none of your business." By the time I finished the sentence, my nose grazed his. He agape and wide-eyed, leaning backward atop his heels, struggling to acquire additional distance between us, but blocked by the immobile beam.

"I didn't mean it, Frank."

"Stop calling me Frank." His fearful eyes within my focus. "Leave me alone." I inched away.

"I care, Sarge. I was just—"

"Leave—me—alone. Keep your mouth shut. Me and you are done."

"I was just—"

"I told you to shut your mouth. Don't speak unless you're told to do so. Look at Geoff." Joe Rook turned his head. "Look how quiet he is. How he listens." Geoff nodded with a smirk. "From this day forward, we're done. We're not friends. We're not anything. If I ever call you, you bring me my stuff, then you leave. Nothing more, nothing less. Do you understand?" He didn't respond. "Do you understand? Answer the question. You're allowed to speak."

"Yes, Sarge. Sorry. I understand."

"I don't believe in apologies, so save them for your girlfriend."

"I will, Sarge. Whatever you want."

"It better be the way I want. Anyway, I have to piss." As I walked towards the bathroom, I overheard Geoff. "I told you so, Joe. I bet you're scared now." Joe Rook didn't respond.

We had reached an amicable agreement to never bother me again. I'm sure Geoff was happy as well, since he no longer needed to hear Rook's rants. I am what I am and will do what I do. As the toilet bowl filled, I swigged some scotch, which quivered me warm. At the sink, I swished a capful of mint mouthwash and swallowed. From my pocket, I retrieved Visine and added a few drops to each eye, then headed to my desk.

"Anything going on today, Rook?" I slipped a cigarette between my lips and spun the Zippo.

"Nothing's going on, yet. I've been waiting for Detective Daniels to show. We'll have more information once he arrives."

"Sounds good, Rook. Isn't it easier to speak when spoken to?" He didn't respond, which was expected.

Attempting to look busy, I fumbled through three-weeks-old paperwork sprawled upon my desk. Not a chance in hell of ever filling out the required information. I slid the flask under the desk and filled my coffee cup. After a few sips, my torso tipped forward, head landing flush against my forearm.

The Precinct door crashed open. Half asleep and blinded by the office lights, I lifted my head in a daze. Two, tree trunks marched towards me, each of their strides clacking against the concrete floor.

"What are you doing, Stark?"

"Nothing," I said, hoping the voice would disappear and that it wasn't Daniels. "Waiting for you, I think?"

"I don't need your sarcasm this early in the morning, plus waiting isn't your job. You should be solving cases, not sleeping. That's your job, Stark. You're a Sergeant for a reason."

"Damn you, Daniels," I said, massaging my eyes. "Can't you see I'm doing paperwork? I'm trying to catch up on all these cases. I didn't get any new leads from the front desk."

"Better check again, Stark."

"You know what you should check, Daniels? Check your shoes. They're too loud for this floor."

"Shut up, Stark. Don't worry about my shoes. They're the best Italian loafers money can buy. You should be out there getting leads. When are you going to learn, Stark?"

"I know what to do."

"Good."

"That's a cute pink tie, Daniels." The tie a blinding contrast to his dark suit. "What's the occasion?"

"Shut the hell up, Stark. It's the best pink neckwear money can buy. Mind *your* business not *mine*."

"I was just saying it goes well with your nice suit. Are you sure you're a cop and not a model?"

"Shut up. The suit's Italian and expensive. Unlike you, I like to look good. That's one of the reasons I solve cases. I don't mess around and waste time like you. Look good, be positive, and always get the cases solved. Take notes because those are three things to live by."

"Whatever... Daniels," I said, scanning him from head to toe. "You look good, but just a little too good, too girlish for my tastes." Daniels's cheeks puffed to the same hue as his tie. "Are you swinging these days, Daniels?" Choking with laughter, I mimicked a bourgeois tea drinker.

"No, Stark. Will you please shut up and focus on work? Maybe if you weren't so attracted to me, then you could concentrate more on what needs to get done with our cases."

"Whatever, man... You're the best money can buy. Anyways..." I huffed a smoke plume. "Do you have any updates or leads?"

"Actually, I do. I put the Narco guys on the Maggie May case, since you turned up nothing. They came back with some leads. People on the streets noticed Maggie May hanging out with a guy named Mario."

"Did they give you any other info on the perp, so I can follow up?"

"I don't have a sketch. No one wanted to come to the Precinct to help. They told me he's a townie and not from our city. Either down south, Geneseo, or from out east, Waterloo or Watertown."

"That's not enough information. Is there anything else?"

"Yes, Stark. He has a large scar on his face and hangs out at some of the bars in the city: Goodman Street or Park Avenue. I think this information should help, since you spend most of your time drowning your sorrows at those places."

"I don't drown my sorrows."

"You can call it whatever you want, Frank. I know you spend most of your time there. Remember, I'm a cop and a damn good one, which means I can figure anything out about anyone, including you."

"Whatever you say, Daniels. Anything else?" I stacked and squared the useless paperwork upon my desk.

"Yes, one more thing. Revisit the shelters. Some of the Narcos told me that Maggie might have hung out on that strip with this Mario guy."

"Will do, Daniels. I'll let you know what I find out. I'll head out a little later. I need to get through some of my desk work."

"Okay. Sounds good."

Daniels walked the RPD with exuberance, showcasing his intelligence. He solved all his cases following the strict rule of law and religion. His religion stated that everyone had a right to live, even criminals. This time I had the upper hand on Daniels without using a stupid law book or religious belief. The answers he needed resided in tote boxes, but Daniels didn't know where to look, and I wasn't going to tell him Mario's secret.

This was one of the simplest leads he ever gave me, since the case was closed. An important reason to visit Shelter Avenue: Desiree. Thoughts of her had crossed my mind many times since our last rendezvous, albeit a formal one. This visit could give us an opportunity to get closer to each other. Hopefully, we'll have dinner and drinks, followed by a nightcap. I need to stay positive for us. Doctor Brazen will be proud of me. Once I can show her that Desiree and I are together, she'll declare me cured. I won't have to visit her anymore.

XVI

Daniels bolted to an armed robbery with Joe Rook riding shotgun. I minded I wasn't pulled from the Shelter Avenue investigation to join Daniels, but it served no purpose arguing with him. I bet suck-up Rook was angling for a promotion at the expense of others, especially me. I had a certain sexy someone to see anyway.

Per Daniels's orders, my trek commenced to Shelter Avenue with a few stops along the way. First at Pat's Drive-In to buy another fifth of scotch and get some advice for my upcoming rendezvous with Desiree. Much to my dismay, Pat wasn't there, replaced by his daughter, Layla. Her dark brown eyes alluring and exotic. She must've been in her thirties. I could've asked her for advice, but I doubt she'd respond. She was born and bred in Little Italy and their kind didn't mix with me. Those girls made it quite clear to me when I was young. I paid, she nodded with an impish smile, and I was on my way.

The next stop at Russ and Philly's on Avenue D. Last names were off limits with these types and most used aliases. They were introduced to me by Jacob Smith after I lost my drug dealer to the Attica State Penitentiary. The three-story home had no street number, only identifiable by olive green shingles and purple shutters. Some rooms on the upper floor dedicated to those getting high. Although they scammed hundreds of people selling fake drugs, they were always honest with me, often inviting me inside with a handshake or a fist bump. They belonged to the LOD, Legions of Doom or Death, an underground street gang. The gang so far off the grid, the FBI had no record of them. I never confirmed the name. A question like that would throw a red flag, meaning they wouldn't sell me drugs.

They led me to a first floor room. The door secured with four bar locks and three deadbolts. Inside, a heavyset man with a shotgun, aimed and cocked, stood guard at the corner, opposite the door. Beside him, two cabinets as wide and tall as the two walls supporting them. Every narcotic imaginable, from pills to liquid, packed their insides. I purchased a couple ounces of cocaine and weed, which they sold to me at wholesale. They offered a few packets of heroin and meth as parting gifts, which I took, but not for personal use. To this day, I'm envious of those who can ingest those drugs just like candy.

Two last stops before visiting Desiree. The first, only a few blocks from the LOD, a welfare check for parolee James Levine. James, a portly, bald man with a face so bloated all its wrinkles had disappeared. A dream for most, but I believe a death sentence in his case. He was arrested for indecent exposure and peeping through his neighbor's window from behind a bush. When the arresting officers arrived, they were shocked to see a stocky man wearing a sequin gown bedazzled in rhinestones with matching lingerie. He wasn't home for the check, but I passed him anyway. It's not like the crossdresser was going to murder a hooker or a stripper.

The final stop at my comfort spot, the Genesee River bank. I needed some shuteye. I tipped back two gulps from the fifth, reclined the seat, and snoozed.

"Hey… baby. Do you remember me?" Her sultry voice beside me.

"Not really. Who are you?" I turned my head while my hand searched the passenger seat.

"I'm Lissa. Are you sure you don't remember me?"

"No... I can't see you. Where are you? When did we meet?"

"Don't you worry, sugar. We met a while ago. Frankie, you've got the sickness of selective memory tonight."

"Huh?"

"It's like it was yesterday. You pulled up alongside me on Lyell Avenue at the corner of Saratoga Avenue, rolled down your window, and called to me. I couldn't understand you at first because the alcohol had taken your tongue. You were my last John that night. I probably should've ignored you."

"I know the area. That's the strip of rundown homes and empty buildings. People walk those streets among the rotting trash and snickering rats. What happened that night?"

"You're spot on with the location. I bet you've been there more than once or twice." She belted a devilish laugh, rattling my bones. "Well… it turned into a stormy night between us. You swerved your way to your place with me in the backseat, almost in the same position I'm in now. You asked me to get naked."

"Why the backseat?"

"You said something about wanting to watch. I saw your eyes in the rearview, while I fluffed my blonde curls and dabbed my lips with a ruby glaze. Those eyes of yours screamed fire and told me otherwise, so I didn't strip. I pulled down my bra straps, which satisfied you enough for the short ride."

"Then what—"

"I'm getting to that, sugar. It all went downhill from that point. We did some lines and must've drank a bottle of scotch. All of a sudden, you jumped on top of me and kissed me. That was good and fine, but then you wrapped your hand around my throat." She wheezed with a whistle.

"I couldn't breathe and you didn't care. You squeezed harder, until my last breath escaped through my nose."

"I don't remember. Are you sure?"

"Yes, sugar. I'm sure. You're just choosing to forget. You even stole the pendant hanging around my neck. Me and my mama were in that picture. You put me in bags, squashed me into totes, and brought me here."

"Where?"

"Here. Where you're parked. The good ole Genesee River. I thought you came back to see me. You better not forget me now. Don't forget...." Her wail blended with the caws of a thousand crows flying to their night roost. "Don't forget..."

Snagging the fifth from the center console, I downed a frantic swig.

Frank. You've had another episode. You'll be fine. You won't be fine.

"I am fine, goddamn you! One more drink and I'll be on my way."

I realigned the seat, started the car, and drove towards Shelter Avenue. The dusking mauve sky losing its battle at the behest of the blackened horizon.

The unpredictable Rochester weather exchanged the cold morning for evening warmth. That difference altered the landscape of the avenue. As I veered the vehicle onto the block, I spotted a pack of homeless people marching the strip like George Romero's *Night of the Living Dead*.

Before opening the door, I chased the alcohol breath away with a gurgle of mouthwash, which I'd borrowed from the Precinct. A couple tugs of the uniform cleared the creases. Glancing towards the check-in counter, Desiree's silhouette stood at its edge in the exact place from my prior visit.

As she made her way forward, her candescent smile welcomed me without hesitation. "Hey, stranger. How've you been?" That southern accent lassoing me towards her.

"I've been good. Busy with work. Crime never stops," I said with a sarcastic grin.

She pyramided her arms against the counter, propping her chin with her fingertips. "I've been thinking about you." She fluttered her eyelashes. "I was wondering if you'd ever come back to see me."

"Just to be fair, Desiree, you never contacted me. Remember, I left my card."

"I'm so bad with keeping track of things. I probably lost it. My apologies, Frank, but you're here now."

She called you Frank. That's a good sign.

A round of applause filled my mind, but I made sure not to show it. "That's right. I'm here now. I bet that card is still here somewhere." I leaned over the counter and sifted through the various papers and magazines.

"Here it is, Desiree," I said victorious. The card was at the bottom of the pile, tucked between a sign-in sheet and *Better Homes and Gardens*. "Now make sure you don't lose it again."

"You *are* a good copper." I handed her the card and she slid it into her pants pocket.

"Yes I am, ma'am."

"Oh please don't call me ma'am. I'm not that old, *sir*."

"Fair enough. Yes... Desiree."

"That's better, plus I like the way you say my name. Look at the positive, I didn't throw the card into the trash like I do with most of them. Come on over here. Come give me a hug." Her dimples, as large as quarters, filled most of her tiny face.

I leaned forward with open arms as hers slithered around my shoulders. Coconut and argon emanated from her satin hair, engulfing my lungs. As our bodies pulled away from each other, our cheeks grazed. She took notice and retreated just a bit, regaining her composure. Our eyes entranced, our lips inching closer and closer—

"Excuse me! Desiree." A male voice called from the sleeping quarters. "Can I get some toilet paper?" His grating tone familiar.

"*Excuse me*, Darnell. I'm busy. You need... what?"

"I'm sorry to interrupt. I just really need toilet paper. Ain't nothing back here? You know Mom wouldn't act this way towards me."

"*Excuse me*, Darnell!" Her voice piercing. "Don't bring Mama into this. You know better. Ask nicely or you're not getting anything."

"Fine, Desiree. Can I *please* get some toilet paper for the bathroom?"

"That's a little better."

She reached below the counter and threw two rolls at him. He fumbled one to the floor and caught the other like an outfielder. "Thank you," he said, vanishing into the sleeping quarters.

"I'm really sorry for that rude interruption, Frank." She continued staring towards the backroom. "You have to excuse my brother." She twirled a finger against her temple. "He's not all there mentally. Some days better than others. Some worse."

"It's alright. It has to be hard dealing with everything."

"What do you mean?"

"You have Darnell and your mom. I can't imagine." And I hope he didn't notice me.

"It is, Frank, but Mom's all set now. She's resting."

"Is that good or bad?"

"I let her rest in peace, rather than suffer in a bed. I thought about what you said that night. Made a whole lot of sense to me the next day. I couldn't continue being selfish. I was keeping her around to make myself happy. I knew she was suffering."

A long pause followed. I scuffed my boots against the floor and tapped the counter's base, breaking the silence. "I'm sorry to hear that, Desiree."

"You don't have to be sorry. I went to hospice and sat with her for hours. I talked to her the whole time and let her know this was the best option. I'm not sure if she heard me. Tears pooled upon her hand while I held it tight."

"She heard you. You're so strong."

She killed her mama. Aren't you envious, Frank?

"Thanks. She did so much for me. I owed it to her. She deserved to rest."

"How's Darnell taking it?"

"He doesn't know. I told him she moved to another facility because the doctors are trying to make her better. Blah, Blah, Blah… I couldn't tell him the truth. I didn't want him going off the deep end. I ended up there for a little while. I knew it'd be worse for him. He'd probably die."

"What happened to you?"

"Well… Frank. I don't think I should tell you, since you're a cop and all."

"You can tell me." I placed my hand atop her shoulder. "I'm not a saint by any means and certainly not here to arrest you."

"Yeah, I guess you're right. You're pretty cool."

"I am most of the time," I said with a gargling laugh.

"Good to know. I'll keep that in mind. Well… I ended up inside a bottle with a white-powder blanket by my side. The drinking and drugs didn't bring me out of my misery. Every time I did them, I loved it, then fell right back into the sadness. Like they always say, you're always trying to chase the high." She bowed her head as if ashamed.

"I understand. It's okay. Once in a while I partake as well, but I try to stay clean as much as possible. Are you still using?"

"Not really. I think I have it under control right now."

"That's good to know."

"It *is* a good thing. I'm going to try and stay clean," she said with confidence.

"I see what drugs can do to people. Maggie May, that girl I came to see you about, died from drugs. I guess we never know."

Unless you're Frank, of course.

She blinked with reassurance. "I know. I see it all the time too. I work in a shelter for chrissake. I'm going to do my best not to have those skeletons haunt me."

"Good point. I never thought about looking at it that way."

Skeletons are bones and bones turn to scattered dust.

"That's laughable, Frank. There's always a way to see things, if you want to look at them."

I scuffed the floor and tapped the counter once more while my finger traced the twisting paths of wood grain. "Yeah, I suppose you're right. Let's change topics. I came here because I'm wondering if you want to go get some drinks or—"

"That's sweet of you. I was hoping you would ask me to do something. I need someone like you to take my mind off things for a while."

"Perfect." I rapped the edge with my fingertips. "I can help you relax and take your mind off things," I said, attempting a southern accent. "I *guarantee* it." We laughed. "When do you get out?"

"Now, if you want. I can just lock up and leave. There's nothing to steal here except toilet paper. Plus, everyone's already sleeping in the back room."

I pressed a standing push-up from the counter's edge. "Well, I have to change. I don't feel comfortable going to get drinks in uniform. People will stare and think I'm working."

"You're right. Go home and change and come back A-S-A-P."

"Okay. I'll be back soon."

As I walked towards the exit, I peeked over my shoulder and caught Desiree's hazel eyes focusing upon mine. We didn't exchange a word, only an amusing smile.

She's beautiful, Frank. This will be good for you.

XVII

The door slammed behind me. With my back against the wall and one boot flush, I lit a cigarette and tipped a swig. The graceful azure moon danced between the clouds to find center stage on the night's canvas. Her acceptance brought relief. It'd been months, perhaps longer than a year, since going on an "official" date. Most of my encounters ended the same night, or the following morning, and required onerous duties. Desiree was different. She liked me, and I wanted her.

I pushed off from the wall and trotted to the car, swinging open the door and jumping onto the driver's seat. I flipped the switch, blaring the lights and sirens, waking the city from a lull, hurrying to the Precinct to swap cars. Once in my personal vehicle, I sped home to change out of my uniform, negotiating each curve like a drunken slalom skier, avoiding signs and jumping curbs like moguls.

Doctor Brazen will be proud of me. No she won't.

"Yes, she will."

Scurrying up the steps, I unbuttoned my shirt. By the time I arrived into the bedroom, my shirt was open and sliding from my arms, my trousers and belt falling to the floor. I kicked them aside and rummaged the closet for my best outerwear. It didn't hold too many options. I owned more meat bags and totes than clothes. I yanked a pair of blue jeans with holes around the knees, probably cut by at an elusive, sweatshop factory somewhere in the third world, and a pleated shirt to match, sans the rips.

I scooped a wad of pomade, adding a couple drops of baby oil, to tame my wild hair, parting it to the right. I spun the faucet, letting it run for several seconds before cupping my hands to splash my fiery eyes, skipping the vanity of course. I swiped a towel and patted my face dry, followed by a dousing of eye drops. Several spritzes of musk finalized the prep.

You need a pick-me-up before you see Desiree.

"Great idea."

From a cupboard shelf, I lowered a blue Maxwell House tin, its coffee had been exchanged for a grab-bag of drug tools. I retrieved a new razor and unwrapped its cardboard sheath. From one of Russ and Philly's baggies, I dumped a few rocks of cocaine onto the kitchen table. With the flair of a Ginsu chef, I diced them into fine, crystal lines, sparkling like diamonds under the beaming lights. I rolled a dollar bill and snorted, using the residue to numb the gums. The powder had lodged in my throat like cake crumbs. Two shots of scotch washed it down and readied me for Desiree.

* * * * * * * * * * * * *

"I'm back," I said, barging through the entrance.

No sign of Desiree at the counter and no response. Odd, she wasn't waiting for me. I switched to cop mode, gripping the handle of my gun, and scanning every inch of the facility. "Hello... I'm here... Where are you?" Still no response. "Desiree. Where are you, Desiree?" As I was about to draw my gun, a response echoed from the backroom, snapping my focus.

"I'll be right out, Frank. Just a minute. I'm in the bathroom."

"You had me worried. I thought something happened to you while I was away."

"Nah. I'm fine. Don't be so troubled. One second. Be right out."

She appeared from the backroom darkness, more stunning than when I had left. A glow surrounded her tightly curled mane that followed her every step. Periwinkle eyeshadow accented her hazel eyes. Parted strawberry lips invited an imaginary sensual kiss, leaving me almost breathless.

"How are you, baby—I mean Frank?"

"I'm as fine as can be. Hope you didn't wait too long."

"Nah. You were quick enough. I thought it'd take you longer."

"You look amazing," I said as she walked towards me.

"Thank you. You don't look so bad yourself. I do have one question: I forgot to ask you earlier."

"Sure… what's that?"

"Why are your eyes so red? Allergies or something?"

"Something like that." Am I not good enough for you now? I've tried to fix them, but the stain won't scrub away.

Frankie, you should check the mirror before you venture out.

"No—just…"

"What is it, Frank?" she said with haste.

"Nothing. My mind… It drifted for a second. Anyway, you have some powder on your nose," I said with a smile, hiding my theory as to what it was. "You should clean it before we go out. Here, let me get it for you." I reached towards her with the swiftness of a ballerina, swiping the residue onto my finger.

"Thank you, Frank." Blushing, she turned away. "Must be leftover makeup."

As she focused on her embarrassment, I slid the powder onto my gums, and they immediately numbed. A cop's hunches are always correct. I'm not sure why she had to lie about the cocaine.

Her unscrupulous gaze complimenting mine. An uncomfortable silence followed. Yelling at her was on the tip of my tongue, but I retreated, not wanting to open Pandora's Box and torpedoing the night. Nothing changed the fact that I wanted, and perhaps, loved her.

"Yeah. It was makeup. It's probably why you look so beautiful."

"Thank you, Frank. You need to stop with all the compliments," she said with a bashful smile. "You had me when you came in to see me."

"Alright. I'll tone it down."

"Don't do that. A woman always likes compliments." She perked up her cheeks, exposing those dimples, entrancing me, forgetting about the earlier faux pas.

"Now you're playing with me." I chortled, stopping mid-breath to cough due to an awkward snort.

"I can't wait to *play* with you." She winked.

"What?" My surprise an understatement.

"Oops, did I say that?" Her sexy grin confirmed one specific outcome out of the hundred flashing through my mind.

"Yes you did, and likewise, I can't wait to play with you either. We better stop before we get carried away in a homeless shelter. Are you ready to go?"

"Yes. By the way… where are we going?"

"I'm thinking the Coliseum Pizza Bar over on Park Avenue."

"Oh... I was there once and loved it."

"Maybe after the Coliseum we can go somewhere else. We'll have to see how it all goes."

We walked towards the exit. She slid her hand around my bicep as I led the way out of the shelter. Her touch soothed any anguish caused by her lie. I never imagined a simple stroke of my arm could invoke such sensuality within my being. Granted, plenty of time had passed since I had closeness from a woman such as Desiree, but I never expected this type of longing for something so real.

As the door closed, she turned towards me. "Hey, wait a minute. I have to grab something."

"Did you forget your purse? Or keys? Or —"

"Be right back."

She flung the door open and sprinted towards the counter, her voluminous curls bouncing like a kangaroo. She dipped behind its edge and returned with a single sheet of paper. It flailed between her fingers as she rushed back to me.

"Sorry. I forgot. I need to hang this on the door so no one starts banging on it and waking the sleepers," she said panting.

It was a laminated handwritten sign using black marker: "Closed - Will be Back Soon. Thank you for your Patience." The bottom-right corner highlighted with a smiley face and a heart. She pulled a roll of neon blue electrical tape from her pocket and affixed four symmetrical pieces to each side.

"Great idea, Desiree. That should keep 'em out. Hope you don't get in trouble for leaving."

"I don't think I will. Who's going to yell at me? The homeless people."

"Yeah. I guess you're right."

She pulled a set of color-coded keys from her puffy winter jacket and slid each one around the ring with precision, stopping at purple. The lock clanged closed.

"We're all set. How come you didn't park out front, Frank? It's a tad chilly."

Although, the temperature was above freezing and substantially warmer than this morning, sporadic gusts of cold wind shivered the bones.

"I didn't want to bring attention to myself. People on this street are sensitive to any car that looks like mine." We turned in unison, walking towards the vehicle.

"I can't handle this cold. Georgia weather is so much warmer." She inched closer, sliding her arm around my waist, mine draped around her shoulder. We didn't exchange a single word during our few block walk, just touches.

"Your car sure does look official minus the lights on top. Good choice with the pitch black windows to match the color. What do they call these?"

"A Ford Crown Victoria."

"Bet no one bothers you when you're driving?"

I led her to the passenger side. As I opened the door, it creaked, bits of orange flakes trickled to the ground. "Damn salt and snow. And yes, you're correct. No issues on the road. Watch your head," I said, guiding her.

"Why thank you, sir. You're such a gentleman."

She sunk onto the plush, leather seat. These cars weren't the best looking and most aerodynamic, but they offered one of the best interiors on the market. The leather as malleable as skin, and the seats padded like feathers, even though it was foam. The carpeting on the floorboards, minus my side, as swanky as the shag inside most middle-class homes.

"No problem. My job is to take care of you." My hand stroked her shoulder and hair as I closed the door.

I situated myself onto the driver's seat and glanced the rearview. *Damn eyes. Damn red eyes.* I turned the key into the ignition, but the car didn't start. Three attempts and still nothing. The engine spun like a broken siren with the radio and lights flickering. I clenched my fists and pounded the dashboard.

"Everything okay, Frank?"

"Yes! Everything's fine."

Everything wasn't okay. My cheeks burned, forehead moist. I ran my hands over my face, but to my surprise, it was dry.

"What the hell? Why is this happening?"

"Sorry I asked, Frank." She dug her body into the corner of the seat.

"Don't. Just don't. Not now." I slapped open the glovebox and rummaged the insides, as piles of paper fell to the floorboard, surrounding her heeled boots.

"What are you doing? The floor is full of garbage."

I ignored her statements and continued searching.

"Frank, are you okay? You're scaring me. Frank?"

A short pause followed. "There it is. I found it." Slamming the walls inside the glovebox, I retrieved it. "I was trying to find the flashlight. Sorry, I overreacted. Be right back. I just have to check something under the hood and maybe get something out of the trunk."

Frankie. You need to relax. Frank.

I exited, slamming the door, and shaking the car. I attempted to lift the hood, but it wouldn't budge.

"Damn it. What the hell?"

The latch had never disengaged. Rust, or the cold, or both had taken its toll. In any event, I needed to act fast. Arching and twisting my fingers like a magician, I was able to jimmy the metal mechanism free. With the flashlight beaming, the battery and the car starter came into focus. The starter resembling a matte, miniature missile, and the wires leading to the battery, Medusa's head. I struck the butt of the flashlight against the starter's casing and hoped for luck. Stressing, with the possibility our date could collapse, I marched to the driver's side, stretched into the car, and turned the key. The engine silent. Defeated, I sighed.

"Are you okay, honey?"

"Yes. Fine. We'll have to see," I said steeled.

"Honey. Honey." She peeked her head out of the window as I walked towards the back of the car. "Are you okay? Frank?"

Her continuous interruptions and questions invited no response. My first grab from inside the trunk was an oversized, flathead screwdriver. I stole it from Chase Pitkin or some other big-box store not too long ago. I whipped it into the corner of the trunk. Desiree continued nagging. "Are you okay, Frank? Is everything alright?"

Stop asking questions. Stop saying Frank. Stop. Stop. Stop.

I dug behind the full-sized spare and located a crowbar. I slammed the trunk shut and marched to the front, stopping at Desiree's window. Her eyes steadfast on the driver's side, presumably waiting for me to walk past. I raised the iron above my head and brought it down with full force, halting just before it crashed through the window.

Kill her Frank. Don't kill her. Kill her. Don't. Killherdont

I tapped the window with its sharpened tip. She snapped her head towards me, startled, and pale-faced.

"Hey, Desiree. I'm still trying to fix the car. We'll be off and running soon. Just a few more minutes."

"I—will. Frank?" Her goggling eyes unchanged.

"It's okay. I'm not going to hurt you. A few more minutes. I promise," I said with an apologetic smile.

My rage exploded against the battery and starter, sending scorching sparks onto the hood's protective shield. Strike after strike the metal clanged, echoing throughout the dormant city streets. I returned to the driver side and flung the door open, then gripped the ignition, paused for a moment to curse the car, and turned it over. The engine, after a bout of clacking and screeching, finally roared to life. I smacked the hood shut. With the crowbar in hand at waist level, my burning eyes met Desiree's through the windshield. Her enticing smile calling me to return inside, to be near her.

"Are we ready to go, baby?"

"Yes, my dear."

I steadied into the seat, lit a cigarette, and floored the pedal, roasting the tires against the pavement. The Coliseum Pizza Bar awaited us. I needed drinks more than food.

"You're driving fast, baby. Maybe too fast for me."

"Don't worry. They won't pull us over. They know me in this city. Don't forget *I'm* a cop."

"Good point. Sometimes I don't know if you're actually a cop by the way you act."

"Well… I *am* so no fretting. I know when *to* and *not to* ignore things." She didn't join my haughty laughter but did offer a faint smirk.

"You're cool. The more time I spend with you, the more relaxed I feel. I've decided instead of putting up a front, I'll let my hair down and be myself."

I turned towards her, confirming her statement with a mischievous grin and a convincing nod. "Let's have some fun." I veered onto the Coliseum Pizza Bar parking lot. "I need a damn drink."

"You got it, Frank. I'm ready."

I met her at the passenger door as she stepped from the car. We gave each other loose hugs and a gentle kiss upon the lips.

"I liked the hug and kiss. Let's go inside, baby." She fanned her hand in the direction of the entrance.

XVIII

Arm in arm, we strolled towards the champagne, stucco façade of the Coliseum. I held open the towering walnut door, hand carved by a master carpenter in Italy and shipped to Rochester via an Italian freightliner. A cathedral arch, with ancient stones from Rome, covered the short foyer. The Coliseum represented its name in full capacity, designed by a crazed flamboyant Italian, Sergio Sicilia, from Las Vegas. On opening night, rumors swirled he had hung out with the Rat Pack during their heyday, a third hand to Frank Sinatra, Dean Martin, and Sammy Davis, Jr. The chance never arose to ask Sergio, but the Italian community says, "Rumors are always true. They're only lies if they can be proven, and lies have short legs to run." No one ever proved it a lie, or perhaps cared to.

Two six-foot marble columns grabbed the attention of any visitor standing at the edge of the anteroom, which opened into an enormous dining area with wall-to-wall Travertine and large pillars hugging each of its corners as well. Each tile as big as a pizza box, some as white as Caribbean sand, and others taupe like the Lake Ontario shoreline. Eight ceiling fans, with blades like a helicopter, spun with fervor, affixed to a copper ceiling.

We sat at an open table at the back of the restaurant, kiddie-corner to a column next to the kitchen. The employees' voices rose and fell like a volume dial, in I—talian, of course. Italians always spoke with passion in their voices, whether love or hate. A trait that my parents lacked.

"How do you like the place?"

"It's beautiful just like I remember. An Italian palace. I love the marble tabletops. I feel like I'm in Italy."

"Have you ever been to Italy?"

"No, but I imagine this is how Italy must be. Have you been?" She traced a figure eight on the table.

"Nope. The farthest I went was Little Italy. I'm siding with you on this one."

"Good evening, Frank. Hope you are well. What can I get for you and the lovely lady?" the waiter asked with a strong Italian accent.

"Hi, Giancarlo. Great to see you again. I need a drink or three." He mirrored my eager laugh. "I'll take two double scotches, no rocks. What would you like, Desiree?"

"I'll take a double vodka on the rocks."

"What kind of vodka, Miss?"

"Absolut with a lime or two."

"Absolutely, Miss. And for food… Shall I order the usual, Frank?"

"Yes, please."

"Will do. Everything will be right up for you." Giancarlo turned towards the kitchen, scribbling onto the order pad.

"What'd you get us, Frank?"

"A large pepperoni pizza with extra cheese. It's what I always order. I hope you like it."

"That's my favorite. I can't get over this beautiful place."

Giancarlo placed the drinks ahead of us on the table.

"Cheers, Frank."

"Cheers. *Cin Cin!* That's what these folks tell me to say whenever I'm here."

Our glasses rose and clinked. The food arrived not too long after.

"Oh my… There's so much cheese. The charred crust is perfect." She licked her lips. Her face raddled under the lights, as if she hadn't eaten in weeks.

"Yes—it—does. Hey, Giancarlo. Can I get another round of drinks? Rocks with mine this time. I'm trying to take it easy." He confirmed with a nod.

The drinks flowed and the alcohol took hold. We chatted, picking at the food between our pauses. A few tables away sat another couple, a plain Jane and John, who'd fit in anywhere and never be noticed. Enthralled, they held hands and laughed, pausing to feed each other. Perhaps, Desiree could make me more like them.

"So... Frank. You have to tell me. This might be weird, but we'll blame it on the alcohol. Do you believe in *love*?"

"Good question. I don't know how to respond. Do I believe in love?" I rubbed my temple.

"Yes, Frank. Do you?" She crinkled her brow.

"I believe in *making love*. Does that count?" I spun the ice cubes within the glass. A diverting glance didn't convince her to change topics.

"Yes, Frank. It's part of it. What about the other part?"

"I do and I don't. I think it's a little too early in our dating process to be discussing this kind of thing."

"It's not. We've already talked about my mom and brother."

"I guess you're right." I let out a wheezing sigh. "I've been hurt too many times. I think, in the end, love's just a game. Sometimes good but most of the time bad, especially when you lose. Is that a better answer?"

I peeked Jane and John and knew they didn't have these conversations. Certainly, not on a first date. Probably, more of a fifth-date topic.

"I suppose it'll have to do. It really *is* a game sometimes. I don't like to lose either. Well, let's not lose tonight. Let's both win." Her coquettish smile brought some relief to the awkwardness.

"You got it. We'll both win."

"Excuse me, Frank. I need to go to the bathroom. Be right back."

As she disappeared into the hallway, I lit a cigarette and surveyed the plain couple. They'd just received their check, reviewing it with content, which suggested they'd been together for years. Desiree wanted to decide our fate in one night. In due time, we'll be just like them, if we're both lucky.

I had ordered another drink and smoked another cigarette. Desiree still hadn't returned, well beyond the normal bathroom time for most. The "I'm just a girl" excuse wasn't going to work. Something else must be occupying her time. Plain Jane pulled out her wallet and paid the tab, which surprised me. Everyone always wanted me to pay. By the time the couple rose to leave, Desiree had returned to the table, sitting with a light sniffle.

"Everything okay?"

"Yes, Frank. Everything's fine," she rambled, wide-eyed, pinching her nostrils, and clearing her throat. "Must be allergies. You know... like the ones bothering your eyes."

My eyes have nothing to do with your allergy to telling the truth. That cocaine drip has a stronghold on your throat. I suggest gargling with some vodka. I passed on the idea to interrogate as not to ruin the evening's potential outcomes.

You need to get your fill as well. You're running low on energy, Frank.

"I'll be right back. I need a bathroom break too."

I locked the door and headed into a stall, hunching over the porcelain tank lid. From my pocket, I retrieved a Ziploc filled with cocaine. The fish scales sparkled like gems and had a slight hint of gasoline. The rule: a hint of petrol, a yellow hue, and crystalline powder equals the purest. Police training was good for some things after all. In fact, that same odor is what attracts the drug sniffing dogs. I tilted the bag and tapped just enough for two pinky-length lines and returned to Desiree. She had just finished her drink. Giancarlo swooped in, picked up the empty glass, and slid another full vodka in its place.

"Where you been, baby? I thought you left." She spun the ice with a swizzle stick.

"Where have *I* been? Where have *you* been? You should've called a search team." I waved to the waiter for another round.

"From the looks of it, I bet it was fun. You need to clear away that powder from the tip of your nose."

"What? Damn it." I attempted a swipe but missed.

"I'll get it for you. Let—"

"No. Stop."

After several failed attempts she said, "Relax, Frank. I'll get it. Don't worry about it, baby." She silenced her lips with her forefinger, as the other stretched to dab my nose. "We're all set. Wasn't that easy?" She parted her lips, wiping her gums.

"Yes. Thank you. Sorry, I was a little tense." I lifted my glass, toasting her with a sip.

Ever since Jane and John left the Coliseum, we became the only patrons, listening to the staff yelling and laughing in "Ital-English" from the kitchen. We nibbled the food, drank more rounds, and took multiple bathroom breaks, separate of course, as not to alarm the employees. Closing time arrived and Giancarlo slipped the check to me, which I paid with a double tip. He wished us goodnight.

"Time to go. Would you like to do something else?" My eyes as hopeful as my smile.

"Maybe. What'd you have in mind?"

"We can go to my place and get to know each other. Maybe fall in *love*."

"You read my mind. Let's continue the party."

She traced a path with her finger across her bottom lip, down to the edge of her shirt, exposing her cleavage. The heat rising between my thighs had to be extinguished by several sips of scotch in order for me to stand. Before they kicked us out, we tipped back the remaining drops from our glasses, then headed towards the arched exit.

Stumbling to the car, and with some cosmic unison, we opened the doors at the same time and flumped onto our seats; our heads cocked and craned towards each other, stuck between the headrest spaces. We realigned our bodies, reclining with just enough space to relax and let out exhausting sighs of satisfaction.

I had to take control of the situation before we fell asleep. Certainly, this wasn't the after-party I was expecting. With urgency, I lunged towards the faux wooden steering wheel, gripping the sphere and pulling myself forward. Manic, I dove into each pocket searching for the keys.

During the slow, short ride to the apartment, her inhibitions disappeared. She leaned over the center console and glided her hand between my thighs. The heat had returned and with it a fury that pulsated within my chest. Her attempt to unbuckle my belt proved to be too complicated for her drunken hands.

I coasted the car into the curb, slamming the shifter into park. A second wind hurried us up the steps, faltering and pawing at each other, almost crashing through the front door as I turned the handle. We wobbled towards the living room, falling onto the couch.

We didn't utter a word, exchanging lazy stares between harmonious blinks. She slinked the jacket from her arms to the floor. Fixated on the blouse buttons, I snapped each one with the accuracy of a drunken surgeon, exposing her flawless olive skin. With utmost care, my fingers roamed her chest and shoulders, removing the silky cloth. She tugged my coat, demanding me to strip, but not before a lustful kiss. I yanked her against me; our lips poised in a desirous duel, which we both lost. Our tongues alternated traversing erratic paths atop our bodies. She lunged, clawing my shirt open, its buttons crashing onto the hardwoods like marbles.

She locked her lips onto my heaving chest, her heavy breaths attempting to fill my lungs through the skin. With one hand, she circled my nipples, the other searched for the belt buckle. Her lace bra within my grasp. Pulling the satin frill freed her breasts from their cloth prison. Sculpted and standing at attention, they invited to be touched. I latched onto them like a teething toddler, heart pounding like an unexperienced teenager. Her approval confirmed with bestial moans.

She unbuttoned my jeans. With her hands steadfast on the raised seams, she jerked them to my ankles, removing the boxers in tow. I, naked for her to view and absorb. We paused, licentious smiles filling the gaps between our gasps.

"Oh… I like what I see." She moaned.

Both hands latched onto me like a broom handle. With each of her double-fisted strokes, her eyes bobbing in tandem, she licked her lips, and simpered. I guided her to stand, rubbing her thighs atop skintight jeans as smooth as wax. I wrenched her waist. She unhooked the latch, shimmying them to the floor and from her ankles. Standing before me she spun, then tore the lace panties from her waist.

"Touch me, Frank. I need you. I want you."

I slid my fingers up her thigh and over her exposed essence, driving them deeper as her groans escalated.

"Oh… Yes, Frank. Yes…"

We panted in unison.

"I want to—"

"No. I want to take care of you, baby."

She forced me onto the couch, my head flinging over the backrest. Her smooth hands glided over me with rapid strokes, alternating with her mouth, bypassing my tip and swallowing me whole. I grabbed fistfuls of her hair, forcing myself into the back of her throat. She continued without gagging, adding gusto. I garnered this wasn't her first rodeo, so I thrusted deeper. She came up for air.

"Keep going, Frank. I love it—you. Give it to me."

I continued per her request, pulling out a few seconds before climax. She slithered up my chest and met my lips, as I massaged her breasts. She retreated, resting upon the couch.

"I want you inside me." She whimpered.

I plunged my fingers into her. Her cries increased, her breaths short like a marathon runner. I cradled her to the bedroom, bouncing her tiny body atop the king bed.

"I want you wetter."

"Fuck me, Frank. I want it now."

I ran my fingers through her soft curls, over her silk thighs, and ended in her swollen, pulsating essence. Her pounding heart quivering my lips as they crossed her chest.

"Yes... Frank."

She guided my sopping fingers into her mouth. I replaced them with my passionate lips. We kissed. As I pulled away to caress her cheek, she stopped me, and directed my hand to her throat.

"Give it to me. I want you to squeeze."

I indulged her request even though she was gasping for air. I had been in these situations many times in the past, except in those, I decided when and how tight.

Don't, Frank. You, we, like this one.

"Fine."

Hesitant, I glided my large hand around her tiny neck, and with it snug, I compressed.

"More, Frank. I need more."

Her request spiraled me into euphoria. I tightened my grip and thrust into her without a hint of resistance. Our thighs twisted and slid, our eyes flushed with ecstasy, a slow-motion gaze on the last throw. I released my grip, her breath fighting to find its normal rhythm.

"That was amazing, Frank," she said, peeling her sweaty body from mine.

She regained her breath, nuzzling her body against me. I didn't respond, lying in a fetal position with my back to her. We fell asleep shortly thereafter.

* * * * * * * * * * * *

I awoke to a nibble on my lower lip that spread to my earlobe. Our sexual escapade commenced for what may have been hours or days, the exact time unknown, only pausing for drinks and toots from a dollar-bill straw. And at some point, our jelly legs annexed that option as well.

"Good morning, baby," she whispered into my ear.

Her long nails sifting my hair like a brush, sending shivers throughout my body. She stopped and rose to her feet, ending my bliss. I scanned the bedroom and found her standing, fully dressed, at the bedroom door.

"I hope to see you soon, Frank."

"Me too. I'm glad we met. That was a good game of *love* for us." I slid a cigarette from a pack on the nightstand and lit it.

"Yes, it was," she said, winking. Her dimples appeared. "We both won this time."

"I hope you don't get in trouble for not showing up at work."

"It'll be fine. There's always someone they call to substitute. I can't lose my job anyway. No one wants to work in a homeless shelter."

"Makes sense. Looking forward to more."

The heels of her boots clopped into the distance and the door closed. On the pillow beside me, her laced panties. I slipped them through my fingers, brought them to my face, and drew her sweet aroma into my chest. A perfect gift for when I need to think about her. I tucked them under my cheek, closed my eyes, and placed my hand below my waist.

May 22

I've decided to write because of the great time I had with Desiree. She's the best thing that has happened to me in many moons. Work has been smooth and I've been keeping to myself.

All is well, but there's a problem.

Melancholia has crept into my being. It may be the drugs and liquor or it may be something more serious. I have to fix the sadness. Coffee and cigarettes don't help enough. My insides are ravaged. I attempted a shot of scotch and a stream of bile burned its path through my nostrils.

The position in which I lay is falling away from itself, sinking like quicksand. As I try to rise, an ocean wave sweeps across my body swallowing me whole. I try to rise again, but this time the Universe weighs heavy on my chest, squeezing out every breath until my body is crushed.

I should surrender to it and push myself into the dark abyss awaiting me, not to have to face more of this misery. I pause, hoping to be swallowed, but it never happens.

My strife continues, shackled to this bed, my alternate coffin, with a felt tip dream in my hand. I must move forward. I must rid the mental anguish, and the drinking and drugs, but I know I cannot. The Universe is a Demon, or I'm the Demon the Universe no longer wants.

Thinking is no longer virtuous. A few deep breaths to remove the negativity, but from nowhere the darkness floods my soul. Everything is disposable, including myself. I can no longer write because my soul is torn, riled with despair.

June 01

Several days have passed since I've written or seen the outside of the apartment. I've taken time away from work. I don't want to see anyone. My only movements within the apartment extended to the bathroom and back to bed. The ashtrays in my bedroom have overflowed, forcing me to use the floor. Miniature mounds of ash have built up across the hardwoods, resembling grey moguls on the ski slopes of Upstate New York. My weighty feet failed to negotiate the proper steps around those mounds, carrying the glued butts and ash onto the already soiled bed sheets. I hesitated to go see Doctor Brazen at first, but have since decided to venture to her office.

I slinked out of bed and made my way to the bathroom to wash up and make myself presentable. I tamed my wild hair and ragged beard with a mixture of water, pomade, and baby oil. Eight drops of Visine in each eye cleared some of the red stains. A douse of evergreen musk masked the liquor seeping from my pores. I stopped at the kitchen, pouring a large cup of cold, black coffee with a splash of scotch into a portable mug. Perhaps, today is the day to show her my journal. In case I decide, I'll bring it with me.

XIX

The brisk drive to Doctor Brazen's office awoke the lull seated within my mind, at least for the moment. With the windows rolled down, the crisp, spring air cleared my lungs and fanned away the remnants of scotch and cigarettes. I parked at a corner spot furthest from the office. The lot vacant again. She's clearly scheduling our visits early to avoid showing the other offices she's treating me. It was a hunch, but the twist in my belly told me it was true.

I sat inside the car for a moment, contemplating if I should stay or leave. The visit bound to be the same old thing, "Frank, take your meds, breathe, and be positive." I straggled to the entrance finishing a crumpled cigarette, making sure there were no crazy people lingering around her office to yell at me. The last episode, or as I put it, real person, frightening. A few minutes passed and no one showed. I continued into the empty waiting room, the moth ball aroma more prevalent today than my prior visits. She stood at the door, hands on hips, with a thin lipped smile teetering between satisfaction and condemnation.

"Hello, Mr Stark. How are you today?" She swung her arm, directing me into her office.

"I'm fine, Doctor. Please call me Frank. I could always be better, but I'm fine." I lowered my head to avoid eye contact.

"Will do, Frank. Your *good* looks tell me a different story, but if you say you're fine, then I'll take your word."

"Really? That's what you say to me? I come for help, not your opinion on my visage."

Appalled by her feral statement, I should've lunged like a cheetah and ripped her torso from her head, but I retreated. I needed to fulfill the visit to account for my time away from work.

"Yes, Frank. It's more of a diagnosis than an opinion. Your inflamed eyes are telling. I expect honesty from you. If you don't feel fine, then you need to tell me. Let's start over. How are you today?"

"I could be better. I said that when I came in. I'm happy-sad. Aren't we all?" I clumped my hair, stretching my forehead like taffy. "You need to be nicer to me. Keep the extra negativity to yourself!"

"Okay, Frank. Glad you brought some emotion this time." She slid a pencil from her prized holder, pretending nothing happened. "Well... I'm doing well. Thank you for asking. Anyway, I'm always clear of mind and seeing my patients to help them. Please have a seat."

"Doctor? Changing topics like that is wrong."

"Please have a seat. We must move forward with your visit, before time runs out." She scribbled a sentence or two, then directed me to sit, gesturing with the pencil.

"Alright. Same chair?"

She folded her hands atop the center of the desk. "Yes, Frank. Please... no sarcasm. Nothing has changed in my office. Let's not focus on your seating arrangement, rather on how you're handling life. How are you dealing with the sadness?"

Well, Doctor... For starters I drink and do drugs. It's the only way I can stay sane. The memories inside my mind scream, cry, and laugh. They're so jumbled I don't know which is which. When those wails are silent, my thoughts take over their spaces, throbbing the walls of each thinking capillary to the point of rupture. Each strand of flesh that keeps them together stretches like a knee scab that never heals.

"Frank... come back to me. I—"

"Yes. I'm here. Sadness."

"Dealing with?"

"I try to breathe, stay positive. If I venture into some bad place, I try to comeback as soon as possible." I hoped that was the right answer for this quiz question.

"Well… that's good progress. At least you're coming back. What's really bothering you? What's making you feel so upset or sad? Please expound."

"Sometimes I feel threatened by friends, family, or strangers. If that happens, I become uncomfortable. I don't like it when others try to take control of situations."

I reclined and stretched my arms, staring every which way but towards her. I was smart to add family and friends to that list. Those two things will tug on her heart strings and she'll leave me alone. She better write that down on her useless notepad for future reference.

"Are there any other triggers that cause you to feel sad or distressed?"

"When I'm told that I'm not acting properly, or to the level of what's expected, I get upset."

"And… Mr Stark."

Her piercing stare delved into my mind like a surgeon's scalpel, raising hairs and tingling my back. I turned to find another focal point on the wall.

"Too complicated to answer, but I'll try to sum it up in a couple sentences. I think people manipulate me. They want me to be a certain way and that destroys all the freedom I have. I'm cornered. People shouldn't act that way towards me because I don't do anything wrong."

"I see how it makes you vulnerable and uncomfortable. Happens to me sometimes."

She tilted her head towards the ceiling with a reminiscent gaze. She was either being sardonic or bothered by her admission. If she was bothered, that's on her. I didn't ask her to be honest with me. If it's the former, she can go fuck herself.

"What do you mean?" I played along. "How can *you* feel that way?"

She snapped out of her hypnosis, then turned her focus towards the notepad. "Mr Stark, I'm not the one seeking treatment. I can't divulge my personal situations. I can tell you we all go through these situations at some point in our lives. We have to assess the situation, then make the best decision to figure it out."

She scraped the pencil onto the notepad. I couldn't tell if she was drawing or writing.

"Doesn't help me much, Doctor. There's been no answer on how to fix my problem."

She aimed the honed pencil at me. "I gave you an answer. Just step back, review the scenario, and make a calculated decision that's positive for whoever is involved." Her voice escalating with each word. "Can you grasp that idea?"

"I'll try." I slid my wet palms over my jeans and sighed with a neck roll, popping the bones.

"Alright, Frank. Great. I wanted to make sure you're with me, even though you're under the influence. The alcohol in that coffee is pretty strong."

"There's no alcohol in this coffee." I balked, raising the mug and almost spilling its contents onto her desk.

"Stop it, Frank. I don't drink that often, so it's easy to tell. Just accept that I caught you and deal with the consequences."

"Fine! Doctor." I plucked one of the pencils from her desk and snapped it between my thumb and finger. "Don't put me in a corner. I'll admit it. I poured some liquor in the coffee." I dropped the splintered halves onto her notepad. "It was just a splash. Enough to keep me calm while you drill me for information. You don't make this easy."

"Come on, Frank. Act like an adult. I'm on your side. I'm here to help you, not put you in jail."

She raised the garbage can sitting behind her desk and swiped the pencil's remains, clanging them against its tin wall.

"Fine. Let's get on with this appointment, and if you don't mind, I'm going to continue to sip the coffee."

I should've used the broken pencil as two shivs and nailed them into your temples.

Frank, I don't think we can kill this one.

"Great." She slapped the desk. "Do what you need to do. I don't need any more outbursts. So... what's new with you? How is that girl that we talked about?"

"Desiree? She's fine. We had drinks one night and got really close to each other."

The mention of her name erased the irritation I had endured from *the/rapist*, bringing a glimpse of contentment into my mind.

"You're almost smiling, which is a feat in itself. I'm guessing she made you a happy man that night. That's a step in the right direction."

"Yes. She's great. I like her. If I stay with her, I'll be cured."

"Well, I hope you can continue the relationship with her, but I wouldn't stretch to being *cured*."

My whole existence summed in one sentence by *the/rapist* of the mind: "You'll never be cured."

"We'll have to see what happens. I can't predict the future."

I shrugged. Of course, I'll be cured. Miss Doctor doesn't know anything about me or my mind. I'll be done with these stupid visits in no time at all. Everyone has hiccups in life, and she can't possibly figure out everyone. I'll be fine. Only a matter of time.

"How's work progressing, Frank?"

"I need to collect a paycheck. I do what I have to do."

"So you're still not happy with work, correct?"

"Correct. Maybe I'll leave some day, or maybe I'll be stuck there for life. I'm not psychic. I promise you'll be the first to know if anything changes."

"How have your mood swings been? Have you had any episodes recently?"

"The mood swings have been controlled. Nothing out of the ordinary. To be honest, I haven't had any problems. No weird feelings and no episodes. I get mad sometimes, but maybe that's because of work stress."

"Have you been writing in your journal? See, I remembered not to call it a diary. Last time, you told me you'd bring it in for me. I need to see it, Frank. You have to learn that sharing with others will make your mind clearer, less stressed."

"I've been writing in my journal *Ms Brazen* from English 101. I write as much as possible. Some days more than others. I don't want to share it with you yet. I need to make it better."

"I'm not looking for a novel. Leave that to Stephen King or J.D. Salinger. I just want to see what you've written. Can you give me any clues?"

"I've written things about my past and present. Things that bother me and make my mind confused."

"You're beating around the bush. Like what?"

"Stop pressing me." I stared at the wallpaper creases beyond her desk. "I don't know. I guess things that happened during my childhood?"

"Oh, Frank. I'm so sorry." Her eyes sprung open as she expelled a heaving sigh. "You never mentioned childhood. Was there abuse?"

"Don't you pay attention? We talked about it in our last meeting. I try to relate those situations to the present day. I—"

"You said you didn't want to go down that road last time. I listen."

"Either way, I guess—the abuses—a little of both. The most severe? I—"

I didn't want to continue. Today was not the time to discuss this information. I suppose if I did talk, she'd get off my case, stop prying about this and that. Wants to know everything about me. Like anything I say is going to make any difference.

"—well—the touching occurred during my early teens. The physical, for the most part, only involved my parents. I could handle their abuse more than the touching." I let out a defeated moan to garner more sympathy from her.

"Oh my, Frank. This is why we need to discuss these things that happened in your past. The more we pinpoint the root of the problems, the more we can reach a solution."

"I don't want to discuss my past any longer."

"We must. That's the only way to remove the negativity. Once that's gone, you can learn to love yourself and others."

I almost fell for her pleasant, nurturing smile, but I took a vocal stand.

"I don't believe in this hippy jargon. Stop trying to convince me. I'll deal with things my way, and only when the time is right. I don't need a doctor to tell me when and how to deal with situations in *my* life. Can we talk about something else? This conversation is annoying."

"I'm just trying to help you, Frank. You have to understand and believe me. Being defensive is not the way to act, especially towards me. I'm not your enemy. I'm not the one that hurt you. I want to make you better, then your life with Desiree will be better, and maybe even your job. Do you understand?"

"I'm done talking. Let's move on. I don't want to get upset today. When I get upset, I end up in that dark place. Sometimes I can't come back from there for a long time."

"We should talk about that dark place. We need to figure out how to get you out of there quickly. Dark places are bad." She wagged her hand as if I was her puppy.

"I don't want to talk about that either. Like I said, I'll figure it out."

"You're making this meeting difficult. Your defensive stance is not allowing us to fix your issues. We need to have an avenue of open communication. I'm not going to judge you about your past, present, or future. We came to an agreement when you decided to see me. The bottom line is to make you better, fix you. There are only two people here and no one else will know what we discuss. Ever. I promise."

"What part don't you understand, Doctor? I don't want to continue this conversation any longer. I'm leaving now."

Thrusting from the chair, its front two legs tilted upwards and the backrest bounced from the carpet. As I marched towards the exit, she called out to me.

"Wait... Frank... You can't just leave. We still have thirty minutes." Her screeching voice expanded into a howl.

Before slamming the door, I peeked into the office. "I just did. Stop crossing lines with me," I said with a growl.

She continued, "Call me. Please. Before you hurt yourself or someone else. Please."

I stormed to the car. Her voice disappeared. I slammed the door and spun the ignition. The engine revved, screeching its belts to find its flow. Cigarette smoke clouded the windshield as my fists thrashed the steering column. I hammered it into drive, pulling onto the main drag and leaving a path of rubber and exhaust. Home, the next stop.

I dashed inside to the scotch bottle, filling a tall glass with the translucent caramel. The weighty drawer squealed as I pulled it open. Three quart-sized Ziplocs occupied its space, but only a portion of one was needed for tonight. I poured a small mound and sliced ten, thin lines, creating a maze on the kitchen table. Raring to go, I dialed Desiree for a date and she accepted.

XX

I had exchanged the day for night where my comfort zone existed. A gentle fog hovered just above the headlights, casting irregular shadows upon the pavement. The moon absent in the heavens. The dark sky splashed with lilac and lava, which was odd because the sun had set hours ago. Desiree waited at the curb of Shelter Avenue, just ahead of New Beginnings. I debated not stopping. That fire sky and mysterious prickling of the skin and bones spoke volumes about how the night might end. The future always unpredictable, then again, always planned.

"Hey, Frank. You put a smile on my face when you called. Thanks for the ride. Saved me a bunch of time walking or taking the bus." She glanced at the shelter door. "We're all set. Looks like the sign isn't going to fall. I thought I didn't affix it well."

"No problem for the ride and you did a fine job with the sign. I see you placed extra electrical tape on the corners this time."

"I did, I did. Did you miss me?" she asked with a longing face.

"Yes, I believe so."

"Believe? Anyway. I missed you, too. We had such a great time."

"Yes, we did. We're off to the Coliseum. Better hold on, I'm going to floor it."

As I lowered the accelerator, she cupped her eyes. Her dimples peeked from the edge of each hand. Acting skills good enough for the local theater but not for a cop.

* * * * * * * * * * * *

Giancarlo greeted us at the door. He offered to seat us at the same table as our prior date. We nodded and followed, he pulling out the chair for Desiree. I ordered the usual pepperoni and cheese pizza and two rounds of drinks as appetizers, she, the vodka on the rocks, and for myself, double scotches. It didn't end there either. She was getting a little jittery and requested, or should I say demanded, that I provide her with the magical powder to give her a boost. I followed the orders. We alternated several walks to the bathroom, snorting our way to the dark side of the moon.

On one particular trip, she'd taken longer than expected. Across from us, where plain Jane and John sat last time, two beautiful women had been seated. One of them resembled Maria with strawberry blonde hair, and the other, Maggie May. I couldn't help staring at Maria. Desiree tapped me on the shoulder, startling me from reverie.

"You like what you see, Frank? *Bless their hearts.* Maybe you should go hang out with them. I'm obviously not enough." She pointed to her cleavage and below the table.

"No. It's not what you think. She looks like someone I used to know."

"Well, you should go ask her. You can hook up again."

"It's not like that. She—they, don't live in this city anymore. I don't know how they can be here."

Divulging Maria's outcome to Desiree, and explaining the alive part, would initiate a line of questioning I didn't want to deal with tonight, especially drunk and high. She caught me gawking a few more times and I had to close the tab. As we exited, Desiree sent them an evil eye, probably damning them with silent maledictions. I should've ended the date, but I wanted my buzz and the party to continue, and I wanted Desiree.

Outside the Coliseum, she grasped my jacket lapel with both hands. "Listen, Frank. If you're into emaciated bimbos with blue eyes, pasty skin, and shoe polish hair, then march in there and go out with them tonight. Otherwise, be happy with an ethnic queen who's got curves and knows how to use them."

She released her grip and spun like a ballerina, rubbing her torso to remind me of the eroticism that existed beneath her clothing.

"Are you sure they have dark hair?"

"Yes, Frank. They're goths." She ran her fingers through her hair. "Anyway, where we going now?"

"Goths? Really? Let's go to Magpie."

We didn't bother with the car. I'd get it later. I lit a cigarette and took a swig to calm my nerves. She placed her arm around my waist with mine atop her shoulder, which ensured a steady walk. We didn't talk. I preoccupied with the gothic mishap and she probably fuming. Maria's strawberry blonde hair and pink tips glistened under the bright lights inside the Coliseum. More of a model than a vampire, although vampires attracted me as well. Our dark mentalities the strongest of bonds. I had my fair share with great memories, although at times, their pallid skin made it difficult to tell if they were dead. I know who I saw. Desiree was mistaken.

I puffed the last drag at the Magpie entrance, flicking the butt onto the street. It caught the wheel of a passing car and cartwheeled to the curb. We entered the bar hand in hand. I nodded in Mike's direction, but he hadn't noticed, continuing to pour drinks for a line of patrons. I espied two empty stools at the corner of the bar. I clasped her wrist and tugged her to the niche.

The bar's atmosphere electric: patrons screaming, kissing, and spilling drinks on the soppy floor. I'd hate to be the mop person after closing time. We didn't need to add to the puddles, but a twitch in my mind suggested the more alcohol the better. Succumbing to the devil's potion always proved wise, whisking any negativity out the back door with the trash.

Mike headed towards us, leaving several angry drunks waving fistfuls of money to wait in line.

"Hey, Frank. What can I get you tonight?"

I leaned across the bar. "Pour some shots, Mike." I realized the slurring too late.

"What? Mike smiled and twirled his finger around his ear. "Can't hear."

"Shots! Scotch and vodka, please."

"What'd you say? Seltzer and cheese?" I nodded with a dumfounded grin.

"I'm just kidding. I got you." Mike drummed the bar and raised his thumb. Less than a minute later the drinks slid down the centerline.

Desiree swallowed the shot first and I followed. Enraptured, probably by the alcohol, we lunged, lips locking, tongues slipping and sliding. The passion contagious, as a crowd of intrigued spectators watched our live pornographic show.

"We probably should tone it down," I whispered into her ear.

She didn't listen. Her kisses ventured across my cheek and neck, eyes closing. Her hand crossed my midriff, gripping my boxers, and yanking me against her body.

"I want you."

I retreated, shaking my head, and removed her hand from my waist. "Not now, Desiree." Her brow furrowed. She punched my chest and ruffled my shirt.

With bartender's intuition, Mike interjected. "Anything else, Frank?"

"Yes. One tall glass of vodka, one of scotch, and two beers to chase."

"No problem."

He lined the drinks ahead of us like trophies. Desiree reasserted herself on the barstool, draping her arm over my shoulder. Her prior contempt washed away by a long sip of vodka.

"I need something from you," she purred.

"And, what's that?"

"I need a pick-me-up."

"Okay. A few more sips and I'll be ready. I can use some too."

I staggered towards the unisex bathroom at the back of the bar. She followed with one hand in my back pocket, and her other on my back for leverage. Once inside, she slapped the slide-lock, wasting no time with her directive.

"Where is it, Frank? I need it. Give me some of that good stuff."

I sighed with a heavy breath. After all the jealous fuss at the Coliseum, she didn't want me, just the baggie in my pocket. This wasn't the same Desiree I knew. She ran her fingers through my hair, pawing my chest.

"Come on, Frank. I need it real bad."

I could've said no, but I had high hopes for us, and Doctor Brazen. This girl was my cure, not my downfall. Convinced this was only a nighttime hiccup, I moved forward. I knew all too well about the drug rollercoaster and the importance of returning to the peak. Those cocaine lows are as easy to escape as a straightjacket. Hell, my high was fading by the second. Frantic, I searched my pockets.

"I found it, Desiree."

Behind her smile, she salivated. A wet counter and stained toilet seat offered no place to pour and cut it. The next best option, the switchblade I always carried, more for its intimacy over guns than cocaine use. I dug into the baggie and scooped a mound, filling most of the blade, then setting it flat against the sink's edge. Her eyes not deviating once from the powdered prize.

"Go first. Careful. Don't spill it."

The blade trembled within her grip as she brought it to her nose and sniffed.

"Baby, I want to fuck you right now." As I refilled the blade, she breached my waist.

"No." I stepped back, lifting the blade and snorting. "We can't do it now. There's too many people."

"Come on, Frank. You're a cop. We can do anything we want. Don't you have the *power* around here?"

"Power? We're in a bar. I don't own the place." I licked the talc residue from the steel and dried the spit against my pants. "Save it for later. Let's just get our drinks."

She continued pressing, relentless. That same energy that drew me, later exploded like a hydrogen bomb. "Come on, Frank. Give me some of that manliness hiding in your pants. Either him, or give me another bump. I'm running out of patience with you. Maybe you need one of those goth girls to get you hard?"

"No patience? I haven't done anything wrong." An urgency existed to change the direction of the conversation before people banged on the door. I clapped and lifted my voice into a cheer, hoping to startle her out of the rant. "Snap out of it. Let's go back to the bar and finish our drinks. We'll have a few more. It'll be fine, Desiree."

"No, Frank. Give *it* to me, or a bump. Those are your only options. If you can't man up, you better pull out the coke now, or leave and go find those girls from the restaurant." She planted her hands on the sink, splashing water against my shirt.

"Here you go." I nodded, scooping another sample and hovering it under her nose.

"That hit the spot. It tastes better than you." A wink confirmed her satisfaction and drove a spear into my ego.

She slid the door latch with such force it clanged against the metal backstop. Flinging the door open, the patrons waiting in line stumbled backwards. Before she exited, I grabbed her arm.

"I'm not happy with you, Desiree. You're being rude, ungrateful and causing a scene. I've done a lot for you. The cocaine's blurring your mind. You didn't act this way before."

She scanned me from head to toe and blew the curls dangling her eyes. "Whatever, Frank. Let's go back to the bar. No sex for me, but at least I got coke and drinks. I don't need you." She stiff-armed through the crowd while excusing herself.

"Better stop while you're ahead, Desiree," I shouted, trying to catch up with her. "No need for this negativity and garbage coming from your mouth. We can get together later."

"Frank," she said, stopping and turning her head with a contemptuous laugh, "you'll fuck me, if I let you fuck me. You don't own me, just like you don't own this place or the streets. You're just a wannabe like all the rest."

I punched the wall, leaving an indentation. "Stop laughing at me, Desiree."

"Fine, Frank. Let's get back to our seats," she said, surrendering with a sigh.

Frankie. It'll be fine. You'll have her home soon enough.

"I know."

We strode over broken bottles, the drunken stumbling fixed by the cocaine high, avoiding jutting patron elbows like a running back. We slid onto our stools, swiping the tall glasses from the counter and sipping. A few minutes passed and I ordered another round. The shot slimed my throat like cough syrup. We each retrieved a cigarette, lighting them from a matchbook atop the bar. All had returned to normal.We'd be back at my place at some point, but I didn't know how it'd play out. The voices never explained anything to me, or I had a habit of ignoring their messages.

Mike rang the closing bell.

"Last call! Last call for alcohol. Everyone... last call for alcohol. You don't have to go home, but you can't stay here. Finish up your drinks boys and girls. Thank you. Have a good night."

Mike approached and slapped the bar like a drummer. "What can I get you two before we close up?"

I turned towards her and she nodded. "We'll take a few more drinks. Make them tall. A vodka rocks, scotch rocks, two shots the same way and two beers to chase."

"So... two talls, two shots, and two chasers?"

"Yes, sir." My lips were too numb to smile.

Mike lined up each drink and hurried away. A scuffle had broken out at the center of the bar. The crowd formed a loose circle. Chairs fell, followed by broken glass and yells. The security detail pounced, lifting them from the floor like empty, cardboard boxes, and dragging them to the sidewalk. One guy had a gash across his forehead oozing blood. The culprit, probably a beer bottle.

Mike turned to us as if nothing had happened, accustomed to the closing-time ruckuses. "Frank, you can both stay as long as you want, or until we decide to leave. We have to count our money and clean up, so we have plenty of time."

I swiveled the stool. "See, Desiree. I told you," I said with triumphant satisfaction. "Thanks, Mike. Really appreciate it. I—"

"Frank," she said, high pitched and satirical, "they must really like you here."

"They do." I shrugged. "They also don't mind having a cop around when they're counting money."

"That's funny." She exhaled a puff of smoke and flung her curls. "I don't think they want a *drunk* cop around."

"Better drunk than none. Stop harassing me," I barked.

I helped myself to a bottle of scotch and vodka from the bar, filling our glasses to the brim. Mike, nor any of the other workers, minded if I poured drinks after hours. They had a problem if I ventured there during operating hours, which I had on a handful of occasions, infuriating them. We drank another refill and decided to continue the party at my place. I yelled towards the backroom, breaking up the money counting huddle.

"Hey, Mike. We're out of here. Better come lock up."

Mike didn't waste a second, placing a stack of bills as tall as a beer bottle on the table, and heading towards us with a wave and raised thumb.

"Alright... be right there. You two make sure you have a good night and morning."

XXI

We toddled along, dawn approaching. Grass blades glistened under the flickering auburn street lamps, soon to be warmed by the radiant slivers of gold cresting in the eastern sky.

"You love those gothic girls and not me."

"Stop it. Just let it go. They weren't *gothic or goths*."

She paced ahead of me, trudging up the steps, using the handrail like a rope to inch her way. Stretching, I latched onto her hand. If I held her, there'd be a possibility she'd forget about the other-girl gibberish and refocus on our upcoming morning together. The plan foolproof for the moment.

Inside, we fondled each other, kissing without restraint. From her midriff, I escalated my hands along her supple stomach and over her chest. She wandered the ridge on my backside, between my thighs, stroking my bulge stretching the jeans. Midway to the living room she stopped. Our blood shot eyes locked. She shoved my chest.

"Why are you treating me like this, Frank?" She backpedaled, leaning against the wall. "Why are you using me?"

"What are you talking about? We went out." Astounded, I inched closer to her.

She huffed the hair dangling her eyes and dug her heel into my shin. "You men are all the same. Probably because you're a cop. My brother warned me. All you do is take and never give anything back. I'm just another fuck to you."

The sting from the kick rose through me like lightning. On reflex, I dug my fingers into her shoulders, and slammed her against the wall. "Desiree—what the hell are you talking about? I've done nothing wrong. If anything, you're the one that takes advantage of me. I buy all the food and drinks, give you all the free drugs, and let you sleep at my place. I think you need to stop this stupid talk. You're high, out of your mind. Don't make this worse."

I clamped her torso between my hands and lifted, her boots hovering the hardwood floor. Glimpses of Maria and the others parading my mind didn't affect my control. Our miscalculations had resolve.

"No... Frank... Stop." Her eyes welled, dripping onto my hand. I released my grip. Her heels clacked the floor. "You have to listen to me, Frank."

I waited, but no follow-up arrived. Leading with her eyes she motioned me closer, parting her succulent lips. As we kissed, a stream of tears trickled onto my tongue. Her hands acquired a second wind, roaming my chest, then yanking the button from my jeans.

"We should stop, Desiree. Your mind is clouded. I don't want you mad."

I wasn't in my right mind either. I did my best to protect the situation, not to let it escalate to the point of no return. I teetered between ravishment and impotence, the latter diminishing by the second.

"Screw you," she shrieked, then paused, then whiplashed to sultriness. "I need you in me right now." The courage to resist her sexual advances vanished. I surrendered, as I had done many times throughout the course of my life. We'd reached that point of no return.

Frank. Take her, but be careful.

"I will."

With one hand I tore her blouse, the other stripped the lace bindings from the bra. I jostled her towards the couch. She fell onto her back. Her crazed gaze as wild as her smile. She unrolled her skintight jeans from her olive thighs, throwing them across the room. No panties tonight. I followed her lead and chucked my pants and boxers onto her pile. Arching atop the cushions, she spread her legs, a curling hand calling me atop her. I thrusted my fingers into her. She guided them to her mouth, licking them clean.

"I want you inside me."

I lunged into her, her sopping walls offering no resistance. As I adjusted to re-enter, drips of her satisfaction dribbled her thighs and pooled below.

"Choke me, baby. I need to feel. Give it to me." Her pleading wails echoing throughout the apartment.

The drug-induced sexual euphoria had taken full effect. *Choke me* repeating within my mind. "Do it, Frank. Do it to me."

Do it. Do it. Don't do it. Choke her. Choke her. Don't.

I could do nothing less than honor her commands. I slinked my hand around her throat and squeezed, gentle at first with a consistent rhythm. The clenches cautious to test her threshold—and mine.

"Squeeze harder. Please. I want more." Faint breaths followed and a subtle froth formed at the corners of her lips.

Do it. Do it. Don't do it. Choke her. Choke her. Don't.

Comprehension departed. The surroundings within the apartment blending between darkness and light. The grip tighter, the light dimmer, the thrusts grew stronger and longer until all went black. My body collapsed upon her. I awoke with her motionless and cool to the touch beside me.

"Wake up, Desiree," I said, caressing her cheek. "Wake up."

Now you did it, Frankie. Now, you really did it.

I massaged her legs, pushing and pulling her body about the couch, but there was no response. I arose, pacing upon the cold hardwoods. I lit a cigarette, and the buzz peaked again, zapping every neuron within my mind. Ahead of me, blinding sunlight breached the window. I stumbled, crashing onto the kitchen table, breaking bottles, and overturning chairs. I regained my composure and reset the fallen items. The scotch bottle hadn't shattered. I tipped a healthy shot and returned to the couch.

"Desiree. Desiree. You have to wake up. It's time to get up. Stop sleeping," I pleaded. No response. I stroked her cheek. Her skin had changed from cool to cold. "I have an idea, baby. Maybe this will warm and wake you."

I kissed her forehead, moved to her neck, then her mocha breasts. With no response, my sensual trek traversed her navel and entered the space between her thighs. I leaned onto my haunches for a brief moment, her beautiful body to behold. The dizzying high returned, spinning untamable thoughts. I clutched her calves and spread her legs. My first attempt jammed on impact. I stroked the pain away.

"What the hell, Desiree?"

I clasped her thighs and slid into her without resistance. She repeated how much she craved me with each lunge of my hips. Her moans not as pronounced, but her calls for me between whimpers clear. Heart pounding, my pace unfettered, each thrust thrashing the couch, its wooden legs smacking the hardwoods. Darkness arrived as I climaxed inside her, my body falling upon her motionless torso.

"Desiree, you're the best I've ever had," I whispered.

Silence followed. I closed my eyes beside her, waiting for Desiree to regain energy. I awoke, unsure if ten minutes or an hour had passed, with a pounding headache matching my heartbeat, fiery needles piercing the eyeballs. I scanned the apartment through a blur and realized the rancid reality.

"Desiree... You're dead. You're gone. Why did you do this to me? You were my cure."

Frankie. You've really done it now.

I should've listened to the omens throughout the day. I hoped to remedy this situation but realized as my vision cleared, it wasn't fixable. I struggled to keep my eyelids open, as if they had been brushed with concrete eyeshadow. I shuffled to the bedroom, leaving Desiree on the couch. The dilemma to be dealt with later.

June 05

Desiree has died within my grasp. She's one of many, but meant more than any. I cannot live in regret and must move forward. She was to be my cure, to free me from the shackles of Doctor Brazen, *the/rapist* of the mind, and rid me of my past. Now she's just become another statistic within my present. I won't give up on finding another cure. I don't know how this has happened to me. It's unfair to be served the shortest straw. I must amend the situation. Reposing on this coffin mattress won't fix it. I'll write again soon, hopefully.

XXII

I slid the hardcover journal, pencil tucked inside, onto the nightstand, exchanging it for a crinkled cigarette. After a few drags, I leaned forward and swung my legs to the floor. The movement dizzying, sending a rush of acid midway my throat and nostrils. Several juggling swallows retreated the sour mix. Hands firm against the mattress, I rose.

I shambled to Desiree disappointed and concerned. Nodding, I lolled my tongue, drier than wool in an oven. "I don't know what to do with you. Baby? Tell me." I perused her body, then caressed her forehead.

Two problems existed: a body needed disposing, and a broken heart needed mending. The latter more difficult than the former.

"I'll do my best handling your body with utmost respect. I'll treat you better than the others. Be right back, baby. I need a drink."

The sunbeams that caused me to stumble earlier had disappeared from the kitchen. A relief to awake in darkness. I poured a tall glass of scotch to soothe my arid throat and sat at the table. The damn cocaine had mixed with the ashes. With a soiled dollar bill, I hunched for a sample, snorting the grey lines. Purity not in my cards today.

Within minutes, the drunken high from the prior night returned with a jolt. Amped, I stood, downing the remaining scotch, and returned to Desiree. Her glossy eyes contrasted that beautiful body, which had since morphed into a darker hue, albeit not for all, perfect for me. She asked for a massage. I obliged, not wanting to be rude, especially after all we'd been through. I began at her breasts and ended at her smooth, firm legs. Although she was cold, the sexual warmth from the prior night flowed through my veins. Her eyelids flickered and mouth parted. I knew she was warming as well.

Bending over her body, I kissed her cheek, then her violet lips. She invited me to graze the contours of her chest. I didn't resist. She suckled me, purring like a kitten. I deviated course to her thighs. At first, they resisted my advances, but after several forceful pries, they opened. Her essence had dried. I didn't want to hurt her. On the bottom shelf of the coffee table sat a bottle of baby oil that I had used on others. I drizzled an ample amount onto my palm and slathered. As I waited for the oil to soak, I traced a swerving path from her feet to her forehead, which ended with a sensual kiss upon her lips. I rose from her body and readjusted myself, kneeling upon the couch and clenching her legs. Uninhibited thrusts ensued, culminating with simultaneous yowling orgasms.

"Did you like that, baby?"

She confirmed with a bluish, bashful grin. Denying her satisfaction would be a crime. I reciprocated with a smile and peck. As I retreated, she twitched, then the oil mix we'd created trickled along her thighs and onto the cushions.

"I like you, even *love* you, Desiree," I said into each ear, then looked into her eyes. "I really do. I wish we could turn back time, but we can only move forward. I'll remember you forever, as I know you will me." I nuzzled her eyelids closed, then kissed them.

I reentered the kitchen, refilling the glass with a finger-length of scotch, and raking two lines of the grey cocaine. Resting my forehead on the edge of the kitchen table, I contemplated the next steps required to clean up this mess. As I staggered to the closet, I couldn't believe what had transpired. But, as I glanced over my shoulder, Desiree's decaying body proved otherwise.

I situated the tarps, totes, and meat bags across the floor and the bathroom. Standing at the entrance, I observed Desiree's hand dangling from the armrest and a surge of warmth overcame me. I let out a sigh and promised Desiree I'd do my best not to desecrate her body.

I cradled her to the bathroom, lowering the limp carcass into the tub. "Oh, you're so beautiful, Desiree." I brushed her long curls away from her eyes and blew her a kiss. "It's time to begin."

I returned to the closet and retrieved the tool bag. Several failed attempts at *psyching* prevented me from selecting the additional tools required to dismember Desiree. Amorous feelings clouding my abilities. Several deep breaths cleared her image from my mind. The last attempt proved successful: a scalpel, hacksaw, pliers, and a butcher knife. The scalpel inherited from Dad. It seems like yesterday he bequeathed that tool to me while wearing a blood-spattered leather apron.

The first incision, using the doctor's tool, carved the perimeter of her hairline. Her face separated just enough to slice through the shiny membrane keeping the skin attached to the underlying muscle. Once the scalpel made its way around Desiree's neckline, her face lifted like a Halloween mask. I draped it over the showerhead. The next cut began at the right breast and ended on her left. Smooth slices into the skin and ligaments continued until each breast separated. Their temporary home, the bathroom sink.

The hacksaw ground through her limbs without hesitation. Dad always said, "Keep the blades sharp and the bones will cut just like butter." They did just as he advised. I separated her hands at the wrist, held them in mine, and with the pliers removed each of her fingernails and pads. The identical process used for her cute little feet. The butcher knife sliced the larger pieces of meat into smaller ones, reducing the mess, which expedited the flesh sorting process into the game bags.

I stepped away for a well-deserved break. The cigarette, absorbing the remnants of skin and blood from my fingers, dried with the heat from each drag. During a random puff, I noticed Desiree's sensual gaze from the showerhead fixed upon me like an angelic face in the sky. A rolling electric wave shimmied every fiber within my body. "Yes, baby. We're almost done." I placed her face and each supple breast into separate meat bags, and with sacred care, lowered them into the totes.

"How can we be together forever?"

I surveyed her cramped torso in one of the totes, a midsection piece that included her stumpy thighs. A few minutes passed and an idea came to mind, which should've been evident all along. I embraced her limbless torso, placing it into the bathtub.

"Yes, this is better than perfect, if that's even possible."

Fondling her essence, she eeked out a quiver from the excitement. As one hand continued to pleasure her, the other held it. Three, swift slices and it dropped into my palm. I continued massaging it between my thumb and forefinger until I arrived at the kitchen, inserting it into a small jar with several drops of olive oil to preserve its beauty.

With a gallon of bleach and a sponge in hand, I returned to the bathroom. The blood turned pink as it sloshed and foamed with the disinfectant. The fumes sending bile from my stomach into my lungs. I mopped the tub and sink with a towel and placed the blood soaked items, including the empty gallon of bleach, into the torso tote. My searing eyes begged to close. Not too long afterward, I spun into a blackout.

XXIII

Desiree's voice interrupted my deep slumber. Shaken and wide-eyed made returning to the pillow impossible.

"I want you. Frank… I need—I love you."

She kissed my cheek, then lips. With fervid hands I roamed all her angles and crevices, ending at her throat.

"Give it to me. I need to feel."

What she wanted I couldn't give and let go. Silence supervened. Her dimples flexed, and as I stretched to stroke them, her hands snarled her neck and snapped it. Then, it rose like a tidal wave, stopping within a hair from my face. Those eyes unforgettable, glossed black. Their penetrating stare charred the remaining sliver of my soul.

"Do you like my face, baby?" Smoke billowed from her every orifice.

The stitching circling her hairline separated, one thread at a time, then her skin peeled to the jawline, each pore stretching and popping, piercing my ear drums. Severed capillaries sprayed my face, streamed my chest, and pooled my lap.

Do you *like* me now, even *love* me?"

"What's happening? What's—Stop," I said whimpering.

Frantic swipes cleared the blood from my eyes, revealing her chest, the breasts rolling onto her stomach. She snatched my hand, guiding it over each of her ribs.

"Do you like how it throbs for you? Guess what?"

"What?"

Her skinless lips paused. "Your Mom sends her regards. You should've been nicer to her."

"I was nice. I swear. Tell her I'm sorry."

Desiree then faded into Mom. Our last night together, well… it didn't go as planned for any of us. After our family dinner, I was sent to the basement to continue Dad's work. Dishes crashed above, then silence. Dad swayed down the stairs cradling Mom, placing her upon the dissecting table. Warm blood trickled over my hand, puddling the corner workspace. A large fan mounted in the corner recirculated the cold, musty air, goosebumps prickling my neck like braille. All went dark.

"I'm back, baby. Do you like my cool breath on your neck?"

Her detached face swung from behind and hovered ahead of me, her black eyes hypnotizing. "Do you still like me—Frank?" I couldn't speak, my only response a weak nod.

She grabbed my hand and brushed it across her body. With each pass, the remaining meat flayed and piled onto the floor, leaving a skeleton. "Wake up. Help. Help!" The screams and pleads existed only within my mind.

Her face, the last addition to the skin pile. Her jawbone snapped open, chiseled teeth like razors craned towards me, latching onto my throat, slicing my jugular.

Blood gushed onto her skull. "What—the—fuck?" My breathing returned in short gasps.

I jumped from bed, stumbling against the walls to the kitchen sink. Distraught and weak, I missed the faucet several times. From the freezer, I creaked ice from the trays, plugging the basin, and filling it with water. Holding my breath, I dunked my head into the slush. With numbing lips and icicles glued to my cheeks, I backpedaled and spun onto the chair. I grabbed the scotch and guzzled from the bottle, then lit a crimped cigarette between my damp fingers.

As I exhaled a plume of smoke, I noticed her essence sitting in its glass home upon the counter. Her teasing stare shivering me sober. I hoped she knew this was the only way to ensure we'd be together forever.

Frank, it's over for now. Dreams are nightmares as nightmares are dreams.

"Snap out of it. Clean up this mess."

Dawn hadn't arrived. I sped to Genesee Park under the cloak of darkness. The river as smooth as glass and the air as thick as a jungle, sweat dripping with each heave. The totes splashed, bubbled, and sank. Desiree to rest forevermore in the depths of the Genesee River, the same place that brought Rochester life and eventually its demise.

Hurrying home, one hand steered while the other propped the eyelids open, attempting to prevent the careening car from smashing mile markers and road signs. Luckily, the streets were clear of any traffic. The time had arrived to acquire the proper rest in order to return to the Precinct.

XXIV

I leapt, spine erect, hands arched against the mattress for leverage. The clock blinking red: 4:00 a.m. I hadn't slept long, but at least there weren't any dreams to rustle the mind. As I sat, staring into the distance, a silhouette with long, wispy hair whisked within the shadows, then hovered, glowing just below the ceiling in the corner. Goggling, I stretched to grasp the blurred image. The motion proved futile. I had no arms.

"How's life treating you?" said a placid, female voice. Her tone familiar and faceless.

"Fine. Who's asking?"

"How's life treating you?" She paused. "My Son."

"Mom?" My hand reappeared. I slid it over my eyes, and just as fast, it vanished.

"Yes... my love, it is I." She grew into focus, dressed in a flowing, red gown. "I wanted to check up on you. I've missed you."

Calm encompassed my being. "I've missed you, too. The last time we spoke was that night with Dad. I'm sorry about what happened. Are you well?"

"Yes." She grinned and nodded. "The place where I live returns the bodies to those who have died without just cause."

"That's interesting. What happens to the ones who deserved to die?"

"Well, those, like your Dad, get partial bodies. Their limbs and organs removed at random." Her grin replaced with a demonic smile, stretching past the width of her face. "They walk with demons amongst the maze of fire and ice. I've never been, but I've been told the darkness is endless and the days are identical." She bellowed a haunting laugh filled with satisfaction.

"Oh my..." My hands reemerged, fingers combing my hair, tugging my scalp. "I feel bad for Dad. I hope he's safe and well."

She extended her arms, palms cupped towards the sky. "Don't worry about him for he signed up for his fate and received it. I didn't come to speak about Dad. How are you doing? How is your job and life?"

"I'm a cop at the RPD, Precinct 13. I haven't been back to work in several days. Trying to take care of my mind." I shrugged with indifference.

"How come?"

"Life has its ups and downs. I needed a break. I'm returning to work soon."

"I understand. Take all the time you need." Her response mirrored the rhetoric she used when I was child. "I always knew you'd become a cop. Remember, we watched *Columbo* while Dad was in the basement tending to his evil deeds. Those were the days when we nestled one another."

"Yes... thank you for reminding me."

"How is Desiree?"

"You know her?"

"We've met once or twice."

"Oh... well, she's fine, but she had to leave me."

"Where did she go?" I did my best to disengage her glare.

"I don't know, Mom. She left me." I swiveled my head opposite of hers. "Can we please change the topic?"

"No. Tell me where she went." No matter which way I turned, her eyes followed like a laser. "Tell—me—now." The incandescence flowing to the center of the wall.

"Oh my..." I gasped, pointing at the wall. "She's standing, hovering next to you."

"Hello, Frank," they said in unison.

A pounding bass drum in a four-beat rhythm interjected in the distance. A faint call from a male voice followed. "Hey—hey. Wake up, Frank."

"Son, do you remember what I said about Dad?"

"No."

The drumming returned, louder. "Wake up, Frank. Wake up." The voice clearer, but I didn't know who or why. "It's important you wake up."

"Son, you have just cause to die. Say hello to Dad when you see him."

The drubbing, this time with chains. They jangled against wood, but neither item found in my vicinity. I saw myself on the bed, body motionless, weeping. A corpse ready for its coffin.

"Wake up, Frank. Wake up. It's important."

"Mom—Desiree. This isn't fair. I've done nothing wrong."

Their baroque response arrived in concert. "Say hello to Dad."

The thundering echoed just as Desiree and Mom dissipated. The reverberations shaking the apartment walls. "Wake up, Frank. Now. Wake up, Sergeant. It's imperative." I'd returned to my body upon the mattress. The noise arriving from the front door. The deadbolts clanking inside their metal casings. "We need to get to work," the voice said with a growl. "We have an important case that just came through the radio. I need your help."

"I'm coming." The words struggled to reach any reasonable volume. Early morning phlegm, combined with tar from too many cigarettes, closed my throat. The humidity and smoke inside my airless room didn't help either. "Give me a minute. I'll be there soon."

"Come on, Frank. Open up."

The pounding ceased. I stumbled along the hallway, struggling to get clothed, wheezing each step.

"I'm coming. One second."

I clacked the two, center deadbolts open and slid the chain lock, pulling the door a smidge. "I'm here, man. What do you want? Why do you keep banging on my door? I'm sleeping. For fuck's sake, it's 4:00 a.m."

"It's Daniels. And it's four-thirty, not four." He grunted, angling his broad shoulder against the door, snapping the chain taut. "Let me in. It's freezing out here. We have an important case."

I propped my arm against the frame and leaned towards the slim opening. "Daniels, you have to slow down. I'm not letting you in. You can't just go around banging on people's doors at four in the morning. Next time you need to call. Go find Joe Rook."

"For the second time, it's 4:30 a.m., and I did try to call, but your phone isn't working. I'm not surprised, since nothing ever works for you. You're screwed up in the head. We need to get moving, so I need you awake. Now!" He forced his fingers through the gap like an octopus, attempting to reach the sliding chain. "Rook isn't going to cut it for this job."

"Hey... slow down, Daniels. You're not reaching that lock. I'll do my best to wake up. Give me a few minutes."

Daniels spun, leading with his shoulder, and rushed the door. The chain stretched against the slide, almost snapping a link. "Whatever, Stark. Let me in. I'm not going to dicker with you. There are more important things. I usually don't make house calls, but this one is important. The pressure from the media and the community is going to create a shitstorm. We have a serious problem in the park."

"Which park?" I said startled, voice cracking. I leaned closer to the door, my lips filling the open space. "Genesee Park?"

"Genesee Park?" Daniels paused, scrunching his brow, and squinting. "No one goes there." Each word sent a cloud of peppermint steam through the opening. "Why would you mention Genesee Park, Stark?"

"I don't know. Just a park that came to mind. I go there, to fish, sometimes. Yes... of course, fishing at the Genesee. Maybe we can go together one day."

"No, Frank. I don't fish, and don't want to hang out either. The murder took place at Maplewood Park near the Maplewood Trail, not the Genesee. It's bad, real bad. We have to go. Now."

"Okay, Daniels. Give me a minute to change. I'll be right out."

"Let me in. I'm not waiting outside. I've been out here for a long time. It's too cold." He shivered, digging his hands into the coat pockets.

"I can't, Daniels. You can't come in here. I'm sorry. Don't take it personal."

"You have two choices, Frank." He slipped his hands from the jacket, clenched his fists, and pounded the door. "I'll break it down and make a scene, or better yet, I'll pull out my gun and shoot my way into your place. Don't forget, you can't say no to me because I'm Lieutenant Detective. I hold rank over you."

"Fine, Daniels." I sighed, popping the ball from the slide chain. "I want no comments from you. It is what it is in here."

"I won't say a thing. Make me some damn coffee."

He strutted about my place, victorious. He sat on the couch that once held Desiree, Maria, and many others, scanning every inch of the apartment, filling me with trepidation. I fumbled the coffee maker, filter, and scooper for several minutes, every so often, glancing over my shoulder to make sure he was staying put.

"What's in that jar on your countertop?"

"Oh... that's nothing. Just a... It's a... snail I found on the porch. Yes. A snail. I collect them."

"That's odd. I've never seen a snail as a pet."

"Oh... yes. They're always around and easy to maintain. This coffee will be strong so I hope you like it, Daniels."

"You don't have to scream. I'm like two feet from you. It'll be fine. You know... you should really put the weed and alcohol away when a cop shows up at your place, especially, when that cop is one of your superiors. Luckily, I don't consider that drug a crime, plus I need you this morning." He cupped his eyes. "You should seek additional help." He paused, peeking through his fingers. "Stark? Is that blood on your floor?"

"Blood? No way. Probably just pizza sauce or ketchup—" I added a chuckle before he could respond. "—Whatever. You said you wouldn't say anything, so don't say any more. I'll be right back. Here's your coffee."

That was an easy excuse.

I placed the mug onto his open palm and scooted the hallway, slamming the bedroom door. Shaking my head, I lit a cigarette and sat on the edge of the bed. Good thing I'd hidden all the other drugs during a manic episode infused with paranoia. I hurried into my uniform, before he decided to use the bathroom or find any other lingering remnants.

"Come on, Stark. Get a move on."

"I'm coming. Relax. Pour a couple coffees in the to-go cups. They're on the kitchen counter." I extinguished the cigarette in the ashtray atop the nightstand, and it glued itself to my fingers, searing the skin. "Damn it, Daniels." I winced and ground my teeth. "Be right there."

"These cups are used, Frank. Unbelievable. Come on. Time to go. Now. We need to get to the park, ASAP."

"I'm ready. Let's go," I said, entering the living room breathless.

We didn't utter a word to each other as we walked to the car. Sitting on the passenger seat, I smiled and lifted my cup towards him. "Thanks for pouring the coffee. Nice, the car is warm. I appreciate you picking me up." He didn't respond, replacing any potential words with grunts and sighs. I pried once more for conversation. "So, what's the deal with this case, Daniels? You almost broke down my door."

He continued the silent treatment for a few more minutes. Hopefully, he wasn't thinking about what he saw at my place. That'd be bad news for me. He was probably just focusing on the new case. You could never tell with him.

"You're probably not going to believe this. An old lady was killed at the park. The preliminary report from dispatch says she's between sixty and seventy years old. She was found by a fisherman on his way to catch carp at the Lower Gorge of the Genesee. I guess they're easier to snag in the early morning hours. You would know more about fishing than I."

"Yup. I *love* fishing." I had no clue about fishing, so it was best if we stayed away from the topic. "Maybe the woman died from a fall. Why are you suspecting murder?" I creased the pinnacle of my beard. It was just as disheveled as my hair, both of which I started growing a few months ago. I was hoping the longer locks would instill a positive mental change. I'm unclear if the trick has worked.

He turned towards me, taking his eyes of the road. A rarity for law abiding Daniels. "This is what makes me a Detective and *you* a Sergeant." He smirked with a condescending snort. "A person that age doesn't die just walking in a park. The chances of a health issue killing her are slim. Her ability to walk means she was healthy. Dispatch also reported that the fisherman said she looked like she was assaulted. That's all I know for the time being. We'll know more when we arrive and check the body. The coroner and forensic team are on their way as well."

He drove onto the empty parking lot, centering the vehicle in a lane nearest to the entrance of Maplewood Park. We crept, in tandem, towards the Rose Garden and Maplewood Trail, our boots sloshing through the manicured greens randomly snapping a loose twig. Every few minutes, a chilly breeze blew through the park, spreading the sweet scent of roses. Each breath as pleasant as a floral shop. The park silent—not even a tweeting bird. In the distance, I heard a faint rumble from the Lower Gorge Falls.

"Fitting, Frank." He sipped his coffee and let out a refreshing sigh.

"What is?"

"The park is like a funeral home filled with a thousand roses." He gazed at the starless sky. "For what it's worth, she's already at peace in this garden. If I ever die, I can only hope my ceremony will include enough flowers to bring the same serenity as this park."

"Well, you're not dying, so we don't have to worry about that now. You've got a long way to go. You're healthy, unlike me." I tapped his shoulder with confidence. "If anyone is dying, it's going to be me, and I don't care what they bring to the funeral. Cheers to that, Daniels." I lifted my cup.

He didn't indulge my laughter. "You never know, Frank. You just never know when we might die. It's a strange, strange world." His melancholy tone atypical. I brushed it off. Maybe the roses or the old lady were bringing him down this morning.

"Yeah... I guess, but I don't think about it. I don't care, and neither should you. Let's get to the body so we can figure out what went wrong." I prodded his muscular back.

"Alright, buddy. Just make sure you don't forget to bring roses for me." I didn't respond, confirming his request internally. No need to continue a negative conversation for a guy who has the perfect life. "Dispatch said she was located in the Rose Garden next to the Maplewood trail. A few more feet and we should see her." He pointed and waved straight ahead.

We retrieved our flashlights and navigated the area, locating the body after several minutes. She rested on her back partially unclothed, her breasts exposed, and her pants pulled down to the middle of her thighs. She'd suffered a heavy beating with multiple bruises surrounding her face and neck. The amount of bruising made it difficult to tell her natural skin tone, which was further complicated by hours of exposure to the elements.

"Looking at this body we're one hundred percent certain this is now a homicide investigation." He tapped me on the shoulder. His smug grin showing why he's the boss. "We need to put a name to her. Check the body for identification while I walk the area."

I slipped on a pair of latex gloves and searched her pockets, trying not to disturb any part of her body. Her shirt and jacket pockets yielded nothing. I found her driver's license buried within her pants pocket.

"Daniels, I found it." I broke the park's silence, setting off a murder of crows.

"Damn birds. What's her name, Stark?"

"Oliva Livelman, date of birth April 12th 19… The last two digits unclear. She's pretty close to the dispatch description. Has to be sixty or seventy. At a closer look, she's in pretty bad shape. Probably went through a horrific struggle with the perp. There's something odd." I pointed across her body. "She has what appears to be tiny holes on her face, breasts, and stomach. They aren't bullet holes or stab wounds. I've seen these types of holes before, I just can't remember where."

"Hey, Stark. I found a weapon. Looks like a gun. Don't worry about the ID. Forensics will get her exact age."

Daniels brought the gun over to me, holding it by the tip of the barrel with his latex gloves. From a distance, the gun looked real. After closer inspection, I realized it wasn't a standard revolver.

"This isn't a real gun. It's a BB gun. You can see the cylinder and hammer aren't the same as a normal revolver."

"That's where I've seen those types of holes in the past." I nodded. "What's weird is he could have done so many more things to her, but he opted not to."

"What do you mean by that?" He raised his eyebrows.

I continued to peruse the body. This guy was a certain amateur and not like me or Dad. He was sloppy at best. I would've tied a rock to her and thrown her into the Lower Gorge. She didn't need to be found, but this guy wanted her found.

"Just stating the obvious, but he seems somewhat creative," I said, readjusting my voice as not to sound blasé.

"You got that right. He assaulted and shot an older woman with a BB gun. You said her name... Oliva—Livelman. Is that correct, Stark?"

"Yes."

"This woman was part of another case not too long ago. She was assaulted and raped a couple years ago by Sten Franking. And now this has happened to her? Too coincidental. Death had a lead on her, and she couldn't get away. It's sad. You just never know."

"I agree. Did Sten serve time, or do you think he's the one responsible for this homicide? Maybe he came after her for revenge?"

"Sten's in jail. He got five to ten and had a few priors, so I know it wasn't him. If my memory is accurate, which it usually is, he has a brother. Lester. Maybe he's the one who came after her to avenge his brother's jail time. We'll bring him in for questioning as soon as possible."

"Sounds good, Daniels. I'm going to take a walk around the park to see if I can find anything else, plus I need a cigarette."

"Good idea. I'll be here trying to figure out Lester's other motives and looking over the body for any other clues. You should quit smoking."

I ignored his comment. The sun began to break the horizon, giving me enough light to make my way around the paths lined with rose bushes. The Rose Garden was created over fifty years ago with thousands of varieties. Each row of rose bushes, with every color imaginable, created a colorful pattern that merged into a cross. I arrived at the center of the cross, and a sparkle on the ground caught my eye. I knelt beside it and cleared a handful of brush from its edges. I scooped it into my hand and angled it against the brightening sky. It was a high school identification card. The name, Mitch Karrsie, junior at Franklin West High School. Perhaps, he'd lost it during a stroll in the park. I placed it into my pocket with hopes of returning it to the owner someday soon, then headed towards Daniels.

"Did you find anything, Stark?"

"No. Nothing special. The only items I found are beautiful roses for Oliva's sad day."

"Alright. Let's get out of here. The coroner and the forensic team have taken over. If they find anything different, they'll let us know, but it's doubtful. Pretty cut and dry case. We'll see what Lester has to say when we bring him in for questioning."

XXV

"Stark..." Daniels greeted me at my desk with a handshake and a wide smile, which was a welcomed change to his dismal attitude at the Rose Garden. "Great job on bringing Lester to the Precinct."

"Hey—no problem." Acknowledgements not his forte, so I obliged with an outstretched hand.

Patrol brought Lester to the Precinct the following day. They found him at his home, a few blocks from the crime scene, wearing a onesie and slumbering on the couch. Good thing they didn't need me. I wanted to go, but I was hung up with a hangover. I convinced one of the guys, who had a habit I fed once in a while, to include my name on the report and give me the update. Lester was so timid, they double-checked his ID to make sure he was Sten's twin. They had expected Lester to act like Sten and resist, maybe even throw a punch or two for good measure, but he didn't.

Sten was a force. His rap sheet as long as a book, riddled with time behind bars since age sixteen. We knew his petty crimes dated back to twelve but had never nabbed him. He stood six-five with hair that hadn't been cut since he was teen. A burly man, he had more muscle behind his three-hundred-pound build than fat, which he threw around like a wrecking ball. His temper as hot as a manic devil playing in a pool of fire. Unlike Lester, tattoos blanketed most of Sten's body: skulls, demons, and crosses, all varying in size. Six officers wrestled to cuff him when he was arrested for the rape and assault of Oliva.

"I had some help. Don't forget to thank Joe Rook and the patrol team as well," I said, cheering a fist in the air. He didn't need to know I wasn't at the arrest party.

"I'll thank him later, since he might be joining me for Lester's questioning. We have to shake this guy down for facts. Hopefully, get a confession. That's if he's guilty, of course. No time to chat. I need to get to the interrogation room."

"Alright, Daniels. Good luck. If you need my help, let me know."

"Well, if you see Joe, send him my way." He ignored my self-invitation.

Even though I'd given my life to Precinct 13, all the hours of overtime every damn day for fifteen years, the only thing I received in return was the label of Sergeant.

We never discussed a damn thing during my yearly reviews, and that was the direct result of an unspoken rift with my superiors. They thought I was mentally unfit, and I knew they were overzealous excuse makers. Big deal, we didn't see eye to eye. No one ever does in life. Perhaps, Doctor Brazen is correct: I need to leave this job to feel happiness and bring tranquility into my life.

Joe Rook barged through the entrance, startling me from my thoughts. Chest out and head high, striding like Daniels. His newfound flair spreading through the Precinct like wildfire. All the officers whispered as he strutted towards me. I couldn't blame him. His inclusion during the perp interview meant my exclusion.

"Hey, Frank. How's it going?"

"It's going... Joe Rook." I rolled my neck, staring at the ceiling. "We brought in Lester. He's with Daniels now. Told me to tell you. Congratulations on being included in the interview. That's a big step at this department."

"I already knew about Lester. Remember, I actually helped bring him in while you skipped out on us. But, thanks anyway. I'm just trying to move forward within the Precinct. I'll be wearing a suit soon and writing the rules." He removed his police cap and placed it onto the corner of my desk. "Stop calling me Joe Rook." He leaned over my desk, gritting his teeth.

"Or what?" I said, pushing off its edge and leaning back into the chair.

"One way or another, I'll get you kicked off the force. Maybe they'll end up finding some drugs in your locker or in your patrol car. I'll take you down. No one even likes you at 13. You won't be missed," he said snarling.

"Is that a threat, Rook? Joe Rook, Joe, whatever the hell your name is." I leaned forward, our chins almost kissing.

"I'd call it a threat. Watch your back, Stark."

"Will do, Joe." As he took a step back, I placed a cigarette to my lips and mumbled *Rook*.

"What'd you say?"

"I said *look*. No problems here, Joe." I splayed my hands, then waved him away. I couldn't deal with him anymore. Fisticuffs with a hangover, this early in the morning, just wouldn't work. "Good luck with the perp. Get in there and take the guy down."

He walked around my desk, then tilted my chair backwards with his boot, causing me to lose my balance in the process. "Look, Frank. I respect you, a little bit. Why don't you come join us? If Daniels won't let you into the room, you can watch from behind the glass."

I slapped his boot from the chair. He stumbled backwards a step. "Are you sure, Joe?"

"Yeah... What's the worst that's going to happen?"

"Well, for starters, they'll kick me out."

"Oh, stop..." He stepped forward, patting my shoulder with disdain. "They won't kick you out because I'm present. You'll be fine."

His trusting grin reeled me in like a floundering fish, even though my gut said no. "Sounds good, Joe. I'll join."

Joe Rook led the way to the interrogation room. I spied him with the malevolence of a thousand witches at the Salem trials, and knew he was doing the same to me. The Rook and I reached a new level of disaffection today, and so did my involvement with the police. I hoped being part of the interview was worth the time, but I doubted it. Perhaps Maria, was right. Some of us are just not good.

Ron Riker, known as the Captain to all, viewed the interrogation with me from behind the two-way glass, deciphering Lester's speech and movements. The Captain crossed and uncrossed his arms, leaning his paunchy body forward, then backwards, then forward again, his pudgy nose nearly touching the glass.

Daniels surveyed the interior of the room, ending his search with Lester. He sat upon a steel chair with an identical empty pair across from him. Between the set, a metal table centered in the room, separating the burdens of guilt carried by each side. The grey, concrete floor had been scuffed by so many soles it turned black. Joe Rook watched from afar, leaning against the wall adjacent to the two-way. Daniels fanned a thick manila folder, most of which held blank papers, excluding a picture or two of the victim. If the perp thought we had a file on them, there'd be a better chance for acquiring the truth.

"Why do you think you're here, Lester?" Daniels began the questioning with calmness.

"Don't know, sir." He sprawled his arms across the width of the matte tabletop. "I just came here because they told me to." He shook his head like a sluggish pendulum.

"Well, we have a problem, Lester." Daniels opened the file folder. "Something happened yesterday and we need answers. That's why you're here." He pulled out a picture of Oliva and set it ahead of him. They locked eyes. "Do you know this woman?"

Lester studied the picture with care, then moaned. "I do not, sir." His steadfast voice void of pitch and presence.

"We know that you know her—Lester." Daniels nudged the picture closer to him with his fingertip. "You may have met her a few days ago, months ago, or a few years ago. Do you know her?"

"I do not, sir." He raised his head and leered at Daniels. "Who's she? What she do?"

Joe rushed from the wall with blurring speed and slammed one of the empty chairs against the table. Lester cringed. "She's dead." He grabbed the picture and waved it in his face. "Murdered, yesterday, at Maplewood Park. Did you have contact with her during the prior days and months?" Joe gripped the lip of the table, his knuckles white.

"I don't know her, sir." His furrowing brow showed confusion and fear. Most criminals showed remorse or surety.

"Yes, you do. You took off her clothes and beat her. She's your brother's victim. Stop lying, Lester." Joe slapped the table with such force its legs screeched the concrete floor.

"One second, Lester. We'll be right back." Daniels shook his head, rolled his eyes, and heaved a nasal sigh. "Come on." He nodded towards Joe. "I need to ask you a question about the case." Daniels yanked open the door. As he approached the Captain and I, he threw his arms up in the air. "Joe! You can't snap and divulge information. We're trying to get the perp to confess, not lead him to answering the questions. He needs to answer voluntarily. That's the law and due process. Do you remember the Oath of Honor, Joe?"

"I'm sorry, Daniels," he said with derision, while glancing at his boots tracing crescent moons on the floor. "We're trying to get answers and an admission at whatever cost." He must've built his courage out of his hatred for me. He glanced at my eyes, then Daniels. Blushing cheeks propped up a defiant stare. "If we lead the perp to answer correctly that's his problem, not ours. He's already guilty. Even the media is reporting his guilt. Do you want to look like an embarrassment to the community?"

"I don't, but we need to follow protocol." Daniels turned, looking for affirmation from within our huddle. "Captain, will you support me?"

"I'll support an end to this case. I don't care how you get it. I just want an end." He slid his bulbous thumbs into his belt buckle and scuffed his boots against the floor. "The quicker, the better, not to mention the thousands of dollars we'll save avoiding a trial. We *are* the good guys. We *are* the men in blue. Don't *you* forget that about us." The Captain jutted his chin and roared, "One less bad guy, at whatever cost, is good for the community."

Daniels clenched his fists against each temple. The creases on his forehead red. "Fine, Captain. Fine, Joe. Do what you will. I'll take a support role. I wash my hands of any wrongdoing. Over my dead body does an innocent man go to jail. There *will* be blood on your hands. Mark my words. There *will* be hell to pay." He compressed his lips and growled.

"Anyway… let's go, Daniels."

He led the way into the interrogation room with a gleaming smile, followed by a shaken Daniels. The Captain and I remained to watch the movie from behind the two-way mirror.

"Alright, Lester." Joe placed another picture of Oliva onto the table. "Are you ready to continue this interview?"

"Yes." Lester's emotionless response lacked even a blink.

Joe sat across from him, drumming his fingers with a beguiling grin. "Cheer up, Lester. This will be over soon, then maybe you can go home. Can we get you anything to drink? Maybe a soda or coffee."

"Sure. I'll take a diet soda. I'm trying to watch my weight," he said with a crazed laugh, more confused than coherent.

Joe tapped the window, nodding towards me to get the drink. I rushed back from the vending machine, opened the door, and Joe swiped the can, slamming the door just as fast.

Lester had slipped into a deadpan daze. The pop from the tab on the can shuddered him back to reality.

"Here you go."

"Thanks." He raised the can, sipped, then released a short belch. "Oops. Excuse me, sir."

"Glad you like it. Let's get back to business." Joe's face intensified, any hint of the prior cordial sentiment revoked. "Do you remember Oliva?"

"Not really. I may have seen her walking around once or twice, but I see a lot of people." He re-entered his stolid state.

"Do you think that boy Lester is slow?" The Captain poked my rib with his bony elbow.

"I don't know, sir." I scooched a step to avoid his reach.

"I believe he is, Stark. Those kinds of people are the easiest to put in jail. I think they call them *autismic* or *autistic.* Something like that... Anyway, I bet we get this wrapped up tonight." He massaged each knuckle with meticulous care. His roguish grin and beady eyes remained resolute on Lester.

"Well, what if he's innocent?" I said, crossing my arms against my chest. I had to conceal my twitching hand that yearned for a sip of scotch. The pooling spit on my gums desired a drink as much as a nicotine shot. I clamped wads from the inside of my cheek, curtailing the crisis while I listened.

Without moving his head or flinching a muscle, he gave me his version of the Oath of Honor. "Don't you worry about that, Stark? Guilty—innocent—innocent—guilty. It doesn't matter in the grand scheme of things. What matters is we place someone in jail. Don't you forget this bit of advice: Cops are heroes when people are put away, especially for life." His haughty laughter juggled his large and distorted Adam's apple.

Surprised by the Captain's diatribe, I shook my head. We'd never spent much time together, and interrogations weren't my cup of tea. I knew he hated all walks of life, except his own, but jailing innocent people crossed all the lines. I had sensible reasons for what I did and all I needed was a cure, but they are cops who are to uphold the law and arrest the guilty. As I watched Joe and Lester, I hoped that Joe was not as evil as the Captain, but I feared the worst.

"So, you've seen her. Where? When?" Joe dangled the picture before Lester, then slammed it upon the table.

"Around the neighborhood. I see different people walking all the time." He swayed his head and closed his eyes.

"That's true. I'm sure you do. There's just one thing about this person." He pounded the table, its legs grating the concrete. "A woman—mother—grandmother. You've taken her from her family. You killed her in cold blood."

"I did not," he said, raising his pitch and jerking his head.

"Yes you did, Lester." Joe lunged forward, wobbling the table. "We know you did it." He swung from anger to calmness, maniacal. "You just have to tell us you did it, so we can close this case. Okay? Tell us, and this will be all over. You can go home and rest afterwards."

"I did *not* do it." He sipped the soda. "Not me. I wasn't there." He knuckled his cheeks and eyelids.

"Really? How come I don't believe you?" Joe inched the table forward, abutting Lester's stomach. "What's your alibi?"

"I was working. Stop, sir. Stop." His crackling voice pleaded for belief. His eyes remained closed, as he pushed the table, grinding the floor.

"Working where, Lester? What were you doing? Come on. Tell me."

He hunched over the can, and with both hands pulled it into his concave chest. "I'm a bus monitor in the morning. I work at Franklin West High School. Call them, please. They'll tell you." Ashen hands held the edge of the table. His eyelids firm against sanguine cheeks.

"I don't believe you, but we'll follow up with the school. There are twenty-four hours in a day. What did you do with the rest of your time?"

"Nothing. I was home."

"You were not. You *killed* Oliva. Admit it," Joe said with a snarl. Pacing, boots thumping, he whacked an empty chair. It jumped and clanged against the table and floor.

"No. I was home. Please." He slumped from the seat, shoulders level with the table.

"What'd you say?" Joe stopped. "Speak up." He butted Lester's head, spewing spit onto his ear.

"Home. Home," he howled.

"You were home doing what?"

"Home." Lester slammed his back against the chair. "I made food and watched television. Cartoons, I think. I don't remember."

"I don't believe you." Joe swiveled his head, cheeks ablaze. "You need to be honest with me."

"Can I go home? You said I could go home. I'm tired." He slid his hand over his brow, squeegeeing sweat onto his long, oily hair.

"We're all tired." Joe Rook ventured to the two-way glass, pressed his forehead and smirked. "We all want to go home, but we're not going anywhere. Once you admit you killed her, we'll all go home. Why are you so tired?"

"I've been awake for almost thirty hours...," he said slurring. His limp arms crashed the table, sliding the can to the center. "All I do is work to pay bills. I didn't kill no one. I was driving a truck before I went to work at the school."

"You did not." Joe picked up the can and paced around the table, tipping it, taunting Lester with each drop. "You killed Oliva. Then, after you killed her, you went home and acted as if nothing happened. Isn't that the truth, *Lester*?"

"No... it's not. Can I please have my ...soda?"

He stretched his hand towards Joe like he held a life preserver. Joe ignored him, and continued his spiteful laps around the table, pouring drops onto the floor.

"It *is* the truth," Daniels interjected, standing against the wall with a brooding expression that could've killed Medusa. His hands in his pockets. "Come on, Joe. Leave him alone." He whipped his hands into open aired fists. "Let's give him some time to think about what he has or hasn't done."

They exited the room. Joe Rook charged towards Daniels waving his finger. "Guys, look at that scum in there." I thought the Rook was going to punch him, but he retreated.

"I think you're wrong, Joe." Daniels kept his cool with tempered confidence. "This guy is innocent. I can feel it in my gut. He has an alibi. No priors, not even a speeding ticket."

"Enough." The Captain hobbled forward, his belly in tandem with each step. Thick creases folded like waves around his ears where a hairline once existed. "Joe's taking this case. He'll close it quicker than you. No need to ruffle anymore feathers finding another suspect. Do you understand?"

"Whatever, Captain." Daniels bolted through the hallway flailing his arms.

* * * * * * * * * * * * *

The questioning continued a few more hours. Alternating investigators allowed Joe and Daniels to rest as well as the rest of us. During the last hour, Daniels and Joe returned to a gaunt Lester while the Captain and I stood at the glass.

"Hey... I want to help you." Joe leaned over Lester, resting a hand on his back. "Do you want to rest?"

"Yes... Please."

"I promise you'll go to sleep when we're done. While I was away I received great news. Not for me, for you. The Precinct got a call from Attica. Sten's already bragging about you to all his buddies." Joe sat across from Lester. The news a lie and a new tactic he and the Captain brainstormed.

"Really? What's he saying?" A smile crept through a wide-mouthed yawn.

"He's saying how you're great for killing the woman who put him in jail." Joe reclined in his chair, giving Lester a thumbs up, and some time to absorb the compliment.

"Yeah. That's good. He's a great guy if you get to know him, but I—"

"I bet he is, Lester. Makes you mad he's locked up because of Oliva. Your brother was walking just like you, then Oliva showed up and probably trapped Sten." Joe rose from the chair. "We know how women act sometimes. They send mixed signals. She didn't have to file charges and get your brother arrested. It was probably her fault. Now he's stuck in jail for the next eight years." Joe slapped the chair against the table. "Wake up, man. Doesn't that make you mad?"

"It does. What happened to Sten wasn't fair."

"I know it's not fair. It made you mad enough to get revenge. Kill Oliva for your brother. Sten's suffering every damn day in a four-by-eight cell, burly men wanting to get in his ass."

"Shut up, man," he shrieked, jostling the table with his knees.

"Am I right, Lester?" Joe parked himself behind him with a hand on his shoulder. "Would you kill Oliva for your brother's suffering?"

Lester closed his eyes. "I suppose I could do that for him."

"I know and it's okay," Joe said, stroking Lester's arm. "We understand why you killed Oliva. You did it for your brother. Just tell us. We can make this all end and you can go home."

"I don't know what to say."

Joe returned to his seat and eyed Lester with a smile more inviting than a car salesman. "All you have to say is that you did it."

"Do I get to go home?"

"You know the rules, Lester. All you have to do is tell me and Daniels. You can do it. I know you can."

He championed him like a rogue reverend in the sin chamber. Joe wrapped his hands over Lester's and held them in prayer. Several minutes of unnerving silence passed. Lester mumbling to himself and Joe Rook grinning through the glass at the Captain.

"Fine... I did it." He stuttered and slurred. "I did it and want to go home. Whatever I say doesn't matter." He turned, digging his chin into his shoulder.

"Oh, but it does. Great job, Lester. See, you said it. I have to show you one more thing and we'll be done. Go get the gun, Daniels."

"No," he replied, turning his back to Joe.

"Fine. I don't need you. I'll get someone else."

The Captain had rushed to get the weapon from the evidence room. Joe opened the door and took possession of the gun wearing gloves.

"Here you go, Lester. Tell me how the gun feels. Hold it. Pull the trigger."

"I've never seen this gun. Ever. Never," he said, fumbling it onto the table.

"You'll need to remember it, Lester, because your fingerprints are all over it, including the trigger. To be honest, there's no way out of this one. I'll get you a soda for your good work."

The Captain turned towards me and nodded, his teeth in full view. "You see, Stark. That's how it's done. That boy is as guilty as a bloodied wolf in a chicken coup," he said, clapping like a seal. "Now, go get the man a soda."

Returning from the vending machine, I cowered into a corner and slugged the flask, the scotch calming my mind. Joe Rook opened the door and swiped the soda from my hand. At the table, he slammed it down and popped the tab. Foam overtook the can.

Those that lie, will lie with Dad.

"Thank you, Joe." His confused smile replaced by a gulp of soda and a sigh.

"Hey, no problem, buddy. You'll be okay now."

Joe lightly embraced Lester's shoulders, then strutted from the room. Daniels followed, hanging his head and hunching as if he'd been struck with a baseball bat.

"How did you like that work, Captain?" Joe asked, his fists shaking above his head.

"Yeah, Captain. How did you like that work?" Daniels interjected with moistened eyes.

"Great job, Joe. Precinct 13 has a great future for you." The Captain turned, his face enveloped with contempt. "And, Daniels, I don't know what the future holds for you anymore." The Captain turned his back on Daniels and extended his hand out to Joe. Their handshake transitioned into a bear hug.

"I guess nothing, Captain. I don't want any part of this Precinct, if this is how we're going to do it. Following the rule of law is more important than any promotion."

Daniels stormed off, punching walls, and slamming doors. He'd never brandished his emotions, let alone desecration for authority. Hopefully, he'd shake off the infuriation and return with a new sense of purpose.

"Stark! Don't worry about Daniels. You need to check on a missing person's report in the homeless district."

"What's her name?"

"I never said it was a *she*, Stark."

"Right... I meant who, Captain. I always assume it's a woman, if they're missing."

"Yes, they *are* usually women. Good assumption." A shiver of relief rolled down my spine. "They told me her name is Desiree. She worked at New Beginnings for Life. Let me know what you find out."

"Will do."

"Joe, let's go back in the room and finalize everything with Lester. Make sure you coordinate everything with the coroner, the District Attorney, and the media. Fix the alibi notes. Oh yeah... And talk to the video guys so they splice the confession tape and make it admissible."

"Will do. I'm ready, Captain. Let's put this guy in jail for a long time."

I watched and listened from behind the ajar door.

"Lester. It's time to go. Come on." Joe smiled and grunted.

"I don't want to go. I want to change my story." Lester's voice cracking as he sobbed. "I didn't do it. I didn't kill that woman. I didn't do anything to her."

The Captain scooped Lester from under his arm. "It's too late, boy. We have everything on tape. Time to go to jail. You'll be fine. I promise. Free room and board. Let's go."

Lester smashed the table with his hand, spilling the soda. "I didn't do anything. Joe, please let me go. I made a mistake and didn't mean to say those things. Nothing happened. I never saw her. I was working. I wasn't near the park or the garden."

"Lester Franking. Time to go jail and join Sten. Two twins in a pen. It's going to be okay. I promise. You're all the same. First you admit it, then cry like babies when it's time to face the music." The Captain grumbled a few vulgarities.

Joe and the Captain forcefully moved him out of the interrogation room. Lester continued to plead his innocence between his screams and cries. Joe didn't care and neither did the Captain. They made their way towards the barred door that led to the dingy holding cells on the basement floor. Lester turned towards me, his sopping eyes begging for help, mine deflecting towards my boots.

XXVI

As the burning sphere rolled into the cliff of darkness, a dense haze rose from its ashes, blanketing the roadways to New Beginnings. I opted to drive my personal car instead of the white and blue. The worn wiper carving its mark into the glass hypnotized me with each stroke. I swigged the flask and lit a cigarette, its cherry tip illuminating the dashboard. I spun the radio knob. Black Sabbath's "Paranoid" shot through the speakers, shocking me from the trance. I needed to tidy up loose ends on Shelter Avenue since I ended with my woman. Better to deal with it now rather than have them trace anything to me later.

I parked in my usual spot. The street lamps had fallen prey to the thick fog, allowing ample cover for my uniform. As I toked a cigarette outside New Beginnings, I harkened to a time plentiful with lust, like, and love. Those beautiful curls, soft lips, and dimples as big as buckets could patter anyone's heart, but not as much as they did mine. I entered the facility and expected to see Desiree standing behind the desk. She had curls, somewhat tighter than hers, but crimson. Her milky, freckled skin, taut on her tall, slim figure, radiated under the fluorescents.

"How can I help you, Officer?" she said, before even reaching the counter.

"Good evening. I'm responding to a report for Desiree. We might have a suspect as well."

"I figured as much. I'm Christie Carlson. If you have any questions, please feel free to ask. I'm at your disposal." Jaunty, she reminded me of a cheerleader turned homecoming queen.

Take her for dinner and drinks, Frankie. She's a keeper.

"I can't."

"You can't what, Officer?"

"Never mind, nothing. Nice to meet you, Christie. I'm Officer Stark. What do you know about her disappearance?"

"Not much. I was hired to replace her. My boss called it in."

"Did you know her prior to being hired?"

"I didn't. I met her only once. The day when I handed her my job application. She took it and told me they'd call if anything opened up. I guess something opened up."

"So you don't know anything about her past?"

"Nope, Officer Frank."

"How do you know my first name? I never gave it to you."

"I found your card tucked under a magazine, plus it matches your name tag. I guess you've been here before."

"It's possible. We always get calls from a homeless shelter. If you don't mind, I'll take that card. I need to return it to the Precinct."

"Oh... okay." She flipped the card between her fingers and handed it to me.

"Actually, Miss Christie do you—"

"Just call me Christie." She giggled. "No need for the Miss, even though I'm single."

"Will do... *Christie*. Do you know Darnell? We've investigated him in the past and he might be here now."

"Is he the *suspect*? That's scary, Officer. I'll check the registry." She zigzagged her finger through each entry, stopping at a name within seconds. "Here we go. Darnell checked in today. Do you want me to go get him?"

"No. If you don't mind, I'd like to get him. He can be aggressive at times, and he's always high. We've been down this road more than once. I know how he reacts to police."

"I don't mind. By all means." She nodded towards the backroom. "You're the cop. I'm just a skinny, little redhead." She pointed the length of her body. "I know I can't help you." Her flushed cheeks rose, their hue matching her hair.

"Can you tell me which cot?"

"Yes. According to the chart, 13C. Right-rear corner. Near the exit."

"Figures, he'd be at the exit. I can't promise this won't get violent. I'll try my best to keep the altercation under control."

"You're a pretty big guy, so I trust you." Her sapphire eyes gestured to stay with her.

Take her home, Frankie. Some drinks and death.

"Stop talking. I'm sorry. I mean... No—thanks, Christie. I'll be right back. Hopefully this won't take long."

I proceeded down the narrow hallway and through a curtain. The rumble of snores masked my boots scuffing the linoleum as I crept the maze of cots. I spotted Darnell just where Christie said. His hands were crossed upon his chest, his body enshrouded by a rainbow blanket. I needed to move fast to prevent an escape or violent scene. I leaned over his cot and grabbed his torso, lifting, and sliding his body against the wall.

"What's going on here? What the hell is—"

"Keep your mouth shut, Darnell." I slid my hand over his mouth.

"—going on here? Leave me alone," he murmured into my pressing palm.

"Darnell." I brought his face to mine. "Keep quiet. We have to do it this way, so no one suspects anything."

I bound his hands with mine against his back and trotted towards the counter.

"Sorry, man," I whispered, shoving him in the proper direction. "Just follow my lead."

"I heard you the first time. Take it easy, man." He flexed, putting up quite the resistance for his small frame.

"Hey, Christie. I got him. He's cooperating. Are you okay?"

"Yes. I'm fine, now. I was hiding in the corner. What's going to happen to him?"

"Taking him in for questioning to see if we can find any clues. I'll try not to bother you again."

"Oh, you're no bother, Officer Stark. I mean, Frank. You can check me out anytime. Good luck with him." She twisted her hair as she popped bubblegum. I was surprised her curls hadn't turned into braids with all the weaving.

"Thanks, Christie. Come on, Darnell. Let's go," I said, nudging him through the exit.

"I still haven't figured out why women and men like you and why they always disappear. Anyway, what's the deal, Frank? I thought we were cool."

"We *are* cool. I had to get you out without them suspecting us." I loosened my grip on his wrists.

"Alright, man. What do you want with me?"

"We have to talk. I got something on my mind that's been bothering me."

"Oh… You trying to go sober on me again? Come on. You know that shit doesn't work on you. You didn't come all the way out here to tell me that, did you?"

"No, man. You're not even close. That's the last thing I need. Let's take a drive and find somewhere private to talk."

"Alright, Frank." He slinked onto the passenger seat, slamming the door.

"Do you need a smoke, Darnell?"

"Yeah, I'll take one." I slid two cigarettes from the pack, handing him one.

"So what do you need this time? Coke, heroin, uppers, downers?" He struck a match, lighting the stick within a cupped hand.

"No drugs, today. I'm here to talk. Just like old times."

Darnell and I had met many moons ago, introduced by Jacob Smith on this same street. I was called to the scene for an altercation between two, homeless people and a passerby. Jacob was lighting Darnell's cigarette when I pulled up to the curb. Darnell peeped my car and was set to run when Jacob grabbed his jacket and convinced him to stay. As I stepped closer, Jacob explained they were approached by a gang member who robbed Darnell of his drugs.

He gave me a sob story about his mom and that he was homeless. After thinking about it for a few minutes, I realized he was an opportunity. I offered him some of my stash. In return, if I was ever strapped for dope, he'd come through for me. He honored his word every time, sometimes free and other times at cost. He'd never mentioned Desiree. I made the connection after she told me the story about her mom. For obvious reasons, I didn't tell her I knew him. With her untimely passing, it'd be problematic if he made the connection between us. Luckily, for now, the heroin kept his mind clouded.

"Just like old times? That means you got the itch to get high. You mind if I smoke?" He pulled out a joint the size of his hand and puffed it a few times to get a clean draw.

"Obviously not. Go ahead. Do whatever."

"Thanks. Where we going, Frank?"

"We're going somewhere where no one will bother us."

"What are you trying to do, have sex with me?" He laughed, gagging on the sweet-leaf smoke.

"Yeah. How'd you know? That's exactly what I need. Some good gay sex," I said with a sly grin.

Darnell turned and ran his fingers through my hair. "I've had a lot of practice. They tell me I'm good."

"You're not my type, but if you were, I would get right up in you. Just need to talk and I don't want any interruptions. Anything new, other than the obvious?"

"I've been hanging with Brandon. Some white guy who fucks around with little boys in that other shelter. Believe it or not, he's a priest. He keeps tabs on me since we started dating. He's a little annoying, but I take what I can get these days."

"That's interesting. Weird?"

"Why? Do you know him?"

"Nope. Can't say that I do."

We pulled into Genesee Valley Park and headed towards the Genesee River. The headlights reflected from the impenetrable mist like aluminum foil, slowing our drive to a crawl.

"Is this place a haunted graveyard?"

"If you look hard enough, you'll find bodies." I parked the car with the trunk facing the river as I had many times in the past.

"This place looks pretty cool, Frank. I don't think I've ever been here. I should bring Brandon here next time. Our kind won't be bothered at this secluded place."

"Maybe you should. I come here quite a bit. It's private. No one bothers anyone here. No sex tonight, but you can do all the drugs you want, and I'll do all the talking."

"Alright. Take a hit of this joint, then we'll talk."

"Sounds good." I coughed after two long drags.

"Are you sure you can handle that weed?"

His laugh lingered in the air like a slow-moving cloud, confirming the potency.

"It went down the wrong pipe," I said, guzzling from the flask.

"Better talk quick, before I start hitting the strong stuff. The weed don't cut it anymore."

"We have a problem with Desiree. She's sort of missing."

"No way. She just talked to me about you. I didn't get into the specifics about us. I just said I knew you from the streets."

He knows, Frankie. He knows everything.

"Well—"

"Well—what do you mean by missing? She either is or isn't. Where is she?"

I couldn't tell Darnell the truth, so I had to play along. I had an idea to resolve this situation, but the circumstances needed to be perfect.

"You're right. She's not really missing. She's sick… at the hospital with the flu. I got a call at the Precinct to find the next of kin. They gave me your name. She's at the same place as your mom. I'm just worried about her, so I needed to talk to you."

"Well, that's good. I figured you'd know since you're a cop. Good you're keeping an eye on her. You drove all the way out here to tell me Desiree is sick? What else do you need to tell me?"

"Nothing. I figured we'd come here, do some drugs, and I could tell you about Desiree."

"Thanks for the ride, but I really didn't need it. Anything else?"

"Yes. Your mom isn't doing well. She might not be here too much longer. Desiree wanted me to tell you."

"What do you mean, Frank? I can't handle this shit right now." Darnell wiped a tear from his cheek, pulled out an eight ball of cocaine, and rested it upon his thigh. "Can I borrow your keys for a second?"

"Sure, no problem."

I handed him the keys from the ignition. He scooped two enormous mounds from the baggie.

"I can't believe this shit with Desiree and Mom. You want some?" he asked, holding one key towards me as the other cleared into his nose.

"Yeah. I'll take a bump." After the snort, I tilted my head back, lips numb. "I'm sorry I had to tell you about your mom and Desiree. Are you going to be okay?"

"Soon enough. When I put the good stuff in me." He rubbed his hands as if he was about to devour a large meal.

Darnell pulled out another baggie. This one stamped with a skull and crossbones on either side. He flicked the contents, draining the powder to the bottom. He reached into his pocket with precision and pulled out a blackened spoon and syringe.

"You got any water for me, Frank."

"One sec." I rummaged the rear floorboard and found a water bottle jammed under the passenger seat. "It's warm."

"All good, man. I'm not drinking it."

He plunged the syringe into the water bottle, sucking a small amount onto the spoon. I gave him my lighter upon request. He heated the spoon, while adding heroin from the baggie, the needle mixing the paste on the glowing ladle. As the mixture began to boil, he tore a piece of cotton, no larger than a Q-tip, from a premade hole on his winter jacket, and placed it onto the spoon. He removed the flame and the cotton ball swelled, forming a heroin sponge. He inserted the needle into the sponge, pulled the plunger, filling it with opium tar.

"This is heaven, Frank." He raised the hypodermic and tapped it. "The high is better than sex. Better than the sun. Better than being alive."

He removed his jacket and pulled out a leather tourniquet, wrapping it tight around his bicep. He plucked the syringe from his lap, and slid the needle into the blue ridge rising on the cusp of his arm, and injected the heroin. A few moments later, he reclined into the seat and sighed.

"No coming back from this, Frank." He closed his eyes. "Did you do any *psyching* with Desiree?"

"What'd you say?"

"Did you do any driving in the driveway?" He hawked a brief laugh, then quieted.

I pushed him, but he didn't wake. His face as pasty as a three-day-old body in the morgue, or my bathtub. Shallow breaths and beads of sweat atop his forehead negated death. I searched his coat pockets and scored a drug jackpot.

"Perfect... Finders keepers, losers don't weep when they're dead." I snorted a heaving bump and swallowed three, purple pills from one of the bags I found.

"What'd you say?" he asked, then faded back into nothingness.

"We're good, man. Rest, Darnell. Just rest. It'll be okay. Soon, I promise."

Follow your instincts, Frank. Great idea to keep you safe. Do it, Frankie.

I followed Darnell's instructions, except I filled the syringe to capacity: fifty units. I poked his ribs and he didn't respond. I wrapped the leather tourniquet around his arm, and as the vein rose, I nailed the needle, releasing all its contents, some mixing with blood and dribbling onto his arm. A few moments passed and a subtle finger tremble transitioned into a full body seizure, snapping his head against the seat, his legs thrashing the dashboard underlay. A pink foam bubbled from his lips and trickled along the sides of his neck. Within minutes, silence.

"Are you okay, Darnell?"

I checked for a pulse and breath, but neither existed. I opened the passenger door. Darnell slumped from the car onto the mud. I dragged his lifeless body to the edge of the river, propping his head on a boulder with his body inline.

"Darnell. Are you awake?"

I raised my leg, and with full force, stomped his head multiple times. Several teeth, mixed with bits of skull and flesh, oozed onto the dirt. I pulled the empty syringe from his arm and placed it into my pocket, then shoved his broken body into the river. I followed the floating carcass until it succumbed to the downdraft of the violent current, and with it, so too did my unresolved issues with Desiree. An unyielding love between a brother and sister resting forevermore in the depths of the Genesee River.

XXVII

A day or days passed. I recall entering my place with a second wind, tearing open the bags of drugs I stole from Darnell. The colorful pills scattered across the table. Their candy allure prompted a pill-popping party infused with alcohol, which produced a blackout.

An urgency arose within me, an unnerving tingle from the bowels, to my throat, expelling breath. Shuddering, I awoke with twitching legs, covered with piss as dark as cola, struggling for movement. Pulling them apart proved another feat, bound together like melting flypaper.

I wriggled from bed, lit a scrunched cigarette, and waddled to the bathroom in a stupor. A strange memory of Daniels flittered about my mind. In a dream, he sat beside Desiree and Darnell smoking a joint. He mentioned there'd be no more pain, then handed me the spliff. Before I responded, he vanished. I avoided the mirror while dousing my eyes with drops, dipped the toothbrush in a glass of scotch, gargled and swallowed, then mopped my face and body with a wet towel. The comb knotted my hair, cutting it free with dull scissors. I scooped the uniform from the floor, spraying it with another layer of cologne. With the buttons misaligned and time abating, I had no choice but to continue dressing as I drove.

Howling winds and a torrential rain overwhelmed me on the way to the car, swishing and swaying my body like a stuffed animal in a washing machine. I whirled the radio dial. A blaring buzz greeted me, recycling itself every few seconds. When it paused, the announcer followed in an urgent robotic voice: "This is a special report. A severe weather warning has been issued for Rochester, New York. Strong winds accompanied by heavy rain and hail are expected. Powerful thunderstorms and tornadoes may develop in certain areas. Seek shelter. If you have an emergency, call 911." The statement repeated two more times, followed by the annoying thrum. No shit there's a severe storm. Damn weather people have the best job in the world, always reporting what's already evident.

Driving to the Precinct posed a mental challenge. Ebony clouds, with spears aglow, rolled low and slow, trailed by its brethren as white as snow, forming vast shelves infinite to the eye. Traffic snarled the main road to work, just ahead of Nick Tahou Hots, the home of the world-famous Cheeseburger Plate with meat sauce. I rubbernecked two mangled cars and a big rig blocking one lane. Their roofs had been pancaked by the semi, doors laying atop the pavement, shards of glass and shrapnel strewn hundreds of feet in every direction. I ogled their upper bodies. The EMTs hadn't tarped them. One occupant in each car, their faces like tomato puree.

As I entered the Precinct, officers bustled throughout the building, attending to calls without missing a beat since my time away—if I was even away. Not more than six steps through the door and the Rook made his presence known with arrogance. "Thanks for making it in, Frank."

"Leave me alone, Joe. I was sick." I lowered my head and walked away.

"You're always sick—in the head."

"Damn you, Rook," I mumbled.

"What'd you say, Stark?"

"I said I have a book… of questions. How long have I been gone?"

"Just a day. But a day too long."

"Odd. It feels like twenty," I said, rubbing my temple. "Daniels... Dream... Is he here?"

"Dream, what? Anyway, he's not. Neither of you work anymore."

"Whatever, Joe. I have a headache. Can you tone it down?"

I slid onto my chair. He approached and hovered.

"Tone? You're both useless. People like me close cases. Someday, I'll move up in this department. Then, I'm going to write the rules."

"Whatever. You play checkers while everyone plays chess. I close cases all the time. At least, I don't lie or cheat."

"Touché, Frank, but you haven't closed a case in years. We do what we have to do. As long as we get the majority of them, the innocent ones will be forgotten."

"That's not how the law works. You should've really listened to Daniels on that Oliva case. If you don't do things properly, they'll come back to haunt you. What's that saying? Karma's a *bitch*."

"I'll take my chances." He pointed towards the Captain's office. "He wants to see you. Now."

"Great. What the hell does he want? I'm not in the mood."

I sauntered to his windowed office, but not before sneaking a swig to help the headache. All the blinds were drawn, including the door. I held my breath and tapped its glass.

"Come in."

"Captain." I peeked around the jamb before entering. "How's it going today? Are you enjoying the great weather?"

"Hopefully, it's not a prediction for how the day develops at the Precinct." He flipped through a stack of papers on his desk.

"I'm with you on that one. Joe Rook said you wanted to see me. What can I do for you?"

"Did you follow up on that missing person's report I gave you?"

"Yes. I went to the shelter and interviewed the staff and some of the homeless people. They all told me the same story. She went back to her hometown, somewhere in Georgia. The manager at the shelter received Desiree's resignation by mail."

"Okay. I'll note that in the ledger and close the case. There's one more thing I wanted to talk to you about, Frank." He scrunched his brow, folding his aged, clubbing hands atop the desk.

"What's that?"

"I know you were upset about the Oliva and Lester case. I saw it in your eyes."

"Yes I was and am. I always side with Daniels. He's the smartest guy in this place, so I trust his judgement."

"I agree with you. He's great at his job. It's just sometimes you have to take a different route with some cases. We needed someone and got them. Case closed. No heat from other departments, the Commissioner, or the media. Sometimes we need to *make* the trail, not follow it. Do you understand, Frank?"

"I do, sir. I won't mention it again." I shook my head with accepted disbelief, scanning the walls of the office. "Have you talked to Daniels yet?"

"No. Hopefully, he'll be here soon so I can explain. Going to tell him the same thing I told you. Have you seen him?"

"I haven't. Once I do, I'll let him know to see you. Strange?"

"What is?"

"Daniels is never a no-show. He's a by-the-book man. Always on time, always about process, always about facts. He'd never leave the Precinct hanging without telling someone."

"Good point, Stark. Try to track him down. I really need to talk to him so we're all on the same page. Don't forget… the Precinct always come first, even if we have to sacrifice a few."

"I'll let you know. One more thing, Captain."

"What's that, buddy?"

"That plaque behind you. 'Pay attention to how you practice, you may get really good at the wrong thing.' I just wanted to remind you."

I rushed from his office without awaiting a response. I stopped at the coffee station, filled a cup with the black gold, topped it off with scotch, and bowled to my desk. With the headache still pounding, I lit a cigarette in hopes of easing the pain.

"Joe. Have you seen Daniels today?"

"I haven't seen him in a long time." He nodded with indifference. "Why, what's up?"

I had no reason to respond to the Rook. Instead of sitting, I ventured to Daniels's desk, hoping to garner some clues to his whereabouts. Perhaps a sticky note or a schedule strewn somewhere. Unfortunately, nothing. On the left corner of his desk, a fish magnet. I'd seen them affixed to cars, usually with "Jesus" in the empty space. Must be some born-again, cult symbol, which fit his staunch views. Beside it, a silver, commemorative plate with the Law Enforcement Oath of Honor: "On my honor, I will never betray my integrity, my character, or the public trust. I will always have the courage to hold myself and others accountable for our actions. I will always maintain the highest ethical standards and uphold the values of my community, and the agency I serve. So help me God." The pens and pencils stood tall like flag poles dipped in concrete, except their base not rock, but a "Greatest Dad" coffee mug. I tugged the drawer handles and they were locked. Rechecking the top of the desk, I noticed an odd book set atop the right corner. Yin-yang embossed on its blue cover. The paper edges lacquered in gold with a button snap. It reminded me of an expensive journal, one a devout writer used daily to spritz the pages with verbs and adjectives—one I yearned to have, if I could just stick to the process of writing daily. It wasn't my property and not my business to read, but it lured me with its exquisite design and the unending possibilities of prose within.

As my fingers secured the book, Joe shouted from the reception area. "Frank, you have a phone call. It's

Daniels. He wants to talk to you. He doesn't sound too good."

"Hurry up and transfer the call to his desk."

The feeling from this morning returned, but instead of a tingle, a rampant shiver. With trembling hands, I raised the receiver against my shoulder, hesitant to bring it to my ear. This wasn't going to be a good-morning call.

"Hello," I whispered.

"Hey, Frank. Daniels." His voice trembled, then faded to silence.

"Hello... You there?"

"I'm not doing well, Frank." He regained some countenance.

"What—" I coughed away the crackle in my voice. "—do you mean, Daniels? What's wrong?"

"I'm not doing well, at all. What I'm about to tell you might shock you, but there's no way you can stop it, or change my mind. It is what it is."

"What's going on? Where are you?"

"It doesn't matter, Frank." He whimpered. "What's done is done." He took a deep breath. "I'll miss everyone. I'll miss my family—the most."

"What's wrong? We can help you, Daniels."

"Frank—listen to me." He reasserted himself, speaking with the confidence I knew. "I called because you're the only one who'll understand. You have issues like me. There's a diary on my desk. Turn to the last two pages. I wrote them specifically for you. They'll explain the why and what of this phone call. Do *not* read the rest of the book. Do that on your own time, if you'd like. Do *not* share the book with anyone, especially my family. They won't be able to handle my truths. They'll only be hurt because of them. Do you understand everything I'm telling you?"

I froze, scrutinizing the Yin-yang etched onto the cover.

This is how it must be, Frank, my Son, my baby, my…

"Frank," he bellowed, "Do you understand? Are you there?"

"Yes—I'm here." I traced a finger over the symbol.

"Thank you. We rarely saw eye to eye, but I did respect you from afar, or else I would've had you fired." He snickered, then abruptly reversed his tone.

"You're welcome, Daniels. Please stay on the phone. Don't do anything drastic. Please."

I kept the phone nudged between my ear and shoulder. An unrecognizable pitter-patter filtered through the earpiece, followed by syncopated breaths, the wailing wind, and passing sirens. If only they would've known to stop at his location. I slid the book from the desk, and carefully turned to the last pages, which had no specific date.

* * * * * * * * * * * * *

August.

Dear Frank. Thank you for reading. I take sole responsibility for all that has occurred and will occur. No one's ever understood what I've been going through because I've kept it to myself. The reasons are as follows:

I've been living a double life. As of today, I will no longer live in what they call "the closet." I've been involved in a relationship with another man for a long time. Giovanni DiBella. He's supported me when others wouldn't. He allowed me to express my true self. I love him more than I've ever loved my wife.

I couldn't divorce my wife because of our daughter. My wife hated me because of my sexual preference. I tried to talk to her, but she refused to understand. Perhaps, her upbringing or religion taught her to hate our kind. Perhaps, she feared for our child. I hope she can now move forward since I'll no longer exist. She can raise our child however she sees fit. I hope she's fair to her.

I cannot deal with the police force any longer. We violate our Oaths of Honor on a daily basis. My last straw was with Lester Franking's innocence. Now there's a guilty party roaming the streets. He will kill again. The Captain, as well as some select officers, including the Rook, are blind to all colors except blue. Note: Make sure you find Oliva's real killer. There must be an overlooked clue.

I couldn't deal with all the deaths and levels of crime. This world is too violent. I believe it'll only get worse. If it does, I certainly don't want to be in the police force. I don't want to be part of this world, if the spiral is downward.

Doctor Brazen, my psychologist, hasn't given me any positive feedback for months. She contradicts everything I say and doesn't listen to any of my suggestions. She tells me there isn't much else she can do for me. She keeps suggesting more medication. I don't want them. Pills are not the solution to every problem.

I can no longer deal with the charade I view in the mirror. The happiness in the reflection no longer exists. My future is grim. The flowers in the springtime are colorless. The birds no longer whistle. Love equates hate. My dreams are all nightmares. The sky is no longer blue. If there's no other side, then to sleep forever will be better than to stay awake for one more minute in this life. I am the Alpha and Omega.

* * * * * * * * * * * *

"Daniels. Daniels." My beckoning reverberated throughout the Precinct. "Are you still there?"

"Yes, but I must go. Remember to keep that diary with you. Don't share it with anyone. Thank you, Frank." His voice removed of all color.

"Daniels! Tell me where you are. Please. We'll save you."

"An apartment—1414 East Ave.—I rented it with Giovanni. He's at work. By the time you arrive, I'll be dead."

"No. Stop. We're coming. It's only a few blocks."

"Joe. Get to 1414 East Ave. Daniels—he's about to commit suicide. Go!"

"I'm on it." Joe stormed out of the Precinct. I turned towards the clock I loathed on a daily basis, and it read 1:03 p.m.

"John. John Daniels... Come on. Respond... Please..."

Seconds later, a thwack and a series of bounces echoed through the earpiece. At 1:09 the approaching sirens no longer wailed, the silence interrupted by a thump. At 1:13 my desk phone rang. It wasn't a coincidence because no one ever called me. Hell, I was barely at the Precinct. The one day I'm at work, Daniels calls with a suicide agenda. I should've numbed that damn feeling this morning with more scotch and stayed in bed. I hung up Daniels's phone and drifted to my desk. Staring at the phone, I hoped it stopped or answered itself. Neither happened, and by the tenth ring, I lifted the receiver.

"Hello."

"It's Joe. I got bad news. He's gone. I tried CPR, but it didn't work."

"What did he do to himself?"

"It's messy. I'm soaked in his blood. He hanged himself, but before doing that, he sliced his left forearm open. I couldn't bring him back."

"Fuck. This is going to be bad. How are we going to tell his wife? He left behind a kid. What the hell are we going to do now?"

"I don't know, Frank. I really don't know."

I hung up the phone and moped to Daniels's desk to gather the diary. I scanned the Precinct. Some silent, some whispered, and some had their eyes on me. I couldn't do anything for them, just like I couldn't for Daniels. I pinched my jacket lapel and stuffed the diary into the inside pocket. Another item to add to the box of memories, except this was not of my doing.

Daniels was smart and everyone looked up to him, even if they didn't like him. He taught me one lesson: even when you have everything, a burdened soul can't be saved. I tipped back a double swig, lit a cigarette, and drove to his home to give his wife, Abigail, the horrific news. She wasn't hysterical, which was expected considering what I knew, but she didn't know that Daniels had shared that information with me. I suppose she really did hate him, probably wishing for his death. I didn't ask if that was the case. It's intriguing to watch how some want others to die, some decide to take that option upon themselves, while others fall prey to someone else's decision. The next few days were going to be tough for the Precinct and Daniels's family, especially with the media coverage.

XXVIII

Daniels's suicide, combined with Desiree's death, removed any optimism I once thought existed within arm's reach. He was a much better man than I, although, in the end, the respect and honors he earned fell by the wayside of his double life. The media castigated him as the Gay Gumshoe, Bisexual Bobby, and Deviant Detective, to name a few. That same negativity spread throughout the Precinct as well. Some cops hated him for being gay, while others sympathized with, as they put it, his "disease." It certainly wasn't an ailment, and some cops like myself, wished he could've sorted all the troubles within his mind and lived. If only I'd known, I would've brought him to the Milky Oyster or Magpie for a few drinks, then introduced him to some of my lovers and friends.

Yearning for an explanation, I scheduled an appointment with Doctor Brazen on Saturday, after the burial, which meant she had to make a special trip to her office for the visit. Her circumstance didn't bother me one bit, since she said she'd be available any day of the week at any time. It was imperative she help me, for better or worse. Hopefully, the/rapist of the mind could console me, give me advice, talk to me like a human being, instead of an injured animal.

I skipped the funeral service. Those concrete sanctuaries and million-dollar, gold domes, sprinkled with Michelangelo inspired frescos, daunted me. Their mega altars always front and center, overlooked by a one story cross with a blonde, bleeding Jesus, who wore a tiara of thorns, nailed to three points of an inverted triangle. A child should never witness such violence, but they did. A man in a robe like Father Brandon instructed the cult to stand, sit, and kneel at specified times, then chanted baroque Latin phrases to an organist playing each note at the lowest octave allowed. He'd trained the masses to accept the illusions that blood is wine, and a wafer, a body. The whole experience was enough to frighten the corpses that I'd left behind.

On the grounds of the Mount Hope Cemetery, I opted to wait in the car for Daniels's arrival. Hundreds of cops interred alongside famous Rochesterians, such as Frederick Douglass and Susan B. Anthony. Some headstones crumbling due to lack of maintenance while others towered two stories. Their intricate carvings begged to be noticed from any distance, just in case the fantastic rapture arrived to save them.

The rain had been nonstop since Daniels's hanging, and intensified during their drive to the graveyard. I didn't want to be part of the symbolic procession where hundreds of police cars beaconed ahead of a tinted hearse. Within that motorcade, and oblivious to all but me, Daniels's wife, who was indifferent to her husband's death, sat in a limousine. They inched ahead, winding the paved path around the cemetery. In spectacular fashion, the spinning lights atop the police cruisers danced through their pellucid plastic housing, partnering with the sliding beads of rain, forming rainbows against the backdrop of a glum sky. As they stopped at his final resting place, the glowing ballet ceased.

I thought about exiting the car to pay my respects at the coffin, but opted out at the last second. Sober, I couldn't deal with the stress. Easier to sit in the car and smoke cigarettes rather than dealing with all the officers, and hearing a missionary reading a nonsensical prayer from a wet book he called the Bible. Hundreds of multicolored roses surrounded the casket, just as he'd wished that day Oliva died. After the priest said the final prayer, they lowered the waxed box into a six foot trench. Bells from the cemetery chapel rang twelve times, followed by a three-volley salute. I left before the final shot to avoid traffic.

Doctor Brazen had parked her Mercedes in the front lot today. She probably didn't want her styled hair to mix with the rain. I took the space next to hers, realizing I owned a part of her expensive car. I dug into the glovebox to retrieve a pack of cigarettes and stumbled upon a flask buried in the corner. I stroked its cold metal surface, the scotch watering my lips, but couldn't bring myself to drink.

Just one sip, Frank. Just one, maybe two, is all you need.

"Fine." I lowered the flask between my legs and eased the cap, squealing the seal free. A quick gulp quenched the gums. I tucked the flask under the seat and headed into Doctor Brazen's office.

"Hello, Frank." She twirled a pencil like a drumstick from behind her desk. I was less surprised, and more offended, she opted not to greet me at the door.

"Doctor Brazen. How are you?"

"I'm fine. Thanks for asking." Her quirky smile accentuated the smeared, red lipstick. "Are *you* well?"

"I've had better days," I said with a shrug before sitting.

"You don't look well."

"Thanks for the unrequested compliment. It's been up and down these past few days. We lost someone at the Precinct. I'm not doing well with the whole situation."

"I'm sorry. I watched it on the nightly news. I didn't know he was from your division."

"Yes. His name was Daniels but *you* already know that. A good man."

"I bet he was. The news didn't release the cause of death. If you don't mind, what exactly happened to him?" She rubbed the pencil eraser against her temple. Her nonchalant attitude suggested she didn't even care he died.

"Well... I do mind. The news isn't reporting it because we're keeping it quiet. It's a very sensitive situation. I'm sure you'll find out soon enough."

She dropped the pencil from her hand. It bounced from the notepad and rolled onto her lap.

"You can tell me, Frank. It's okay. We have doctor-patient privilege. I promise not to ever share it with anyone," she said, batting her mascara-matted eyelashes. She must've forgotten to look in the mirror today. "It's best to get it off your chest. I'm here for you. Talking is always the best option."

"No. It's sensitive."

"Well... keeping it in and not talking about it isn't going to make you feel any better. By the way, I can smell the alcohol. Do you have to hit the bottle every time you see me? If we talk about it, you won't need to reach for a drink."

"It wasn't a—bottle. It was a—flask."

"It's all the same, Frank. Stop acting like a child. You need to face reality, not drink it away. Talk to me. It's my job to help you."

"That's a joke. Right, Doctor? The same way you helped Daniels. You know he mentioned your name to me?" She probably thought Daniels would just kill himself and go quietly, leaving her exonerated.

"Look..." Pensive, she sunk into her chair. "I do all I can for the patient. If people choose to do things on their own time, then I can't help them. He didn't reach out to me. Tell me what happened."

"You're peddling excuses. He fucking killed himself," I said, slamming my palms against the armrest. "How's that sit with you?"

"Again, I can't change what happened, but I'm surprised and sad. Why did he mention me? Did he leave a note?"

"No. He told me over the phone. He said you didn't help him. You don't even know how bad his body looked. You only care about your damn self."

"You're wrong, Frank. I'm sorry for your loss. How did he die?" she asked, lacing her hands with an exaggerated curl of each finger.

"Daniels sliced his arm open, then hanged himself. He made sure to leave no chance of being saved."

"Oh my..." She gulped, jaw clenched, digging each fingernail into a knuckle. Her rosy complexion faded. "That's horrible. I really don't know what to say to console you, other than I'm sorry you had to experience it."

"Of course you don't, Doctor. You didn't know what to say to him either. You should've saved him. You could've saved him."

"I couldn't save him F—"

I should grab those scissors from that pencil holder, and tear through both of your arms. Blood will pool on the plush shag beneath your expensive heels. Too surprised, you won't even realize what's happening until you've lost your breath. You'll be like Daniels, Desiree, and all the rest. Globs of mascara, mixed with tears, trickling your cheeks like strips of tar, strands of hair sticking to them like feathers. For good measure, I'll finish you by nailing each pen and pencil from your desk into your skull, starting at your eyes, then following the dribbling trail on either side of your face to the ridge just above your neck.

"Frank—Frank. Are you with me? Did you just have another ep—"

"I'm here. What the hell were you babbling about?"

"I called out your name. You disappeared. Another episode. I said don't blame me for the actions of others." She let out a tedious sigh. "I offer to help everyone. If that person doesn't want help, then there's nothing I can do. Each person that comes here must be honest with me. I can only help people that want to help themselves. He didn't want my help and wasn't honest with me. If he was, then he'd still be alive. He made a decision to take his life because he wanted to take his life. There was nothing any of us could do to save him. Ask yourself if you're honest with me. I doubt you are."

"I *am* honest with you," I said, jutting my chin and digging my nails into the armrest.

"You don't tell me anything about your personal life." Annoyed, she tilted her head and rolled her eyes. "Where's your diary—I mean journal?"

"I've told you everything." Damn Doctor putting this on me. I flailed my hands in protest.

"What happened to Desiree?"

I paused for a moment and held my breath, remembering Desiree's last moments on my couch. "She left town to be with her family. Hopefully, she'll be back soon. What else do you want to know?"

"Your journal, your problems, the people outside work. These are the things you never talk about."

"Never mind about that damn journal. I've always been honest with you. I go out with friends and have drinks. That's my simple life in a nutshell."

"You have the right to be or not to be honest. If you're not, then your mind will catch up to you eventually, just as it did for Daniels. We're not going to have this argument, just because you're upset about him. I'm upfront with all my patients. I've had plenty of success stories walk out of my office, even children. It's your choice if you want to succeed or continue on the destructive path. Let me help you. What can—"

"Nothing. I don't need anything from you."

"Why do our visits have to be so volatile? You need to figure out a new approach, if you want to move forward. Let's change the topic a bit. Maybe that'll help clear your mind."

"Okay... Go ahead."

"Stay calm. Have you seriously thought about taking medications? We've talked about it and I'm hoping you'd consider that route."

"No way. Maybe, you need those damn meds, but I don't. I'm happy with the drinking and whatever else I do."

"That's not the right approach, Frank, and I certainly don't need them. The medications will relax your mind and body. You won't want to drink as much either. It's something positive to consider."

"So what you're telling me is that I take these meds and I'll have a relaxed mind? I won't be bothered by anything and I'll always be calm. Hot dog... sign me up." I slapped my thighs with exaggerated jubilation. "I don't want to be comfortably numb. I'll pass." I kicked my boots against her desk. She jolted backwards, her hair grazing the bookshelf encompassing the wall. "No way. I want to live as the true me. Daniels was smart. He chose his way out. Not to be controlled. Pick another topic, damn it."

She extended her arms across the desk like two balance beams. "I *will not* say this again, Frank. I helped Daniels as much as he allowed. He chose to take his life because that's what he wanted to do. I didn't make him take his life, nor did I force him to take medications. He *chose* what he wanted to do. I'm trying to help you now." She leaned across the desk, a finger pointed at my face. "I don't want you to go down the same path he took. I want you to get better. You're the one in control. How to fix it is your choice. Let's start over. How can we address Daniels's death?" She retreated into her seat, plucking a pencil from her desk, spinning it like a baton between her hands.

"We fucking can't. One thing's for sure... I can't disagree with his logic. He was right with what he did."

"Taking your life is never correct, Frank." She jotted something onto the paper.

"For once, you should take all your psychological mumbo-jumbo and shove it up your ass. Look at things for what they are. Sometimes death is the only option to save yourself from this evil world."

"Don't try to justify suicide. What Daniels did was completely wrong on every level."

I rose from the chair, grabbed one of her pencils, holding it within inches of her face. "Listen, you damn Doctor. For once in your life, listen. He had the courage to take his life and leave what this world had to offer him. You can't tell me he was wrong, if he had that kind of strength."

"I understand your point. I'm just stating what he did *is* wrong in my eyes. I strongly advise against suicide for anyone. Are you thinking about suicide?"

"No. I don't have the fortitude," I said, hanging my head and huffing.

A long silence followed. She raised and lowered her brow several times, scribbled a few more notes, then continued.

"Good, Frank. How about your job situation. Have you thought about what you're going to do?"

"Don't change the topic. You screwed Daniels. Forget my job. I'm taking some time away to think."

"I'm truly sorry about him. I can't change what happened. Try to stay positive."

"Can't promise I will. Daniels has sent me into melancholia. I'll try to get out of it as soon as I can."

"You have to try to work through the depression. You don't want it to get out of control. I recommend writing in your journal to alleviate some stress. Then, you can bring me that journal to read."

"Nice try, but that's not happening. I'm fed up with all of this fucking garbage in my life, including you. I need to leave. I need a drink and a smoke."

"Alright, Frank, but we still have some time on the clock. I'd like to offer you more, free of charge. We can focus on Daniels or any other topic."

"I don't want to hear his damn name anymore. That's all that echoes in my head right now." I clutched my hair, attempting to rid the incessant thumps filling my mind. "I really have to go. I can't take this anymore. If I need you, I'll call you."

"Okay, Frank." She lowered her head and scribbled. "Stay strong. Stay healthy." She offered a faint wave without glancing towards me.

Screw her, Frank. You don't need this demon in your life.

I jumped from the chair and dashed from the office. As I frantically sifted the floorboard for the flask, the car filled with smoke from my cigarette. The first swigs of scotch like water. The last time it was that refreshing was when I stopped going to those useless AA meetings. One hand held the cigarette and the other the flask. Steering with my thighs, I guided the speeding car through red lights and over graveled shoulders, stopping with the wheels against the curb in front of my apartment. A half-gallon of scotch greeted me at the kitchen. I swallowed a quarter of it with a single tip, adding several colorful pills and lines of cocaine for entrees. Before I could contemplate my next move, I passed out.

XXIX

"What are you doing, baby?"

A muffled female voice, its location unclear, forced me to roll to other side of the bed. I fluffed the pillow and repositioned my head, hoping it'd disappear.

"What are you doing, baby?"

The voice clearer this time. I rolled to the opposite side, but she reiterated her question from the darkness. I had no choice but to engage.

"Nothing… Sleeping. Why you asking?"

"I need you to come over here and talk with me."

"What do you want? I haven't slept in days. I'm tired."

"Frank. Frank…." The blurred image crept into focus. "Don't you want to talk, then maybe touch me? Don't you miss me?"

"Is that really you? Of course I miss you."

"Yes, baby. It's me. I miss your lust."

"What's going on, Desiree?"

I stretched to touch her face, but it was just out of reach. She inched closer. I swiped once more, and just as I was about to make contact, she darted.

"We need to talk about you and Daniels."

"Not that name again. About what?" I pulled away, confused and surprised by her mention.

"About how they sent the wrong person to jail. You have to fix that, baby."

"Fix? It wasn't my doing. There's nothing I can—"

"Oh… but there is. You have to find the clue to link the guilty party to Oliva."

"I don't know what you're talking about. I have no leads and the cops don't like me, so they won't help."

"You have what you need already. Think harder."

"Where, Desiree? I presented my hand, twisting and turning it. "I don't have anything. I need more rest."

"Never mind sleep. You do know. Place it into your pocket. You'll figure it out, once you see it."

"Yes. The only thing in my pocket is hard, and it's for you. Our last night together was amazing. I want to feel you again, suffocate within your aroma, and be inside you."

"You're too sweet. I miss you too, but you must focus on helping Daniels."

"I want you. Let's forget about him. He's long gone. It's just us now."

"You have to find the real killer." She approached my lips, swept over my cheek, hovering at my earlobe. Her breath cold. "You must find him, baby."

"Right. The real killer. Where?"

"I know you have the answer."

"What answer?"

"It's where my hand resides. Can you feel it? Remember, look in your pocket and you'll find the real killer."

"My pocket?"

"Yes, Frank. You placed it into your pocket after lifting it from the brush. Remember?"

"The ID card?"

"Yes, now you're remembering. Daniels will be happy."

"Okay… if I find the ID, I'll find the killer. Thank you for the clue."

"You're very welcome." In that instance, she disappeared.

"I'll miss you, Desiree."

I awoke with one hand grasping the space where her face once lingered, and the other moistened between my thighs. The warmth soon replaced with a frigid prickle. A few seconds later, the damn siren blared from the nightstand. I didn't recall even setting the alarm, and to the best of my memory, I'd thrown it into the closet after the last mishap. I sent it to the floor with a violent swipe, silencing it.

I picked the crust from my eyelids, then jutted from the bedroom into the kitchen, avoiding the scotch for the water tap. As I waited for the glass to fill, I noticed Desiree's essence upon the countertop. I'd forgotten to pack her away into the box of memories. All of its perfect texture and color still intact within the olive oil. I brought the jar to my lips and kissed it. I closed my eyes, picturing her grandiose dimples, which had welcomed me at the shelter not too long ago.

Finding the ID held priority over storing her essence. A frantic search ensued, sifting all the uniforms scattered throughout the apartment. The first set of pants and shirts provided nothing, but the third proved a charm. From inside a small auxiliary pocket, which usually held single bullets, I found the ID and raised it to eye level.

"Mitch Karssie. Junior at Franklin West High School. I'm going to get you Mitch—Karssie."

I exchanged the glass of water for scotch, but didn't overindulge, chasing it with only a small line of cocaine. I rubbed Desiree for good luck, stuffed my pocket with a full flask, and headed to Precinct 13 to browse the Person Search Database (PSD).

* * * * * * * * * * * *

"Hey, Frank." Joe Rook greeted me at the door as if awaiting my arrival. "How've you been?"

"I'm better," I said with a wink and a nod. "Not perfect, but better."

"Good. You've been away for a while. We're all still hurting for Daniels." He shook his head with disbelief and frowned.

"I don't mean to rush you out of your thoughts for Daniels, but is the PSD available to use?"

"Slow down, buddy. Yes, it's free. You show up at work out of the blue and need to search for someone. Doesn't make sense. Why do you need it?"

"Oh… I have to look up an address for Abigail. It's for one of Daniels's friends. She needs to contact him." I escalated my pace towards the research room.

"Okay. No problem. Anything for Daniels, or his wife. She sure is pretty." His voice faded into the distance as I entered the room. "Let me know if you need my help."

"Will do. Thanks man." He couldn't have heard me, nor did I care.

The sensors detected my presence, lighting the fluorescents like a rolling wave. Good thing he didn't follow me. I didn't have any logical reason to explain the search if he was standing behind me. I flipped the switch on the back of the antiquated computer and waited several minutes for it to boot. A blue screen with a blinking white cursor greeted me. Using my fingers like hammers, I inputted each letter for his name. I should've taken those damn typing classes when they were offered. The longer I stayed in this room, the more of a chance Joe Rook or some other straggler would show up and find out what I was doing.

A quick sip of scotch while I waited for the computer to think. Only one result popped onto the screen: Address 1026 Maple Ave, no priors, age 16. An asterisk highlighted a side note: Individual detained at the Olympus Arcade for smoking weed. No ticket issued. Released.

"You need any help, Sarge?" Joe called out from his desk. "I'll be there in a second."

"No. All set." Hopefully, he heard me this time, but the thumping of his boots suggested otherwise. He was probably on his way. Damn Rook.

I smacked the print key and rushed to the door, peering from the jamb. The page rolled onto the tray and the coast was clear. I snagged the paper, tucked it into my pocket, and rebooted the system to wipe the search. At my desk, I strategized Mitch's capture. The cops weren't going to be involved. The only parties: me, Mitch, and Daniels.

Without fail, the Rook interrupted my tactical planning. "I was on my way to join you in the PSD room. You were taking a damn long time to get that name. Did you get everything you need?"

"Yes."

"Can I see what you printed?" He craned his neck across my desk.

"No. It's private. How about this? Let's have a coffee the next time I'm here. My treat." I offered a gracious smile.

"Sure. Sounds—"

"I have to go, Joe. Going to check on a missing person at the shelters. I'll see you later."

"Okay."

"Oh, I almost forgot… Can I borrow two things from you?"

Yeah. What do you need?"

"I need one of your Precinct business cards and a pen."

"What for?" he said befuddled.

"Well… in case someone at the shelter needs to contact you for a big case. The pen. Well, that's pretty obvious. It's for writing."

"Sure. I'll take all the big cases I can get to move up." He handed the items to me and I slipped them into my pocket. "If you need anything, call me. Great job following up on those leads. I'm looking forward to that coffee. I like flavored."

I rose from the desk without responding, heading to the exit with a limp wave from the back of my hand. I had some ideas for his flavored coffee, but nothing set in stone. I'd played a good diversion game with the feebleminded Rook, one of the most annoying men I'd ever met. Not only was he a crooked cop, but his arrogance unjustified by his reputation or lack of intelligence. Those wanting to touch the sun on false pretenses always get burned.

I changed into street clothes outside the car. Tonight was the night to find Mitch and any hint of a cop would scare him off. That's if he was the perpetrator, but the ID at the park couldn't just be a coincidence, plus I had Desiree and Daniels to confirm. They couldn't be wrong.

XXX

I set up surveillance inside my car on Maple Ave, one block south from Maplewood Park, which meant Mitch had easy access. The murder scene presented no evidence of vehicle involvement. The perp had to be someone familiar with the park, who possibly lived in the vicinity. The only part that didn't fit: he's a high school junior.

I kept my drinking to a minimum—a sip here and there—but the smoking to a maximum to stay alert. Cocaine would've been a better alternative.

No one had entered or exited the house after several hours. Frustrated, I quit and started the car. As I was about to drive away, the front door opened. From it emerged an individual wearing dark jeans and a hoodie. The gender undetermined, but they did have shoulder-length, shaggy hair. As the individual stepped from the illuminated porch, I determined the person a he. I held the ID under the dome light and the two faces matched. He hopped on his bicycle and rode away. I tailed at an undetectable distance.

About a mile down the road, he popped a wheelie and veered onto the Olympus Arcade lot. He scanned his surroundings for a moment, then chained his bike to the rack. I waited for him to enter, then snuck my car, headlights off, into a scarcely lit spot furthest from the entrance. I ventured throughout the arcade securing exit doors, as well as confirming the number of individuals present. It was empty, except for the attendant, who was busy talking on the phone and smoking a joint.

I located Mitch, mesmerized by the colorful blinking ghosts, at the Ms. Pac-Man game. I timed my approach to the open paths of dots on the screen.

"Hey, man. What's going on tonight?"

"Playing games. What do you think it looks like?"

"Alright… Don't get all riled. Do you mind if I play next?"

"No, but I'd rather play against you. Put up your token."

"Do you come here often?"

I slid four tokens onto the game's tapered ledge.

"Yup. It's my hangout to get away from my stupid home. I've never seen you here. What brings you?" His eyes never lost focus of the screen. The yellow sphere, with a red bow, swallowing the blinking ghosts and dots.

"I'm here every couple months."

"We all need a change sometimes." A pink ghost swallowed the Pac-Woman. "You're up. Hope you're ready to lose old man."

He retreated from the console and waved me in. I latched onto the joystick, slamming it every direction.

"What's your name?"

Distracted by his question, I turned from the flashing maze on the screen. The yellow orb then falling victim to three ghosts. "Damn it. See what you did? I'm Frank—Frank Stark. What's your name?" No need for aliases tonight. The kid too young to know me from anywhere in the city.

"Move over. I'm up again. Mitch—Karssie."

"Nice to meet you, Mitch."

"Likewise, Frank. I'm going to crush you."

Four tokens later and the game staled. A perfect opening to offer another option.

"I'm heading to Maplewood Park. You ever been?"

"Yup. Favorite spot after the Arcade."

"Cool. I have some drinks and weed. You want to join me?"

"Yeah, man. I'm in, if you're bringing the party."

"Good. Leave your bike and ride with me. I have to make a quick stop to buy beer. I only have the strong stuff on me."

"Okay, that works too."

He didn't put up any resistance, which was a good sign. His demeanor older than his age, but behind his eyes existed something off-kilter. I couldn't quite place it. We stopped at Pat's Drive-In to buy beer and a couple packs of smokes. Pat wasn't working again. I made a mental note to stop there soon. He had a special concoction I needed to purchase. Mitch and I didn't exchange a word during the ride. To counteract our silence and offset the whistling wind through the open windows, I turned up the radio. Ozzy Osbourne's "Diary of Madman" came through the speakers, which commanded me to spin the volume louder. Each of his lyrics denoted my everyday life, my being. He wrote and sang those words for me. The only person on earth that understood and cared for me, enough so, to send me an ode through the radio for all to hear. Mitch was oblivious to my anthem, but as we pulled into Maplewood Park he brightened, as if he were home.

"I like this place, Frank. It's so peaceful."

"Yeah, almost like a cemetery."

"It's exactly like a *cemetery*. That's why I love it. If only the trees could talk," he said with a deliberate laugh.

"If only they could. Not too long ago, they found a lady murdered in this park."

We exited the car and strolled towards the vicinity where we found the body. We sat on an empty bench on the perimeter of the Rose Garden, he on one end, and I at the other.

"I guess she was at the wrong place at the wrong time. You should always be prepared in the park. When it gets cold at night, you need to keep your clothes on."

We never released specific information about the body to the public. At this point, I knew Mitch committed the murder, but I wanted to know the motive before I went any further. Perhaps he deserved to be saved. I opened two cans of beer and handed him one.

"It does get cold at night." I plucked a pre-rolled spliff from my jacket. "Do you come here at night often?" I licked the paper to smoothen the joint and lit it.

"Yup. It's the best time because no one's here to bother anyone."

"Do you ever run into people that shouldn't be at the park?"

"What do you mean?" He took a long drag, held his breath, and coughed a cloud.

"Gangs or crazy people?"

"Not usually. I used to hang with a guy your age, so he watched over me. Made sure nothing bad happened. His name was Sten. Almost twice the size of you. He was a good guy, but then he went away for something he didn't do. Now, I come alone and hope nothing goes wrong."

"It's always good to have someone else around. What happened to Sten?"

"Well… he's not returning for a long time. He got in some trouble at this park." He took a sip of beer and raised the can in the air. "Here's to you, Sten."

"Were you really that close?"

"Yup. We'd drink and smoke weed together like we're doing now. He always gave me advice on growing up and taught me things to make me stronger. I've had a rough time in high school. The kids are always making fun of me, bullying me. Sten was the only guy who understood me, and got me through all that high school stress and bullshit."

"What happened?"

"I don't like to talk about it."

He turned away, staring into the park's emptiness, in the same direction where we found the body.

"Come on, man. You can tell me. It's always best to talk about it. That's what my psychiatrist tells me. Here… take a hit."

We laughed as we alternated drags from the joint.

"That's funny. You don't look like the kind of guy who needs one of those shrinks. Aren't they like grownup, high-school counselors? I see one of them all the time, but they don't help." He sipped his beer and let out a sigh. "I know *more* than they do."

"We all have problems, Mitch. Mine are just different than yours, but she says talking is the way to fix them." If there was ever a time to use that stupid, psychological mumbo-jumbo, it was now. I respected him for saying he knew more than they did. "I don't agree with her because I still have problems. She can't help me, either. One of my friends recently committed suicide because of his problems. She said she couldn't fix him. I think she didn't want to."

Reel him in, Frankie, but I think he's just like you.

"That's too bad. I don't know, man. I guess.... I can tell you about me. You seem cool." His voice retreated as he lowered his chin to his chest. "I'm... bisexual. It's difficult for me in high school because they don't like my kind. I like both, but have only been with Sten. I'd hang out with him at this park or his trailer. We'd drink, smoke weed, talk, and then get together sometimes. He cared about me a lot and now he's gone. Sucks for me."

"I understand. I'm that way too. I don't like labels, but I guess I'm what they call "bisexual" as well. As long as someone's got something to offer, then I'm taking it," I said with a proud laugh.

I sauntered to Mitch and caressed his shoulder, then ran my hand through his straggly locks. I ended with a soft brush upon his neck. He withdrew and gazed at me, startled. "Thanks for understanding. I was hesitant at first, but I'm glad I met you tonight." His astonishment turned into a familiar invitation. "You remind me of Sten."

"No problem. Tell me, what really happened to him?"

"Long story. I'll make it short. This old hag had him arrested. She was horrible and only cared about herself."

"What's her name?"

I didn't expect this to go as smoothly as it did with confirmation right around the corner.

"I don't really know or care to remember. I think Ollie or Olive Oyl. I only know her by face. Old like my grandma. She lived somewhere near here."

"What happened to Oliva?"

"How do you know her name?"

"Oh, the news."

"Well… she made Sten go to jail because she was jealous. She didn't like that me and him would hang out and do things."

"What kind of things?"

"You know… She didn't like me and Sten getting close. Oliva and Sten used to have a thing. They'd get together once in a while and you know… have sex. Once she found out Sten and I hooked up, everything blew up between them. Bitch!"

"What'd she do to Sten?"

"Sten told me. One day they were walking in this park and they started to get hot and heavy. They were all over each other, then she snapped, yelling at him about me. She said she was going to get back at him for playing around with me. The next day, or a few days after, she called the cops and said she was raped." Mitch's hands shot through the air with bravado, his beer spilling onto the ground. "What the hell was wrong with that bitch? The cops came and arrested Sten while I was at school. I never even got a chance to say goodbye. Every few months, I take the bus and visit him at Attica. She ruined his life and took my best friend. It's not fair."

"That's horrible." I stroked his cheek. "I'm sorry."

"It's the worst thing in the world. She ruined the best thing that ever happened to me and needed to pay for what she did to Sten."

His initiative impressive and admirable. I would've done the same thing, but that didn't change why I was here. Paybacks are never-ending.

"What did you do to her?"

"I don't remember the day. I followed her to the park one morning or it could've been nighttime. Once she arrived at the same spot where they hooked up, I jumped atop her and beat her. She screamed. I punched her in the mouth to shut her up. Everything went dark. I pulled out my BB gun, grabbed the barrel, and hit her on the head with the handle several times. The more I pounded her, the quieter she became, until she was sleeping. That's when I stopped."

"What else happened?" I wanted to applaud his natural talent.

"I needed to show Sten and the world what I did. I lifted her shirt, exposing her tits, and pulled her jogging pants down to her knees to fake a rape. Now everyone knows she's a whore. I loaded the BB and shot her full of pellets until the gas emptied from the cartridge. After I was done, I went home, washed up, and went to school like nothing ever happened."

"What the fuck? Were you exhilarated?"

You know those feelings all too well, Frankie.

"I know Sten appreciates what I did for him. She deserved it. I was so high my pants bulged as I killed her."

We smoked another joint and drank a few more beers. A couple swigs from the flask completed the buzz and took the edge off the admission. It was time to get him to my place. Revenge for Daniels's death was due and deserved, regardless of my appreciation for his actions.

"Hey, Mitch. Let's get out of here. It's starting to get cold."

We rose to our feet. He swayed at first but caught himself on the edge of the bench.

"Where do you want to go?"

I approached from behind and ran my fingers through his hair. "Let's go back to my place. We can have drinks and smoke inside. Maybe afterwards we can play around."

"I don't know about that." He stepped back, waving his hands with defiance. "I just met you. I don't know if that's a good idea."

"Come on... It'll be fine. I'm just like Sten. We're cool with each other. Having fun." I clapped his shoulder and ruffled his shirt near his belly. "I just want to continue the party at my place where it's warm. You can kick back and relax. Don't worry about it, man. I have a nice apartment."

"Alright... Fuck it. Let's go. I don't feel like going to school tomorrow anyway."

"Great. You won't regret it. I promise."

XXXI

We rambled to the car, my arm around his waist playfully tugging his jacket, his hand atop my shoulder. I led him to the passenger side and opened the door. He crept his fingers along the steel roof like a spider, eyeing his final destination like a hawk. Once he found the spot, he released the metal ridge and plopped onto the seat. I straightened his body against the backrest, placed an open beer between his legs, and handed him a joint. We exchanged a smile, mine more tempting than his. At the rear of the vehicle, I stopped and turned towards the Rose Garden, inhaling the sweet scents of a thousand blooms, and thought about the day Daniels and I strolled the orchard. If only I'd known how that story would end. I took a swig, lit a cigarette, and entered the vehicle.

"How's it going, man?" I said, popping open a can of beer, then placing it into the cup holder. He didn't respond, too occupied with puffing the joint and staring into the darkness of the Rose Garden. Perhaps, he awaited Oliva's visit at the window.

I started the car, revved the engine, and sped onto the street. We didn't exchange a word for most of the trip, the radio filling the gaps of conversation. He ventured towards me twice to rub my thigh and blow the remnants of the blazing joint into my face. His eyelids fluttered. Falling asleep wasn't an option for him. A long night awaited him to enjoy every dreadful minute. I slalomed the car from the off ramp, skidding across two lanes of traffic, and with a violent spin of the steering wheel, cut the rear end into a straight line. At that moment, he awoke.

"I love this song. I love fast cars."

He slapped my leg, turned up the volume on the radio, and reclined into the seat.

"I thought you'd disappeared on me. Guess who sings this song."

"I don't know, man. Don't care for trivia. I just like it."

His humming attempted to meet the pitch of the chorus but fell noticeably short.

"I like it too," I said, pounding the steering wheel to the beat. "The answer to the trivia is "Rev on the Red Line" by Foreigner. Did you know the guy singing this song is from Rochester? He's too I—talian to use his real name, so he shortened it from Lou Grammatico to Lou Gramm. He's one of the best singers of all time."

The chorus kicked in and I floored it, bringing the car to a hundred-miles-per-hour on the narrow streets. Good thing the song ended as we approached my place, or I would've had to keep driving in order to drain the adrenalin. We still had a portion in our veins as we rushed from the car, slamming the doors. He'd grabbed the beer from the backseat and lugged it up the steps while I straggled with the drugs in my pockets. With his backside facing me, I swarmed his body, thrusting him against the door.

"Whoa... slow down, Frank. We'll have time for that when we get inside."

"I know. I wanted you to feel what you're missing. By the way, I think you're cute. When I look at you, I see a younger version of myself."

I unlocked the door. He bumped it open with his forearm and staggered towards the kitchen, lunging the case of beer onto the table. He flung his jacket onto one of the empty chairs. Ubiquitous lines of cocaine occupied random sections of the table, which he'd avoided when dropping the beer. He either had a good eye or pure luck.

"Frank." His eyes widened. "I didn't know you liked powder. Sometimes, me and Sten did it before hooking up."

"Go ahead, man. Take a line, or two, or three. I have more of everything."

"Is that a promise?"

"Of course." I marched to the counter and grabbed a bottle of scotch.

"Yes… that hit the spot." He raised his head from the table, his eyes as crazed as his smile.

"Always does. Do you want some scotch, vodka, beer?"

"I'll take two shots of ScoVo and a beer to chase."

"Good choice. That's my pick too. We have so much in common. This is going to be a good night for you."

I poured two shots and placed each glass at the head of the unfinished lines on the table. Simultaneously, we huffed, lifted our heads, glanced each other, and swallowed the liquor. I stepped away from the table and surveyed him for an opportunity. He sipped his beer and let out a fading sigh, sprawling the chair in a drunken stupor, then swiveling his head towards each wall of the apartment. I wanted to pounce at that moment, break that tiny, teenage neck, but as I lurched towards him, he disrupted my thoughts.

"Nice place. It's better than Sten's trailer." He slurped the remnants of an empty beer and popped the tab on another.

"Thanks. I have to piss. Be right back." I hoped to regroup with a more skillful plan of attack. "Why don't you get more comfortable while I'm away?" I said with a cajoling chuckle.

"Maybe I will, then when you return, we can play."

"That's exactly what I was thinking. In the meanwhile, don't be afraid to lose some of that clothing. I know it's hot in here."

As I entered the bathroom, I glanced over my shoulder and caught him removing his shirt. I locked the door and the buzz overcame me. I gripped the edges of the sink and leveraged my body. Inching my head higher, the reflection in the mirror slid into focus. Crimson starbursts exploded in every direction around my pupils. I opened the vanity for the eye drops, then quickly slammed it shut, deciding the remedy served no purpose. I'd take care of them after obliterating Mitch. I regained my composure, focusing on the task at hand, hoping the mirror would divulge the answers to my next steps.

"What are we going to do to you, Mitch? Daniels deserves quintessential revenge. He told me to find and kill you in his suicide note. I can't let him down. Your death is his glory. Revea—" That piercing buzz had returned, sizzling all the minute crevices within my skull. With one hand I grabbed a fistful of hair, the other pummeled the tiled wall. The pain eased for a brief moment.

"Are you okay in there, Frank?"

"Yes... I'm—fine. I... the rug." Goddamn it, man. For fuck's sake, Frank, get with the program. Figure this out. The mirror silent. With a finger, I traced the reflection of my seething eyes. "Fuck you. Damn you. I don't need you."

Sub-due him, Frankie. Then kill him, Frank.

I gripped the door handle, turning it with silent precision. My other hand steadied the weight of the wood against the hinges, inching it open. I surveilled, not jumping the gun on this attack. Mitch stood shirtless at the table pouring a shot. He tipped it back and winced, then stumbled backwards, catching himself against the back of a chair. He twitched his head and poured another drink, then dipped the plane of the table, rising with a smile, and gulped another shot. My opportunity arrived with clarity.

"Hey... Mitch." I exited the bathroom.

"Frank... What's up?" he said stunned, bouncing his hip from the chair.

"I see you're feeling good. Hope you're ready for me."

I approached with determined eyes, my body towering over his bare chest. I grazed his shoulder. With my fingers, I crawled across his body to his waist line, then up to the bony ridges at the base of his neck. I feathered a kiss upon his nape and he responded with a seductive gasp. His sexual exhilaration offered a chance for attack. I slithered one arm around his feeble throat, my bicep locked into place by my other hand. His body squirmed within my grasp, inadequate to escape. Within seconds, the chokehold limped his body into my arms. I lowered him to the floor.

With the first part of the process completed, I returned to the bathroom to brainstorm the next steps to destroy him. He deserved to be tortured with flawless exuberance. Mitch, the special case for Daniels to watch and scrutinize from wherever. Standing before the mirror my reflection, and all that existed, tunneled into a mesmerizing black hole. I faltered and Dad appeared. His teeth, now riddled with pus and maggots, had darkened as well since our last visit.

"Hello, Son." He grinned and a swarm of worms fell from his lower lip. "What brings you to see me?"

"Dad! I'm glad you're here. What do I need to do with Mitch?"

"Son... The answer is simple. You need to remember the past."

"I don't remember all of it. I thought you always took care of the torturing. I just did the cutting."

This mirror, now a swirling black hole, transported my being to another realm. I found myself back in the basement of my childhood home.

"Glad you could make it, Son. I'm surprised you don't remember what you did with some of those patients you brought to our dungeon." He propped himself upon the dissecting table and pulled out the scalpel I inherited, resting it upon the bloodied wood.

"How did you get my scalpel?"

"I've always had the scalpel. Just because you hold the scalpel in your hand doesn't mean that I'm not there in spirit. Your grandfather is also in its spirit. We're always there to hold it with you and watch you use it. Now, remember what you did to that beautiful girl, Aliyah Gomez."

"Oh yes... I hogtied her and crushed her skull."

"You have your answer. Goodbye, Son. I hope to see you soon."

Without notice, Dad disappeared. I stared at my reflection with ember eyes aglow. The plan: hogtie Mitch, sodomize him with a broom, then cut the flesh from his body. Piece by piece, all while alive. Pop his genitals from their sac like an avocado pit. Once out, stuff them into his mouth. Scoop out each eyeball and cram them into his gaping, blood-soaked rectum. He'd die somewhere in this process, but at least he'd enjoy some of this fantastical journey.

Peering from behind the bathroom door, I sought to get an accurate view of Mitch, an owl sizing up their prey. Astonished, I found the chair empty, the one liter bottle of scotch upon the table missing, and the front door ajar. Furious, I charged towards the living room.

"Mitch... Where are you? It's time to party. Mitch..."

I taunted him as I paced through the kitchen and to the front door. A glance outside provided no evidence of him. "Where are you, baby? It's time to play with your Sten." He didn't respond. My goading transitioned into rage. "I'm going to find you, Mitch. Once I do, there'll be nowhere to hide."

I pussyfooted into the bedroom, checking below the bed, then the closet, but no one. I swung the door and spotted the missing scotch bottle. It hit me square on the forehead and bridge of my nose. I plummeted to the floor with blood blurring my vision to the point of blindness. Spinning and crawling, I searched for the exit.

"Where are you, motherfucker? Show yourself." I growled, as blood filled my mouth. I spat a glob into the air.

"Fuck you, cop. I found your uniform and badge. Fuck you."

"I'm going to find and kill you, Mitch. You can't run and hide. There's nowhere to go."

"Screw you. You're just like the people that put Sten away." His shrieks deafening.

"I'm going to get you. Fight me like a man."

I mustered enough strength to stand, swaying and staggering, but tumbled to the floor after a few steps.

"You set me up. Why don't you fix that nose and forehead, loser?" He jeered. "You can't fight me. You can't even crawl. You're a loser."

His footsteps pounded towards me. My head spun and arms flailed, hoping to grab him from where I knelt, but as I stretched and twisted, my knees caved, balance waned, and my chest bounced from the floor.

"You're a piece of shit. You tried to kill me."

He rammed the points of his boots into my ribs.

"You don't understand. I did it for Oliva and Daniels." I gasped for air, blood burbling in my throat.

"Fuck you—cop. I hope you die. I'm lucky the snow woke me up, or I'd be dead."

As my face rested against the floor, his blurred body hunched over me. "Don't ever come near me again. I'll have you put in jail or killed. Don't ever find me. You got that cop?" His kicks continued to my ribs and face.

"Whatever," I murmured with a titter.

"What'd you say?" He grabbed a fistful of my hair and arched my neck.

"I said... yes."

"Yes to what?" Jabs from his boot spread the length of my body.

"Yes... I'll leave you alone. It's over. I'm done with you."

"Good. Just know that I could've killed you tonight like you were going to kill me. I'm not going to kill you, so you better not come find me."

"Fine. It's done. I give. We'll never see each other again."

I curled into the fetal position, hoping for his departure. The beating stopped. His tromping steps faded. Chairs crashed to the floor and the front door slammed. I pawed at the wall to gain leverage to rise. After several grueling minutes, I rose to an upright position. Tottering into the bathroom, I lunged for a towel, wrapping it as a facial tourniquet while I sat upon the toilet seat.

Hours passed before the bleeding stopped. Arms shaking, I gripped the edge of the sink for stability. The blood blurring my reflection cleared just enough to perceive the damage. Of course, Dad didn't show this time to assist. One eye swelled blue and black, sealed against a golf-ball cheek. The slash from the bottle created a jagged gash along my forehead, skin curling. The bridge of my nose split in two, the white cartilage gleaming through the red. Ichor formed crusted trails along my neck and chest.

Driving to the hospital doped up and naked would land me in jail, especially since I'm a cop. From inside the medicine cabinet, I pulled out a suture kit and a handful of OxyContin. The pills slid down my throat with a long swig of scotch. With the help of liquor and pills, I spent the next few hours stitching each serrated piece of skin into a seam. After soaking the towel in cold water, I rewrapped it around my face and collapsed onto the bed.

September 6

I can barely see the lines upon the pages. They want to be filled with linked letters to form words within their confines. I'm doing the best I can to fulfill their request, but it's pointless. This entry weighs heavy on what is left of my soul, if I even have one. Daniels is dead and the planned revenge has failed. Mitch will forever live in my memory. I hope he doesn't kill again. I cannot err in the future. I must pay attention, be more careful with my actions.

XXXII

I called the Rook a day or two after my mishap, explaining in a voicemail I'd be away from the Precinct to heal from a severe stomach ailment that required hospitalization. Once I hung up the phone, I realized they might request proof of the hospital stay. Hopefully, one of the black-market doctors would forge a note.

Professional care would've been better than self-treatment. An ammoniacal sweat browning the mattress roused me every morning, a cue to exchange the tourniquet towel for a new one. This method was easier than venturing to the store to buy gauze with a deformed face. I soaked it in cold water, then wrapped my head. Some days, when I slept longer, it desiccated, unable to absorb water. My only option, which included a shot of scotch, peeling the dried cotton from the wet wound.

A few days later another problem arose; a never-ending migraine pounding against my forehead. Removing the towel revealed an opaque discharge. Applying a vodka cleanse failed to clear it, which meant a burrowing infection with only one cure. I chased several pain pills with a bottle of scotch and doused a cloth with alcohol. Numb, I removed twenty sutures, then washed the wound. Luckily, the infection hadn't spread to the bridge of my nose. I chugged more scotch. With tweezers, I latched the frayed skin, tearing each section open, globs of pus spraying the mirror. This process lasted hours. I disinfected the area and sewed the wound. A week passed before the skin gained a foothold, forming scabs, which I lathered with Vaseline to reduce scarring.

In bed, I snapped the soiled linens from my body with Desiree circling my mind. I latched onto the headboard with one hand, the other reaching between my legs. Undulating, the bedsprings creaked in tandem with my heaving breaths. Arching my back, I convulsed and gasped, adding remnants to the soiled mattress. I stretched for a cigarette from the nightstand, then thrusted my legs over the bed like a drunken gymnast. The hardwoods frigid against my bare feet as I doddered to the bathroom for one final inspection of my face before venturing into the public domain.

A wormlike ridge had formed atop the bridge of my nose. That damn bottle had carved my skin like a meat slicer. The dark imprints around my eyes stamped with a cookie press while the red starbursts around my pupils expanded into a supernova.

The wounds were healing, but my internal pain swelling. I'd disconnected the phone after leaving the Rook that message, and as the days passed, no one came to rattle the deadbolts. My absence was of no consequence to the Precinct. I entered the living room, an adequate space not long ago. Its floors now buckling from the weight of broken bottles and garbage. The walls crumbling upon my chest, chunks of mortar squeezing each breath. Any moments of clarity short-lived. I reveled in the comforting confines of darkness and horror.

I accepted the reality, wobbling onto a chair at the kitchen table. Absolution splashing the walls of a tumbler. The wafting aroma bubbled bile into my throat, forcing me to scurry to the sink. I hurled a speckled mess, which snailed along the basin and into the sewer. Another go at the scotch proved successful, numbing the lips.

Abutting the bottle rested a razor. Carving figure eights into the table, I pondered if I should partake. The angelic powder demanded consumption. I rose, kicking the chair across the room. My shirt rippling with every heartbeat. Euphoric, I gyrated towards the counter, espying Desiree. Once in my grasp, I spun the cap of her glass home.

"Desiree... I miss you."

I retrieved her essence and cradled it upon my fingertips, stroking its ridge with utmost care. I lifted her to my heart, then my lips, and closed my eyes for a kiss.

"I miss you too, Frank."

"You've come back to see me."

"Yes, I was speaking with Julia."

"Julia Sarinksy?

"Yes, I believe that's her name."

"We spent a few good nights together. She was always open to trying new things. But as you know, all good things must end."

"I do, Frank. I've come to remind you of something."

"And what's that? Your love for me?"

"No, Frankie. You must take care of Darnell's friend."

"I'm sorry that happened to Darnell. I had no choice. Who's his friend?"

"I can't forgive you, but I understand. Baby, what would you do without me? Father Brandon. He'll punish you, if you don't punish him first. He knows what you did. I must go now."

Drips of olive oil tickled my chin, startling me. I cupped her essence and guided it along the glass wall. With her resting, I opened the closet and deposited the jar within the box of memories, snug against Daniels's diary. I left the apartment shortly thereafter in full uniform, determined to remove anything standing in my way.

I veered onto Pat's parking lot too hot, skidding the car to a halt. I clenched the cigarette between my lips, sucked the last drag, and chucked it onto the street. I stormed into the store. The glass door bounced from the wall, its abused chimes rattled a deadpan tune. Pat sat atop a bar stool behind the counter, unfazed by my explosive entrance.

"Hey, Pat. How's it going?"

"I'm fine, I suppose." He tilted his head towards me.

"Are you alright?"

"Yeah… I guess it can always be worse. This store… this city… this weather… it's all taking a toll on me. Sometimes happy and sometimes sad. How are you?"

His eyes widened. "What the fuck happened to your face?" He stood, his protruding gut thumping the cash register.

"Well… I—fell, chasing a perp. Some back alley. Tripped and crashed. They stitched me up. Had me in the hospital for a few days."

"That's too bad. Hope they caught the guy."

"We did, but let's not worry about that right now. Back to you. Let me get three packs of smokes."

"I think you can use a drink." He reached below the counter, gathering a bottle of generic whiskey and a pair of shot glasses.

"Of course. I'll take a shot, or two. I never say no to free booze."

We nodded and grinned. I wondered about the thoughts behind his smirk. Perhaps, there were none. Mine, a bit more complicated. If he only knew the things I've had to do or will do. I couldn't tell him. He wouldn't understand, especially since those actions, most of the time, are out of my control. I raised my glass. He followed. We toasted midair, then gulped.

"That was good, Frank. Let's have one more. Fuck it. We'll figure everything out later. Can I get you anything else?" He winked and refilled the glasses.

"I think the second one tasted better than the first. I need—"

"They always do. The first one numbs you and the rest just make you feel good." His devious grin suggested more shots, which seconds later came to fruition.

"—drinks. Now that liquor is flowing, let me get a couple fifths of scotch and some sleeping pills. I'll be on my way. I have a busy night ahead. I need to follow up on a lead for a pedophile."

"I don't believe there are people out there like that. How do these guys do that kind of stuff to little kids?"

Pat slammed the bottles of scotch onto the counter. We had drank about half of the whiskey by this time.

"I don't know. This world is fucked. It's only going to get worse."

"You should kill them all, Frank. Fucking kill them all."

"I'll do my best. Always better to sacrifice the sum for the whole."

"I agree one hundred percent." He refilled another set of shots.

"I better get going, Pat." I handed him the money for the smokes and liquor. "Don't worry about the change."

"Alright... I could drink with you all night. Great talking again. Come back soon," he said, slamming the register drawer shut.

"I don't know if I'll see you again. I think I need to get away from all the negativity filling the air we breathe. You know what? I actually do have one more question before I go."

"Sure, buddy. Go ahead." He refilled another round.

"Do you have any more of that special powder you gave me a few years back for the rats?"

He perked up with pride. "Do you mean the *cherolean* powder?"

"Yes, the good stuff. I want all of it."

"You must have some big *rats* to kill. Did you know I'm the only person in the city with this powder? I was taught how to make it in Italy: eat a cherry, then grind the pit, adding a hint of oleander, and voila, you have natural cyanide. A few of my friends working with the Cosa Nostra told me this is how they'd taken care of some of their enemies, including politicians and priests."

"Amazing, and yes, I have big rats to exterminate." I growled, then smiled.

He pulled the vials from an improvised, safe-deposit box located under the counter and handed them to me. "Here you go, Frank. Free of charge. A gift from me to you. I'm going to tell you a secret, but you didn't hear it from me. Two-tenths of a gram will kill a full grown man, which equals one or two cherry seeds. I recommend using about four-tenths just to make sure." He placed a finger over his lips.

"Perfect and I didn't hear a damn thing from you. Thanks."

"You're very welcome. If I don't see you again, have a great life."

Our gazes lingered for a few moments. He poured another round of whiskey. There was less than a quarter bottle left. I hesitated at the door, then exited with authority, entering the car with the same fervor. Before lighting a cigarette, I noticed Pat at the window. A rarity for him to leave the register. We stared at each other for a moment, my eyes sending him a permanent goodbye. I took a long drag as he turned away, screeching the tires as I drove from the parking lot. Next stop: Father Brandon at the Catholic Open Arms Mission.

XXXIII

I parked in front of the shelter, not bothering to hide the vehicle tonight. Standing before the wood door, with its intricate, Christian carvings, I hoped it wasn't locked this time. My prior visit had introduced me to the horrors occurring behind closed Catholic gates. The lock disengaged with a gentle tug. I peered into the foyer. Empty. I crept the hallway, the eyes of Jesus on the posters following my every move under the luminous, bronze sconces. The counter unmanned. I waited for a few minutes. No one showed. Someone had to be here, somewhere.

Tiptoeing, I edged the wall towards the sleeping quarters. A quick glance into the tenebrous room showed all the cots were occupied except one. Still, no sign of Father Brandon or any staff. A faint hiss caught my attention, then a rustle of clothing, a whisper, and the grind of a zipper.

The sounds emanating from behind a set of camouflaged drapes. I leered through their slit and discovered an unlit room with Father Brandon, kissing and fondling a young boy who couldn't have been more than thirteen. Shocked and furious, I stumbled backwards almost falling to the floor. I marched towards the counter, made an about-face to the curtain, then back to the counter.

Stay in control. Don't screw this up, Frank.

I drummed the woodgrain. The intensity increasing to pounds, echoing throughout the shelter.

Fucking prick couldn't resist temptation. I warned him last time.

"Be right out," he said frenzied. He murmured to the boy to get dressed and hide. "I'll be right out. One second, please."

He slinked between the curtains, tucking his clerical shirt into his pants. The white collar hanging over his shoulder.

"How can I help you, Officer?" He gazed towards the floor, realizing I'd returned.

"Hello, *Father* Brandon. Don't be scared. Do you remember me?"

"Not really—maybe. Cops are at the shelter all the time." He attempted to hide his tremulous hands inside his pant pockets.

"Not too long ago, I came here looking for Maggie May's partner. I'm sure you remember. I'm Officer Stark. Frank Stark. Ring any bells?"

"Oh… yes, Mr Stark."

"You can call me Frank. I wanted to personally thank you for helping me find her killer. She's resting in peace because of you."

"That's great, Officer. I mean… Frank."

"I probably stressed you out that night, so I'm here to make it up to you."

"It's quite alright. I'm all set. Just happy I could help."

"I really want to make it up to you, *Father*."

I leaned over the counter and placed my hand on his shoulder. I hoped a gentle touch could break the ice. I realized I didn't have the allure of a child, but I had to try.

"That's very sweet of you," he said, extending his arms towards me, palms facing the ceiling, "but you don't have to repay me. *He* will take care of us."

"I understand how that magical stuff works, but you must accept my gratuity. Isn't that whole church thing about accepting gifts if they're offered?"

"I presume we do, but in this case, we can pass. I'm glad I helped Maggie."

I inched behind the counter. "Father, you must reconsider."

He turned to face me. "It is fine, my son. You don't owe me anything. I will be repaid in due time." He retreated a few steps, his back grazing the wall.

"Father. You don't have to be scared. Everything's okay." I offered a handshake. He refused, fanning it away.

"What's the matter? You can tell me." I extended my hand once again.

"Nothing, Officer. The last time you were here you scared me. I thank you for returning, but I'll have to decline the offer."

"Oh, Father. Is that all? Last time, I was riled because of the case. I never followed through on any of those promises I made. We're perfectly fine. I want to repay you for Maggie May, and because I like you. It's all good. I promise."

Towering over him, I pressed his body against the wall, my breath feathering his hair. My plan taking longer than expected. If it didn't work, then I'd be the victim. I'd lasted this long in life. There'd be no way some rotten-toothed pedophile-priest was going to ruin me.

"Come on, Father. Let me show you a good time tonight. It'll be fun. You deserve it." I leaned closer, placing my hand in his. He reciprocated the embrace. "That's better. Does this mean you'll let me make this up to you?"

"Yes. Fine," he whispered, hanging his head.

Good thing he accepted my offer because I had no backup plan. Most of the people I dealt with were either upon the dissecting table in my dad's basement, or in my bathtub. I'd never thought about handling them in a public place, let alone a homeless shelter for Catholics. It'd be too tricky. And dealing with the children as well. This place would turn into a house of horrors, and that's assuming I could get them all.

"Good answer, Father. Do you have any ideas in mind?"

"I don't. How about you decide?"

"That's an even better answer. I have a few things in mind for us. Drinks and maybe something extra here and there. I promise you won't be disappointed."

"On second thought, I shouldn't."

He released my hand, slithering the small space between me and the counter. Now, standing in the open hallway behind me.

"Look, Father. If I may, Brandon, be blunt. I understand what you're going through. I've been in the same place as you not too long ago. I know it must be difficult resisting all the young boys that come through this shelter. We went through that the last time I was here. I want to give you what you can't get from those young boys. I strongly suggest you go with a man tonight. Do you know what I mean, Brandon?"

"I do. I just don't believe you. Put yourself in my shoes. When was the last time a cop showed up at your workplace to proposition you? Never. I'm a little apprehensive. I'll have to decline, Officer."

"Come on, Brandon. I wouldn't lie to you. Okay. I'll be straight with you. Darnell told me to show you a good time while he's in hospital."

"But, he's missing like his sister, Desiree. All the shelters received a memo about her disappearance. It said to call the police if we have any information. I bet if they find her, they'll find Darnell."

Frank, he's on to you. You better not let him go.

"Well, I'm here. I can assure you they're not missing. We found them at hospital and cancelled that memo."

"That's good to know. I'm so relieved."

"So... let's do this for Darnell and Desiree. Yes?"

"Alright. I'm in. Make sure you tell Darnell I said hi when you see him."

"I promise you'll be able to tell him yourself pretty soon. Let's go get some drinks and maybe afterwards we can hang out. That's if you're cool with everything. No pressure."

He squared a few loose papers on the counter and rearranged a set of pens and pencils into their holder. He pulled a ring of keys from his pocket, fumbled them onto the counter, then picked them up.

"Let's go, Frank. I can use a drink to unwind."

I led the way out of the shelter. He followed, bobbling the keys. I stood on the sidewalk watching him find the correct match for the lock. Growing impatient, I lit a cigarette.

"What's wrong with you? Don't you know which key it is by now?"

"I'm sorry. I'm a little nervous. I've never done this type of thing before."

"Sure you haven't. You've done worse, but it's alright. Let's go."

The deadbolt snapped shut and we proceeded. I swapped my uniform at the rear of the vehicle and hopped into the car.

"If you don't mind, I'm not going to call you Father for the rest of the night. Are you ready, Brandon?"

"Yes, and Brandon is fine. How come there are no lights on the top of this car?"

"It's my personal car. I try to stay low key."

"Where we going?"

I leaned over the center console and tugged at this shirt. "Take off that white collar and put it in the glovebox. Don't look like such a priest tonight. I'm going to take you to heaven and hell." I followed with a nefarious chortle.

"What do you mean heaven and hell?" He lifted his trembling hand and placed it over his heart. "You're making me nervous."

"I'm just kidding for now. The Milky Oyster or Magpie Irish Pub?"

"Oh, I can't go to the Oyster for obvious reasons. Someone might recognize me."

"Alright. We're heading to Magpie on Park Avenue. They make good drinks for me, and since we're friends tonight, they'll treat you well too."

I lit two cigarettes, handing him one, and spun the radio knob. The Doors and Jim Morrison bellowed "When the Music's Over" through the speakers. He turned it off and explained they aren't allowed to listen to the devil's music. I wasn't expecting that response, but I suppose that's how priests reasoned with all their misdeeds: the children, drugs, alcohol, and prostitutes were not of the devil. They were all twisted Jesus attributes in their minds. I could've convinced their cult I was the new savior, carving up bodies for a human sacrifice. For fuck's sake, I'm their closest bet to a god. I decide whether to giveth or taketh life, even providing a proper burial when the time arrives. Because of his outburst, I scared him with reckless driving until we reached Magpie.

"Slow down, Frank."

"Whatever, Father-fuck-off."

"Come on. Please..." He covered his eyes. "I don't want to die on the way to the bar."

"You'll be fine and we're here." I slammed the brakes and turned off the ignition. "One second, Brandon." I reached into my jacket, pulling out a baggie of cocaine. "Do you want some?" I placed several mounds on the armrest, forming them into thick lines with my business card.

"I shouldn't but..." He paused. His knee began to bounce. He placed his hand atop of it, attempting to hold it down. "Okay, I'm in. I do like that stuff, but it's been quite some time."

"Sure it has. You'll be fine."

The bar had a handful of patrons scattered throughout, some seated at tables and others standing. We took two available stools at the corner. Mike served a couple at the other end of the bar. He waved with a thumbs-up. His grand smile suggested a good night, possibly with a date or hefty tips.

Kitty-corner from us sat Jack and Chuck. I acknowledged them with a nod. Two average stocky gents who, depending on the amount of alcohol one consumed, could be handsome. The array of etchings upon their face suggested hard times and long roads travelled. We had exchanged enough conversation throughout the years to make us friends. Our talks usually comical, sprinkled with psychological healing, minus the office setting. The more we drank, the quicker they learned how much I hated the Precinct. On more than one occasion, they offered their experiences to soothe my pain, followed by more drinks.

Chuck sipped his staple drink, a scotch on the rocks with a splash of soda, and Jack drank vodka neat. I got along better with Chuck because he was a retired cop with an endless bar tab. No one knew if he paid it, nor did we care. I don't think he cared either, so we always piled on the orders. Every so often you'd hear random people blare, "Put it on Chuck's tab." Mike always obliged the request and the party never ended. Jack, the neighborhood drunk, had been employed by almost every company in Rochester. Working was not on his top-twenty list. Rumors said his family had enrolled him in a trust fund because he was set to fail from birth.

"Hey, Chuck. Jack. What are you guys up to tonight?"

Chuck swayed his glass towards me, eventually finding half a lip for a sip. "We're getting drunk. How about you? Who's your friend?" He lowered his tumbler, squinting at Brandon. "Who's this guy? He doesn't belong here." The comment brought a laugh from Chuck, Jack, and I, but not Brandon.

"We're here to get drunk. This is my buddy Brandon Biloxi. He works undercover narcotics. Brandon—Chuck Bukowski and Jack Torrance."

Chuck's eyes perked up as his prior suspicion turned into trust. "Good man, Brandon. Make sure you get all the drug dealers and users off the streets."

Jack chimed in with his slurred opinion and swinging arms. "Yup—per, Brandon. Go get them bad—guys..."

Chuck slapped Jack upside the head. "Ignore him. That's how he acts when—" He lifted an invisible glass to his lips. "—he's had too many. Hey, Mike. Get these two a drink on me. Put it on the tab."

"Thanks, Chuck." He responded with a nod and grin. "We'll be right back. We're going to the back to smoke."

Chuck raised his glass, then turning to Jack and restarting their drunken banter. I called Mike over to the backroom, ordering four drinks, two on Chuck's tab and two on mine. I pulled out a pack of smokes and waved

Brandon closer. I flipped the Zippo, the flickering flame setting our faces aglow long enough for the cigarettes to burn. The drinking continued like a determined fever with sporadic bathroom breaks to inhale some energy.

During one of our lulls, he slid across the polished booth, abutting his body to mine. "You're cute, Frank. I like the scar. It's sexy, manly." His fingers trekked up my thigh, stopping at my waistline. "I mean it, Frank. You're very cute and nice." He batted his eyelids at a turtle's pace as I brushed a piece of ash from his clerical shirt.

"Thanks. We should leave. Continue the party at my place."

Mike rang the closing bell. "Last call! Last call for alcohol. Everyone… last call for alcohol. You don't have to go home, but you can't stay here. Finish up your drinks boys and girls. Thank you. Have a good night."

We approached the bar and two shots were lined up, courtesy of Chuck, per Mike. "Let's shoot 'em up." We gulped the shots, slamming the empty glasses atop the bar.

XXXIV

Out the back door we went. A gentle mist and light wind chilling my face produced a false sense of sobriety. Father Brandon, on the other hand, complained every stride. I attributed his diatribes to the consequence of the alcohol, cocaine, and priesthood. He slipped and slid across the glazed grass separating the sidewalk and street. His pair of secondhand shoes no match for his wobbly legs, marching as if on a funhouse floor. His fingers clawed my arms each time he lost footing, and without fail, his knees scraped the pavement. I kept reaffirming the short distance to the apartment, but he wouldn't listen, too occupied convincing the road to stand still. We arrived at the door, he hanging on my back like a concrete cape. I managed to find the keyhole, rushing into the living room and tossing his body onto the couch. I told him to sit still and headed to the bathroom.

An urgency filled my being to bring this night to an end. I patted my pockets and found the sleeping pills, but they lacked a potent mixer, Ambien. I used them last with Elena Gatsfield, a tall, voluptuous redhead from England. I'd met her at Magpie. We spent a couple great nights together, but luck had its way and the third didn't end well. If I loved anything on this earth, it'd be British accents. Rummaging the cabinet, I found the Ambien tucked into a corner, wrapped in foil.

"Wake up, Father," I said as I entered the kitchen.

"Wake up from what?" He waved a weak hand. "It's time for bed."

"No, it's not. Time to party. I'll get you a drink."

"Okay, but I just want the bed."

"You'll go to sleep when I tell you. Soon. I promise."

Thinking of all the children's lives he ruined roiled me: assaulting them, raping them, using them for a diabolical, self-satisfaction, Christian scheme. The kids, emotionally and physically scarred for life, then turned to the allure of drugs, prostitution, or murder. They'd end up at homeless shelters, eventually dying by a needle, a rope, or at the hands of a serial killer. I ground the Ambien and sleeping pills using the edge of a glass and sprinkled the concoction into a sweet drink.

"Come on over, Brandon. I have something for you. You're going to love it. Cranberry vodka."

"Trust me when I say I don't want anything." Torpid, he turned his head, eyes shut.

"Get over here. Now. We made plans and you're honoring them. Pretend I'm a little boy. You'll rest after the drink, asshole. I promise. I'll even swear to your god."

He boosted himself from the couch and pigeon-toed towards me, grunting with each step.

"What do you have for me, Frank?" He steadied himself on my shoulder.

"Drink this juice and you'll be fine. Just like *heaven*."

Trembling, he lifted the sugary blend to his pursed lips. "This tastes so good." He slurped every last drop from the glass. "Thank you for making the drink." Less than a minute later, he spun and crashed onto the floor.

"You should be dead soon, *Father*, but not from the pills. Hope you enjoy." I leaned over his motionless body. "Can you hear me? You're going to have to suffer. You can't get off easy like the others." I knelt beside him and stroked his hair. "Be right back, baby."

I rushed to the bathroom, swiping a comb from the sink, then parted his hair so he looked presentable for his new beginning. The ending far from being realized. His head thumped against the walls and floorboards as I pulled him by the ankles into the bathtub, handcuffing him to the grab-bar.

"I need to get some tools. See you soon."

I set the tool bag cater-cornered to the edge of the bathtub, took a deep breath, and initiated *psyching*. The selections immediate: a Bowie knife, the sturdy sledgehammer, the scalpel, and a filleting blade.

I sliced his clothing with the Bowie knife and stripped him naked. The sharp tip of this knife included a semicircle, which allowed cutting from both sides, and if talented, artistic lacerations. I scored crosses on each of his limbs and torso. The larger the skin canvas, the bigger the cross, ending with a prominent mark atop his forehead. At the center of the crosses, I carved a full circle, then drew a V. A bloodletting trick with artistic flare. He didn't wake, so I followed with a right hook to his face.

"Brandon, you're doing very well. Keep resting because we're going to get creative."

I drew back the sledgehammer like a baseball bat and swung at his right knee, hitting a homerun. His kneecap separated and spun to the back of his leg. His facial expression remained unfazed, confirming he wouldn't wake this evening.

"Father, I have an idea. I want you to be like your favorite person."

I dug into the tool bag searching for nails, then to the closet. Buried behind the box of memories sat a bagful of spikes. Stroking their pointed shafts, I angled his knees together and whacked them with the sledgehammer, repeating the maneuver with his feet, hands, thighs, and ankles. The last one driven into his stomach just below the ribs. I barreled to the basement for a final addition to the masterpiece. Combing between cobwebs, dust, and animal droppings, I located a short piece of barbed wire I'd taken from my parent's home many years ago, never thinking it could be used. I wrapped it around his head, mashing it into the scalp. Jesus would be envious and proud.

A cigarette and scotch breather awaited at the kitchen table, his body in full view from my chair. Blood trickling from his thorn tiara dribbled upon his chest, coalescing with the other open wounds and pooling the tub. From the drain roared a torrential wave that rose to the ceiling, then merged and whirled like a hurricane upon his stomach. Desiree's Georgian accent appeared with identical fervor, echoing throughout the apartment.

"Baby, you need to take care of him real good. He was going to have you arrested and he hurt Darnell."

"You always help me to sort my mind. I've kept your essence smooth, soaking in olive oil."

"I noticed, baby. Thank you. We must focus on Father Brandon, not me. I know you have many ideas for him, but only one is important."

"Tell me, please."

"You must regain your love for human flesh. You don't have to eat all of him, just some of him."

"Which parts, Desiree?"

"His most prized possessions. That same demonic tool he used to hurt all the little boys. Cut it off and split it down the middle. After you've grilled it, slice it into little pieces and add ketchup and mustard. The other item is his heart. It's all muscle, lean. If you eat a raw, human heart, you'll become invincible. You may cook it as well, but eat it raw first. Invincibility is the goal. You have nothing to lose, Frank. Only everything to gain."

"I don't know what I'd do without you. Thank you."

"I must go, baby. We'll talk soon."

I jumped from the chair, spilling the glass of scotch and knocking the ashtray to the floor. I retrieved a frying pan, olive oil, salt, and pepper from the kitchen cupboard, then returned to Brandon. His position unchanged. His head hanging and shoulders caved, his body like a porcupine. Portions of his body jaundice, others highlighted with hints of blues and reds. Surprisingly, his pulse had a faint throb.

Cut him alive, Frankie. The meat's always best when it's fresh.

I locked the scalpel under my index finger and created several long incisions, targeting the arteries in his arms and legs. As I waited for the blood to empty, I smoked a cigarette and sipped a glass of scotch. A hot stream from the showerhead sluiced the plasma pool into the drain.

I clutched the head of his most prized possession, stretching it taut while my other hand placed the filleting knife at its base. One quick slice detached it from his body. At that moment, a liquid as dark as cola sprayed onto my face and chest.

"Damn it. Fucking priest piss. Damn bladder."

I regained my composure and cleansed my body with warm water. I traded the filleting knife for the scalpel and pierced his jugular, draining all the remaining blood.

With the Bowie knife in hand, I stabbed the hollow of his neck just above his chest, the spinal column stopping the penetration. Violent twists dislodged it from the backbone. I continued the Bowie along his chest and into the abdomen until the intestines poured free. I pried open the thin space created in his ribcage with my fingers and ripped it open. Tendons and ligaments stretched and tore like Saran wrap, exposing his heart. It pumped two more times, then went still. Gooey blotches sticking to my hands.

I topped the glass with scotch, filling a small tray with the bits of Father Brandon. At the stove, I stood waiting for the oil in the frying pan to shimmer and smoke. With the filleting knife, I removed the outer layer of white sheathing from the meat. I tossed his prized organ with olive oil, salt, pepper, and a dash of flour, then rolled it in the pan, charring each side, remnants popping and spraying across the stovetop. Within minutes, it resembled a seventh inning hot dog. The ketchup and mustard gave it an extra kick. The meat melted in my mouth like braised pork.

The heart came next. I sliced it thin against the grain, salting three, raw pieces, placing the first onto my tongue. The initial taste bland, but after a few moments the meat liquefied. The remaining portions I cooked to medium rare, more succulent than any tenderloin I'd ever tasted. Invincibility, salvation, and a cure for my disease just around the bend.

An idea came to mind as I chewed the last piece. While searching the cupboards I noticed a cheese grater. Holding the remaining chunk of his heart, and with careful strokes, I slid it against the scalloped edge. Shaved heart piled upon the cutting board. A dash of salt and pepper and a quick fry. More exquisite than the sirloin strips.

Dinner ended with several scotches and cigarettes to help digest Father Brandon. I tucked his clerical collar into the box of memories. Too sluggish with a full belly, I retired to bed. The dismemberment to continue at a later time. A hint of rejuvenation crept through my mind. Closing my eyes, I hoped the heart had cured me.

Letter to Doctor Brazen—November 02

Dear Doctor Brazen,

Happy Day of the Dead. If you're reading this letter, I've left Rochester. Its surroundings have sent me spiraling with no point of return. Your treatment has failed. You are the failure. You wanted to medicate me, but their voices want to be alive, need to be alive.

I've included my journal entries for your reading amusement, but they're only a fraction of the whole story. Don't judge their content. The entries tragic because the Universe wanted them to happen. The end always justifies the means for the greater good of the individual. As you suggested, perhaps, one day, you'll read my memoir and grasp the full picture.

I want to kill myself, but I *cannot*. I want to revive Daniels and Desiree, but I *cannot*. I *cannot* have anything I desire. My world is as dark as the waters of the Genesee

River. The paths crumble below my feet when I walk the streets.

I may or may not contact you in the future. Don't share any of my information with anyone. Remember, we have doctor-patient confidentiality. You won't find me, so don't bother searching. I hope you'll treat patients better than you treated Daniels and myself.

I have concluded people like me don't have any issues. We are sane and people like yourself are actually insane. I hope you find happiness in your dismal world. Good bye and good riddance.

XXXV

A hint of winter pushed through Rochester with single-digit wind chills, a dusting of snow, and icing roadways. Body dumping during these months posed a challenge and not because of the cold. The city diverted water from the Genesee River to reduce bank erosion. From years of experience, I'd charted the deepest sections. The desolate park alleviated any worries from onlookers. I chucked his remains into the frigid waters and watched them sink. With the disposal complete, it was imperative I leave Rochester as soon as possible. It should've begun six hours ago but a brutal hangover hindered progress.

I stuffed the letter and diary entries into a manila envelope and mailed them to Doctor Brazen. The next stop, Rochester Charter One Bank. The larger establishments had squeezed this one dry. Half the letters on their sign were unlit, attached to a crumbling brick façade. A better option would've been an acronym, but bankers aren't creative writers. They'd miss my funds, but I didn't care. Money provided the only route to afford a new life.

Heather LaSalle, a petite, blue-eyed woman with auburn hair welcomed me at the counter. Chiseled cheeks rose above her quirky, sometimes maniacal, smile.

"It's been a long time since we've seen each other," she said.

We dated years ago. Our tumultuous breakup torpedoed any possibility of a friendship. She instilled within me indescribable emotion, which prevented me from butchering her. She had accompanied me to those basement meetings, usually at a church, where everyone sat in a circle describing their addictions and menacing traits. For the first couple weeks, she held my hand like a compassionate warrior. I believed she loved me. I received a thirty-day coin, but once she learned I was only sober during the meetings, all bets were off between us. If only I could've removed her, then I wouldn't have to deal with her condescending attitude today.

"How've you been, Frank?" She twisted her hair, rolling her eyes.

"I'm doing well, and you?"

"Good. Have you sobered up, yet?" Our encounters always as pleasant as walking barefoot in a park littered with hypodermic needles.

"Am I sober? Well, if I have to see you, then I'm not, otherwise, I am."

"Whatever, Frank. I know the true you. What do you need today?" She shuffled some papers on the counter, then tapped the keyboard without looking at the screen.

"Well… a full withdrawal. I'm leaving Rochester. Starting over in another state."

"Where you heading, Frankie?"

"None of your business. Just need the money. Don't call me Frankie. Let's leave it at that, nothing more, nothing less."

"No, Frankie. Where you heading? I promise not to follow you. Tell me and I'll make this easier for you."

"Fine, Heather." I sighed, rapping my fingers along the counter. "I'm moving to Florida, but I'm not telling you the city. Hell, I don't even know."

"Good for you, Frank. Enjoy the white sand and sunshine."

"I will. Can I have my money now? Large bills, please."

"I can't handle a large withdrawal. Looks like you have sixty thousand in the account. I need approval from the manager, then I'll be back with your money. I don't think we'll have any issues. At least, I hope not."

"Fine. I'll wait. Remember, large bills, *please*."

She strutted, accentuating her backside, which I missed, into the backroom. The manager stood behind bulletproof glass, protecting her and the vault. A black outfit didn't flatter her scrawny frame and gaunt face. Dark eyeliner highlighted her beady eyes, glaring at me between wisps of silver hair. Her retirement date well overdue, and if up to me, she'd be more than just retired. I deflected her derogatory stance, scanning the bank for other customers who might delay the withdrawal. The only one, an old lady ten years beyond her expiration. Empty chairs abutted plaid wallpaper atop a matching carpet as old as disco. Thirty minutes ticked at a crawl on the oversized clock ahead. My heart raced. Sweat, probably reeking of alcohol, forming atop my forehead.

"I'll be right there. We're all set," she said, peering from behind the safety glass.

"Finally, you hag," I mumbled, raising my thumb and waving.

Several minutes later, they exited the backroom. The manager lurching from the weight of the black duffle bag. She heaved it atop the counter, cursing me with her stare, then retreated to her office, adjusting her disheveled hair.

"It's all there. We counted it several times. You're welcomed to count."

"I'm all set. I'm sure the machines didn't make a mistake."

"Have a great rest of your life, Frank. The bank and I thank you for your business. Try to stay sober and take care of those eyes."

She always had to get in the last word. Arguing at the bank would only delay me further. I winked with a spiteful smile and rushed home to drop off the money. I gathered the police uniforms from the closet and the ground cherry seeds.

I hurried through the Precinct to the Captain's office with my head lowered, ignoring everyone.

"Captain, we need to talk." I slammed the door and dropped the uniforms beside me.

"Go ahead. I don't think I'm going to stop you but I have a—"

"Anyway, I've been doing some thinking." I avoided eye contact. "I'm resigning my post as an officer."

"What the hell happened to your face, Frank?"

"Never mind that… I'm quitting."

"You can't just quit. You barely even work as it is."

"Whatever. I work. Anyway, I need to leave this place. It's not healthy for me."

"You've been on the force for fifteen years. What's bothering you? Is it the Oliva case? The drinking? What's your psychiatrist say about this?"

"No need for all the questions. Doctor's orders. This job and city are killing me inside and out. I can't deal with it any longer."

"Why don't you take some more time off to think about it?" He nodded. "That's the least you can do before making any rash decisions."

"Sir, I've made it. Time to go." I placed my gun and badge on his desk and slid them towards him.

"This doesn't make any sense, Sarge. You're not the quitting type. You have a lot of invested time. Something else must be up."

"Well, Captain, I guess you don't know me very well." I leaned over the desk, our eyes locked in a blinking duel. "Screw this place. Take that damn badge and gun. Let's close this chapter of our lives."

"Alright, Sarge. If your mind's made up, then I accept your resignation. Good luck with everything. Hope you have a great life. Where you headed by the way?"

"Going to throw a dart at one of the fifty states. When I get there, I'll know."

I lifted the uniforms from the floor and threw them onto his desk.

"Alright, Sarge. Pleasure working with you." The Captain offered a handshake and I obliged. "Did you ever have these cleaned?"

"Sometimes."

"More like never. They smell like shit," he said, fanning his face. "You realize laundry is a free service at the Precinct?"

"Doesn't matter."

"I suppose it doesn't, but we're going to have burn these things. You ruined them. What the hell? Did you wallow in a bucket of manure and cologne? You have some serious issues, Stark."

I stormed from his office, lowered my head, and headed to the Rook's desk.

"Hey, Rook. How about that coffee I promised?"

"Thanks for remembering. What happened in the Captain's office? Your face is—"

"Don't worry about that. I'll be right back with your coffee. Have a seat. Do you like your coffee sweet?"

"Yes, of course."

I filled two, large cups, mine black, and his loaded with cream and sugar. From my pocket, I retrieved the vial of cherolean powder. Several stirs dissolved it into the Rook's coffee, which was enough to take care of a two-hundred-pound man. Good thing he weighed thirty pounds lighter. I marked his cup with a blue stirrer and returned to the desk.

"Here you go, Rook. Hope you enjoy." I handed him the cup with a welcoming grin and a wink.

"Thanks, Sarge. Remember we talked about this. I prefer to be called Joe." He took a long sip. "This coffee tastes really good with a hint of cherry."

"My pleasure, *Joe*. The cherry is from the cream. Drink up, Rook."

"How've you been? We've missed you at the Precinct. And your face?"

"Never mind about that. I've been well. I don't know what the future holds but so far so good." I sat across from him and lit a cigarette.

"I want to apologize for the Oliva case and for what happened to Daniels."

He stood and extended his hand. I didn't bother shaking it, instead blowing a cloud of smoke in his face. He didn't like that too much. Swallowing the last gulp of coffee, he slammed the cup atop the desk.

"Don't bother apologizing." I kicked my chair against the wall. "Leave me alone, Rook. I quit this damn job. I'll never have to see your ugly, annoying face again."

"Whatever, Stark. Too bad for you." He slapped the empty cup onto the floor. "If you were a little smarter, you would've stayed here a little longer. Maybe a promotion was in your cards. Now, I'll have to take your position. I'll be the king of this palace."

"Take it, Rook. You're nothing but a crooked suck-up. This city doesn't need any more of your kind. I promise it'll catch up to you in the near future. You won't even know it hit you."

"What's going to catch up to me?" He inched closer to my face. "Don't you threaten me. I'm not like you, Frank. You—" He gagged with one hand on the back of the chair, the other on the edge of the desk. "—you're the one that'll be chased down and haunted. Good luck getting away from your demons. Daniels was right about that devil ring you wear. Belial is going to be the end of you, just as it was for him."

"Screw you." I shoved him and rushed towards the exit. A few minutes longer and a fight would've ensued. "In a few hours you'll pay for all that you've done." I forced the door open, bouncing it from the concrete wall. It slammed shut.

Outside the entrance his voice whirled. "What the hell is he talking about? I'm not paying for anything. That guy is nuts. Good bye, Stark. Moron. To hell with you."

At home, I filled a suitcase with everything I owned, loading it into the trunk, along with the sacred tool-bag and money. I stopped at Pat's to offer one last goodbye. Unfortunately, he wasn't there and neither was his daughter. A teenage clerk explained Pat had taken some time away to spend with family.

"Ten cartons of cigarettes and two cases of scotch. Tell Pat, I'm headed to find a new life with white sand and sunshine."

I handed him a few hundred dollars and told him to keep the change. His gaping mouth suggested he'd won the lottery.

PART TWO

XXXVI

The trip to Florida took longer than expected. A simple two-day trip extended into weeks, venturing through multiple states along the east coast with stops in each one, at times to rest, and others to fill the box of memories. I-95 South delivered me across the Georgia-Florida line into Jacksonville. A blue sign with shimmering white letters greeted me: Welcome to Florida, The Sunshine State. A series of unexpected turnabouts, too many sips of scotch, erred esses, and missed off-ramps deviated my trek to Fort Lauderdale, placing me onto I-75 South. After driving about a hundred miles, I realized the accuracy of their slogan. The sun had nowhere to hide and the temperature must've been a hundred. Several blurring mile markers later, and this time, an oversized orange billboard gleamed: Come to Fort Myers & Visit the Salty Marina, Turn Left before the Matanzas Bridge SR 865. I followed its lead, running low on energy.

SR 865 brought me south. The road, I later realized, transitioned to San Carlos Boulevard. Not more than a mile or two, and another sign welcomed me to South Fort Myers, Estero Island. Florida should be considered the "Sign State" as well as the Sunshine State. Glancing out either window, the sun beamed the turquoise Intracoastal canals, which led to the revered Gulf of Mexico. In the distance, straight ahead, the Matanzas Bridge. Its towering height made viewing the other side impossible.

I lowered the window to glimpse the last stretch of water before arriving at the destination. A sudden chill filtered through the car, crawling across my chest like a centipede. I swatted the skin, but the tingling persisted. The air conditioner off, I scanned the canal, and floating above its calmness, Desiree, Maria and Juliette. Their feet skimmed the surface. In unison, they dove its depths. The water rose, a red tidal wave as tall as a house followed, pursuing the car. I swerved, almost clipping the concrete median, then accelerated, realigning the fishtailing wheels. The water surged, the crest crashing the roof, cascading the sides, and filling the interior. I gasped a breath before it squeezed my chest and rose above my head. The car sped, walloping my body against the interior. Submerged, I pawed to find an exit. The water now blood, burning my eyes, then without notice, the car screeched to a halt. I gulped, craning my head over the steering wheel. A shoddy sign affixed to a wooden post leaned against the bumper and hood, illuminated by the headlights. Its dripping black letters appeared drawn by a finger: The Salty Marina, Access to the Gulf. An arrow pointed away from the parking lot.

I tumbled from the car, hunching to regain a breath, and lit a cigarette. Standing, I gulped a swig from the flask, and in the distance heard Doctor Brazen bickering about episodes. I left my belongings in the trunk in case they didn't have any accommodations. The marina silent, not a purring outboard-motor, nor a wandering sailor cackling.

As I tromped towards the main entrance, devious limbed shadows flitted about, some descending from the sky with elongated legs, some stretching from the ground, and others encircling the flickering tiki-torches lining the walkway. One broke free from each pack, three in total, and rushed towards me, whisking through my hair and knocking me to the pavement. They swarmed, hovering, whispering with a high-pitched whistle, each incoherent word boring into my skull, drips dribbling across my earlobe and down my neck. Each attempt to sit impossible. My jaw locked open, unable to scream. A prickling wave rolled the length of my arms, both pinned to the ground. The whispering pitch rose, then silenced. A shadow, on either side, flipped my arms, palms facing the ether. The third rolled my sleeves to the bicep and strapped them with a tourniquet. For a brief moment, they lifted my arms to show me their plotting. Each pulsing, muscle fiber plucked through the skin, stretched and twisted like licorice. They smacked my arms against the ground. The third shadow flew the night sky, and just as I thought it disappeared, it returned with an urgency, floating above my chest, then throwing hundreds of syringes like daggers into every exposed fibril atop my arms. I fainted, regaining consciousness much later. Several of the tiki torches had expired. I rolled onto my side and lit a cigarette, taking a few deep drags, then rose to my feet and shook my head. They must've been tricks caused by Florida's setting sun against her sky, a much different sky than New York. I tipped another swig and walked onward.

Frank, I think it was an episode. We can't have those anymore.

"It's fine. I'm cured. Leave me alone."

A stout man with squinting eyes, surrounded by well-oiled wrinkles, met me at the front desk. He greeted me with howdy and a peculiar look, probably because I was mumbling to myself. His bloated, peeling cheeks had spent too many days in the Florida sun. The rest of his face was hidden behind an untamed, peppered beard. He reminded me of someone, but I couldn't quite place him. Multiple tattoos lined both of his large arms. His left bicep was covered with two bleeding swords that penetrated a skull, and on the other, a naked Betty Boop being raped by a robot holding a spear. Both forearms were stamped with various portraits, interwoven skulls, and crossed daggers. Certain sections were blotted black and others were covered with burn scars, a sure sign his former motorcycle gang gave him a pass to avoid the morgue.

"How can I help you, bud?" His deep, southern voice had endured many years of drinking and smoking.

"I moved to Florida from New York. Looking for a place to stay, preferably on a boat." Our hoarseness an initial commonality.

"Well, bud. I can probably help you. I got everything you want and need in Florida."

"Good to know you have it all. Does that mean you can get me drinks, drugs, and whatever else I need?"

My throaty chuckle and sarcasm wasn't well received. His welcoming tone whiplashed into castigation. "Hey, bud. You better slow down here. Are you a cop or something? We don't want any trouble down here in Florida. We do it our own special way and don't need Yankees coming down here starting trouble."

"I'm sorry, man. Just joking. Didn't mean anything by it. I'm not a cop. I hate cops. I left the north because of them."

"Alright... good. Then we're going to get along since we both don't like cops." His beard rose with a smile. "Remember, I don't want any trouble around here. What type of boat you have in mind?"

"A big boat." I stretched my arms the length of the counter. "So I can sail the Gulf and the Atlantic. I want to be free."

"Well... A big boat is going to cost you. Hope you have money." He combed his fingers through his beard. "I have a thirty-foot yacht out on the dock. It's old and just repossessed with two bedrooms, one bath. One bedroom's still wrapped, never been used after the renovation. You know that's a big boat? You ever sailed?"

"Sure, of course, I can sail. If you've driven one boat, you've driven them all." Freedom moistened my lips as I licked them. "How much?"

"It'll cost you thirty thousand. Cash. Thirty by check, but we don't take checks. It's your call, Yankee."

"I'll take it." I extended my hand across the counter and we sealed the deal with a handshake. "Since we made a deal, I need something else from you." Still holding his hand I pulled it towards me.

He tightened his potent grip, his cheeks blushing, as an uneasy silence lingered between us. "What do you need, boy? I don't play games." He surveyed me with his grey eyes. "I don't need any trouble or cops around here. Remember?"

"You don't have to worry. I'm not a cop. Remember? I just want your name before I bring you the money—and of course, the keys."

"Oh... okay, bud." He released his grasp. "My name is Brock—Brock Youngblood. I'm not so young anymore. And yours?"

"Funny joke. Okay, Brock Youngblood, my name is Frank—Frank Strongman. I'll be right back with your money."

I counted the money into piles under the trunk light, then stuffed the bills into a paper bag, and headed to Brock. "Here you go." I slid the bag across the counter. "Money's all there. Count it if you want."

He removed the bills from the bag and stacked them atop the counter, covering every inch of it. He counted through half the pile. "I don't need to count the rest. I trust you, bud. Looks all there, plus I know where to find you. Glad we can start a friendship with a boat deal. Follow me. I'll take you to your new home, so you can get some shuteye."

The walk from the front desk to the floating dock measured several hundred feet, passing the marina bar, Shrimps 'N' Drinks. The hanging sign depicted a tattered shrimp dipped into a Martini glass. The paint and images battered by the relentless sea spray from the Gulf of Mexico. The bar faced a wooden pier leading to a plethora of boat slips and my new home.

"Is that place any good, Brock?"

"Yeah, bud. It's got good strong drinks and televisions all around. Good food too. Jenna's been here for years. One of the best bartenders in town."

"Are there any hot people that come through here? You know… nice looking."

Brock turned towards me and stopped. "Yeah. I suppose so," he said, tilting his head. "You put enough drinks in you and they all look good." He restarted his stroll and I followed. "We get all kinds down here in Florida, young to old, all colors of the rainbow. Some passing through and some staying. Like Key West, we're an open community and accept everyone, except cops. A word for the wise: you'll always find what you're looking for in Florida, if you let it find you. Sometimes better not to search."

"I'll keep that in mind."

"I've been meaning to ask you. How come your eyes are so red?"

"Oh… just allergies or something."

"Better get some of those eye drops. Here we are, Frank." He handed me the keys. "Slip C 103. Boat's name is *All Behind Me.* The name didn't work out so well for the last guy, or I suppose it did. Anyway, as you can see, it's fully furnished," he continued in a salesman's voice, his dancing hands too quick to follow, pointing and turning throughout the cabin, "beds, fridge, stove, and couch. Everything you need, except a mirror. The other guy stole it. Moving on. Bathroom is at the back of the boat. We have two cockpits on this boat: one under the canopy on the wide-open second floor, and the other enclosed on the first. Both cockpits have two radios: standard and Ham. One's used for listening to the news and weather, and the Ham to talk to other boats." He pointed at the room with its door closed. "That room is the wrapped room. We can take the wrap off for you, or you can do it yourself."

He opened the door. Every inch of the room layered in bubble wrap and cellophane. Somewhat homey. I should've had a room like this in Rochester, instead of using tarps, totes, and a bathtub. Then again, rewrapping it every so often might be a hassle. Those situations are long gone.

That's a nice room, Frank. We're all going to love our new home.

"Perfect. Thanks for everything. I'll take care of it myself. Do you want to grab a drink, Brock?"

"Yeah. Shrimps. Least I can do is buy you a drink for spending the big twenty. Jenna's gone home for the night, but I can serve them just as good."

"I'm looking forward to a few drinks. It's been a damn long ride from New York."

"Screw that kind of driving. I'll show you around the waterways someday. We can go fishing for sharks."

"Great." I wanted to say no way in hell. Sitting on a boat for ten hours doing nothing isn't my cup of tea. I'll do the drinking, but no way am I holding a fishing pole for that long.

We drank until the early morning hours. He stumbled to his living quarters and I snaked to the parking lot. I found a proper spot for the car away from the entrance. With all my belongings in hand, I dragged them to my new home, weaving and wobbling atop the maze of floating docks. I'd make a wholehearted attempt to forget my prior life in Rochester because the future offered better opportunities: new friends, new home, and no negativity. I situated all my important items into the wrapped room, drank a few more, and fell asleep atop my new bed.

XXXVII

The Florida sun and a liquor indulgence obscured the days and weeks. The large stash of drugs untouched. The vodka had even taken precedence over the scotch, which I deduced to be a major contributor to the debauchery. One certainty existed within my life: everything is always too good to be true. The struggles in Rochester had receded into unreachable areas, until they showed up, but with all honesty, it wasn't my fault.

Jenna rang the midmorning bell, signaling the start of happy hour. Shrimps charged a flat rate to drink all day, but they gouged me on the boat slip rental fee. I wrenched the final bolt on the mast of a touring boat. From its bow, I noticed Brock waving. He'd hired me for various menial jobs that paid well with a handful of drinks as a perk.

"Come on, Frank. Break time."

"I'm ready for a drink." I confirmed with a salute, then trotted to Shrimps to sit upon my usual center stool.

"Are you going with the same or are we changing it up today?"

Jenna smirked, indifferent to our prior drunken interactions. I nodded, a cigarillo between my lips, its ashes feathering the countertop. The pull was much smoother, and per Brock, healthier than cigarettes, although health really didn't matter to me. Based on my daily rituals for the last few decades, I'd been dead for over a hundred years.

"Same, Jenna—Jenna Loving. I still can't get over that name of yours. Suits you well. Vodka rocks with two limes. I don't want to sway the boat too much with the scotch."

"Good pun, Frank. Coming right up. Let me know if you ever want to switch."

My buzz kicked into overdrive, swaying the stool beneath me. Hours had passed with dusk approaching. From the end of the bar, a slender twenty-something clopped atop the planked floor wearing heels and a string bikini. Free-flowing raven hair bounced above a toned waistline. The Caribbean queen slithered upon the stool beside me, wafting coconut from skin basted with suntan oil.

"Excuse me." I grazed her arm as I inched closer. "Let me buy you a drink."

"Alright. By the way, I love the beard and long hair. I'll take a rum on the rocks with lime."

I hadn't cut my hair or shaved in months. The curls lingered below my shoulders and my beard resembled a lumberjack. My inner Samson roused with her appreciation. I raised my glass with unabashed exuberance.

"Perfect, just like you." Her ebony eyes lured me into her soul. "You know... you're really beautiful."

"Thank you, sweetie. What's your name sexy man?"

"Frank." Mesmerized by her spell, I proposed the lamest question imaginable. "And your name must be gorgeous?"

"You're too sweet." Her bronze cheeks swelled. "My name is Des—"

"Let me guess. It's... Des—iree."

"No..." She smirked. "But who's this Desiree?"

"Someone I used to know. Never mind. Let's get back to you. My apologies."

"Well, they call me Delicious Destiny. Just like... *I'm* your destiny. And the other... well, you can guess." She licked her upper lip.

"What if *they* don't call you? What's your name then?"

"That'd be Destiny Petit. It's French."

"*S'il vous plait,* Destiny," I said with a mismatched accent. They were the only French words I knew, learned from a tourist.

"How did I know that was coming?"

"I'm just trying to break the ice. Let me get you another drink."

"Of course. And, I forgive you."

"Let's start over. Where are you from, Destiny?"

"I'm from everywhere, mostly Cali, born in Martinique with family in France. I'm doing a photoshoot on the white sand beaches. Unfortunately, I'm enjoying it all alone." She pouted, then grinned. "I may need some company tonight."

"A model? That was my first guess. They tell me I make for good company."

"Perfect, because I have a question for you. Do you like to *ski*? I really could use some." She pointed to her nose, then stroked my back, twirling my hair. Her touch tingled the space between my shorts.

"I suppose I can oblige." I attempted to say no, but I couldn't resist the sexuality. Those eyes, those heels, the bikini like dental floss. "I believe I have some on my boat. Let's go have some fun and find out what's under that swimsuit." And in a blink of an eye, my prior life under the cloud infested skies of Rochester returned with a fury.

Her nails skimmed my shoulders, down my back, and circled upward, raising more than just arm hair. I adjusted my seat, hoping to hide the bulge between my legs.

"Sounds like a plan. I need to get out of this bikini anyway. It's too tight." She flicked the strap of the top, then yanked it down for a peep. "I'm pretty sure you're going to like what you see underneath."

Jenna approached. "These are your last two drinks. Sorry, I'm closing up. You can take them to go," she said, filling the glasses.

"Thank you, Miss Loving. We'll guzzle them now. Put them on my tab, give yourself a hefty tip, and have a good night."

"You have a goodnight as well. I'm thinking it'll be better than mine."

We headed to the boat with our fingers interlocked and her ankles like jelly. A rule to live by: Don't drink and high heel. She bounced between me and the ropes lining the planked walkway. I guided the small of her back through the hull. She crawled the fiberglass walls until she reached the couch, then fell onto her back. She arched her long, tanned legs, soliciting me to sit beside them. I didn't hesitate, helping her remove the straps to her top. She flung it across the room. It had been so long, the beauty of a naked woman had escaped my mind. My arousal immediate. A moistened finger from her lips traced each breast, then fondled each nipple.

"Bring me some of that snow so I can ski."

"Yes. I'll be right back."

I obeyed like a submissive servant, rushing into the wrapped room. In the corner, below a set of shelves and behind a camouflaged, carpet door, sat all my valuables. I flipped the latch and slid out the box of memories, placing

Desiree upon a shelf. I hadn't viewed her essence since leaving Rochester. From deep within the compartment, I retrieved a large bag of cocaine and a spoon, scooping a few mounds onto a small mirror, the only one I'd purchased for the boat and never used. Between the sprinkles of snow, Desiree's reflection appeared, just as youthful as when we made love.

"Hey, baby… Do you miss me?"

"I can't talk right now. I'm busy."

The olive oil within the jar bubbled and the mounds of cocaine shivered. My head snapped backwards, skull quaking, unknown hands stretching my scalp. The powder atop the mirror levitated, then blasted up my nose. My body thrown against the wall. I shuddered to regain consciousness, snaking the cellophane wall to regain footing.

"Are you okay in there, Frank? I need you to hurry up with the snow."

Better come up with an excuse, Frankie.

"Yes… I'll be right out." Vision blurred. "I'm making drinks." The oil had stopped bubbling, which hopefully signaled a stop to this madness.

"You need to do something special for me tonight."

"Please let me be…" I shook my head with disagreement, but my response opposite. "What do you want me to do?"

"Have sex with Destiny after you've fed her the cherolean powder."

"I've been doing well. I don't want to go back. Please, Desiree…"

"Do as I say. They all say you must. You cannot change who you are, Frank. This is your *destiny*."

Like a robot I extracted a vial of cherry powder from the box of memories, mixing some in the vodka cranberry and some with the cocaine. I set the drink upon the coffee table and held the mirror beneath her chin. She shoveled the mounds into her nose with a long, manicured fingernail, then sighed and reclined.

I handed her the vodka cranberry. "I don't have any rum, but it'll chase the drip in your throat just the same. A sweet drink for a sweet girl."

The drink disappeared as fast as another shot of powder. She scooted next to me, and threaded my hair, tugging me to venture between her legs. As I made contact, I realized why they called her delicious. A medley of pineapple, strawberry, and mangoes flooded my tongue. Her moans escalated to uninhibited howls. She clawed my back and arms leaving her mark, culminating with fistfuls of hair as she climaxed.

"It's my turn."

She knelt between my legs. Enraptured, she held me, then dipped a finger between her legs. Dampened, she swiped the cocaine from the mirror and brushed her gums. "Do you like this? Do you like me?" I could only muster a moan as her tongue glided over me. Insatiable, she clamped her nails into my thighs and swallowed me whole.

I thrusted, baying like a wolf, expelling weeks of pent-up lust. She retreated, sitting upon her feet, tears of pleasure streaming her cheeks while creamy remnants trickled her chin.

"You need to be inside me now."

I obeyed, sliding over her body and into her ocean. As my hand inched around her neck, she convulsed with a pink foam driveling from her mouth. Each of my repeated thrusts invoked a gasp while her quivering ebony eyes disappeared.

"How does it feel, Des—iree? Do you want it harder, deeper?" I thought I heard a faint yes. No turning back. I clamped her neck with both hands. "Wasn't that amazing Des—tiny?" What little was left inside me burst into her motionless body. She didn't respond.

I checked her pulse. None existed. She had succumbed to the cherolean powder quicker than I imagined. I must've added too much. I gentled her lips, her breasts, her supple stomach, and those smooth, tanned legs. Nothing good ever lasts long. Grasping her ankles, I dragged the body across the abrasive carpet to the cellophane room, leaving a sticky trail of spit, hair, and skin.

"Destiny... Destiny... Can you hear me?"

An unwavering seductive beauty still existed in her glossed eyes. She couldn't be dead. She had to be alive. Her gorgeous body probably resting after our sexual escapade.

"Do you still like me?"

She nodded with confirmation. Eyelids flittered, then a whisper. "Yes, Frank. Make love to me."

I lifted her limp legs, fondling the space between them. The lingering juices affirmed her enthusiasm. Oddly, she wouldn't respond to any questions, although her spastic body conveyed the pleasure. My final thrust met by the rising sun through the porthole. I nestled beside her in a post-sexual trance.

"Hey, bud." The hull door clacked and shuddered. "We have some work to do. You ready?"

"Fuck. Fuck. Fuck." No time to panic and no need to approach the door. "Hey, Brock. All good. I can't make it this morning. I'm hungover and need to... pick up a... buddy at another port thing. Yes. A buddy at a port."

"What do you mean? We have plans. We got work to do."

"I'm sorry. He flew in from Rochester and took a cab to the wrong marina. I have to get him. I'll be back later to help you. Sorry for the short notice."

The door creaked open, his sandal snapping against the first step. "I can help you go get him. Do you need my help, bud?"

"Stop! I'm all set. Don't come down. I'm naked. I'll see you later. I promise."

"Okay. Talk to you later, bud." The door closed and his flip-flops thwacked into the distance.

"See you later, Brock," I said, nuzzling within Destiny's hair.

I removed the tool bag from the compartment and stood, wondering the reasons for my comeuppance. Life had been well, except during the drive to Florida. I closed my eyes, held my breath, and initiated *psyching*. The tools for Destiny: a cleaver, a carving knife, and the Santoku blade. I dismembered Destiny in much the same way as the others, a cut here, a chop there, although, I left most of her torso intact. The wrap unappreciated until this moment; the stacked body parts not seeping their fluids into the carpet. During my stops to Florida, I accustomed myself to an *à la carte* process. Ingenuity replaced the old methods, some disposed in the woods and others in marshes or landfills. Today, I graduated to a yacht, much different than the rowboat I paddled on the Cape Fear River in North Carolina.

I exited the slip and set sail to find a perfect location for her remains. Several hours of navigating the serene waters didn't bring me to the Gulf of Mexico, but a fortunate wrong turn led me to a swampy inlet. The only onlookers, a pack of wide-eyed alligators sunbathing on the bank. I learned long ago if you put out the grub, they'll always nibble.

I scattered her parts across the inlet as the boat trolled. The alligators swam towards the floating remains, snatching them up in a wrestling frenzy. Easy as making tea. I washed my hands in the clear, warm water and headed home. The orange orb creeping the horizon disappeared as I pulled into the Salty Marina. Brock stood at the dock, as if waiting, watching for me all day at that same spot.

"Where you been, Frank?" He tied the mooring line to the boat cleat.

"Sorry, man. My buddy sent me to the wrong marina, then I got lost on the waterway. I'll make up the work tomorrow. I need to get some rest from sailing. Do you have any bleach and garbage bags I can borrow? I ran into some muck."

"Sure. Just one question. Where's your friend?"

"Good question. Well... he... he decided to stay at that beach for a couple more days. You know how it is, Brock. Friends just aren't reliable."

"Odd, but I'll take your word for it." From a canopy shed he returned with the items. "Will this do, bud? Do you need more?"

"No. That should do the job. Have a goodnight. See you in the morning."

"Okay. Have a good night."

Simple cleaning turned into feverish scrubbing across the plane of the cellophane and carpet floor. Flesh, bone, and blood-soaked rags filled the garbage bags. I discarded the items into the dumpster, then stumbled through the hull. With Destiny's bikini secure in the box of memories, I sipped a tumbler filled with scotch and drowsed.

XXXVIII

The walk to work, only a few hundred feet, sluggish with a pounding headache. Considering all the drinking-practice I'd had in life, I still found shaking its effects impossible. The stagnant air saturated with brackish humidity didn't help either. Panting, I toweled the pooling sweat from my brow and beard to no avail. An unrelenting spigot under the midday sun burning shadows onto my skin. The day no different than any other, spent wrenching on various engines and sorting miscellaneous issues from the marina customers. As I secured a damaged aluminum hull from a small boat to a couple sawhorses, Brock shouted, signaling from the service desk.

"Hey, bud. Can I talk to you for a couple minutes?"

"Yeah. No problem. Be right there."

I confirmed with a wave, wondering what the hell he wanted, knowing all too well the difficulty drying from a swim in a liquor bottle. I suppose there's never a good time to talk, but it hurt more than usual today.

"Is everything going well for you at the marina, Frank?"

"Yeah, sure." I shrugged with indifference. "I like it here and appreciate the work. The extra funds help."

"Good to hear, bud. I wanted to ask you about the bleach and bags." He eyed his boot kicking the base of the counter. "Did you need them to clean the boat or is there something else you need to tell me?"

"Yes, of course, I cleaned the boat. And no, there's nothing else to tell." I squared my shoulders and held a poker face. "I have two complaints, which may or may not be your problem: the dumpster is too far of a walk, and the bleach inside the boat is too strong."

"What do you mean *inside* the boat? You said the outside got cruddy."

"Yes, I cleaned the outside, but the odor somehow floated inside. Where else would I clean? Maybe the toilet, but I didn't."

"I have another question." He flexed his tattooed arms across his chest with an inquisitive grunt. "What happened to that girl from the bar?"

"Well... we had some fun together, then she bolted. Some modeling thing in... Miami."

"That's odd, bud." He leaned over the counter and sized me up. "Miami doesn't make sense since we just received mail for her."

"I don't know anything, man." I raised my hands. "She said she's a model from California or France. Somewhere. Anyway, beauty like that is always crazy and unpredictable. They come and go as they please. They own the world." I recoiled my arms, resting them upon the counter and whispered, "Between you and me, I'm upset. I had a pretty good chance with this one. Her ride probably came by this morning. She was gone when I awoke."

"I guess you're right, Frank. Those types *are* crazy. Reminds me of my three exes, each marriage worse than the prior. Odd, her mailing address is the Salty Marina. She must've had a better option in Miami. I bet when she returns, you'll both hook up again."

"I don't think she's coming back," I said, twisting my lips.

"What makes you think that?"

He probably thought he had me, but I'm always trying stay one step ahead. Lie on the fly. I did her a favor, saving her from the inevitable cocaine overdose in some dingy hotel room.

"Miami versus Fort Myers. I'm betting she stays in Miami. That's what I'd do."

"Good point. Forget I asked. Let's go get a drink, bud." Brock stepped from behind the counter, drilling his fingers into my shoulder, guiding me towards the bar. "I'm glad you're here. Always nice to have good people around. Hey, Jenna, a round of drinks for us, please."

"No problem, boss. You buying the next couple rounds?"

"Of course. Put 'em on the house tab. A quick shot for me and I'll be right back. Have to take care of something. Lady complaining on Dock Ten."

"Will do. How about you, Frank? Do you want the same, vodka lime?"

"No. Let's switch it up. Scotch, please. I wouldn't mind a little extra," I said with a wink.

"You doing alright and liking it here? You look pretty rough." She poured a double. "Those eyes of yours look like they're bleeding."

"I'm okay. I forgot my eye drops today. Allergies or something. I've been keeping busy with all the work Brock gives me and enjoying the weather at the same time." I retrieved the aviators from my pocket and slipped them on.

"Always great weather while you work, and during the summer—" She nudged my elbow. "—you're cooled by an onshore gust with a short downpour."

She snapped the bar towel towards the ceiling. It fell like a parachute, sliding over her hand like a glove. Swift strokes soaked up the spilt alcohol atop the counter. Across the way, a paunchy older couple, guessing early eighties by the depth of their wrinkles and thinned platinum locks, drank Bloody Marys. Never understood why older women always decide to cut their hair as short as their male counterparts. It's as if their mirrors only reflect one blended image. They'd bicker for a bit, which resembled a sibling spat, pause for a sip, then return to their heated rants. I guess at that age there's nothing left but alcohol and bitching. Jenna spun towards the wall of liquor and wiped down a bottle, then swung her head upwards, her mane whiplashing behind her, and did a double take at the television screen above. The ancient couple silenced, then the woman blurted that's my city.

Jenna sprinted to the other end of the bar, grabbed the remote, and turned up the volume. "Oh, gosh. Oh my g—. Do you see that, Frank? It's a special bulletin. Breaking news! I just love these things."

I nodded, taking a long sip, and followed her lead. What I saw on the screen didn't bode well for me. The images too familiar as well as some of the people. I rested the drink, exchanging the cigarillo for a cigarette.

CBS, with its affiliate WROC, reported the news by Dan Pass as follows:

"We're bringing you late-breaking news. This is a special report. Late-breaking news. We have a series of unfortunate events in Rochester, New York. There's a crime scene unfolding at the Genesee River within Genesee Valley Park. This murky river runs parallel with the city of Rochester and was, at one time, its lifeblood. Just in—we've confirmed two bodies have been recovered. They were chopped and stuffed into totes. There may be more, but it's unconfirmed.

"We're being told the police were tipped by the assailant's former doctor. Her name is Doctor Matilda

Brazen. She's a well-known and respected psychiatrist in the Rochester community. Doctor Brazen went to the police with a letter sent to her by the assailant. The assailant's name is Frank Stark. I repeat, Frank—Stark. The letter included detailed diary entries of people he'd killed. Doctor Brazen stated and I quote, 'I couldn't abide by the doctor-patient confidentiality clause because these lives mattered. The families of the deceased need closure. Mister Stark must be brought to justice for the heinous crimes he's committed.'

"I apologize if I keep interrupting the story, but this is a fluid situation, and we're receiving new information by the minute. We are being told that Mister Stark included his possible whereabouts in the letter. He may be in California, Arizona, or Las Vegas, Nevada. Those areas must be considered as possible, not actual, locations. The police are saying Mister Stark could be anywhere, and he may have included that information to throw police off his trail.

"They're telling me that Frank—Stark was a former police sergeant at the RPD, the Rochester Police Department. We've placed his picture on the screen. Note: the picture is a few years old. The police said their artists are working diligently to create updated sketches, which will include what he may look like with a beard and long hair.

"This just in from the RPD... Frank Stark is also accused of poisoning and killing Sergeant Joe Russo. Joe was new to the force and had just been promoted to Sergeant. We, at WROC, offer our condolences to his family, friends, and brothers in blue. Frank Stark is ruthless. Back to our report.

"This is Dan Pass. The police are asking if you know his whereabouts to please contact the RPD by dialing 585-254-3230. He's considered armed and dangerous—this just in—the scuba team has discovered two more bodies. The RPD expects the number to climb. 585-254-3230 if you have any additional information regarding Frank Stark or any missing persons. Do not—I repeat—do not approach the assailant. Call your local police. Frank—Stark is considered armed and dangerous. The police are stating he's just been classified as a serial killer. Please, everyone, be careful. Do not approach this man. Contact your local police department. We don't need any heroes. This man is a serial killer who's armed and dangerous—Dan Pass signing off—I'll be back with updates as soon as they're made available. Stay safe and let's bring these families justice."

My heart raced, stomach tightened, a thousand bayonets attempting their escape through my skull. Jenna turned towards me. Her expression teetering between astonishment and fear. "Frank! You guys have the same first name. Isn't that scary?"

"Yeah, we do. Luckily, we have different last names. I think we're safe. I promise to protect you, Jenna."

Relax, Frankie. No one knows about you.

I sipped my drink and lit another cigarette. She didn't know I was Frank Stark. I'm Frank Strongman, plus the news posted an old picture. A thinner, beardless, short-haired version of me who no longer existed. The news lied as well because I never told them my final destinations. Regardless, the unfolding events were still too close for my comfort. Good thing no one else saw the news at the bar. The old couple didn't matter, nor did they approach me. Brock never returned either. I hoped the lady on Dock Ten would bother him indefinitely. I realized, for once in my life, the news is not your friend.

"It's all good. Don't fret. The news said he might be in California, Arizona, or Nevada. Those States are far from Florida. Can you top off my drink?"

"Sure, and good point, Frank. Sounds so weird to say your name, but I'll get over it. Hopefully, he's far away. You know... I think you both have the same nose." She smirked, topping my glass with a generous pour, not suspecting a damn thing.

"Good it's only a nose." I lifted the tumbler to my forehead, attempting to skew her view.

I kept my back to the bar for the rest of the night, concealing my face as best I could. Once the bar closed, I retreated to the boat for safety. I continued drinking from a new bottle of scotch until my vision blurred into darkness. Best to numb the mind and not ponder the potential consequences.

XXXIX

I stayed on the boat as often as possible, drinking scotch and smoking cigarettes to pass time. The days following the media reports complicated my mind more than reality. The news stopped showing Frank Stark's picture on replay, and better yet, the RPD must've had a teenager for a sketch artist because the updated picture didn't resemble Stark. Still, my gut twisted like a snake, an untold omen imminent. A Florida police officer, or, by pure chance, a snooping tourist, who watched too many episodes of Sherlock Holmes, stumbles upon Frank Stark and ends him, me. Two weeks, give or take a few days, normalcy returned, and perhaps for once in my life, the gut erred. Back in the swing, I approached the service desk early one morning, waving to greet the boss.

"Hey, Brock. How many boats today?"

"Hey, bud. Where you been?"

"Sick with the flu or something," I said exaggerating a cough.

"I've been under the weather too." He cocked his head and snarled. "Damn northerners spreading diseases. They should know better not to come here. Anyway, we have ten to fifteen boats. Clean 'em up and fix 'em. You okay with the workload?"

"Yeah, I can handle it."

In the distance, an unmarked police cruiser whirled dust as it drove onto the parking lot. Brock hadn't noticed yet, but I knew those vehicles all too well. Out stepped a well-dressed man resembling Daniels. Another red flag because most Floridians didn't wear a suit and tie. That damn wringing gut returned. I excused myself before he reached the desk.

"I have to piss and do whatever. Can I use your office bathroom?"

"Yeah," he said, fanning his nose, "go ahead but don't stink it up. Use the spray when you're done."

Abut to the ceiling, a square vent overlooked the service desk. I emptied a milk crate filled with magazines and toilet paper, and slid it against the wall beneath the opening. Straddling its edges, I teetered, leaning against the wall. The slits wide enough to view a bit more than a silhouette and perfect for eavesdropping.

I hoped Brock wasn't lying when he said he hated cops. His vitriol could give me an advantage. He slammed his fist onto the counter as the detective's footsteps approached.

"What do you want, boy?"

"Slow down a minute there, son. I'm Detective James Parkland. I'm not here for you. I'm looking for some information on a case."

"Information about what? I don't need your kind around here. Didn't you get the memo at your office? You're bad for business."

"Look, Brock. They've already told me at *my* office that *you* don't like cops, but I need your help. I won't take up too much of your time."

"Alright. Go ahead." Brock sighed. I think he knew cops never stop prying.

"We found a decomposing body in the swamp. A couple guys were hunting crocs and gators. After skinning and gutting one, they found a female torso inside its stomach. We searched the area and found a putrefied head floating in a swamp."

I punched the stucco wall on reflex, which, unbeknownst to me, reverberated throughout the office.

"Are you alright in there?"

I dropped my voice an octave. "Yes—I'm fine, Brock."

He continued, deflecting from my interruption. "Oh, man. That's pretty intense. So why are you here? Shouldn't you be out there finding her other pieces?"

The detective ignored Brock's questions. "Who's in the back room?" He eyeballed the vent, but the angled fins obscured me.

"There isn't anyone in the back room. That's the bathroom. It's one of my employees taking a dump."

"Alright, fine. Let's move on. I brought a picture. Her family filed a missing person's report and we received a match. We tracked her to California, then South Florida: Fort Myers and Miami. Her name was Destiny. Beautiful transgender woman. I believe they said she was a model. This case may be treated as a hate crime as well." He pulled out the picture and slid it towards Brock.

Brock wasted no time with his response. "Yeah, man. She's smoking hot. Never seen her. If I had, she'd be with me. What makes you think she came to the Salty Marina?"

"We don't know she came here—yet. We're checking every business in the area for leads. The family needs closure. Can I ask your employees?"

"No way, cop." Brock folded his arms across his chest. "You can leave the picture and a phone number. I'll show it around the marina. If they know anything, I'll call you."

"Alright. We can do it that way." He pulled out a business card and set it atop the counter next to the picture.

"Anything else, cop? If not, I believe it's time for you to go."

"I do have one more thing. We found a piece of jewelry wedged between her mouth and throat. Well… the upper part of her jaw and a piece of the lower, considering the circumstances. We don't know if the ring got stuck before or after she was dismembered. The ring is for a male based on its size. The image on top looks like a gargoyle and on the inside are the initials FS. Do you know the ring or anyone with the initials FS?"

"I do not," he said with a firm tone. "Never seen that ring."

"Alright. I'll leave a picture of the ring as well. Just give me a call if any information comes to mind."

His footsteps faded. Once he started his car and pulled out of the parking lot, I returned to the counter, acting as if nothing had happened.

"What was that all about, Brock?"

"Don't mess with me, boy. I know you heard everything. Ain't the first time I spied people from that bathroom. We have a big problem between us." Brock retrieved the pictures from underneath the counter and slid them towards me. "I know you know the girl, and the ring. That's the ring you *used* to wear. Belial. I'm guessing you're not wearing it anymore because they found it inside her."

I looked down at my right hand and it was gone. I hadn't even missed it. Brock paced behind the counter, then halted, his beady eyes steadfast upon mine.

"Fuck," I said, grinding my teeth.

"You've got that right, boy." His fist struck the counter. "*You are fucked*. Now, we have to talk and we're making this quick. I'm going to throw out these pictures, maybe burn them. After that, you get on your boat and head out to the Gulf of Mexico. Sail far, far away. Do you understand, boy?"

"Why do you want to do that for me?" I scratched my forehead. "Why aren't you calling the cops?" I wanted to grin but decided to refrain.

"Pretty simple, boy. I don't like cops or bad press. If they arrest you, well, this marina will always be known as the place where they caught the crazy killer. That's bad for business. Someone else can deal with the hell you're going to bring 'em. I don't want no memory of you at this place or in my mind. Get the fuck out of here."

"I want you to know I didn't hate her, nor did I know she was transgender. She was angelic, beautiful. I liked her a lot, but the voices… I can fix this. I know I can. Give me a chance," I implored with clasped hands.

"Get out. Now! Take what you need and leave the money under the counter. I'm leaving. When I come back, you better be gone."

"I guess this means you're not taking me fishing?" I said, elevating my brow.

He didn't respond, just stormed the exit. I returned to the boat and sat on the couch. As I extinguished one cigarette, I lit another, gulping from an open bottle of scotch. Certain occasions are glassless. My overpowering buzz met by an unnerving reality; my time had arrived to leave with nowhere to go. So much for sinking my toes in the white sand.

Frankie, time to go. Move forward, not backward.

"Sure is. Screw it."

I hustled through the marina gathering all I needed for the long haul, filled the fuel tanks, and reimbursed Brock. Inside the cockpit, I prepared for the trip to Neverland, opening a drawer to extract a map, and instead, finding a stencil kit and heat gun. At the stern, I changed the name of the boat from *All Behind Me* to *Point of No Return*. I altered the registration number to match the number of an almost identical boat a few slips from mine.

At the helm, I steered the boat through the Intracoastal and onto the Gulf of Mexico. The water was smooth as a mirror for miles. Traversing the Caribbean Sea would lead to the Atlantic with an unknown final destination. Perhaps, Europe, Africa, South America, or the good ole United States. I spun the dial on the Ham radio, searching for handles to gather weather and news. One station crackled and squealed, finding clarity within a few knob adjustments.

The news report went as follows:

This is a special bulletin from Amateur Radio News Line. We are ARNL. They've apprehended a killer in Rochester New York for the murder of Nali Koulpot. Nali was a gentle four-year-old girl who was brutally murdered by strangulation, then stuffed into a water container at a local factory. The killer worked at that same factory as a part-time security guard. The alleged killer of this beautiful little girl is Mitch Karssie. Our condolences to the family. May you rest in peace Nali.

My lungs burned and throat blistered as I shrieked at the open, dark waters. "Damn it. Damn you, Joe. Damn you, Captain." The helm spun as I pounded it with ferocious jabs. "Mitch Karssie. If that night could've been different, then Nali would be alive."

I stomped into the cabin, grabbing a bottle of scotch and a pack of cigarettes. Jim Morrison chanted "The End" through the speakers. I spun the volume to maximum. Revenge was not an option in the middle of nowhere. I reclined into the Captain's chair, staring through the Clearview screen into the infinite darkness, pondering my future. If only Poseidon could appear and wash me away into the depths of the water.

Frankie. You'll be fine. We promise. We'll see you soon.

The End

Epilogue

This is a memoir by Frank Stark. A glimpse into the mind of a serial killer. Additional entries exist, but only time will tell if they're released.

National Suicide Prevention Lifeline

If you are suicidal, thinking about hurting yourself, or are concerned that someone you may know may be in danger of hurting themselves, Please Call 1.800.273.TALK (8255).
https://suicidepreventionlifeline.org

For TTY Users: Use your preferred relay service or dial 711 then 1.800.273.8255.

Veterans 1.800.273.8255, then Press 1 or Text 838255.
https://www.veteranscrisisline.net

All services are confidential.

SAMHSA's National Helpline

SAMHSA – Substance Abuse & Mental Health Services Administration.

Please Call 1.800.662.HELP (4357).
TTY: 1-800-487-4889

SAMHSA's National Helpline is a free, 24/7, 365-day-a-year, treatment referral and information service (in English and Spanish) for individuals and families facing mental and/or substance use disorders.

https://www.samhsa.gov

All services are confidential.

About the Author

Thank you for reading. I am flattered as well as grateful. This will not be the "typical" about-the-author page.

I've been writing since I was a child, and remember it as if it was yesterday, even though those days are far removed. I grew up and lived in Rochester, NY for over forty years, then moved to the Cape Coral / Fort Myers, FL area. I love animals more than humans because they aren't judgmental and know what they want. That being said, I support all humans who promote love, equality, and acceptance. I am vocal about the aforementioned and have been since I was five. The best analogy to my prior statements about love is when you nuzzle a kitten, puppy, or newborn. That exact moment is nirvana.

On writing: I hope to have additional novels out soon. They will not be limited to any genre.

If you liked Stained Mirror, or have other questions, etc..., please feel free to contact me.
www.giannifranco.com, Twitter: @giannipetitti,
IG: gianni.franco, FB (love/hate): Author Gianni Franco, for now. May delete again.

Made in the USA
Columbia, SC
11 December 2021

51109495R00257